PRAIRIE GHOST

A NOVEL

DOUG KRIVANEK

First edition, 2022.

ellen road press

ISBN 979-8-218-12492-2

In Memory of Jenna

PROLOGUE

October 22, 2010

The pulsing ambulance lights cast a macabre light show on the house and the somber crowd mingling on the lawn; spotlighted the man seated on the porch rocking the limp body in his lap. When EMTs rolled two gurneys carrying wrapped bodies out the front door, a mournful wail pierced the night air, a raw expression of grief that haunted neighbors for years.

July 17, 2011

Jacob Fines flattened himself against the car seat. *A ghost town? Father was driving through a town filled with ghosts?* Could this trip get any worse?

Mother and Father had announced this morning that they

were detouring through the black hills to see Mount Rushmore and Crazy Horse. After having to run away from grasshoppers and cows oozing strings of snot out their noses yesterday, Jacob wasn't interested in meeting famous people and an Indian. And black hills? Jacob wasn't about to play in any black dirt. His shoes were red with white stripes, and he wanted his new first-grade friends to see them before they got ruined.

Even the gravel road his father had turned onto wasn't any fun. The ride was too bumpy to color a straight line or play any of his games, so Jacob could only sit with his seatbelt rubbing the underside of his chin. Worse, the car kept jerking sideways like it would slide into the ditch. When he raised to his knees and looked outside, he discovered a swirling cloud of dust following them, blocking his view.

Father finally slowed the car, allowing Jacob to relax. That only lasted until Mother said, "Oh, look. It's a ghost town."

That's when Jacob dove for the car seat.

Mother laughed at the sight of Jacob's seatbelt smashed against his face. "There's nothing scary here, Jacob. 'Ghost town' is just an expression for an old town that nobody lives in anymore."

"Everything falls apart because nobody's left to take care of things," Father explained, stopping the car. "See that collection of old cars, Julie? That Cadillac must be forty years old."

A regular town, except empty and messy. That didn't sound so bad to Jacob. He imagined broken windows, like the kitchen window he and his friends had hit while playing baseball at Jeff's house. And trash scattered over their yard, the same as after that windstorm tipped over everybody's trashcans.

"I promise you no ghosts live here," Mother said. "Sit up and have a look."

No ghosts. Comforted, Jacob raised enough to peek out

the window.

The old town looked much worse than he had imagined. The building directly out his window was missing a large section of one of its walls, leaving a hole large enough to see the yucky old furniture piled inside. The ceiling over the front porch had collapsed onto a pair of rusted metal porch chairs, while a fallen tree had punched a hole through the roof.

The next house—Father insisted that people had once lived in them—had collapsed like Jacob's card house after Petey stabbed it with his finger. The house's tattered roof had tipped sideways, and Jacob could look directly into the old brick chimney.

Jacob raised to his knees and peered through the windshield. There were two more rows of tiny houses beyond a blacktop road. One of the houses had collapsed to the ground, trees grew out the roof of another, and the rest looked sadder than the house Jacob and his friends had built using washer and dryer boxes after it got rained on.

Purple and yellow flowers partially concealed a trash dump. Jacob could see metal barrels, an old stove, wire coils, a metal cabinet missing one door, messy piles of metal bars and pipes and tubes—even a rusting tractor. Next to wire fencing strung between wooden poles as crooked as Jacob's great grandma's fingers, rusted cars sat parked like bumper cars at the finish of an amusement ride.

Jacob slid to the other side of the car for a closer look at a larger building. "What was that?" he asked.

"A store, perhaps," Mother said. "Or a hotel."

Jacob looked around and spotted only one other large building. "Where were all of the other stores?" he asked, naming the places Mother and Father had taken him.

"Or a police station or fire station?" Mother added.

"Small towns lack many basic services," Father said. "But don't worry, Jacob. Price has everything we'll need, even a great donut shop for our Fun Saturdays."

Reassured, Jacob remained on his knees to peer out his window as they turned onto the smooth road and sped up. There were two more old homes along this road, and Jacob saw that they were in as bad a shape as the rest.

Just before he looked away, the ghost floated into view between the two homes, large and menacing, a long stick slung over its shoulder. When it turned its head and scowled at them, Jacob ducked down in his seat and squeezed his eyes shut.

Dan Stuart watched the car speed away along the highway. The driver hadn't spotted him, too busy watching the road, but the close call spooked him enough that he hurried behind the old house.

Sweating more from the rising panic attack than physical effort, Dan shouldered the door open and stepped inside. Closing it behind him, he slid to the floor and pressed the heels of his hands hard into his eyes.

Once again, the tragedy consumed him. His fingers were so chilled that he could hardly feel his lifeless daughter in his lap. The EMT's light touch on his shoulder and the promise, "We'll take care of her," served only as an indictment. Compound mistakes intensified his guilt: the cap, the painting, the windows, the headache. All his fault. It took a moment for him to realize that the anguished cry he heard when his wife and eldest daughter were rolled from the house covered in white sheets was his own.

As the attack subsided, Dan took a deep breath and slowly exhaled. He recognized what he was going through, but a part of him insisted that he deserved the punishment.

He pulled his hands down his face. The light filtering through the broken windows showed a small room cluttered with filthy, torn furniture rotting beneath a coating of fallen plaster. Peeled and torn wallpaper littered the floor. A brass table lamp sat useless, absent a bulb and electricity. He turned his head toward a faint scurrying sound and watched a mouse climb over his belongings piled in the corner.

Dan flinched as another car rolled past. It was safer to remain inside, but idleness only aggravated his symptoms. He decided that fixing up the place a little wouldn't harm anything.

CHAPTER 1

"I know you."

Dan flinched at the unexpected voice below him and nearly lost his balance. Standing high atop an extension ladder leaning against rotted, rickety boards, hammer in one hand and several nails in the other, he sacrificed the nails and grabbed the ladder rung to steady himself.

Once he was secure again, Dan peered down to meet the upturned gaze of his intruder, a young man in a fitted T-shirt, blue jeans, and hiking boots, with an overstuffed backpack slung over one shoulder. Twenty years old, if that, with wavy brown hair and deep brown eyes accentuating a handsome face, and an athletic build likely purchased with a gym membership. God's gift to women, no doubt. Dan half-wished a nail had scratched one of those flawless cheeks on its descent.

Practicing his customary motto, "That which you ignore will go away," Dan returned to his work. Time was at a premium. The line of thunderheads building to the southwest wasn't bluffing.

"I said, I know you."

Frustratingly, his intruder wasn't receding like did the pain after hitting his thumb with a hammer. Dan rewound the last minute, and the sound of the slowing southbound car finally registered. Since a vandal wouldn't check in to introduce himself, Dan most likely faced a vagrant.

"I'm not deaf," Dan said. "I'm trying to beat the storm." Meaning, *go away*.

"Don't you want to know how I know you?"

Subtlety wasn't going to cut it, either. The roof was steeply sloped such that just a nudge would start something sliding off. If Dan were lucky, he could bean the lad.

"I was just a little kid," continued the jabbering from below. "We drove through here on our way to Mount Rushmore. I thought you were a ghost." He finished the last line with a little chuckle.

Dan took stock of his potential projectiles: a small box of nails, but only if heaved en masse, boards, and his hammer. The hammer would send the clearest message, though it also might knock the lad senseless.

"You looked directly at me."

Dan picked up a board and flung it off the roof. Its arc was true, but his intended target sidestepped the projectile.

"You dropped a piece of wood. Do you need it back?"

"No!"

Dan wedged another thin board in position and tacked it in place.

"What are you doing up there?"

Reconsidering my reluctance to bean a jabber mouth with a hammer. "Are you blind? I'm fixing this roof before it starts raining."

"I mean big picture. As a kid, I thought you were carrying

a club. It was a piece of lumber, wasn't it? You were already working on these buildings."

Dan thought about tossing a handful of nails as a diversion and *then* fling the hammer.

"My parents told me this was a ghost town. It *still* looks like a ghost town."

"This isn't a town," Dan said. He reached for the last board that wasn't there. It lay buried in the weeds at the base of the ladder.

"You live here all alone?"

Enough with the Twenty Questions. And Dan needed that board. He thrust his hammer into his tool belt and descended the ladder. Face to face, the lad was even taller and more handsome than when viewed from above. Undoubtedly, a few girls *did* grant him Godly sway.

"Yes, and I prefer it that way," Dan said. "You got a name?"

"Jacob Fines."

"Out of my way, Jacob Fines."

Jacob stepped sideways to let Dan pass. "You've lived alone in a ghost town for nearly as long as I've been alive."

"This isn't a town," Dan repeated.

"Whatever." Jacob pulled at his crotch. "Got a toilet around here?"

Dan nodded at the house across the road. "Help yourself."

Jacob tilted his head to match the lean of the tiny building. "No way you live in that."

Dan accepted the compliment. His present home *was* one of his better masquerades. Split and broken sun-bleached gray siding covered the square ruin, while the front door hung visibly crooked in its frame, and few intact windowpanes remained. Hail-beaten roof shingles and shabby overhangs completed the deception.

Jacob hesitated, expecting a joke. "Or you can relieve yourself here," Dan said, leaning down to grab the board.

With an "Okay, I'll bite" shrug, Jacob hurried across the road. Dan rested a foot on a ladder rung and waited as Jacob disappeared inside. Predictably, the lad quickly reappeared.

And just as predictably, after rushing back, he started chattering again. "It's a real home inside," Jacob said. "Walls, flooring, lights, fans, furniture—a kitchen. Your work?" He grabbed at his crotch again. "No bathroom, though."

"Didn't say there was one. Go around back. If you need to go 'one,' choose the greenest weed growing along the back wall and start spraying."

"Against the back of your house?"

"Weeding," Dan said. "Urine is toxic to plants. If you need to go 'two,' the outhouse is straight back fifty feet."

Dan trudged back up the ladder, shaking his head at the absurdity of someone stopping just to chat. The luminous tops of the anvil clouds didn't fool him. Those roiling black bases dared him to finish before rendering his efforts useless. He set extra nails.

Jacob reappeared just as Dan had descended the ladder to gather the shingles. "Have you lived here alone ever since—"

Dan spun on the lad. "Why are you here?"

"I was hitching a ride to Denver for a job and recognized the place. Once I saw you on the ladder, I decided to stop and say hi. Who wouldn't be curious about someone putzing around a ghost town for ten years?"

"And what about your job?"

"I'm in no hurry. I can easily hitch another ride."

"Then hitch it."

Dan turned away and climbed his ladder. Against a stiffening wind, he worked his way up the roof, interleaving the new shingles into the old ones. When he spared a glance down the ladder, the lad was gone. *Good riddance.*

Dan finished the repairs, gathered his tools, collapsed the ladder, and toted everything to his maintenance shed. Hustling around the corner of his house to get indoors before he got soaked, he smacked straight into Jacob's shoulder.

"Are you okay? Jacob asked.

Dan rubbed his sore sternum. Now he knew what it felt like to run into a brick wall. "I think this qualifies as adding injury to insult."

"Sorry. No cars yet."

The penalty for living alone for so long is the presumption that you're alone. Though Dan couldn't have guessed that Jacob was lurking around the corner, he knew, if only subconsciously, that Jacob was still about.

"I suppose you'll be needing me to start walking," Jacob said.

As pain went, colliding with Jacob didn't rank with other injuries this place had dealt Dan. That didn't impact the lad's fate, though. "You suppose right—"

A bolt of lightning struck too close for comfort, followed by rolling thunder that echoed back and forth across the sky. The thunderhead's front edge curled up in a straight line where it collided with an invisible mass of cooler, denser air. The sweet, pungent smell of ozone promised rain.

No matter how compulsively Dan craved solitude, his old training kicked in, and he found he had no stomach to deny shelter from this weather. "But you're not going to."

Jacob looked up into the threatening sky and huffed. "Getting stormed on or scolded by an old grouch. Some choice."

Dan shrugged. "So I'm set in my ways. At least I'm not

dangerous."

Jacob looked at him. "And *I'm* not afraid of a little rain." He slipped his free arm through the second backpack strap and clipped the chest strap.

As if Jacob's challenge had drawn the storm's ire, thunder from the next lightning strike boomed before Dan could begin counting. Dan could easily show Jacob and his dangerous curiosity on his way. But his younger self's standards again intruded and insisted he help. Dan had been a young man— generations ago, admittedly, but some aspects of boyhood you never forget—and he knew he could do the storm one better.

"Hungry?"

Jacob looked at Dan for a moment before lowering his head and nodding. "Starving."

"This way," Dan said, motioning for Jacob to follow. "We'll dump off your stuff where I'm putting you up and round up some supper."

"I remember the old cars, too," Jacob said as they stepped over the fallen fence bordering the rusting shells, slowing when he realized where Dan was leading him. "Why bother? The hole in that roof is big enough to drive a truck through. I might as well sleep outdoors."

Dan felt an odd satisfaction at Jacob's reaction. "Look at the hole and tell me what you see."

Jacob stared up at the hole as they started across the gravel road. "Nothing," he said. "Total darkness."

"Look more closely."

"I still don't see anything."

"Two shades of black," Dan answered. The color variation was clear to him because he had created it: a lower expanse of deep gray-black topped by the black of nothingness.

Jacob paused again, this time to study what Dan was

describing. "I guess so. What am I seeing?"

"The new roof, shingled in black, built inside and underneath the old, holey roof."

Jacob hooted in amusement and shook his head. "What are you creating here? A haunted town attraction? Aren't you a little too remote to get much business?"

"Sometimes too close," Dan commented.

Dan led Jacob up the wooden steps and through the heavy front door. Feeling for the wall switch, he flipped on the lights, six bare bulbs spaced across the ceiling.

"Spacious," Jacob said. "But a little sparse."

"It was originally a hotel," Dan said. "I've only gotten as far as demoing the interior and finishing the perimeter walls."

"Are you renovating all the buildings in this town—place?" Jacob asked.

"I've completed a couple of them. A few are in progress, while nearly the same number are too far gone to salvage."

Jacob took a slow turn. "This is a mansion compared to that shack you call home. Why don't you move in here?"

"Too big to heat in the winter. Drop your pack, and let's grab something to eat."

Jacob propped his backpack against a post and followed Dan back outdoors. The wind was picking up, and more anvil clouds had lined up to the west. They were in for a long night.

"If you're not building some sort of haunted town," Jacob said, "then why *have* you been living here for so many years?"

Questions, questions. "You're worse than a two-year-old."

"Certainly not for fun—living here, I mean."

"No?" Dan hoped that had come out as a question.

"No. Fun isn't living as a hermit surrounded by fallen-down houses and rusted-out cars, spending your days repairing roofs. Fun is movies and parties and games—and girl. Lots of girls."

Dan flinched at the mention of girls. Storm or no storm, the lad was pressing his luck. "Hartman's," Dan said when they reached their destination. "The old general store."

Entering Hartman's was stepping back in time into an antique mercantile shop. To their right, glass-fronted red oak display cases ran front to back the length of the store. Two rows of double-sided oak shelving ran parallel to the display cases, flanking a massive cast iron stove that squatted dead center of the store. All manner of hooks and shelving covered the walls. The plank wood floor was worn and widely gapped.

"Wow," Jacob said. "Did you build this?"

Dan shook his head. "All original. Mr. Hartman ran this store for over fifty years." Dan motioned for Jacob to follow. "I keep my supplies towards the back."

Dan preceded Jacob along a creaking floor to where he stored his dry goods, close to a refrigerator shoved against the back wall. "Hope sandwiches are okay," he said, handing Jacob two bottles of water.

Jacob twisted open his bottle and mumbled "umm" through a long drink.

Dan loaded a corrugate box with bread, ham and roast beef, and cheddar cheese from the refrigerator and added a bag of chips and a package of cookies from the shelves.

Jacob recapped his bottle. "Get much business in here?"

Dan hoisted the box. "None paying yet. Grab a sleeping bag from the corner, and we'll head back."

The bruised thunderheads had drifted directly overhead, and the light and sound show had intensified. It had started drizzling.

Dan lifted his head and yelled, "You're just teasing."

"Whatever happened to Mr. Hartman?" Jacob asked, looking around. "And to everybody else?"

"Mr. Hartman, I made up. The others, I have no idea. Ghost towns don't tell their secrets."

Dan pointed at the mound of debris across the gravel road. "That was once a post office."

The sky opened up.

"Let's get inside."

CHAPTER 2

A tap-tap-tap on the ladder drew Dan's attention. He looked down to find Jacob using a twig as a drumstick.

"I didn't want to risk startling you again," Jacob said.

"You just wake up?" Dan asked, noticing Jacob's disheveled hair. "I figured you'd taken off."

The storm kept me awake all night. Things kept banging against the walls."

"Happens quite often around here," Dan said. "Lots of loose stuff lying around."

Jacob pointed his twig. "More repairs?"

"Lifted shingles. The wind again. After that, it's back to the walls."

Jacob shook his head. "Shingles and walls. I'm assuming you haven't built a fitness gym. If you feed me breakfast and point me to some heavy lifting, I'll stay the day and help."

Dan's impulse to tell Jacob to get the hell out of his sight dwarfed yesterday's urge to fling a hammer at the lad's head.

Solitary life suited him to a T, and he didn't need anybody—helper, moocher, or otherwise—underfoot. But Jacob's behavior raised alert flags. And Dan *could* use the help.

"Grab yourself something to eat from Hartman's, and I'll get you started."

Dan had just collapsed the ladder when Jacob reappeared, white dust dotting his lips and fingertips.

"Nothing like powdered donuts for breakfast," Dan said.

"I found cornflakes but no milk."

"That's tomorrow." Dan turned. "Last evening's storm reminded me that some salvaged siding needs to be stacked off the ground. A great task for you while I reattach some loose siding." He pointed at a line of trees five hundred feet to their east, running parallel to the highway. "Hat Creek runs through there. I've been cutting up dead logs for firewood at that tall cottonwood with the double top. Grab eight split pieces and meet me at the boards. You'll spot me."

While Jacob hustled off toward the creek, Dan walked the shoulder of the road south past his house and two similar buildings before turning onto Brule Street, an east-west-running rut road of two parallel dirt paths straddling ground-clinging weeds. Its regulation street sign attested to an active past of homes with yards and flower gardens; of family picnics and celebrations; of community gatherings. Following the ruts, he preceded Jacob to a pile of weathered gray boards strewn over the ground.

Jacob dropped the split logs to the ground and pulled on the leather gloves Dan offered.

Dan spaced the logs along the ground. "Stack the boards three across on top of the logs, leaving an air gap in between."

Jacob lifted a board from the stack and dropped it onto

the logs, kicking it into position. As he reached for a second board, a telltale warning sounded.

"Rattler!" Dan yelled.

Jacob reacted with youthful speed; a fraction of a second later, the rattlesnake struck the spot Jacob's hand had vacated before slithering away into the dense weeds.

"Damn you, Mabel!" Dan yelled. "You didn't get bit, did you?" he asked Jacob.

Jacob stared back, wide-eyed. "No."

Dan worked his way around the stack, lifting boards and letting them drop loudly.

"Mabel?" Jacob mocked. "You have a pet snake?"

"I don't know if it's the same snake, but I have frequent skirmishes with a rattler that size."

"But still, naming a snake? And should you be reaching into the pile like that?"

"Got a better idea?" Dan snapped. "Think it would stay away if I asked kindly?" He declared the pile clear and slunk away, hoping Jacob twisted an ankle climbing over it.

"Boards stacked," Jacob said, catching Dan taking his customary afternoon siesta behind whatever house he was renovating. "And why are you resting in the sun?"

Dan peered into the cloudless sky. *So passersby didn't spot him.* "Hadn't noticed."

After relocating into the shade, Jacob dropped to the ground, struggling to find a comfortable sitting position. "You need to plant some grass."

Dan eased his tired body to the ground. "Lawn grass takes care, which I don't." Rattlesnakes, ridicule, sunstroke, lawn grass. Jacob certainly had a knack for reminding Dan just how little he cared about anything.

Jacob pointed at the water tower butted against the creek just south of the gravel road. It was a traditional cylinder style with a spherical bottom and a conical top, elevated on four spindly legs. A ladder ran up one of the legs, leading to a catwalk that ringed the cylinder. "I cooled down using your spigot beneath your old tower. I swallowed water when I washed my face. I hope I won't get sick."

"Heavy in minerals but safe to drink," Dan said. Admittedly, he had tested the well water himself using a swimming pool test kit, but he had never suffered any ill effects.

"I thought about climbing the ladder to look around," Jacob said, "but that tower looks as rickety as everything else around here."

"It's fine. The rust is only superficial."

"Only superficial. I was unaware there were different types of rust."

"Different *levels* of rust. The inspector assured me that the structure wasn't compromised."

Jacob stared hard at Dan. "You had the tower inspected?"

Dan nodded. "To make sure it would be worth the effort to repair."

"Worth the effort to repair," Jacob repeated dubiously.

"For running water. And if you repeat me one more time, I'm sending you to bed without supper."

Jacob held up his hands in surrender. "Can I ask what's involved in repairing a water tower?"

"Though the visible rust is only cosmetic, *any* inside rust is toxic, so I sanded it to bare metal and epoxy sealed it. Took me years to complete."

"Years to complete," Jacob said, trance-like, unconscious of how close he was to losing his meal. "I assume there's a second ladder?"

"Two more. One ladder extends up the backside to the tank from the catwalk to the roof. The other descends down into the tank through an access hatch."

From Jacob's expression, he thought Dan was loco. "That tower must be a hundred feet tall. You climbed up and down it every day for years?"

Dan nodded. "I could only work for an hour or so in one stretch; the paint strippers and industrial coating give off noxious fumes."

"Warning," Jacob droned, "Repairing water towers can be hazardous to your health."

"Unfortunately, noxious fumes weren't the worst of it." Dan rolled up his right sleeve to reveal a jagged scar extending from his wrist nearly to his elbow.

"Holy shit!" Jacob howled, quickly turning his face away from the disfigurement. "That is one ugly wound. Do I want to know how it happened?"

"I was working high up on the curve and lost my footing. Slid clear to the bottom. A protruding bolt caught my forearm and ripped it to the bone."

"That must have hurt badly."

"Still does." Dan had used his shirt as a tourniquet to stem the bleeding and fought off shock long enough to climb to the ground. After regaining consciousness, he cleaned the wound and bound it best he could, determined to keep working. But unbearable pain eventually forced him to the emergency room, where he was admitted and pumped full of antibiotics. Doctors performed two surgeries to clean out the infections. Dan had arrived soon enough to save his arm but too late to avoid scarring.

Jacob slowly surveyed the surroundings. "So what you've got to show for years of drudgery and"—he pointed at Dan's disfigured arm—"agony, is a tiny home—with running water, but no bathroom—a grocery store, a partially-renovated hotel, a rusting water tower resembling an old rocket ship—"

"An old rocket ship?"

"Look who's repeating who now. Your tower is a dead ringer for the rocket ships pictured on those old fifties science magazine covers."

Dan remained unconvinced. "I've always thought it resembled a coffee pot."

Jacob snickered.

"I'm serious," Dan said. "Your basic old-fashioned model: silver cylinder with a shallow domed lid—what am I saying? Long before your time. Your generation grew up on coffee *machines*."

"I've seen plenty of pictures of coffee pots. Enough to know your basic model seems to be missing a handle and spout."

"Believe it or not, I've seen them added as decoration, grafted right onto the tower. Small town advertising gimmicks."

"Remind me to steer clear of those places," Jacob said. He adjusted his seating position. "Allow me to continue: a rusty water tower resembling an old rocket ship, a fleet of junk cars, an outhouse, stacks of split firewood—oh, and a rattlesnake named Mabel. You have the makings of a great town."

"This isn't a town."

"So you keep insisting. How do you receive mail?"

"I have a PO Box in Edgemont. The town's twenty miles northwest of here."

Jacob pointed south. "How far along the highway belongs to you?"

"A couple of hundred feet beyond the last building, all the way back to the creek. Why do you ask?"

"That grassy area just beyond the stacked boards is a great

place to build a bonfire. Mind if I burn your downed limbs and brush?"

Dan weighed Jacob's idea for a bit of amusement. The only real danger was drawing attention. But with so much accumulated underbrush, the next dry lightning strike was apt to start a larger fire on its own, with more severe consequences. A major clean-up might be in order.

"Have at it," Dan said. "You'll find matches in Hartman's."

Jacob grabbed his gloves and jumped to his feet. "Do you own a log splitter?"

Dan shook his head. "I split by hand."

"Even those lengths of huge tree trunks?"

"No. They're too big. They'll rot where they lay."

Jacob nodded. "Matches are in your store, you said?"

"Yes. Just don't burn the firewood I've already split and stacked. I'd prefer to survive the winter."

"My parents heated with wood for a couple of years before switching back to propane," Jacob said. "They claimed propane was cleaner burning. I think they tired of hauling wood."

"You won't catch *me* switching to propane or natural gas," Dan said. "I'd rather freeze first."

Jacob rolled six large logs from the creekbank and arranged them into a ring. Once his bonfire blazed, Dan raided Hartman's for hotdogs, buns, and fixings, and they enjoyed an old-fashioned weenie roast.

Afterward, staring into the mesmerizing orange embers, Dan considered his aching arms and Jacob's impressive show of strength. "Interested in helping out at a local ranch tomorrow."

"Doing what?" Jacob asked.

"Herding cattle, stacking hay, maintaining equipment, delivering feed—hired-hand work, primarily. My weekly barter for eggs, milk, and meat. It wets the Cornflakes."

"Sounds strenuous."

"Very."

Jacob laughed. "So, you *do* have a gym. Count me in."

CHAPTER 3

Dan tipped his hat down to block the early morning sun and strode toward the old hotel. His gut had begun churning last evening watching Jacob's youthful antics around the bonfire, the discomfort continuing unabated through the night. Though Dan had gorged himself, he suspected a more sinister culprit than indigestion: he was enjoying Jacob's company. It had taken a chance intrusion to make him realize how lonely he'd become.

Dan entered to find Jacob still in yesterday's clothing, sprawled on his stomach across his sleeping bag with the soles of his shoes pointing at the door. Defenseless against being returned to that evening and finding his daughter prostrate on the floor, the bottoms of her shoes pointing at him, Dan slumped against the door frame and moaned.

"Jacob!" he called out sharply. "Jacob!" Please let this not be a repeat.

Jacob rolled onto his side and attempted to squint his eyes

open. Dan pressed his palms to his eyes and forced a couple of deep breaths. *Sleeping. Jacob was only sleeping. Don't be a fool.*

"What time is it?" Jacob mumbled.

Dan dropped his hands to his sides. "Almost seven."

Jacob groaned. "Didn't we just go to bed?"

"A little early for you?"

"A little?"

"Well, it's late for me, so come on."

"Your truck is in no better condition than any of the wrecks," Jacob said.

Dan considered his transportation. Old, dirty, and beat up, plus religiously parked amongst the junkers to escape attention. "Bought it off a rancher. Ugly, but reliable."

Jacob rubbed at the dust coating the truck's fender. "Bright blue. Excepting the rust on your oversized coffee pot, it's the first color I've seen in this entire town."

"This isn't a town."

"Place. In this entire place."

Jacob had to pull hard to jerk open the stiff passenger door. "When was the last time anybody used this door?" he asked, shutting it to a loud, long squeak.

Dan shrugged noncommittally—not since he owned it. He started the truck and backed it onto Brule Street. Pulling forward, he turned west onto the gravel road and crossed the blacktop, accelerating into pastureland stretching to both horizons.

"Desolate," Jacob commented, shaking his head. He peered back at the dust cloud swirling in their wake. "I remember that, too."

After ten minutes of jostling and shimmying, Dan turned off at a cattle gate and steered along a meandering rut road running a mile to a set of buildings. "The Childress Ranch," he said. "Tom and Nadine."

The Childress's home was a simple two-story box with second-story dormers and a wrap-around porch. A small root cellar peeked out of the rise leading away from the house. Across the grounds and facing the house, a large faded-red wooden barn backed up against the line of trees marking Indian Creek, metal-fenced corrals flanking both sides. To the north of the barn, a deep open-sided shed sheltered several tractors. Smaller buildings dotted the grounds, including a chicken coop, maintenance shed, and feed storage. The Childress's truck was parked beside the creamery well directly in front of a scythe mower and a hay rake arranged in tandem. A gas tank on metal stilts flanked the gate into the south pasture.

Nadine stepped outside as they approached, cradling a stainless-steel bowl in one arm. She was short and wiry, in her late forties, with shoulder-length brown hair streaked in gray, wire-rim glasses resting on a button nose.

"Good morning, Dan," she said.

"Morning, Nadine," Dan returned. "This is Jacob. He's helping out today."

"It's a pleasure meeting you, Jacob. Give me a moment." Nadine stepped off the porch into scruffy weeds.

Of the same mind as Dan, the Childresses didn't bother with lawn grass. A brood of white hens, familiar with the morning routine, gathered around her. "Greetings, ladies," she said, scattering the breakfast scraps over the ground.

The scent of pancakes drizzled in maple syrup with notes of fried bacon wafted into the air. Jacob perked up as if wishing he could have saved Nadine from the trouble of wasting food on the chickens.

"Cream goes to market this morning," Nadine told Dan.

"Strap them into the truck's bed, and I'll be off. The men baled the pasture across the creek last week. Fit what you can in the hayloft for the horses and stack the rest in the hay yard. And a couple of heifers escaped from the north pasture, likely through a loose corner post. See if you can find it."

"I know where Tom keeps his fencing supplies," Dan said.

"I figured you did. Eggs and milk are in the fridge, help yourself; wrapped meat is in the freezer."

Taking their leave, Dan led Jacob to the creamery well. "The Childress's milk only for personal use," he said, "except for what I confiscate. They separate and store the cream below ground to keep it fresh until it's ready to sell."

The creamery well was a cement-lined pit with a shingled-roof wooden frame supporting a hand winch. Cool air touched Dan's cheeks when he opened the access doors. The temperature at the bottom of the well remained unchanged year-round. He cranked the winch to raise a wooden platform loaded with the cream cans. While Dan strained to lift a single can, Jacob hoisted one with each hand. Leaving Jacob to retrieve the remaining cans, Dan grabbed a ratchet strap from the truck cab and secured the cans into the truck bed.

After Dan alerted Nadine that she was good to go, he led Jacob to the tractor shed and hitched the smaller Ferguson to the Childress's flatbed trailer. "Ever driven a stick shift?" he asked.

"No."

"No better time to learn." Dan traded Jacob the tractor seat and familiarized him with the simple controls. "The clutch is the only tricky part. Let it out too fast, and you'll give both of us whiplash."

Dan scrambled onto the trailer and held on tightly as Jacob drove across the building grounds, the length of the south pasture, and across the simple steel bridge spanning Indian Creek. Dan hopped off the trailer and loaded rectangular bales of alfalfa while Jacob inched the tractor forward. After a pass, they traded jobs. Jacob took pleasure in demonstrating his physical prowess by hoisting fifty-pound bales with each hand and tossing them through the air onto the trailer. Dan, in retribution, quickly released the clutch while Jacob stood on the trailer, tumbling him into the stacked bales.

Clearing the field nearly filled the wagon, and Dan drove the heavier load back to the grounds. Traditionally, Tom refilled the barn hayloft from the trailer, and stacked the remainder of the bales onto a supply he kept under a tarp behind the chicken coop.

"The lunch menu is fried egg sandwiches," Dan said, opening the refrigerator door.

He handed Jacob a half dozen eggs and rummaged through a choked shelf for cheese and ham. While he cooked, Jacob gathered bread and mayo, a bag of corn chips, and a couple of Nadine's home-baked blueberry muffins. Dan assembled and loaded their meals into empty bread bags, and they returned outdoors for Dan's usual lunch spot in the barn hayloft.

"It reeks in here," Jacob complained after Dan slid open the barn door and ushered him inside.

Dan pulled in a lungful of hay, cow manure, dirt, feed pellets, leather harnesses, and aged wood. "Classic barn," he said. The odor had grown on him over the years. "The stairs are at the back, to the left. Watch your step, though," he warned, noticing a covering of fresh hay in one of the cattle stalls. "Some of these cow pies may be moist."

"Yuck."

An unframed wooden staircase led to the hayloft. It

was noticeably hotter at the top of the stairs. Darker, too, illuminated only by light leaking through the gaps between the boards. Dan opened the rear hayloft door to brighten the area and admit a cooling breeze.

"Anybody hiding up here?" he called out.

He got no reply.

"Were you expecting someone?" Jacob asked.

"Some*thing*." Dan handed Jacob their meals and scrambled across a deep stack of hay bales. "Come on out, ladies." A pair of squawking hens jumped into view. Dan shooed them across the floor and out the hayloft door, then lowered himself to the floor, dangling his feet out the open doorway. "Roosting hens don't lay eggs. Can't have them stealing my lunch."

Jacob dropped down beside Dan. "What a bleak place," he said, swatting at the dust kicked up by their arrival. "If the loneliness and boredom doesn't kill you, the dust and cactus needles and snakes and cow pies and—"

A *high-pitched "kee-kee-kee"* sounded from a nearby tree.

"That was spooky," Jacob said.

"City slicker," Dan huffed, unpacking their lunches. "That was a golden eagle. My resident golden eagle is quite vocal, too."

"Have you named your eagle, as well?"

Dan ignored Jacob's dig and gazed into the pasture beyond the trees. "It *is* a stark beauty, I'll admit."

"Stark beauty?" Jacob mocked. "Stark, I'll buy. Beauty? Uh-uh."

"Look carefully enough, and you'll find it," Dan said. "The pastures sparkling like golden seas in the early morning sunlight; a winter rancher astride his horse, its breath frosty in the frigid air; the summer snowstorm of cottonwoods releasing their seed pods; cows lowing for their calves; the pungent, earthy odor of freshly cut alfalfa—"

Jacob was staring like he thought Dan had lost his marbles. "I had an English teacher who often lapsed into verse. They eased him out the door the following year."

Dan shrugged and unpacked their lunches. "I find solace in the solitary."

Jacob shook his head. "Not me," he said. "Tomorrow, it's off to the big city. I enjoy people, excitement, opportunity." He unwrapped his sandwich. "Is bartering how you earn your living?"

"No. It's just a ready supply of fresh food. Mostly, I'm retired."

Jacob laughed so hard that he choked on his first bite. "You call working every day retired? And how did you get exiled here? Did your wife kick you out of the house?"

"I have no family. I'm just a sixty-year-old—"

"Spending his days putzing around in an old ghost town. At least the ranchers *work* here. Are you telling me you *chose* to retire here?"

"Eat your lunch," Dan snapped to shut Jacob up. "We have work to finish." He unwrapped his sandwich and took a bite he didn't taste. Never in a million years would he have chosen to live here.

It was pitch black outside before they started back home.

"Aren't you concerned about getting robbed while you're away?" Jacob asked.

"Nothing of value to steal."

"What about the gear in your general store—I saw fishing poles leaned up against the wall. Do you catch many fish in your dry creek?"

Dan nodded out his side window, a useless gesture in the

dark. "There's a dam a couple of miles off to my side stocked with largemouth bass. They grill up tasty."

"And your tools. Of course, it helps that everything looks deserted. Is that the *real* reason you keep it looking like a ghost town? So, nobody will steal anything?"

"You haven't told me anything about yourself," Dan said to change the subject.

"I was born in Grand Junction, Colorado. My father sells insurance, and my mother was a nurse until my kid sister came along. We moved to Price, South Dakota, when I was just a little kid."

"Never heard of the place."

"It's a Podunk town north of Sioux Falls. I was anxious to move back to the mountains, so I answered a help-wanted ad from a Denver replacement window manufacturer. I'm headed there tomorrow."

Dan turned onto Brule Street and parked his truck in its usual spot. Shutting off the headlights submerged them into total darkness.

Jacob immediately opened his door and climbed out. "I can't see my hand in front of my face," he complained. "You need to install a few streetlights—oh, that's right. This isn't a town."

Dan remained seated until his eyes adjusted. Stars filled the sky, twinkling in the clear air. Mars was rising, and the gauzy Milky Way arched overhead. There was nothing "stark" about this beauty.

"Look up," Dan said.

Jacob craned his neck. "Wow!"

CHAPTER 4

Dan's daily routine hadn't varied in over ten years: rise at six a.m. and breakfast on pancakes and eggs, ham or bacon, depending on his latest bartering; work until noon before pausing for lunch, usually a simple sandwich along Hat Creek; after a short siesta, labor on through to dinner time; retreat indoors, prepare a hearty meal and collapse into his favorite recliner to read; around ten p.m., hit the sack.

Dan had had no trouble keeping busy. Each building salvage started by erecting a rebuilt core within the wrapping of decayed exterior materials, after which he began interior renovations. Water well restoration had followed the water tower repairs, after which he trenched running water to his home. He electrified his house and Hartman's; he'd recently started on the old hotel. Splitting enough firewood to heat his home and Hartman's through the winter required dedication.

He seldom traveled other than bi-weekly trips to Edgemont for groceries, mail, or the bank and runs to the lumber store in

Hot Springs. He had met with his lawyer in Rapid City three times and trekked as far as Scottsbluff for repair parts. Of late, he had begun hiking long distances, usually along Hat Creek.

He had faced prolonged inactivity only three times—each self-inflicted. He blistered several toes on his right foot on a bitterly cold day, obliging him to recuperate in front of the warm fireplace until the frostbite healed. And three years after mangling his left arm inside the water tower, he'd fallen off a ladder, breaking his right foot.

On his bad days—early on, they had been frequent—he skipped the afternoon nap and outworked the melancholy. On his bad nights—those had stubbornly relented—he settled into his recliner and stared into the fireplace or wandered outside and gazed into the night sky until exhaustion lulled him to sleep.

His memories had never dulled.

Which left Dan conflicted as he strode toward the old hotel to offer Jacob a hot breakfast. His initial loathing at Jacob's intrusion had readily softened to ambivalence, dare he admit, amusement. He had had little occasion these years to smile or laugh; happiness was a foreign emotion, one he had thought permanently banished.

This morning, Dan found Jacob slumbering comfortingly inside the sleeping bag, clothes strewn on the floor in a jagged line leading from the front door to the makeshift bed. Seeing that Jacob's wallet had fallen out of his pocket, Dan stooped down and picked it up, intending to drop it on top of Jacob's jeans. It opened as he lifted it and Jacob's grainy learner's permit photo, hardly recognizable, stared back at him. *Learner's permit?* Dan located Jacob's printed birthdate and did the math.

"Jacob!" Dan barked, cursing himself for missing the obvious clues: Jacob passing through here a decade ago as a "little boy," no driving experience, peach fuzz for a beard, hungry from missed meals, hanging around instead of pushing on.

Jacob raised to a sitting position. "What?"

"You lied to me."

Jacob scowled. "When?"

"You told me you're on your way to Denver for a job."

"I am."

"You're a fifteen-year-old runaway!"

"I turn sixteen in a couple of weeks—how did you find out?"

Dan tossed the wallet into Jacob's lap. "From your learner's permit."

"You had no right going through my stuff," Jacob said, collecting his wallet.

"I didn't need permission because I didn't invite you here. Get your clothes on and meet me at my house."

Dan turned away and returned outdoors. "Not twenty years old," he complained aloud to the weeds. "Only a boy of fifteen."

If only Jacob had been preoccupied for a measly twenty seconds when they sped through. Dan sighed. Jacob would be none the wiser and delivered directly into the bowels of a big city, where he might already find himself walking the streets, easy prey for seasoned predators.

"No child should have to face that danger," Dan muttered. He had no excuse for letting self-pity overshadow Jacob's well-being. Difficult as it was to admit, *fortunate* circumstances had delivered Jacob to the base of his ladder.

Dan entered his home and stepped into his kitchen. Remembering Nadine's breakfast scraps, he dropped two skillets onto his stove and grabbed a slab of bacon and the pail of eggs from the refrigerator. He peeled off several strips of bacon into one skillet, greased the other, and poured pancake mix into his measuring cup, this time doubling the portion.

Dan left the skillets to heat at Jacob's knock and ushered him inside. "I salvaged much of it from the old homes," Dan explained when Jacob glanced critically at the furnishings. Weather and animals had ruined the fabric-covered items, but wooden pieces like his side tables and bookshelves were in better supply, and his chrome kitchen set must have been all the rage. His stuffed chair was a garage sale find.

"No television," Jacob noted.

"No television."

Jacob shook his head. "No bathroom *and* no television. An outhouse is one thing, but what do you do for entertainment?"

"Mostly, I read," Dan said, pointing at his bookshelf.

"That's some stash of books. Did you stumble upon a library, too?"

Dan shook his head. "Bought them by the pound from a second-hand store. Drop your pack and grab a seat at the table."

Dan returned to his kitchen and tilted the greased skillet to spread the hot grease. He stirred milk into the measuring cup and poured two circles of pancake batter into the skillet.

"I have a question to ask, Jacob, and I need the truth."

Jacob gingerly lowered himself onto the padded vinyl seat as if worried he might ruin Dan's tape job.

"Are you running away from an abusive home?" Dan asked

"No."

"The truth, Jacob."

"That *is* the absolute truth!"

Dan picked up a fork and flipped the sizzling bacon. "So, why are you running away?"

"I'm not running away. I finished tenth grade; I've done

my time. Call me a high school dropout if you like, but I'm no flunky. I despise school, so I applied for a job in Denver rather than waste my time sitting in a classroom for another two years."

Dan flipped the pancakes. "And what did your parents say about all of this?"

"I never told them."

Dan spun on Jacob. "So, you did run away?"

"I didn't run away. I'm moving on. And I left them a note."

Dan shook his head in dismay. "Left your parents a note. Jacob, I guarantee they're worried sick."

Dan forked the cooked bacon onto a plate and broke two eggs into the hot grease. Remembering Jacob, he broke two more eggs, added a little milk, and scrambled.

"So, a company in Denver offered you a job?"

"I answered an online ad. It's an entry-level position, stock handling. Nobody can outlift me."

"And they're aware you're only fifteen years old?"

"Sixteen in a couple of weeks. I can easily pass for a grownup. You thought so."

"Your learner's permit says otherwise."

"I won't show it to them. I brought my Social Security Card."

"Which they'll input into the system to gather the same information. Jacob, companies are required to follow federal labor laws. Minors aren't allowed to work more than three hours a day during school days, nor after seven p.m."

"How do you know that?"

"Everybody knows that."

Dan set two plates on the counter and slid a golden pancake onto each. "What will you do when this company turns you away?"

Judging by Jacob's frown, he hadn't considered that scenario. "I'll survive."

Dan shook his head. "Trust me, Jacob, living on the street is a fate you want to avoid. No roof over your head, nothing to eat, with unsavory people attempting to take advantage of you. You'll scurry home faster than a rabbit chased by a fox. Picture your friends laughing their asses off at your foolishness."

Dan turned off the burners and portioned the scrambled eggs and bacon onto the plates. He placed one in front of Jacob and the other at his place, then grabbed the butter and syrup from the refrigerator before taking his seat. "Salt and pepper," he said, nodding at the shakers.

"I applaud you for taking your future into your own hands, Jacob," Dan continued, buttering his pancake, "but your timing is off. You're only going to turn your dreams into a nightmare."

Once Jacob poured syrup over his pancake, Dan helped himself and dug into his meal, granting Jacob a moment's reprieve. He couldn't remain silent for long, though, because he must convince Jacob to return home before they finished eating.

"Mind if I offer you some advice?" Dan asked.

Jacob swallowed his mouthful. "Something tells me I have no choice."

"Consider it the penalty for trespassing. Here's my advice: return home and finish high school. Work evenings to save enough money for a car. With a diploma and a set of wheels, you can settle wherever your heart desires, this time with a legitimate chance of success."

"Two years," Jacob mumbled. He bit off a chunk of bacon as if it were jerky and chewed it down. "That's like twenty years in the state pen. Do you have a high school diploma?"

"Yes. And a college degree—two of them."

Jacob huffed. "Look where that got you."

Dan suffered the dig but didn't let on. "Don't just try to endure your remaining high school years, Jacob. Enjoy them. If you can't find much entertainment, then make your own. Take me, for example. Where else can you build a bonfire as big as a house without worrying about the fire department showing up?"

Jacob only huffed again, but Dan didn't dare press the matter further. Universally, teenagers think they're immortal and adults are stupid. If Jacob decided Dan was preaching to him, he might ignore Dan's advice out of hand, or worse, take it as a challenge rather than the intended warning. Jacob finished his meal in silence, though, staring a hole through his plate. Dan's words had left an impression.

After cleaning his plate, Jacob wiped his mouth with his sleeve. "You're a good cook."

"Thanks," Dan said. "I've had years of practice." He finished his meal. *What to do? What to do?* "I can't harbor a minor," he told Jacob. "But I can't send you on your way, either. Laws cover those responsibilities, as well."

"Meaning what?" Jacob asked. "You'll call my parents and have them pick me up?"

Dan nodded. "That *would* be the responsible next step. I don't own a phone, though."

Jacob's mouth flopped open. "What else do you live without?"

Poorly timed admission. Dan was attempting to convince Jacob to return home rather than encourage him to play twenty questions about Dan's spartan living standards. A computer? No. Internet? No. Air conditioning? Enough! At least I own a coffee maker.

"It's useless trying to understand me, Jacob," Dan said.

"The facts are, I can't let you stay here, and I'm certainly not going to send you on your way. The next step is up to you." He stood. "I trust you'll make the right decision."

Fear, ridicule, reason, advice. Dan had seeded Jacob's thoughts from several angles. Now let Jacob try on responsibility for size.

Dan stepped into his kitchen and poured himself a cup of coffee, figuring Jacob finally understood that life wasn't as simple when you're driving the car rather than riding in the back seat. With only himself to blame should circumstances sour, was he willing to risk ridicule from his friends by pulling such a stupid stunt? An important question to ponder when you're fifteen, going on sixteen.

Dan relaxed as Jacob continued to reflect, more convinced Jacob knew he had no choice. On cue, Jacob turned toward him.

"I think I should return home," Jacob said. "I didn't know about those labor laws."

"No way you could have," Dan said, happy to help Jacob save face. "Do *you* have a phone?"

"Of course. Everybody does—well, except you."

Dan smirked at Jacob. "Then phone your parents. I'll step outside to give you some privacy."

Jacob joined Dan a few minutes later, his phone tight to his chest. "My father wants to talk to you. He's in Denver. He was already searching for me."

Dan laughed. "Is he relieved or pissed off?"

"Pissed off, mostly." Jacob handed Dan the phone.

Dan deflected Roger's apologies and politely accepted his thank you's, assuring Roger that Jacob had behaved responsibly and hadn't posed a burden. Dan finished the conversation by providing directions.

He returned Jacob's phone. "Your father is on the way. He should arrive in about five hours."

Jacob spoke briefly to his father before ending the call. "Father told me to find out how much I owe you for food and everything."

Charging room and board! How amusing. Dan would fend off Roger by insisting Jacob had more than paid off his debts helping at the ranch, which was close to the truth. Just a few weeks of Jacob's strong muscles could clear a year's worth of Dan's backlog.

They only had five hours, though, and busying Jacob with hard labor would constitute punishment. A more entertaining use of Jacob's strength came to mind.

"Are you game for an adventure while we wait for your father?" Dan asked.

"Sure."

"Follow me, then."

Dan stepped behind Hartman's front counter and unrolled a set of blueprints onto the countertop. "These are the original prints for this building. I found them during renovation." He grabbed a few knickknacks to hold down the corners. "This top sheet is the plan view—the top view." He pressed his finger to a detail near the center of the building. "Those symbols indicate a staircase."

Jacob looked over his shoulder. "To the second floor?"

"No." Dan turned to the second page. "This elevation view—side view—shows a one-story building with no attic, just a truss roof."

"So, the stairs go down?"

Dan shook his head. "The drawings don't indicate a

basement, either."

"Nothing up and nothing down." Jacob looked at Dan. "So, is there even a staircase?"

"Bingo," Dan said. "That's the puzzle I'd like to solve. This way." Dan led Jacob between the two rows of oak shelving to the black cast iron stove squatting dead center of the room. It stood nearly seven feet tall and likely weighed over five hundred pounds.

"The staircase—if one exists—descends directly beneath this stove."

"Why would anybody place a stove over a staircase?" Jacob asked.

"To conceal the buried treasure, obviously," Dan said with a chuckle.

Jacob dropped to his hands and knees and pressed his face to the floor. Dan had already tried peering under the stove, but its legs were missing, presumably to fit it into the building, leaving only a tiny gap on either side of the frame.

"No way to see," Dan said.

Jacob stood and studied the stove. "I assume you're proposing we move this thing."

"You assume correctly. That's where your muscles come in." Dan retrieved a step ladder from the back corner of the room and climbed it to disconnect the stove pipe. "Now then, let's see if we can slide this monster."

Standing shoulder-to-shoulder, they positioned their hands and feet for best leverage and, with a "Now" from Dan, pushed. Dan immediately realized his folly; they might as well have tried moving a mountain. Jacob, though, had no interest in being bested. He moved his hands higher, then lower; faced the stove, then turned sideways to use his shoulder; silently, his cheeks puffed out, then aided by sustained grunting;

finally pushing so hard that his feet slipped from beneath him, dropping him to his knees.

"It was a long shot," Dan admitted.

Jacob slumped to the floor, panting heavily. "Nobody slid this stove out of the way to get to any staircase. If there is a trap door, they lifted the stove aside."

"We're short a few strong people to do that."

Jacob rose to his knees and turned to face the stove. "Archeologists think the Egyptians moved the heavy pyramid stones using logs as rollers."

Dan laughed aloud. "School isn't so useless, after all. Rollers, I have. Back outside."

They walked the gravel road beyond the water tower to Dan's pile of scrap steel. After burdening Jacob with five suitable lengths of round steel pipe, Dan collected several stub pieces of lumber and his truck's tire jack on their return trip.

Standing again before the stove, Dan located the jack beneath a protruding ledge in the ornate frame and tilted the stove high enough to slip boards beneath both corners. Repeating the lifting process on the opposite side of the frame, he spaced the metal pipes evenly beneath the stove.

"Imagine what the Egyptians could have built if they'd had hydraulic jacks," Jacob said once the stove rested on the pipes.

"Most likely, larger pyramids," Dan said. "Here's the plan. It'll take both of us to get this thing rolling. Once it starts, you keep pushing while I recycle the pipes."

They positioned their hands on the stove, each moving a foot back for leverage. "Ready?"

Jacob nodded. "Ready."

It took little effort to start the stove slipping sideways, their makeshift roller bearings grinding loudly over the wooden floor. Dan knelt when the first pipe cleared the bottom of the stove, quickly feeding it into the opposite side. "Those Egyptians were geniuses," he declared.

Jacob maintained a slow advance. A narrow kerf appeared in the flooring when Dan removed the second pipe, perhaps thirty inches long, with similar kerfs extending from either end and disappearing beneath the stove. The two parallel kerfs continued lengthening as Dan transferred more pipes until the fourth kerf appeared to form a square.

"Your trap door!" Jacob said excitedly.

"Let's hope so. Step around to the other side of the stove and start braking. It's time to stop this thing."

Dan fed one last pipe beneath the stove while Jacob parked it. The newly exposed flooring was unworn and deeper in color than the surrounding floor, evidence that it had been covered for untold years.

Jacob knelt beside the door. "Do you mind?"

"Not at all," Dan said.

Jacob hooked his finger into a small notch cut into one edge of the door and lifted it. "Wow," he said, setting the door aside.

Dan peered down at an unframed wooden staircase descending into blackness. Within seconds a cool updraft like the Childress's creamery well lifted a stale, desiccated odor, accented by an inert tang promising nothing living—or dead.

Dan retrieved two flashlights from his camping supplies and preceded Jacob down the steps onto a dirt floor. Primitive wooden shelving, all stocked, ran the length of the two long mortared rock walls.

"Honey," Dan said, lifting a dark orange glass jar from the nearest shelf. "Old honey."

"Why would somebody hide a jar of honey?" Jacob asked.

"No idea. Let's have a look around."

They scavenged through the shelves, discovering typical

general store wares from a bygone era: glass canning jars, a metal contraption with a crank handle Dan identified as an apple peeler, metal utensils, cards of buttons, faceted glass doorknobs and drawer pulls, iron skillets, leather boots, nails and wire, wrenches, shoe polish, boxes of matches, scissors, pins and needles. The persistent covering of dust further attested to the room's extended isolation.

"Cha-ching," Jacob said.

Dan spotlighted Jacob as he lifted a pocket watch dangling from a gold chain out of a box.

"Father collects old watches," Jacob said. "There's probably $200 worth just in this one box."

"Stuff a couple of them in your pocket for your father," Dan told Jacob. "But they don't explain why someone took such trouble to conceal this cellar. Back then, those watches were just common goods."

"Good point."

Dan was sorting through a wooden crate packed with tableware when he heard clinking glass. "More canning jars?" he asked.

"No," Jacob said. "'Chateau d' … Something-or-other.' I think it's French."

Dan carefully rewrapped the porcelain teacup he had been admiring and joined Jacob. "French wine," Dan affirmed when Jacob handed him the bottle. "*Old* French wine." He spotlighted the bottom of the label. "Vintage, 1922." Dan shone his flashlight onto the shelving and counted at least four cases of identical bottles.

"Is it drinkable?" Jacob asked.

"Wine can retain its flavor for hundreds of years when stored properly. And a cool, dark place like this certainly qualifies."

Dan found more spirits on the adjoining shelves: two cases of narrow-necked bottles with shorter, bell-shaped bottoms that turned out to be Scotch whiskey—real Scotch whiskey; a cache of English brandy, long-neck bottles of stout bodies tapering to a slightly smaller diameter at the bottom; Jamaican rum in tall square bottles; three cases of vodka bottled in classic clear glass; varieties of Italian wines. Every label Dan checked was dated between 1920 and 1925.

"The merchandise stored down here would look familiar on the shelves of a general store," Dan said. "A general store from a hundred years ago." He looked over the impressive collection of spirits. "I think I know why my Mr. Hartman was concealing this room."

"You do?" Jacob said.

"Yeah, here's my hypothesis: Mr. Hartman opened this general store in the early teens, let's say 1920." Dan held the bottle close to Jacob's face. "And tell me what's relevant about this bottle to that era?"

Jacob looked from Dan to the bottle and back. "Maybe that's covered in next year's history class."

"Prohibition is what's relevant," Dan said. "Alcohol was illegal, both to possess and to sell. And these bottles were high-quality, high-dollar spirits concealed from the authorities. Our Mr. Hartman was the preeminent supplier of quality spirits for the entire Black Hills region, but his business collapsed when the economy crashed in 1929, and this stash went unclaimed. The general store owner that the ranchers knew was unaware of this cellar and its buried treasure."

"Hypothesis or otherwise," Jacob said, "what are you going to do with everything?"

"For the time being, close this place back up. It's the best way to preserve everything." He nodded toward the stairs.

"After you."

Bottle in hand, Dan followed Jacob up the stairs.

It was noon by the time Dan finished reconnecting the stovepipe. He decided to lunch at his truck, eating outdoors to watch for Roger.

Dan dropped the tailgate and slid their meal into the bed.

"Grab a seat," Dan said, removing the twist tie from the loaf of bread.

"Your truck isn't much newer than some of these old cars," Jacob reminded Dan. "Are you sure this tailgate is strong enough to support us?"

"Bought new chains a couple of years ago," Dan said, flicking one of them with his finger. "I'm hoping to get a hundred years out of them."

Jacob chuckled and added his weight to the tailgate. The chains held, though the truck's springs complained.

Jacob assembled a sandwich before removing his phone and one of the old stopwatches from his pants pocket. Episodes of feverish two-handed thumb typing alternated with bites. Dan could only shake his head. This generation's skillset was different than his.

"I was wrong about the value of these stopwatches," Jacob said.

"Worthless trinkets?"

"The opposite. Two hundred dollars. Apiece."

"Apiece?"

Jacob nodded. "I bet some of your other buried junk is valuable, too."

Jacob assembled a second sandwich. "My father will be arriving soon. Have you got any more advice for me?"

Dan would have bet his life against hearing Jacob ask that

question. He laid down his sandwich and wiped his mouth.

"Firstly, as I said before, return home and finish school."

Jacob screwed up his face.

"Sorry," Dan said, "but a high school diploma opens more doors than you can imagine. Secondly, between now and graduation, squirrel away every penny you earn. Big cities are expensive."

Jacob nodded in agreement with that idea.

"And lastly," Dan said, "start considering your career."

Jacob frowned as if Dan had suggested he give up dating.

"There are alternatives to colleges," Dan said. "Trade schools, night classes, even applying yourself to the task at hand. I'm saying, Jacob, to set yourself up for success. Life can and will throw some nasty curveballs at you.

"I hope that helps."

"I guess," Jacob said, shrugging. "But I meant advice on surviving the trip home."

"Ah."

Dan ran his hand over his stubbled cheek. "Saying 'sorry' is a prerequisite. And thanking your father for picking you up could go a long way—and hand him a stopwatch as soon as you climb into the car."

CHAPTER 5

"Thank you again," Roger told Dan, shaking Dan's hand for the fourth time. "My wife and I are grateful for your compassion." He climbed into the car, adding with a relieved chuckle, "We'll make sure Jacob doesn't bother you again."

Dan watched the pair depart before returning to his house. He was proud that he had chosen to turn toward the difficulty, acting honorably to impact Jacob's life positively. Dan firmly believed that his intervention had placed Jacob in a far better situation.

The unfamiliar buoyancy aroused the lighthearted fantasy that more needful souls might stumble through. Perhaps a pair of college coeds the ages his daughters would now be, with car trouble, needing rescue. He smiled at the thought. Didn't this renewed willingness to help others prove he had *some* redeeming quality?

Dan peered into the corner of the room at the small safe he had discovered buried under the post office's collapsed front wall. He had lugged it into his home to secure his valuable documents and his priceless photo album, a Father's Day gift from his daughters, never opening it again. Some memories were too painful to relive.

A relentless yearning fortified by his good deed induced Dan to fish the safe key from the glass bowl resting on his bedroom dresser. He removed the photo album to his chair, recalling his daughters squeezing into his recliner on either side of him. "Open it! Open it!" they had implored. Just as on that day, he complied.

The captivating photo took Dan's breath away. She was more beautiful than the vision his memory had preserved: hazel eyes, calm and serene, a button nose sprinkled with freckles, full lips curled into a smile hinting of shared intimacy, and a heart-shaped chin, all framed by wavy auburn hair. He cursed his inability to return to that morning.

"Hello," he said, sliding a fingertip over her cheek. She deserved an apology, but since he hadn't planned this reunion, anything he said would come out wrong.

"I talked a runaway off the dangerous path he was following," Dan said. "Jacob might have ended up on the street if I hadn't been here."

He shook his head. "I don't know why I was allowed to be in the right place to help him, but not you." Tears welled in his eyes. "You would have been so proud of me," he added, the words catching in his throat.

More than his blurry vision, guilt stilled Dan's hand and prevented him from turning the page. Retrieving his album had been a mistake, exposing his old wounds of self-loathing and shame to the harsh light of day. He replaced it in the safe and returned outdoors. No longer in any mood for accidental company, he veered through the thick weeds behind his house, away from the road and any prying eyes.

Dan considered what had possessed him to risk his mental equilibrium by dredging up his past. The obvious answer was that he wished to see his family again. "Hah!" he yelled. Pure fallacy. He had *always* cherished those photos—why else had he brought the album with him? —yet he'd left it untouched these ten years.

He stopped and dropped his truck's tailgate to stress his shiny new tailgate chains. A more accurate assessment was that he had erroneously assumed a single good deed would magically right all the wrongs locking his album away. That he had been in error was an admission nearly as painful to swallow as the anguish forcing him to return it into the safe. It spoke volumes of his momentary bout of stupidity.

Dan shook his head. Enough degrading himself. He hadn't been wrong in hoping he was up to facing his memories, merely premature, a blunder facilitated by the rehabilitative effects of dealing with Jacob. Youth had always affected him so, only he had assumed their presence in his life one more permanent absence. Considering he'd just contemplated a needy pair appearing on his doorstep, apparently not.

Dan focused on the empty spot beside him that Jacob had last occupied. Seeing no reason to leave this intrusion of the past incomplete, he conjured up his younger, professional version: driven, compassionate, and unwavering in his belief that everybody was worth saving.

What do you want in life? his younger self asked. And direct, too. Dan had never been one to beat around the bush.

Dan knew the answer: to face his family again, a proud husband and father. Only then could he smile at the wealth of memories preserved in each photo, deservedly joyous as any ordinary husband and father.

Then earn it. Dan could have predicted that line. His younger self disdained charity, prescribing to the dictum that people derive lasting benefit only through active participation in their treatment. Gift someone a house, and they will trash it. Empower that same person to build their new home, and they will defend it as their castle. Dan's opinion, considering it anew, hadn't mellowed.

He laughed aloud at a sudden realization: From Jacob's arrival to Roger and Jacob's departure, from Dan's initial flight responses to embracing his role as a responsible adult, from ingrained hopelessness turned hopeful optimism, this entire affair had demonstrated that he *could* and, more importantly, *wanted* to earn the right to pull his album from its hiding place and display it proudly, announcing to all, "This was my family."

Dan pulled his hand down his face and scrutinized the gray buildings he had made standing again, malignant growths of his compulsion for concealment and insulation.

Even Jacob had seen through his work as aimless, sedating toil to suppress traumatic memories as securely as burying his photo album behind that locked door. But recent events had opened his mental lock, and his foolhardy attempt at the album had exposed his goal, his dream. There was, he understood, no turning back.

How, then, could he earn his goal, his dream? He dug his fingertips through the dirt-filled crevasses of the corrugated steel tailgate, understanding that the deeds inciting his attempt with the album had also taught him the currency: helping more Jacobs.

Easier said than done. While erecting a convenience store along the highway would advertise his presence, serving fountain drinks wouldn't earn minimum wage. "You're a lifesaver!" Roger had exclaimed. Broadly defined, that was the minimum standard to guide Dan's conduct.

Restating his last question: How could he "save lives" while living miles from nowhere? Jacob's constant harping on "your town" grabbed Dan's imagination, and the idea formed fully fleshed out, so audacious that Dan sprung to his feet to take quick stock of his unintentional rebuilding project. Between his home and the hotel he had ample living quarters to get started, plus electricity and water sources to render them livable. Of course, the legal hurdles would be tall, so too, the layers of regulations. Looking critically at his assets, addressing those two areas might require creative solutions. Dan had no delusions about the enormity of his task of making this place livable again, but laboring for a purpose would be a welcome challenge.

Jacob had asked if Dan was creating a haunted attraction. Another vital clue. To passersby, this must remain a ghost town. And, with a nod to his younger self, bare existence should be challenging, nothing soft or easy.

Dan raised the tailgate and strode purposefully towards his home, shedding the shackles of his self-imposed exile. It was time to put this place back on the map.

CHAPTER 6

Dan's first two state inspections had been painless, his efforts limited to digging out record books and preparing lunch. Hank Hutchings, the well-seasoned inspector, signed off sight-unseen on most items after chatting over a sandwich and a beer.

But the immaculate white Chevy truck pulling into town in place of Hank's beat-up green Ford suggested today would be different. And Dan knew lunch was off when a young man attired in a dress shirt and khakis exited the truck, clipboard in hand, a tape measure clipped to his belt.

"Todd Sterner," the younger man announced. Todd was thirtysomething and slightly built, with neatly trimmed hair, a beak nose, and a receding chin.

"Dan Stuart," Dan said in a friendly tone. "Subbing for Hank?"

Todd shook his head dryly. "Hank retired two months ago." He eyed the buildings dubiously. "Why am I here?"

"We've incorporated, now," Dan answered. "Puts us on the inspection schedule."

Todd remained unconvinced.

"It's a work in progress," Dan admitted. "I envisioned Hat Creek as a wellness retreat for people who could benefit by escaping the complicated, fast-paced, often suffocating real world."

That only earned Dan a raised eyebrow.

"Through the guise of living in a ghost town," Dan finished.

Todd rapped his clipboard with his ink pen. "Let's get started, then."

Dan lamented Hank's retirement quicker than a frigid winter blast burns exposed skin. Hank had quenched his thirst from the nearest faucet and declared that all was well, seeing as the water was clear and he was still standing. Todd, conversely, produced an impressive water test kit equipped with an array of small plastic dropper bottles and plastic vials. Armed with a laminated sheet peppered with color charts, Todd commenced a battery of water tests at the pumping station beneath the water tower.

"You're borderline on both turbidity and toxicity," Todd said. "Turbidity is merely aesthetic, but toxicity will shut you down." He nodded at the water filter housing. "When did you last change the filter?"

"Three months ago," Dan replied, though the truth was closer to a year.

"Good filters don't foul that quickly. I suggest you check your seals."

Dan confessed that he hadn't started a preventive maintenance log. Todd drew one on a blank sheet of paper and inspected every motor, water valve, and pump seal, citing Dan for a broken lockout handle and the missing log.

The most attention Hank had ever paid to Hat Creek's holding pond was advising Dan on using a fountain as a water circulator to control odors. Todd donned chest-high waders and, posing as a deranged trout fisher, traversed the length of the wastewater. "Three-foot depth is what we're looking for," he told Dan, explaining the fluorescent orange stripe across the front of the waders. "Most ponds require periodic dredging." Todd collected a water sample and swabbed the spill tube before citing Dan for the missing "keep out" signs.

Among Hank's stated positions was that rural drivers had the brains to check for oncoming traffic at intersections. Todd required Dan to replace the gravel road's damaged stop signs. Of Todd's recommendation that Dan paint crosswalks, Dan remained tight-lipped, imagining the ranchers' jibes should such white lines ever disfigure the landscape.

After inspecting Hartman's and Westside and recording every refrigerator and freezer's temperatures, Todd applied the final flourishes to his paperwork. "I've listed your action items on top; seven citations, three monetary that I've suspended pending compliance by your next inspection."

"You've done Hank proud," Dan said, straight-faced. If Todd expected gratitude for being lenient, he was mistaken. Dan would betray Hat Creek's occupancy with a dancing water fountain before stooping so low.

"Let's wrap this up," Todd said. "I just need your records binder."

Hank always left it to Dan to collate the inspection paperwork, so the binder remained in Dan's safe. He hustled to his house to retrieve it, vowing to carve out space for it on his bookshelf to avoid a repeat of glimpsing the corner of his photo album. Todd was eyeing Grange Hall's deteriorating roof when he returned, so Dan hurriedly pointed out the actual roof, fearing the inspector would demand to inspect his buildings.

"There's still the issue of falling debris," Todd said. "That's city responsibility, though, so I assume it meets your building codes."

Todd took possession of the binder and leafed through several forms. "Everything rubberstamped, same as I found in Slater and Hampton. Hank worked a few years too long." Todd flipped back to the front of the binder and snapped his additions inside.

"We'll treat your next inspection as an initial inspection," Todd said. He returned Dan's records binder and eyed the ruins of the former post office. "Starting with your building codes."

The fast-approaching whirlwind caught Dan's attention. Once he made out the blue eagle logo and red and blue stripes of a US Postal Service truck racing along the gravel road, he started for the mailbox he had mounted along the road facing Grange Hall. Time to meet the mailman.

He rested his forearm on his rusted steel mailbox to await the truck's arrival. The garbage dump find was too dented to shut, plus missing its little red flag. But function was secondary to complimenting the town décor.

The mail truck slowed to a stop alongside. Make that meet the mail*woman*. She had a round face with high cheekbones and crow's feet at the corners of her eyes, making her look happy even though she wasn't smiling. She wore little makeup, and her skin showed the aging Dan's might if he wasn't out in the sun all day. Short, wavy, gray-streaked brown hair stuck out below a well-worn cowboy hat.

She reached out her window to hand Dan two envelopes and a folded circular. "At first, I didn't believe this was a town again, but here you are."

"Here I am," Dan said.

"How many mailboxes?"

"Just this one."

"One?"

Dan smiled. "Just one person."

"Just you? A town of one?"

Dan nodded.

The mailwoman nodded back. "Ain't that novel. That must make you the 'Dan Stuart' in the address."

"That it does," Dan confirmed.

"Maggie Johnson," she said, offering her hand. "It's a pleasure to meet you, Dan."

Her palm was softer than Dan had expected. "Same here."

"You also received a package," she said, releasing her seatbelt. "Large and thin, almost too heavy to lift."

"That would be my road signs."

"I'll meet you at the back," Maggie said and disappeared between the seats into the bowels of the truck. After loud jostling, she swung open the rear door and pushed out a corrugated box. Dan wrestled it vertically and propped it against the mailbox before meeting her back at the cab.

"I haven't driven these parts for years," she said, climbing back into her seat. "Your stop more than doubles my daily route."

"Weekly deliveries would suit me," Dan said. "I receive little mail and send out even less."

"We're required by law to provide daily service, Monday through Saturday." Maggie stared at Dan harder than necessary, visibly distracted by something about his face. Dan wondered if he had cut himself again.

"At the very least, I'll be stopping by every day you get

mail," she said, her words trailing off. "My, but don't you have the brightest green eyes." She flashed a friendly smile and shifted the truck into gear. "Here's hoping you get mail every day," she said with a playful laugh before driving away.

A great horned owl greeted Dan with an early morning salutation as he finished securing the sign to the square metal post. He nodded in return and knelt to shut his toolbox. A bee buzzed absentmindedly amongst a stand of fragrant purple asters to his left, while a grasshopper inches behind his boot chirped fretfully. A soft breeze stirred the nearby field of wheatgrass into undulating waves and rustled through the cottonwood trees lining the now namesake creek. After a dozen years of uneventful solitude, for better or worse—for better *and* worse, likely—Dan's life was about to undergo a second upheaval.

He stood and stepped back to read the road sign that, along with its twin mounted at the opposite end of town, would greet passersby and each temporary resident: Hat Creek, Population 1.

The First Flower of Spring

Dan peered at his front window and watched Hat Creek Retreat's newest residents cautiously exit their car. Vanessa Peterson hoped the change of scenery would alleviate a prolonged bout of postpartum depression. Vanessa's husband, Max, walked around the car to join her, and they warily eyed the nearest dilapidated building—Dan's original home.

The couple's reaction was amusingly common. The scattering of decayed buildings, junked cars, and tangles of menacing weeds suggested that their map or taxi had deposited them in the wrong place. Even when the couple gazed across the road directly at Dan, they remained unaware of his attention.

Dan had constructed his home's new front wall inside the crumbling original, a vertical duplicate of Grange Hall's roof. Peering out a ragged hole in the weathered boards, Dan watched Vanessa turn to open the rear car door and lean inside, momentarily straightening and clutching an infant to her chest. An infant? The Petersons' application hadn't mentioned anything about bringing an infant!

Dan cursed his stupidity. Of course, the Petersons would bring their child. Postpartum depression indicated pregnancy followed by childbirth—big clue, Dan—and parents didn't board infants like cats and dogs. Dan stepped outside into the crisp spring afternoon, making a mental note to add a crib to tomorrow's shopping list.

"Welcome to Hat Creek," he called out.

The couple turned, their apprehension dissolving. "We were beginning to wonder," Max said.

"Dan Stuart," Dan announced, crossing the blacktop. "You must be Max and Vanessa."

"Yes," Vanessa said. "And this is Lily."

The tiny girl, dressed head to toe in pink, smiled at Dan and began bouncing up and down.

"I think Lily likes you," Vanessa said.

Dan stepped to place Max between himself and the vivacious bundle.

"Your website *does* describe Hat Creek as an old ghost town," Max said. "To be honest, we weren't expecting something quite so … literal."

The couple further relaxed when three residents spilled out of Grange Hall, transitioning the deserted ghost town into an occupied Wellness Retreat. Just as quickly, though, Vanessa's eyes widened in alarm.

"That's Grange Hall," Dan said, knowing the source of Vanessa's concern. "Our boarding house and laundry facilities."

"People *stay* there?" she asked, instinctively pulling Lily closer to her chest.

"I'm putting you in a cabin, though, to give you a little more privacy," Dan said.

Max pointed across the road. "And the building you appeared from?"

Dan nodded. "My home."

"Your home?"

Vanessa burst into laughter. "Now, I know we chose the right place. Lily can't possibly make a mess here."

"I'll show you to your cabin," Dan said. "First, though, let's get that shiny car out of sight. It's standing out like a sore thumb."

Dan dispatched his Hat Creek residents to Rapid City for Garage Sale Saturday after the next morning's breakfast in Westside, the cafeteria-style diner Dan had slapped onto Hartman's west face. Arming the group, now five adults and one infant strong, with a wish list and a supply of cash, Dan invited them to spend any leftover funds towards Hat Creek's "general beautification." Not all challenges need to be serious.

The Peterson's cabin squatted along the east side of Brule Street, facing Dan's original home. Peering out its front window typically offered a panoramic view of Hartman's through the collection of junkers and a peek at Dan's present home from behind his old one.

But a pink plastic bird perched atop a metal rod marred today's view. The garage sale group's haul from their Rapid City expedition included for Hat Creek a tarnished copper rooster weathervane, a wind chime—and a pink flamingo. Lily was so enamored with the long-necked bird that Dan insisted they place it in front of the Peterson's cabin rather than his. But the garish decoration was destined for Dan's trash pile once the responsible parties departed. No respectable ghost town flaunts its pink flamingo.

The unsavory duty of babysitting placed Dan at the Peterson's front window, roped in by Vanessa's promise that she and Max would return before Lily awoke from her nap. That hadn't stopped Dan from pacing the floor, a nervous wreck. Was Lily uncovered? Sucking her thumb instead of the pacifier? Sleeping on her stomach? Tangled in the crib railing? Dan had checked in on her once but didn't dare again, fearing he'd wake her.

He'd spent the fretful time considering the inherent dangers of children of *any* age staying in Hat Creek. What if a child were injured, fell ill, or suffered an allergic reaction? Medical resources were far away, and it was impractical to make Hat Creek child-safe. The prudent course of action was obvious: immediately after relieving Hat Creek of its pink embarrassment, Dan would modify his application rules to prohibit children.

Soon peace of mind outweighed the risk of waking Lily, and again Dan tiptoed into Lily's room. She was lying on her side in the middle of the crib pad, hugging her blanket to her cheek, her tiny chest rising and falling in peaceful slumber. Before leaving the room, Dan cracked open her window to let in a little fresh air.

Promises, promises. Lily was awake, as in babbling "ba-ba-ba-ba" awake. If Dan showed his face, she would demand to be held. But if he ignored her much longer, she'd likely start screaming. *Damned if I do and damned if I don't.*

The front door unexpectedly swung open. Dan started for the bedroom door before being caught cowering, saying "Great timing. Lily just awoke," with credible enthusiasm as Vanessa stepped inside. "How was your outing?"

"It was wonderful," Vanessa said, closing the door behind her. "Max stopped by Westside to fix Lily a bottle."

Dan followed Vanessa into the bedroom. Lily's face lit up when she saw her mother, and she reached skyward, fingers fluttering.

Vanessa swept Lily into her arms and kissed her repeatedly. "And how is my little lady?"

Lily bounced and babbled in reply.

"Let's change your diaper before we go see Daddy. Hold Lily for me, will you, Dan?"

"Um," was all Dan got out before Vanessa dumped Lily into his reluctant arms.

"She won't break," Vanessa laughed, reaching for the changing pad.

"It's been a while," Dan said before forgetting the remainder of his excuse. Lily was remembered lightness, a priceless treasure incapable of mistake or meanness. She grabbed a fistful of Dan's shirt and probed his face, squeezing his nose before trying to poke his eye.

"Lily's never seen such bright eyes," Vanessa said. "Neither have I."

Memories surfaced of ultrafine hair, flawless skin, wondrous eyes, pouty lips, tiny fingernails, and sour baby smell; a bundle of stolen goods returned. Perhaps Dan should reconsider this ban on children. Lily smiled back into his smile and spoke to him. "Ba-ba-ba-ba."

"Yes, he *is* a wonderful man, isn't he, Lily?" Vanessa squeezed Dan's shoulder and kissed his cheek. "I haven't felt this good in so long."

Lily wriggled in delight at her mother's affection and opened her mouth to plant a wet kiss on Dan's cheek.

CHAPTER 7

Dan stepped to his front window when he heard the car slowing along the highway and watched as a white sedan passed his house at a crawl before crossing the median to park off the blacktop just short of the gravel road. Hat Creek's first intern stepped out and hurried through the weeds to the safety of the shoulder of the road, swatting at the grasshoppers her arrival had stirred. Attired in a fitted T-shirt and jeans, with her muddy brown hair tied back in a ponytail, she looked every bit the innocent nineteen-year-old coed. But Dr. Malkovich, Michelle Drake's sponsoring psychology professor and Hat Creek's professional consultant, had cautioned Dan against underestimating Michelle's intensity. And the good doctor had expressly invited Dan to challenge the young New York City native's idealism.

Knock the young lady down a peg, in other words. Hat Creek had gotten off to a flying start on its own: tall weeds, pesky grasshoppers, hot weather, and no residents in view.

Michelle crossed her arms over her chest and slowly turned to take in the scenery, her face contorting with disdain and trepidation. Nicely done, town!

Dan stepped outdoors and showed his face. "Dan Stuart," he called out, soldiering through the weeds the young woman was specifically avoiding. Dan had learned that tall, dense, and unkempt weeds such as this stand contributed greatly to Hat Creek's aura. "You must be Michelle Drake."

She turned at the sound of his voice and smiled, finding amusement in his struggle through the tangle.

"Those weeds nearly swallowed me up," he said when he reached the road.

"I'm more accustomed to traffic jams," Michelle said, staring at her feet. "And sidewalks. I'm accustomed to sidewalks."

"Sorry," Dan said, "but the best we can supply is dirt paths. Since the weeds have the run of the place, foot traffic determines our dirt paths' placement. A democratic process."

A large flash of green alighted on Michelle's leg. She jumped with a startled squeak and swatted it away.

"That was *huge*," she said.

"Our grasshoppers grow quite large," Dan admitted. "They also have the run of the place. As you discovered, they're particularly fond of weeds."

"Anything else fond of the weeds?"

"Mosquitoes, after a rain; rattlesnakes, during hot spells."

Michelle warily eyed the weeds ringing her car.

"Residents are in little danger from snakes unless they get too adventurous," Dan assured her.

"In other words, stay on the paths?"

Dan couldn't help piling it on. "Except when cattle wander through town. Then, I recommend remaining indoors, especially if a bull is present. And mountain lions have been spotted in these parts, though I've never seen one. Plus, the official flood evacuation route is climbing the water tower."

Before Michelle could recover, Dan directed her attention across the road at his original house.

"I'm putting you up in there."

Michelle only shrunk further. The cabin's exterior had aged another year since the retreat's opening, a full dozen years since Dan first occupied it, but the interior met Todd's strict standards.

"Take your time getting settled," Dan said. "Meet me in Westside for a cup of coffee, and I'll introduce you to Hat Creek." He pointed at Hartman's. "The diner is attached to the far side of our general store.

"Oh, and one last thing." Dan pointed out the rusted-out Buick with the torn landau roof amongst the junkers. "Before you join me, please move your car behind that one."

"I don't understand."

Dan chuckled and swept his arm the breadth of his town. "Shiny rental cars most definitely do *not* have the run of the place."

Michelle entered Westside and shook her head, clearly bemused. "It's going to take me a while to adjust to Hat Creek, Mr. Stuart—"

"Dan, please," he said, standing from his seat.

"Dan. Arriving at my rickety front door, I noticed the broken window and rotting siding and said to myself, 'Mr. Stuart can't intend for me to stay here.' But I let myself in and—you know what I found.

"Then, on my way here, I peeked inside your general store and discovered a museum."

Dan chuckled.

"I have so many questions," Michelle said with a laugh of her own.

"And I'm here to answer them." Dan made an ushering motion. "First, though, coffee."

Michelle deposited her notebook on the square table and shadowed Dan to the coffee pot on a wooden table placed along the dining area's back wall. Cici Decker and Stella Beal sat deep in conversation at Hat Creek's computer hub along the left wall. Alik Popov occupied one end of two long tables butted end-to-end cafeteria-style to their right, preparing his cameras for this evening's photo session. Afternoon sunlight streamed through the west-facing double-hung windows onto plank flooring salvaged from the same buildings as the siding and shingles. Overhead, two ceiling fans turned lazily.

Michelle stirred creamer into her coffee and peeked into the doorway leading back to a kitchen equipped with a double sink, two stoves, and two refrigerators.

"Westside is Hat Creek's only contemporary building," Dan said. "I didn't have a suitable dining room space."

"It *looks* old," Michelle commented as they returned up the aisle. "It's spooky being unsure what you'll find on the other side of any door."

Dan smiled. "Things will make more sense once I show you around." They took their seats. "First, tell me what brings you here."

"Long story short," Michelle said, "a high school teacher introduced me to psychology through a summer class at Columbia University, sponsored by Dr. Malkovich. That's how I met her and why I decided to attend Columbia."

Michelle's last statement addressed Dr. Malkovich's reverent comments about her budding protégé. Dr. Malkovich said the university's undergraduate acceptance rate hovered around seven percent. Columbia decided whom to accept, not the other way around.

"I pestered Dr. Malkovich for a summer project, so she suggested I check out your retreat," Michelle continued. "She described Hat Creek as a non-specific wellness and recovery center employing unusual and innovative techniques and tasked me with understanding how your retreat functions to assist her in developing methodologies to measure its effectiveness."

Dan chuckled inwardly at Michelle's ease with the jargon, recalling Dr. Malkovich's initial "you wish to do what?" reaction to his proposal. Dan guessed the good professor also hoped Michelle gained insights into what made Dan "tick." Dr. Malkovich's enthusiasm to participate in Dan's innovative experiment had suspended her curiosity about him spending a decade rebuilding a ghost town before considering how to exploit it, but assuredly hadn't extinguished it.

"I hope we interest your fascination," Dan said. "We'll start your tour here while you finish your coffee. Westside is open twenty-four-seven. I supply traditional breakfast fare: eggs, bacon, toast, muffins, yogurt, and fresh fruits. Supplies only, though. Residents cook for themselves. Same as Hat Creek is not a resort, Westside is not a restaurant.

"Residents are on their own for lunch and dinner; most dinners are community efforts. We receive fresh food deliveries twice weekly, excepting extreme circumstances, such as last winter's blizzard that stranded us for over a week."

Michelle's eyes widened. "Did you run out of food?"

"No, but the precarious situation prompted one of the residents to take the lead in managing a rationing program."

"Self-help," Michelle said. "Dr. Malkovich said that was Hat Creek's hallmark."

"Yes," Dan answered. "Dr. Malkovich's most valuable

contribution was organizing my ideas into a coherent plan."

"How did you meet her?"

"Let's head outside, and I'll fill you in."

Dan deposited their coffee into the dirty dishes tub and met Michelle, notebook in hand, at the front door. "I knew how I wanted Hat Creek to function," he said, ushering her into the summer heat, "but clueless about how to pull it all together. I stumbled onto Dr. Malkovich's work while researching and liked what I read. So, I contacted her.

"Let's step inside Hartman's," Dan said. "I orient every new resident, so they know where to find supplies."

Dan continued his story inside the store. "Dr. Malkovich flew out and lent her expertise. She felt the quirky isolation combined with an absence of resident professionals—I employ no psychologist or psychiatrist staff—dictated that Hat Creek operate as a self-help retreat."

Dan led Michelle down the far-left aisle. "You'll find staples, meats, snacks, and condiments on these shelves and in the coolers along the back wall." He pointed out toiletries, lightbulbs, cleaning supplies, and other miscellaneous necessities as they returned up the center aisle.

"Dr. Malkovich reasoned residents would gain limited benefit in being handed a room key and told, 'enjoy your stay,'" Dan continued, "no matter how far removed from home. To promote healthy introspection, she recommended we provide access to challenging duties, activities, and situations. So, in addition to staples, you'll find supplies for a broad range of pursuits here."

He pointed at the drawing tablets, paints and pencils, sculpting tools, and clay. "Creative supplies have proven popular. Highly therapeutic."

"People pictorially expressing their issues?" Michelle

guessed.

"Yes." Dan walked around the end of the last cabinet and started down the central aisle. "Found materials; items collected during renovations. Everybody loves this junk."

Michelle picked up one of the picture frames crowding the top shelf. "Did these come from the old homes?"

Dan nodded. "Lots of memories." Three of the old frames now occupied places of honor on Dan's fireplace mantle, displaying photos sent by appreciative residents. The tangible evidence that Hat Creek provided a valuable service was satisfying.

"Lots of stories, too, I bet," Michelle said.

Dan moved on to distance himself from *his* old memories. "Hiking and camping are popular activities," he said as they neared the back of the store. "I've stocked backpacks, tents, sleeping bags, mess kits; you name it. Residents are free to hike wherever they wish, though most follow the creek: zero chance of getting lost, a ready supply of firewood, and"—he picked up a cartridge water filter—"access to water when the creek is flowing.

"Fishing gear," Dan announced, making his way along the oak shelves. "Rods and reels, fishing tackle. There's a stocked dam within walking distance."

Dan pointed at the contents of a large barrel. "Work gloves and hats. Weekly, residents help at a local ranch. Our next trip is on Monday."

"Count me in," Michelle said.

"Great."

Dan escorted Michelle outside. "Motivated residents invent new occupations," he said as they crossed the gravel road. "One resident proposed a community vegetable garden, even staking out a suitable spot."

Michelle nodded. "Self-sufficiency. Dr. Malkovich mentioned that aspect of Hat Creek, too."

Dan led Michelle close to ruins sagging over ragged stubs of a block wall. "This was once the town's post office," Dan said. "It's not stable, so it's off-limits."

"Is it on your list to rebuild?" Michelle asked.

Dan shook his head. "Too much effort."

"A source of materials, then?"

Dan smiled. "No. Its presence helps preserve Hat Creek's ghost town feel."

Michelle faced south. "Same as the ruins I noticed when arriving."

"Exactly."

"Placed in the middle of nowhere …" Michelle nodded. "'Hat Creek's isolation and appearance as a ghost town are its enablers,' Dr. Malkovich told me. 'Transport people far away from their problems, both in distance and time, to the simplest, most unpretentious surroundings imaginable, concurrently unburdening them from the pressures of modern life.' Her words are already starting to make sense."

Michelle turned back to face Dan. "How much snow fell during last year's blizzard?"

"Over three feet."

"Your residents had to dig their way to the food, didn't they?"

Dan nodded. "And to the firewood. That's how Hat Creek operates."

"Nothing like rescuing yourself from real-life danger to place your other issues in proper perspective," Michelle said.

"You're very perceptive," Dan said. The post-storm celebration had been a high point of the retreat. "Dr. Malkovich assured me you would appreciate the not-so-subtle subtlety."

Michelle smiled, obviously pleased at the praise.

"Shall we continue our tour?" Dan said. "Finishing the story of Dr. Malkovich's contributions, she assisted with administrative details such as retreat rules, application forms, records keeping, regulatory compliance—the list was extensive. Once I established an inhabitable living environment, I opened the retreat."

Dan nodded ahead of them across the highway. "I typically assign singles a room in our boarding house. Grange Hall was the first resident living space I renovated."

Michelle's step suffered that familiar glitch when she noticed the gaping hole in the old hotel's roof. She was still craning her neck, trying to understand the gash, as they climbed the stairs and stepped inside. Dan had framed three small rooms on either side of a central hallway while plumbing a community bathroom and two pairs of washers and dryers at the far end. Dan opened the door to one of the rooms for a quick peek. Finished to the same standards as Westside and Michelle's cabin, it was spartanly furnished: double bed, dresser, desk and chair, padded chair.

"No television," Michelle said.

"No television. No cable. No wireless internet—just a wired installation at the computer hub inside Westside. And no data service. We're too far away from the nearest tower."

"Does anybody complain?"

"Everybody complains. But the retreat needs as much help as it can get. Physical separation isn't the severe isolation it once was."

Michelle hummed in amusement. "Nor the form that affects people the greatest anymore."

"Exactly."

"How do you screen potential residents?" Michelle asked

after they had returned outdoors.

"It's less rigorous than you might assume," Dan answered. "No life story, no doctor's referral, and only enough explanation to filter out vacationers. Hat Creek isn't a dude ranch."

Michelle laughed at that.

"Having said that," Dan continued, "I've recently expanded my definition of self-help. A writer contacted me seeking a little solitude, which proved beneficial to Hat Creek; she used the written word to draw out a few residents. Alik, the photographer you saw sitting with his cameras at the table inside Westside, is attempting similar therapy through pictures.

"And, as a matter of principle, I don't turn anybody away. Two people have shown up unannounced."

They reached Brule Street's twin ruts. "Hat Creek's sole residential street," Dan said, pointing at the old street sign. "As it were."

"I can't tell which buildings you've rebuilt and which you haven't," Michelle said as they strode along the ruts. "All of them? None of them?"

"In addition to Grange Hall, I've rebuilt five cabins, your place and mine included." Dan nodded at the last cabin in line. "That's Alik's place. He requested a quiet environment within this quiet environment, something about sensitive hearing."

Michelle paused and turned a slow three-sixty. "Dr. Malkovich told me *you* rebuilt Hat Creek, working alone."

"Yes." Dan was proud of that, proud of those he'd already helped.

"To temporarily shelter troubled people and provide an environment conducive to relief and recovery." Michelle furrowed her brows. "But not to earn a living."

"No," Dan agreed. "There is a fee structure, though it's means-based. Acceptance to visit Hat Creek isn't dependent on the ability to pay."

"*Not* to earn a living," Michelle confirmed. "But *for* a reason." She nodded at her epiphany and walked on.

Dan ushered Michelle onto the dirt path leading to Jacob's fire ring, already leery of where her latest train of thought might lead.

"Bonfires are popular," he said, evidenced by the residual heat of last night's inferno. "I recommend you introduce yourself at dinner this evening—Alik is bringing his cameras for his project—and check for flames after dark.

"And a tip: ditch the notebook. I've alerted the residents to your presence in a research capacity, and they're apt to clam up if they think you're documenting their life story."

"Got it," Michelle said.

Once they had circled back to the blacktop, Dan gestured south. "The ruins you noticed when you arrived, the old church foundation—and Maggie."

"Maggie?"

"Our mail carrier."

The postal truck, camouflaged in Black Hill's signature tan dust, squealed to a stop in front of them.

"Good afternoon!" Maggie called out brightly, her smile as inviting as cool shade on a blistering hot day. Acknowledging Michelle's presence, she withheld one of her customary playful advances: "Work up that sweat just for me?" or "Your emerald eyes are more precious than jewels," or "No mail today. Just the mail lady."

She settled for making eyes at Dan, then shifted her attention to Michelle. "Dan told me an intern was arriving today. Michelle, is it?"

"Michelle Drake. Yes, and Dan's taking me on my introductory tour."

"Then I won't interrupt. But I insist you join us for dinner tomorrow."

"Maggie and I dine together most Sundays," Dan told Michelle. "We'd love for you to join us."

"Then I accept," Michelle said.

"Wonderful," Maggie said. She looked at Dan and smiled. "I'll arrive early and make a cheesecake."

After Maggie sped away toward Hat Creek's mailbox, Dan and Michelle followed slowly, aiming for Michelle's cabin.

"Maggie seems friendly," Michelle said.

"Very," Dan admitted.

"And?"

"And?"

"I saw her making eyes at you."

"Maggie and I are just friends."

Michelle rolled her eyes. She wore exasperation as comfortably as her ponytail. "Enthusiastic roadside greetings, Sunday dinners—perhaps long, secluded walks through the trees?"

Dan dropped his jaw in mock shock. "A tad forward, are we?"

Michelle shrugged her shoulders. "You can take the lady from the university, but you can't take the university from the lady."

"I assure you, we're just friends."

Michelle snickered. "Maggie wants more than 'just friends.'"

Dan laughed. "Based on what evidence?"

Michelle raised a fist and uncurled a finger for each point. "The delight in her voice, how her eyes smiled at you, lamenting my presence, anticipating tomorrow's dinner, offering to arrive early." Out of fingers, Michelle raised an eyebrow, daring Dan to set her straight.

Except Dan could add more fingers to the effort: Maggie's

propensity to stand intimately close when they talked or walked, leaving her foot touching his when they bumped under the table, kissing his cheek when they hugged goodbye. Dan only regretted his inability to return Maggie's affections. Someday, perhaps.

Dan nodded at Michelle's splayed fingers. "All that from a short introduction?"

Michelle put away her markers and dropped her hand. "Maggie's easy to read."

"And me?"

They had reached Michelle's rickety front door. "You're guarded," she said, "more of a mystery. But I've only known you for an hour."

With a mischievous grin, she opened her door and disappeared inside.

CHAPTER 8

Alik Popov, the eldest son of Bulgarian immigrants, wasn't the first Hat Creek artist, just the first to propose using the residents rather than the scenery as his subject matter. Alik planned a coffee table book filled with faces expressing hope and fear, joy and pain, longing and loss. As refugees, the homeless, and random people plucked from Big City streets already graced the pages of published books, Alik proposed focusing on a novel subset of American culture: temporary residents of a remote South Dakota ghost town.

His efforts thus far had proven fruitless. Each time Alik pointed his camera at Cici Decker, she made silly faces. Stella Beal, meanwhile, shied away from his approach. Graham Jefferson wouldn't or couldn't sit still long enough for Alik to get a good shot, and Brooke Young masked her distress behind cheesy photogenic poses. Only the departing Jeffersons—"Emigrating!" they had declared with corny zeal—had willingly participated.

"Participation must remain voluntary," Dan told the frustrated photographer. "But nothing says we can't coerce them. I believe a welcome dinner for Michelle Drake is in order."

Alik, to plan, had claimed the head of the joined tables, a pair of his ever-present cameras resting on the table. Graham and Stella had found seats to Alik's right. Graham was a thin and wiry man with fidgety dark eyes and sunken cheeks that made him appear malnourished. Stella was more petite than Michelle and even thinner than Graham and had the knack of disappearing from any scene. Across the table, Cici and Brooke fashioned an image filtered to black and white, save a single spot of defining color. Cici's chocolate skin and black curls contrasted Brooke's fair complexion and silky blonde hair, with Brooke's captivating sky-blue eyes promising who would always garner adoration and envy.

Dan loaded his plate and slipped into the chair to Stella's left, directly opposite Michelle. Her notebook was nowhere in sight.

The first flurry of camera clicks and Cici's subsequent cackle paused the dessert forks and quieted conversations. When Alik pointed the lens at Brooke, she stared defiantly into the whirring camera before looking away. "Don't you dare," Stella warned Alik as he turned.

Alik lowered his camera and frowned at his obstinate tablemates. "I've met each of you, yet you remain strangers. *I* communicate through images; my photography tells stories. I didn't make this trek to clutter my hard drive with this desolate scenery, and none of you will cure whatever ails you closed up tighter than hermetically sealed packages."

When Cici shrieked at Alik's flowery, tough-love language, Alik lifted his camera and peered at her through his viewfinder. "As for you, I want to capture the turmoil masked by your playful guise." He focused on Brooke again. "I want to peel away your anguish to reveal the beauty hidden beneath." Despite Stella's earlier protestations, he placed her in his crosshairs. "I want to know what you're ashamed of." He snapped Stella's photo before she could erase the surprise from her face.

Sparing Graham, Alik lowered his camera. "I want to tell *your* stories. Considering we're all gathered, starting now would be convenient."

"Starting now," Cici mimicked. "Dan, Dan, Dan," she scolded, shaking her head. Dan wasn't surprised she had seen through the charade.

"Okay, Alik," Cici said. "I'll play along and spill my guts." She looked around the table. "But only if everyone participates. We're flying together."

"I'm game," Graham said, accepting Cici's challenge. He looked at Stella and added, "I only hope I won't disgust anybody."

Stella, emboldened by Graham's attention, agreed to follow Graham. That left Brooke, who reluctantly nodded. "I'll join in."

"Great," Alik said. "Just be yourself and focus on the camera. Forget everything else."

Cici stared into the lens, her face a blank slate. With Alik poised, she assumed her familiar character: composed, inquisitive, and flippant, yet indignant, with an undercurrent of pain. Alik's camera began whirring.

"Stupid!" Cici barked forcefully, causing Stella to jump. "Worthless, disappointing, lazy—oh, and overweight!" She spit out the words like mouthfuls of Hat Creek dirt. "That's me. So say my *respected* parents. You've likely heard of them. They're the 'Deckers' of Decker Devices."

Dan had forsaken high-tech fifteen years ago, yet even he knew of the Deckers and their renowned Silicon Valley corporation.

"It seems I've offended them by declining to follow in their illustrious footsteps," Cici continued. "I attended Stanford only because they insisted. After I flunked out, they shipped me off to Europe for six weeks before dumping me here to 'find myself.'" She leaned closer to the camera. "That's Decker vernacular for 'you'd better get your head screwed on straight.' Wait until they learn I've spent my days posing for a coffee table book." Cici's mischievous, wide-eyed glare prompted another flurry of clicks.

She stuck out her tongue at the camera. "That's all you get." Alik continued snapping photos as Cici scooped up a spoonful of ice cream and stuffed it into her mouth.

"Parental expectations can be difficult to meet," Brooke said calmly, ignoring Cici's antics.

"As can our own," Graham mumbled. He took an audible breath. "Your next patient is prepped and ready, Alik."

"One moment." Alik lifted an elaborate camera bag to the table. After detaching the camera lens, he dropped it into the bag and produced another lens in the same motion, which he mounted with a quick twist.

"Ready," he said, sighting Graham through the new lens.

"I'm a recovering drug addict," Graham announced. Camera whirring, he turned to Stella, contrite, before turning back to face Alik. "I've tried to stop using several times. I finally checked myself into rehab, and I'm clean for the first time in years. The clinic sent me here as a waystation to avoid returning directly to any bad influences. No temptations, no access, and a positive environment."

He nodded. "So far, so good. My urges are still safely held at bay. I hope to find something in Hat Creek to give me the strength to survive the challenge of returning home.

"And that's my story."

"My college roommate, Eddie, had a similar problem," Cici said. "He was a chocoholic.

"I'm serious," she said when everybody snickered. "Eddie consumed entire bags of chocolate—*large* bags—in a single sitting. Despite the weight gain and constant stomach pains, Eddie couldn't help himself. He tried quitting cold turkey several times, going so far as avoiding stores that sold chocolate, but his addiction was too strong, and before long, he was gorging himself again. Sound familiar, Graham?"

Graham nodded.

"So, I suggested Eddie substitute his compulsion with a new one, one absent the bad side effects: diet soda."

Even Alik found it challenging to stick to his task.

"Caffeine-free, at that," Cici continued. "And it worked. Eddie slimmed down, his health improved, and both his face and our bathroom cleared up. On the downside, he burped non-stop.

"My advice to you, Graham, is to follow Eddie's example. And I think I have just what you need." Cici glanced around furtively before reaching into her purse. "Does Hat Creek have a cop force, Dan?"

"Another service Hat Creek lacks," he admitted.

"Good. Graham, stick out your hand." Cici palmed a tiny package into his hand which Graham revealed to be a pack of gum.

"Sugar-free," he said, Alik snapping the little joke that

wasn't. "Thanks, Cici."

While the levity played out, Alik switched cameras to a smaller, less imposing model. The photographer knew his job. "When you're ready, Stella."

Stella faced Alik's camera but, her face blushing to bright pink, quickly dropped her head. "It's starting already," she whined.

"Relax, Stella," Cici said. "Unlike dogs and certain parents, cameras don't bite."

"And you've got us," Graham said.

Stella pressed her hands together and lifted her head, Graham's words of encouragement infusing her with needed courage.

"I suffer from Social Anxiety Disorder," Stella said. "Any social setting can trigger a panic attack: crowds of every size, restaurants and shopping centers, parties, talking to strangers, making phone calls; you name it."

She faltered at a flurry of camera clicks. Alik lifted an apologetic finger and paused long enough for Stella to compose herself.

"I'm seeing a therapist," Stella said. "She's helping me to develop coping strategies and teaching me how my thoughts and emotions influence my behavior."

She rubbed her palms on her thighs and continued.

"Hat Creek is part of my therapy: small group interaction." She looked at her palms before placing one to her chest. "My palms are sweaty, and my heart's racing, but at least I didn't skip this evening's dinner. And I'm sitting here, even speaking without vomiting or passing out. For me, that's progress." She managed a proud smile, a moment Alik's camera recorded.

Stella took another deep breath and slumped back into her chair. The camera whirred.

"You survived," Graham said.

Stella nodded. "I did, didn't I?" Dan noticed Stella's hand find Graham's.

Attention naturally turned to Brooke. "After everyone else, I feel foolish," she said nervously.

"Feeling is good," Cici said.

"One second, please," Alik said, switching camera lenses again. After pressing a few buttons, he lifted the camera to his eye. "When you're ready, Brooke."

"Craig and I started dating in junior high," Brooke said, speaking to the camera. Alik snapped photos at a benign pace. "While still in high school, we knew we'd eventually marry, so we didn't rebel when our parents encouraged us to wait. 'Start your careers first,' they insisted, 'You'll be on much firmer financial footing.'"

"*Persuasion*," Dan muttered.

Brooke managed a weak smile. "It's a Jane Austen book," she explained to her tablemates. "The heroine's best friend 'persuades' her to call off her engagement because her beau has yet to secure an income.

"What concerned our parents," Brooke continued, "was that Craig and I would mature into different, perhaps incompatible, people. That didn't happen, though. Craig and I attended college together and, after graduation, found good-paying jobs in the same city. Only then, still very much in love, did we marry."

Brooke paused, her eyes watering. Tears leaked down her cheeks.

"Craig and I never discussed children. I just assumed …" Brooke swallowed hard. "I wanted a family. Craig didn't. The issue slowly festered into a chasm we couldn't cross." She folded her arms across her chest and wiped her face. "Finally,

Craig divorced me."

Brooke looked away until she regained enough composure to face the camera again. "Craig is the only man I've ever held hands with, the only man I've ever kissed, the only man I've made love to. My children were to be his; my whole life to be shared with him." She shook her head. "What am I supposed to do now?" She looked at her tablemates. "I told you I felt foolish. It's because I don't even know why I'm here."

Cici reached out and embraced Brooke.

Dan looked from the pair to his other residents and then at Alik's cameras. Dan knew the power of the printed photo. The memories they preserved had both haunted him and driven him for years. Now he had evidence that *taking* pictures also held therapeutic potential—another tool to help him reach his goal.

Cici picked up the smaller of the two cameras. "How does this contraption work?" she asked Alik.

"Point the top at me," Alik said. Once Cici tilted the camera, Alik turned a dial. "Now it's on auto," he said. "Simply point and shoot."

Which Cici did, at Alik. "You didn't think we'd forget about you?"

Alik laughed. "As in, 'So, Alik, what brings *you* here?' Okay, I'll play along." He adjusted himself in his chair and gazed into the lens. "Killing two birds with one stone brings me to Hat Creek." Cici began snapping pictures. "My book, primarily, but also to complete another project that my editor keeps bugging me to finish. Quiet surroundings allow me to focus better."

"Life's all hunky-dory, huh?" Cici asked, using the camera like a machine gun.

"Married and divorced twice, a daughter with three

children from three different men, living for weeks at a time out of my car, and a bum knee injured falling off a mountain during a photoshoot. Can't complain."

Cici huffed and pointed her new toy in the opposite direction. "Lean back, please," she told Brooke. "And you?" she asked Michelle.

"I don't have any issues worth mentioning," Michelle said in a stuttering cadence, almost in apology.

"Foibles, then. For instance, I bet you've never had a boyfriend."

Cici duly recorded Michelle's gaping mouth.

"Elaborate, if you please," Cici said with a grin.

"Simple." Michelle focused on the shiny glass through another burst of shutter clicks. "I've never had time for a boyfriend." She paused, reconsidering her words. "Okay, I seldom get asked out, so I pour all my energy and time into my studies." Now she frowned, her words making little sense even to herself.

"Ah," Cici said from behind the lens. "Blurred Cause and Effect Syndrome. And you're afraid you'll never have a boyfriend."

Cici's final snap captured Michelle's resigned shrug.

"Don't worry," Cici said, offering a comforting smile. "You and I, we've got lots of time. There'll be somebody out there for us." She started laughing. "Likely *despite* our best efforts."

Dan didn't need a reminder that he was the only person at the table yet to be interviewed. He stood and picked up his plate. "And I claim proprietor immunity," he said before Cici could point the camera his way. "I have a serious plumbing leak to fix."

"Chicken," Cici called after him as he retreated to bus his dishes.

Guilty, as charged.

Dan loosened the hose coupling from the water pipe and cleaned the pipe threads. After applying two turns of new sealant tape, he reattached the coupling, wrenched it tight, and turned the water back on. No more drips to annoy Alik's sensitive hearing.

Before leaving Alik's cabin, Dan instinctively unlocked the doubled-hung window and cracked it open. Guessing that Alik would reclose it to block out unwanted noise, Dan wondered about methods to allow air exchange without compromising the soundproofing.

CHAPTER 9

Michelle smiled, seeing Dan and Maggie seated at a shiny new patio table sheltered from the sun by a broad umbrella. "This would do a New York City corner deli proud," she said.

The patio had been an unplanned addition, using leftover concrete delivered during the construction of the new water pump base. Dan hadn't protested Maggie's donation of the new outdoor dining set because it was out of view of passing motorists.

Maggie offered Michelle the seat next to her. "Dan's single compromise to outdoor modernity," she said.

Michelle peered west. "This is a peaceful view. I can't see this far looking down Broadway."

"Are you enjoying your stay?" Maggie asked, unstacking the dinner plates.

"Immensely." Michelle nodded when Maggie offered her a serving of potato casserole. "Yesterday's dinner certainly brought Hat Creek into focus. Dan, are group sessions common?"

"Group *activities*, such as cookouts and bonfires—tomorrow's workday at the ranch—yes. Group sessions such as yesterday's, no. Hat Creek's style is less structured."

"I suspect everyone wanted to speak," Michelle said. "Alik's cameras helped them escape their shells. I captured my thoughts last night while everything was still fresh. It'll be part of my report to Dr. Malkovich."

"Our young scientist," Maggie said. While Dan dished out the pork loins, she poured wine for Dan and herself. "Wine?" she asked Michelle.

"Um ... I'm only nineteen."

Maggie laughed. "I'll take that as a yes." She poured a little Chardonnay into Michelle's glass. "Give it a try. It pairs well with pork."

Michelle lifted her glass to her lips and took a small sip, grimacing at the taste.

Maggie laughed again. "Dan, I don't think we'll have to worry about finding this one passed out in the weeds after a night of binge drinking."

Michelle sipped her water to cleanse her palate. "Today, Alik posed us among your old cars. The juxtaposition of troubled but hopeful people with broken and hopeless objects was striking, though I doubt anybody else noted Alik's symbolism. Stella and Graham certainly didn't notice," she chuckled. "They were too busy paying attention to each other."

Michelle looked from Dan to Maggie and back. "I never considered how the seclusion could inspire relationships."

"Little seclusion in New York City," Maggie said. "Are you taking in the ranch tomorrow?"

"I wouldn't miss it," Michelle said. "Have you worked there?"

"Only the one time. You'll love the manure spreader."

"Manure spreader?"

"It's a farm implement that flings dried cow manure over the ground as fertilizer," Dan said.

Michelle looked dubiously at Maggie.

"No joke," Maggie said. "Don't get caught in its path."

"I doubt they'll rope you into loading the manure spreader, though," Dan said. "Besides milking cows and collecting eggs, you'll likely haul hay or clean pens. Nothing gross, but physically challenging."

"You mean for a city girl."

Maggie took Michelle's hands and turned them palms up. "Yep, city girl. Make sure to wear gloves. And that's no joke, either."

Michelle picked up her earlier conversation while Maggie served dessert. "Back to today, Dan. After Alik's photoshoot, I braved the weeds and grasshoppers to explore.

"Thank you," she said as Maggie handed her a slice of apple pie. "I figured immersion was the quickest way to understand Hat Creek. Putting myself in your resident's shoes helped me truly appreciate what you've accomplished. You've created a facility that removes your residents from the societal and environmental pressures contributing to their issues *and* the modern comforts of life. Remoteness empowers self-reliance, almost demanding that they take charge of their recovery. Now I understand Dr. Malkovich's enthusiasm."

Maggie glared at Dan in mock alarm.

Dan masked the pride Michelle's insights validated. He *could* help people. Instead, he nodded and said, "Dr. Malkovich predicted as much."

"I walked as far as the creek," Michelle said. "Why is your

pond full while the creek is nearly dry?"

"The pond's water source is the water tower and the cabins rather than rain," Dan told her.

Michelle nodded. "An obvious question came to mind while I wandered: How did you purchase an entire ghost town?"

Maggie choked on her pie. "Obvious question? To you, perhaps. Now that you've brought it up, though, I find I'm curious, as well. So, Dan, how *did* you purchase an entire ghost town?"

Only one meal and Michelle had already recruited Maggie as her accomplice. Michelle was the young woman Dr. Malkovich had described: intense, inquisitive, and insistent. Evasion would only increase her scrutiny.

"Simple," Dan said matter-of-factly. "Land deeds are available for view at the county courthouse. I purchased a sizeable parcel to legally reincorporate the town and informed the absentee owners about the upgraded building standards. Those costs, naturally, far exceeded their land values, so they sold out to me."

"A tad underhanded," Maggie elaborated.

"A tad," Dan admitted.

Michelle had her fork to her mouth before pulling it away. "But how did you find Hat Creek? Search the 'ghost towns' section of the real estate listings?"

"I just stumbled onto this place," Dan said over Maggie's giggle.

Michelle speared a sugary apple slice and chewed contemplatively. "What about money? Buying out the other owners, renovating the buildings, plus all the other costs involved in kickstarting a town, couldn't have been cheap."

The truth escaped Dan's lips before he considered the consequences. "I sold everything I owned and used the proceeds to start Hat Creek."

"All in," Michelle said reverently.

Dr. Malkovich, too, had puzzled over Dan's choice of residence until her enthusiasm for their grand experiment subdued her curiosity. Michelle's furrowed brows suggested the student wouldn't be so easily distracted.

"Where did you live before founding Hat Creek?" Michelle asked.

"That's unimportant." Dan tried to attack his dessert to end the conversation, but Michelle had nothing of it.

"As I said, a man of mystery."

"Good luck with that challenge," Maggie said.

Eyes narrowing, Michelle raised her elbows to the table and steepled her hands under her chin. "You stumbled onto a place so far off the beaten path that rusted-out tractors outnumber people. After selling everything you owned to raise the money to purchase and rebuild it, you established a unique self-help retreat, one you now administer as a selfless volunteer, laboring twenty-four-seven assisting troubled people. Have I missed anything?" She had asked the question rhetorically, confident in her observational prowess.

When Dan didn't respond, Michelle smiled smugly. "I should have taken Alik's camera from Cici last evening and asked *you* a simple question: Why?"

I want to tell your stories, Alik had said. *Starting now.*

Michelle's intense gaze morphed into Alik's camera; her blinks, the winking shutter. Hat Creek's residents had met Alik's challenge. Michelle, too, through Alik's surrogate. They deserved—Maggie deserved—for Dan to show the same courage. That fact didn't ease his pain, but it shouldn't have taken a curious student to coerce his story into the public light. If he couldn't or wouldn't speak, he might just as well shut this place down.

"*Why?*" Dan repeated. He looked down at the remains of his dessert. "Because I couldn't stay in that house."

"What do you mean, Dan? What happened?"

Dan placed his fork beside his plate and lifted his head to face his camera's twin lenses. "I lost my wife and children in a tragedy," he said.

Michelle's face contorted in horror. "Oh, Maggie, what have I done? Help me, please."

Maggie reached across the table and took Dan's hand. "I'm afraid I can't be of much help, Michelle. I'm only divorced, but my daughter rightfully blames me, and I doubt I'll ever get to meet my little grandson." She looked compassionately into Dan's eyes. "I'm sorry for your loss. Know that I'm here for you."

Dan squeezed Maggie's hand. "Thank you."

Michelle covered her eyes with a hand in shame. "I apologize. To both of you." She slid her chair back and stood. "Please excuse me. And, again, I'm sorry." She walked away, disappearing around the corner of the house.

Maggie stared at the space Michelle had left vacant before turning to Dan and squeezing his hand. "Someone needs to teach that girl some manners."

Ruby Woodstone wrote Dan that she had controlled her temper through the court hearing, crediting the week of cooling her jets in Hat Creek to keep her out of jail. But losing her job concerned her, and Ruby hoped the added stress wouldn't cause her to spiral out of control again. She lamented missing Dan's ready supply of rotted wood to punch but said she had purchased a boxing club membership as a substitute.

Ruby's levity gave Dan hope. He had predicted demolition

would be an effective stress reliever for Ruby, though he hadn't previously considered her bare-knuckled approach. Boxing—with gloves—seemed a more humane alternative.

Dan slipped Ruby's note back into its envelope. Looking at the bills stacked on the desk in front of him, he leaned back in his chair and admitted defeat. Busying himself with administrative tasks wasn't blunting his torment any more effectively than Maggie's well-intentioned handholding or the long solo walk he had taken following their meal. He stretched his right leg and bumped his knee against the side of his safe, the steel block now an integral part of his desk. Unlike his photo album, he had no secure place to conceal the panic and terror of that night.

For better AND worse. Dan had envisioned the likes of Ruby and Hat Creek's current residents, people whose lives he could improve. He had also foreseen circumstances inclined to make his life worse. But would he have opened Hat Creek knowing the act would lead to this evening's dinner? A pointless question since he couldn't reverse time. Equally meaningless to close shop and revert to his hermit existence. Human nature dictated that Maggie and Michelle wouldn't compose an exclusive club for long. Word would inexorably spread like hot lava flowing across the landscape.

Despite his sour mood, he smiled at the polite knock on his door. He had predicted regrets to be issued tomorrow morning at breakfast.

"Come in, Michelle," he called out. He tidied the nasty clutter inside his mind to a state resembling his desktop and leaned back to make eye contact as she entered.

Michelle stepped momentarily into the tiny alcove serving as Dan's office. "How did you know it was me?" she asked.

"Firstly, because I neglected to inform you of an important

Hat Creek rule: Knock only if you feel obligated; otherwise, open the door and enter. Seeing as it doubles as city hall, my house is required by law to be accessible to all residents."

"Even after dark?"

"And, secondly, none of the residents would pay a visit this late in the evening."

Michelle sighed dejectedly. "I should pack my things and leave."

"I'd rather you stay," Dan said. He motioned at the slat-back wooden chair wedged between Dan's desk and the wall. "Dr. Malkovich would be disappointed in both of us."

Michelle plopped down into the chair. "She would be disappointed only in me. After my antics at dinner, nobody would fault you for kicking me out of town."

"You don't think our good doctor would question my abilities if I couldn't handle a meddlesome intern?"

"Meddlesome," Michelle said, shaking her head. "You're too kind." She looked at his stack of envelopes. "I'm interrupting your work. I'll come back tomorrow."

"Just paying bills and answering correspondence. What's on your mind?"

"My behavior at dinner, obviously," she said. "My curiosity ran amok."

"You couldn't have known my unfortunate circumstances."

"That's no excuse. I was selfish and inconsiderate."

Though Michelle's disgust at her earlier behavior appeared genuine, Dan was under no delusions that Michelle's painful retreat had permanently satiated her curiosity. He had seen the gears turning in her head, a self-described snoop trying to puzzle out his motives. And if, as he expected, the information would eventually become public knowledge, he preferred controlling the conversation.

So, he took a deep breath to steel himself. "My family's passing created a chasm in my life. Work became meaningless, and my home constantly reminded me of all I'd lost. Building and running Hat Creek is my attempt to turn tragedy into a positive."

"You're a strong man."

"I wouldn't go that far."

"Noble, certainly. Still, I'm sorry about causing you so much grief."

"It's done now. We'll put it past us so you can get on with your stay."

"Thank you. And I'll let you get back to work."

Michelle stood, only now noticing Dan's unique desk. "I can't say I've ever seen a filing cabinet and a safe used as desk legs."

Dan rapped his knuckle on the desktop. "Nor, I bet, a wooden entry door for the top."

Michelle hummed in amusement. "You make do with anything you can find, don't you?"

"Cheap and stout. A mantra of necessity."

She looked past Dan's shoulder. "Your bookcase, conversely, is beautiful."

Dan had relocated the ornately carved red oak piece from Hartman's. A mix of hardcover and paperback books littered its shelves.

"Reading is my evening hobby," Dan said. "Do you read?"

"Only textbooks," Michelle replied. "I have little time for anything more." She tipped her head to read some of the titles. "What are your interests?"

"I focus on a specific genre until I fill the bookcase, then donate the lot and start over fresh. I've covered American history, historical fiction, and mystery. Currently, I'm midway into my classic literary phase."

Michelle fingered a couple of the books, tilting them out to view the covers. "Any recommendations?"

"They're all well written." Dan's finger found a book on the third shelf. "Virginia Woolf should appeal to you. She experimented with a narrative style termed 'stream of consciousness,' writing out the character's thought process as if you're inside their minds. Interested?"

"Sure," Michelle said, "though I don't know how much spare time I'll have to read."

"I'll start you out with *To the Lighthouse*." Dan slipped the book off the shelf and handed it to Michelle. "If you finish it, let yourself in and grab another."

"I will—without knocking if I can remember, and at a reasonable hour. And I promise to behave myself."

Dan wouldn't give even money past a few days. "I predict your tomorrow will be downright mundane."

CHAPTER 10

Dan stepped from Westside into the early morning warmth. The rising sun revealed sparse cottony clouds becalmed by the still air and a forecast of stifling heat—ideal conditions, to his admittedly sadistic thinking, for a resident workday at the Childress Ranch.

Michelle burst from her cabin as Dan crossed the road toward his truck, her nose wrinkled as if she knew how badly she would reek when she returned.

"Dan!" she yelled, pointing behind her as she ran. "Someone is—" She reached his side, panting. "Someone is urinating on my back wall."

Dan could vouch for his innocence, and he had left Alik and Graham sitting inside Westside finishing breakfast, meaning—

The perpetrator appeared around the side of Michelle's cabin before Dan could venture a guess. He was a tall, handsome young man with wavy brown hair wearing a fitted shirt accentuating his ripped arm and chest muscles. Only the backpack was missing.

"Jacob!"

"Hey, Dan."

"What were you doing back there?" Dan asked.

"Weeding, naturally. You've been dogging it. They've taken over the entire wall."

"I installed indoor plumbing two years ago."

"Ah."

"Michelle, Jacob Fines. Jacob, Michelle Drake."

"Pleasure," Jacob said, turning on the charm.

"Hello," Michelle responded sourly, dismissing Jacob's advance with a curt frown. "I'll be ready in a minute," she told Dan and returned to her cabin.

Jacob turned back to Dan. "Was she inside while I …?"

Dan nodded.

"That's funny."

Dan snickered despite himself. Michelle's wildest imagination couldn't conjure *that* Hat Creek challenge. "Very funny, actually. And, by the way, welcome back."

"Thanks," Jacob said. "I wondered if you still lived here and pulled in when I saw your truck. The new cars surprised me, though."

Dan nodded. "You are now standing in Hat Creek, South Dakota."

"A town? Whatever happened to 'This isn't a town!'"

"Times change, people change. I converted it into a retreat for people who could benefit from a little solitude. Michelle is an intern, a protégé of the university professor I consulted to design the retreat."

Jacob raised an eyebrow. "Get bored swinging a hammer, and all hell breaks loose." He glanced around. "Four years later, and nothing's changed. Everything still looks as desolate as I remember."

"On purpose. What brings you here?"

"Returning home, unfortunately. You'd be proud of me. I took your advice and finished high school before packing my bags for Denver. Everything was hunky-dory until one of my roommates decided to shack up with his girlfriend, and the other packed up for Florida." Jacob shook his head. "I couldn't afford the rent, so I thought I'd crash at home for a few months."

"Long story short, you ran out of money."

"I ran out of money."

Michelle reappeared in jeans and a fitted long-sleeve shirt, Dan's recommended attire for the day.

"Meet at the truck," Dan told her. "I'll round up the stragglers from Westside."

As Michelle crossed in front of Jacob without acknowledging his presence, Jacob pivoted to watch her pass, grinding tiny rocks under his boot as his head tipped sideways. Dan peered past him and regarded Michelle through the younger man's eyes: a slender figure accentuated by tight clothing, a long neck exposed by her ever-present ponytail, and that decidedly feminine trait: a sexy butt wiggle pulled off without the slightest effort.

An interesting thought occurred to Dan. If Michelle could be kept busy fending off Jacob's advances, she wouldn't have the time to snoop into his past.

"Jacob?"

No response.

"Jacob!"

Jacob blinked out of his stupor and turned to Dan. "Huh?"

"In a rush to get home?"

Jacob screwed up his face.

"Do you remember the way to the Childress Ranch?" Dan asked.

Jacob nodded. "A few miles west, left at the cattle gate, follow the road to the buildings."

"Interested in chaperoning Michelle and my other city slickers for the day?"

"Sure."

Dan handed over his truck key.

A heavy-set Black girl opened the squeaky passenger door as Jacob climbed behind the wheel. She slid in after shepherding Michelle inside, shoving Michelle tightly to his side.

"I'm Cici," she said brightly.

"Jacob," he announced.

"And this is Michelle."

"We've met. Twice." Laughing at Michelle's frown, Jacob watched through the rearview mirror as four others climbed into the truck bed. The flat-chested waif with the short black hair didn't warrant a second glance, but he wouldn't mind curing whatever ailed the stunning blonde—except she was wearing a ring.

He waited for the thumbs up that everyone was seated before starting for the ranch, forcing Michelle's legs apart when he pulled the floor shifter into second gear.

"How long have you known Dan?" Michelle asked, removing Jacob's arm from her lap.

"A few years," Jacob answered. "I stopped by just once. Denver is too far away to get here often."

"You live in Denver?" Cici asked.

"Yes," Jacob answered. They didn't need to know that the true answer was "formerly." "I moved there after high school, working odd jobs at restaurants and loading trailers to make ends meet. Mostly, I hike in summer and ski in winter."

"I like your style," Cici said.

Jacob glanced at a building Dan had slapped onto the backside of Hartman's. "But this place wasn't a 'retreat' then, whatever that means."

"A 'retreat' means us crazies populating the town while trying to get our heads screwed on straight," Cici said. "Don't worry, though; Michelle isn't one of us. She's a brain sent here to study us."

"I am not," Michelle complained. "I'm studying psychology at Columbia University, and I—" She squeaked when Jacob slid his forearm into her crotch while shifting into fourth gear.

A tad homely for his tastes, but seducing Michelle would be fun. Cici, as if privy to Jacob's musings, giggled loudly.

"We'll need two in the truck bed stacking bales," Jacob said. "The rest of us will pass them up."

"Don't stand there like a bumpkin, Graham," Cici said. "Help Stella up."

Jacob tossed a bale onto the flatbed as the pair clambered up. "Drag it to the front corner," he told Graham. "I'll get you started stacking once we get a few loaded."

When he turned around, Michelle was attempting to bearhug a bale.

"Use the twine as a handle," he said.

Michelle grabbed two twine handholds and successfully dragged the bale off the stack but couldn't lift it without Brooke's help.

"It's heavy," Michelle complained when Jacob scoffed at her struggle.

"It's heavy," he mimed. "That's the problem with today's colleges. No phys ed classes." Jacob hoisted a bale with each hand and heaved the pair into the truck bed.

Cici placed her hand on her forehead and swooned dramatically onto the stack of bales. Alik, evidently Hat Creek's resident photographer, snapped her picture, followed by a flurry of photos of Jacob flexing his biceps.

Jacob located Michelle in the milk barn's storeroom, struggling to lift a large bag of cattle feed. Another bag, torn open and trailing brown chalky streaks from being dragged across the concrete floor, was surrounded by pyramids of leaked brown feed pellets.

"You're supposed to lift with your legs," he said.

Michelle startled and spun around.

"What are we doing?" he asked.

Michelle wiped the sweat from her eyes. The storeroom was as hot as inside any trailer Jacob had loaded. "I'm supposed to stack ten bags at each milk stanchion."

Jacob counted six stanchions. "Sixty fifty-pound bags."

"And another stack outside needs to be moved inside."

"And you were going to somehow manage this all by your lonesome? You're lucky I showed up."

Michelle wrinkled her nose. "Except you stink."

Jacob buried his nose into his shirt sleeve. Grease, oil, dirt, straw, and animal crud. "At least I smell better than Stella. She broke a rotten egg in the hayloft. I'm guessing she rolled over it while making out with Graham."

"Must you *always* act so juvenile?"

"Egg was plastered all over her butt," Jacob said. "*You* tell me how it got there."

Michelle groaned and attacked the bag again.

Jacob shouldered her away. "Like this," he said, bending at the knees to reach under the bag. "Knees bent, back straight.

Don't they teach you anything in college?" He stacked the bag atop another and lifted the pair. "I'll handle the bags on the floor and up high. You stick to the ones at waist height. Knees bent, back straight."

Jacob carried the feed bags along the narrow accessway that extended along the backside of the stanchions, crossing paths with Michelle on his return as she strained under the burden of a single bag. "Drop it at the first stanchion," he said, squeezing past her.

Jacob hoisted two more bags, forced to stack them at the first stanchion because Michelle was blocking his path, struggling with her load further down the accessway. Obstinate as well as conceited. After his third load, he removed his shirt and wiped the sweat out of his eyes. Michelle was staring open-mouthed at him when he pulled his hand down. Sweat dotted her forehead and top lip and ran in rivulets down her cheeks and neck to darken her shirt. He wondered what she looked like with her hair down.

"Don't any real men attend your fancy college?" he asked.

"You were standing in my way." She sucked her sweaty upper lip into her mouth. "Besides, I prefer brains over brawn."

"And yet, you can't keep your eyes off me."

Michelle smirked. "You are so into yourself."

"You're the one into yourself," Jacob said. He posed, one arm on his hip. "'I'm pursuing my PhD in psychiatry at Columbia. Have you heard of Columbia University?'" He wiped at another line of sweat running down his face. "I couldn't get a word in edgewise during the ride over this morning."

"I'm studying psychology, not psychiatry—"

"You mean playing."

Michelle's mouth dropped open. "Playing? *Playing*? College

isn't 'playing.'"

"Parties, football games, sleepovers—art exhibits and symposiums. College is all fun and games."

"I work my ass off at school."

"No. *I* work my ass off."

Michelle stepped closer. "Let me guess. You did poorly in high school."

"My grades were okay."

"And you started working the day after you graduated—"

"I was already working—"

"—because you couldn't stomach college. You've been wasting your mind at dead-end jobs while I've been training mine for a rewarding profession."

Jacob grabbed Michelle's hand and slapped it to his pec. "This is the result of *real* work."

Michelle snatched her hand away and wiped it on her jeans. "That's just gross."

Jacob turned away with a frustrated groan and squatted three feed bags in one lift. Daring Michelle to get in his way, he lugged them to the last stanchion.

Jacob finished loading the stations and hauled the feed bags indoors before slumping to the floor beside Michelle. "Lifting three bags at a time was a mistake," he said, feeling the deep ache in his muscles.

"My back hurts," she said, leaning into him. "My arms and legs, too." She held out her gloved hands before dropping them onto her lap. "Why would anybody choose ranching as a profession?"

Jacob shook his head and adjusted his position to fit Michelle comfortably. He must have dozed because Alik knelt before them, snapping pictures. Brooke and Cici stood on either side of the photographer, wearing tall black rubber boots covered in slimy green cow manure.

"Don't they make a cute couple?" Cici gushed.

"If I had any strength left," Michelle said drowsily, "I'd throw something at you."

"Allow me," Jacob said, reaching for a handful of stray feed pellets. As he leaned, Michelle followed, nuzzling closer.

"They're bonding," Cici said in a singsong voice.

Jacob tossed the pellets, chasing away the three intruders. Looking at Michelle, he chuckled. She hadn't nuzzled closer. She'd fallen back asleep. He relaxed with her, content to enjoy the sensation.

Dan was restocking Hartman's shelves when the squeal of truck brakes signaled the return of his volunteer ranch hands. He paused and listened to doors open and close, the tailgate drop, and a cacophony of tired laughter and moans.

Thirty minutes later, he found Brooke, Cici, Stella, and Graham seated inside Westside, squeaky clean and shoveling food into their mouths as if they hadn't eaten in days. Jacob, they told him between bites, had grabbed food as soon as they returned, determined to haul off Michelle somewhere. They were unsure if Alik had eaten.

Dan decided to check on Alik before packing dinner away. Dan got no response to his first knock on the cabin door but, confident the photographer must be inside, knocked harder.

Momentarily, the door opened, and Alik appeared wearing over-ear headphones. "Come in, Dan," he said, pulling them down around his neck. "I hope I didn't make you wait long."

Dan stepped inside. "Just checking to see if you'd eaten."

Alik wiped away the sweat from where the headphone padding had pressed against his cheeks and pointed at a half-eaten dinner sitting on his desk. "I grabbed a plate when we returned."

Dan noticed that the headphones were cordless. Wireless technology, he supposed. "Headphones or a radio?"

"They're earmuffs, actually," Alik said. "The sound protection kind."

"Ah," Dan said, remembering Alik's preference for solitude. "Sorry, I don't have quieter accommodations."

"Your accommodations are fine." Alik eased onto the corner of the desk. "*I'm* the one with an issue. Doctors diagnosed me as a child with a severe hearing sensitivity called hyperacusis."

"Never heard of it," Dan said.

"It's quite rare. Before the diagnosis, doctors classified me as developmentally challenged. Little wonder, considering I was prone to fits of screaming, violence, boxing my ears, and running away. How was I to know that the painful noises were normal to everybody else?"

Alik fingered the earmuffs. "My life greatly improved after I received my first earmuffs. I've outgrown the worst of the affliction, though. They're mostly a crutch now, an old habit."

Dan took his leave and headed back to Westside to pack the leftovers. The red rings on Alik's cheeks convinced him that Alik's earmuffs were more than "just a crutch." Dan guessed a soundproof booth would be more to Alik's liking. Unfortunately for the photographer, remote Hat Creek couldn't meet *that* standard.

Dan paused in front of the next cabin, stripped down to bare studs. What would it entail to rebuild it to Alik's standards? The task appeared straightforward: fill the walls, ceiling, and space beneath the floorboards with soundproofing insulation; install a heavy, air-tight front door; remove the front window and install a modern window on the side. Sealing everything so tightly meant he'd need to install an air exchange system, but that was doable. Then he could entice Alik to return, plus offer other artists—

Faint voices disrupted Dan's musings. He searched for the source and sighted Jacob and Michelle's heads over the top of the pond berm. "Don't tell me," he muttered, hurrying toward them.

Dan crested the berm and, as he had feared, found Jacob and Michelle sitting waist-deep in the water. He could excuse them from noticing the water's green sheen this late in the day. At least their hair was dry, evidence that they hadn't dunked their heads.

"What are you doing?" he asked.

"Skinny dipping," Jacob answered.

"We are not!" Michelle complained, needlessly pulling at her bathing suit straps.

Jacob snickered and cupped water onto his chest. "Dan, you've done yourself proud: modern homes with electricity and running water, a dining hall, a park, and a pond to soothe our aching muscles."

Dan shook his head. "Let me offer you two a primer on city infrastructure. The water well taps a dependable supply, piped to buildings through trenched water lines. The sub-station south of town distributes electricity. Hot water heats the buildings wherever a stove or fireplace is unsuitable. Mail is delivered six days a week, trash is collected every two weeks, and Hat Creek depends on satellite for phone and internet service.

"That brings us to waste plumbing. Sewage treatment plants are prohibitively expensive, so small towns like Hat Creek typically depend on individual septic systems. Unfortunately, our soil isn't permeable enough—porous enough—to drain septic tanks, dictating a holding pond. Raw effluent from the various toilets, sinks, and showers drains into the pond, where sunlight breaks it down. A holding pond"—he looked out over the water and then back at Jacob and Michelle—"like this one."

"Shit," Jacob said.

"Yep," Dan said. "Yours, mine, and ours."

Michelle let out a bloodcurdling scream and leaped from the water, racing for her cabin without bothering to wrap up.

"Scrub thoroughly," Dan yelled.

Jacob stood, revealing blue plaid boxers.

"Skinny dipping?" Dan said.

"I tried. Michelle's a prude."

"Best you failed."

"Probably," Jacob admitted, climbing out of the pond. He thumbed his hand toward Grange Hall. "I think I'll take a shower, too."

"That would be wise," Dan said. Also wise that he posted Todd's keep-out signs.

CHAPTER 11

Jacob approached Michelle seated on a bench in Hat Creek's cozy park, tapping away on her laptop. A flower garden bordered by small rocks enclosed a sculpture created out of tractor parts—or maybe it was just an old tractor. His fire ring was still in use.

Jacob dropped onto the bench as if climbing into bed, warning Michelle to "lose the electronics" before stretching out to rest his head in her lap. "Better," he sighed. "I'm still exhausted from yesterday."

"And I'm trying to work," Michelle complained, holding her computer aloft.

"Well, now you can. Analyze me."

"Psychology," Michelle said sternly. "I'm studying psychology, not psychiatry. I'm not reminding you again."

"Psychology. Psychiatry. Sociology. They all start with an 's.'"

"You're ridiculous."

Jacob looked into Michelle's stern brown eyes. "You can do better than that."

"Okay. You're childish, inconsiderate, discourteous—"

"I'm assuming that last word means handsome and dreamy—"

"And, conceited. Now, sit up!"

Jacob sensed Michelle might repurpose her computer as a weapon, so he rolled to standing. Noticing a half-burnt stub sticking out of the firepit, he kicked it back into the ashes. "I built this fire ring for Dan," he said.

Michelle closed her computer. "You said you were last here a few years ago."

Jacob nodded. "Four."

"Dan opened the retreat two years ago," Michelle said. "He must have been working on it before you arrived."

Jacob shrugged his shoulders. "Puttering around fixing things seemed to be Dan's whole life—that and injuring himself in the process. He made no mention of any retreat, though."

"Dan had his reasons," Michelle said. "Both for living here and building Hat Creek. Did he ever tell you what happened to his family?"

"Dan told me he didn't have one. I figured he was too ashamed to admit that his wife had kicked him out of the house." Jacob kicked at another coal. "He's endured this place for the past fourteen years for some odd reason."

"Fourteen years? You just said four."

"I *met* him four years ago. But I saw him ten years earlier than that." Jacob chuckled at his memory. "While riding through here on the trip to our new home. I raised to my knees to look at this ghost town, and the first thing I saw was a ghost walking between the buildings; Dan, of course. He scared me half to death."

"You're telling me Dan has lived here for fourteen years?"

"At least. Who knows how long Dan lived here before I saw him."

"But Dan told me he sold everything he owned and moved here to start Hat Creek because he lost his family."

"Dan lost his family? His entire family?"

Michelle nodded.

"Poor guy. Did he say how?"

Michelle shook her head. "Only that their passing was a tragedy." She frowned. "Something doesn't add up. Dr. Malkovich started working with Dan only three years ago. What was Dan up to here for all those years *before* that?"

Michelle ran her fingertip around a knot in one of the boards. "Dan insisted that he stumbled upon this place. I thought he was joking. But what if it's the truth? I'm beginning to suspect Dan didn't originally intend to set up a retreat."

"A conspiracy theory?"

"Can you make sense of anything?"

Jacob looked past Michelle. Everywhere was the same gray, crumbling, dusty, weed-infested emptiness he remembered. Now, though, only the appearance of abandoned decay remained. Beneath the surface, this town was alive again. "You're asking the wrong person," he said. "Nothing made sense to me back then, nor does it now."

Jacob glanced at the maze of water pipes beneath the water tower. "But something certainly happened since I was last here. All this modern, to use Dan's term, 'infrastructure'? Little of it existed yet. And Dan has changed, too. He was a grumpy eccentric living off the grid who talked aloud to himself. He didn't even own a phone. Now he's engaged and committed and managing a town and health retreat."

Michelle stood and stepped around the fire ring to Jacob's

side. "Dan and the town have changed that much?"

Jacob nodded. "That much."

A gray blur—Jacob only caught sight of a long, thin tail—darted from between two logs and scurried across their feet. Michelle shrieked and attempted to run away but stubbed her toe, fell to her hands and knees, and instead crawled to safety.

"Are you okay?" Jacob asked amusedly.

Staring at the ground, Michelle nodded. After several seconds, she leaned back on her heels. "I wonder if Dan was running away from something."

"You mean other than his whole family dying in a terrible tragedy?"

After a pause, Michelle looked up at him. "Yes. Loved ones die. You're depressed, naturally. You withdraw to grieve." She flipped her ponytail off her shoulder. "I can't speak from experience. My parents and sisters are alive and well. I haven't even lost a grandparent yet. But where does escaping here fit into Dan's recovery?"

Jacob helped Michelle to her feet. Her hands were academically soft. "Your guess is as good as—"

"I'm going inside to work," Michelle interrupted, retrieving her laptop. "Later," she added, walking away without a backward glance.

Jacob folded his arms across his chest and watched Michelle's delicious butt wiggle fade from view. Food, a comfortable room, and now, a pursuit. Jessica and Aubrey could pine for a few more days.

CHAPTER 12

Dan popped into Westside to print Todd's warning signs. Michelle was the diner's only customer, nursing a cup of coffee and a pastry.

"Was breakfast called off?" she asked. "Or have I been dumped?"

"Graham and Stella grabbed an early breakfast before heading north to tour the monuments. Alik is cleaning out his RV; said it was beginning to resemble the Childress's pigpen. Brooke, Cici, and Jacob have yet to make appearances. I presume they're sleeping in—I've invited Jacob to stay. I can always use strong muscles."

Dan dropped into a seat at the computer table. Michelle and her coffee cup joined him.

"I've got two hours before the inspector arrives to post warning signs around the holding pond," Dan said. "He takes fanatical pride in issuing violations, and I have better places to spend my money than sending it to the state."

Michelle huffed. "I've taken five showers in the last two days."

"Lack of imagination on my part." Dan leaned closer and sniffed. "You smell clean."

"Little consolation. I looked it up. Do you know the diseases I could have caught?"

"Then I bet you're proud that your suffering was the catalyst for this public safety measure." Dan laughed when Michelle threatened to swat him. "How about 'Keep Out of The Water'?"

"I'd suggest 'Keep Out! Raw Sewage,'" Michelle said. "Direct and succinct."

"That'll do." Dan typed the words in large font and printed three copies.

"For once, I'll be prepared," he said, inspecting the prints.

Dan's luck ran out when he stepped into his supply shed to grab a new water filter and instead found an empty box. Cursing his forgetfulness, Dan stepped outside to ponder quick fixes. Blasting the fouled filter with high-pressure water would only loosen trapped particulates, contaminating the water. Stuff the filter housing full of towels? Unwise. A towel sucked into the discharge tube would force him to disassemble half the piping to remove it. Operate without a filter and pray for the best while preparing for the worst? Even worse.

That's when he noticed Alik's RV.

Dan guided Alik off Brule Street toward the water tower. After Dan signaled Alik to stop, the photographer shut off the RV's engine and climbed out of the cab.

"Tell me again how this scheme will fool your Evil Inspector Todd," Alik said.

Dan unscrewed the RV's water tank drain cap and attached a garden hose, laughing at the moniker Alik had given the inspector. "I've connected this hose from the taps where Todd draws his water tests to your tank. He'll think it's the garden hose you're using to wash your RV. Instead, when Todd opens the other tap, he'll fill his vial with clean water from your RV tank instead of Hat Creek's water supply."

"Devious!" Alik laughed.

"I'm banking on him ignoring the reduced water pressure," Dan said.

Todd emptied the test vial into the weeds and refilled it with water from the tap. Music blared out the open RV window, masking the RV's water pump, while Alik attacked the accumulated Black Hills dust with a soapy yellow sponge. A green garden hose identical to the one supplying Todd's samples lay at Alik's feet as a prop, snaking away in plain view toward the tap.

Todd added three drops of clear liquid from a tiny plastic bottle and shook the vial. "Your water mineral content is great," he said, comparing the color of the sample to his laminated chart. "What brand of water filter are you using?"

Dan hadn't the foggiest idea. "I switched to Acton Bell," he said.

"Acton Bell," the inspector repeated. "I've never heard of that brand."

"I'm surprised," Dan said. "It's a classic."

Todd issued only a pair of minor code violations. After he departed, Dan thanked Alik for heading off Brooke as she approached in a pink bathrobe and slippers, questioning why there was no water for a shower.

Dan stepped out his back door into the night air and settled into a patio chair. The Milky Way arched across the night like the gossamer contrail of a galactic-sized starship, stirring the stars in its wake. Dan never wearied of the awe-inspiring grandeur.

Closer to home, a dim glow showed through Westside's rear kitchen window, likely a resident having left on a light after grabbing a late snack. Dan rose from his seat to turn off the light.

Instead, he discovered the diner occupied. "A fellow night owl?" he asked, finding Cici seated at the computer table.

"I counted on being the *only* one," she answered.

"Are we up to something nefarious?"

"Alik told me about the stunt you pulled on the state inspector, so this might be right up your alley."

Dan accepted the offer to join her when she slid the other chair back from the table. On the computer monitor, images of Brooke lined the bottom of an online dating site.

"She's very photogenic, isn't she?" Cici said.

"Alik's in cahoots with you, too?"

"A willing resource." Cici began typing. "Occupation: Pediatrician and fashion model. Age: twenty-eight—close enough?"

"Close enough," Dan said.

Cici resumed typing. "Interests: sports, especially football and basketball; attending concerts (rock, alternative); dancing; cooking."

"I'm smitten already," Dan said.

"Brooke mopes all day long, wounded and sad. But the past is the past. She needs to understand that her life is still in front of her."

Dan shook his head. "Between you and Michelle—"

"Don't associate me with Michelle," Cici said sternly. "She's cast from the same die as my family, interested only in her advanced college degrees, prestigious-sounding titles, and highfaluting plans. Pompous and bombastic, all."

"Language to make an English teacher cringe! I was referring to Michelle's efforts at hooking me up with Maggie. While I admit that she approaches things a little more clinically than you—"

"A *little* more clinically?" Cici huffed, though her tone was more conciliatory than dismissive. "Are you and Maggie an item?"

"Back to Brooke."

Cici smiled. "Help me select a pose."

After choosing a suitably alluring image to adorn Brooke's fantasy profile and another flurry of typing, Cici clicked the mouse a final time. "Done."

She turned to face Dan. "Next subject. What more can we do for Stella and Graham?"

"We?"

"My compulsion, your retreat. Beyond a cattle ranch and Mt. Rushmore, what does Hat Creek offer in the way of romantic getaways?"

Though Dan had never ranked his activities by their romantic potential, a venture immediately sprung to his mind. "I maintain hiking trails in both directions along the creek. How about an overnighter? Hiking and camping might lead to something."

"Promising," Cici said, nodding. "Especially the overnight part. But we need context and cover. Otherwise, Stella might balk."

Cici's request dovetailed nicely with one of Dan's ongoing projects. "I've established a series of hiker boxes at five-mile intervals along the trail," Dan said. "I'll propose a hike to resupply the two boxes to the north and establish a third box fifteen miles out."

"Can one person haul everything?"

"Carrying supplies—food, pots and pans, and a first aid kit—plus a new supply box kit, sleeping bags, and a tent?" Dan shook his head. "Impossible."

"Perfect. Graham and Jacob will supply the muscles, and Michelle will make it a foursome. You'll propose this adventure in the morning?"

Dan laughed. "I'll catch everyone at breakfast. If they're game, I'll gather supplies and outfit them later in the afternoon."

"Sounds like a plan."

"What about you?" he asked.

Cici patted her stomach. "I'm allergic to hiking. Seriously, I need some quiet time to choreograph my arrival home. My parents' interrogations require preparation."

Cici's language spoke of complicated family dynamics.

"Excuse me for prying," Dan said, "but isn't Stanford a difficult school to get accepted into?"

"I was a shoo-in," Cici said. "I graduated top of my class—my parents would accept nothing less, nor to attend university anywhere else."

"And yet you flunked out?"

"Purposely. The lowest test scores aren't suffered by the stupid. They're achieved by the smart intentionally answering incorrectly."

Dan guessed her real goal. "And scoring so poorly, you couldn't get accepted back into school."

Cici made a mischievous "Who, me?" face.

"Such a rebellious child."

"Not rebellious. Stupid, worthless, disappointing, and lazy.

Remember?"

Dan also remembered Cici clamming up at the dinner table after spitting out her parents' unflattering opinions.

"Romantic getaways aren't Hat Creek's only devices, Cici. Don't hesitate to ask for suggestions."

"You're already helping, Dan. Hat Creek isn't judgmental. I'm free to be who I am. I could stay here forever."

A sad yip escaped her closing lips, and the brash young woman shrank into a vulnerable child before Dan's eyes. "I don't want to go home, Dan. I don't know how to face my parents."

Dan regarded Cici as a child for but a moment. Though it may appear callous, Dan couldn't allow Cici to hide in any comfort Hat Creek might afford her.

"I want to show you something," he said, holding his left hand between them. The last joint of his middle finger angled unnaturally toward his index finger.

"What happened?" Cici asked.

"A loosened board of a building I was dismantling swung down and nearly scissored off the tip of my finger."

"Ouch."

"Big ouch. I straightened it the best I could, splinted it to my index finger, and returned to work, disregarding the pain I knew would be temporary."

He wiggled his finger. "It functions properly. I can still do everything I used to do. My point, Cici, is that your issue, too, will mend if you deal with it."

Cici smiled but remained unconvinced.

"Don't run from your problems, Cici," Dan said. "I learned that lesson."

CHAPTER 13

Jacob rummaged through the camping supplies strewn across the Hartman's counter until he found a black plastic cylinder with rubber hoses dangling from either end. He unscrewed the cylinder cap and dumped out a porous carbon filter.

Michelle stepped beside him and hoisted a corrugated box onto the counter. "What's that?"

"It's a backpacking water filter," he said, installing a fresh filter. "Using this, we'll be able to draw our drinking water from the creek. It beats hauling our water."

Michelle removed plastic bags of penne pasta from the box and stacked them on the counter. Reaching into the bottom of the box, she produced a short length of wood molding.

"I doubt we'll need picture frame supplies," Jacob said.

"It was already in the box when I picked it up. It must have fallen off the shelf." She turned the molding in her hand. "Have you ever been inside Dan's home?"

Jacob nodded. "His old cabin. He served me breakfast."

"Did you see any pictures of Dan's family?"

Jacob shrugged. "All I remember is that Dan scrounged his furniture from the other houses—and that he didn't own a television. Why do you ask?"

"Dan has no family photos on display in his house—his present house, I mean. I looked everywhere." Michelle shook her head. "Who wouldn't want remembrances of their loved ones?"

"Maybe the memories are too painful—" Jacob placed the filter on the counter. "You've been snooping around Dan's house."

"No, I haven't."

"You looked 'everywhere?'"

"Dan lent me a book and said I was free to select another one."

"Okay," Jacob said. "But that doesn't permit you to wander through his house."

"His house is so tiny that it requires more effort *not* to look around."

"And, if I were to inform Dan of your intrusion?"

Michelle's eyes flared. "Don't you dare."

"Ah, so you *are* guilty! It's going to cost you."

"What?"

Jacob considered a suitable penalty. "A kiss."

"I'm not kissing you."

"No?" Jacob held his fist as a phone to his ear. "Dr. Malkovich, Dan Stuart here. I'm sorry to inform you that I've insisted Michelle leave Hat Creek. I don't tolerate vandalism."

"That's blackmail," Michelle complained.

Jacob dropped his phone and laughed. "Call it what you wish."

"Unbelievable," Michelle said, shaking her head in disgust. She turned the molding in her hand and studied its cut ends. "I'd been thinking Dan was hiding something." She looked at Jacob. "Do you think, instead, he hasn't been truthful?"

"You mean about what happened to his family?"

Michelle nodded. "Or that he even had a family."

Jacob smirked at her. "What possible motive would Dan have for creating a fictitious family, only to kill them off in—how did you describe it—some tragic event? Sympathy? As an excuse to create Hat Creek? Uh-uh."

"Point taken," Michelle said. "Strike my last thought. But I'm—"

"Still snooping."

"Still curious. There's a big difference."

"It seems a little online research might be in order," Jacob suggested. "Family tragedies usually make the headlines. We'll look into it together tonight in your cabin."

"Hat Creek's internet works only in Westside and Dan's house." Michelle returned the box to a shelf and started up the aisle. "I'll round up Graham and Stella to begin packing."

"Wait!" Jacob said.

Michelle spun around.

"Aren't you forgetting something?"

"What?"

"My kiss."

"Oh, yeah." Michelle hurried back and pecked him on the cheek. "We'll be right back."

Jacob leaned against the counter and watched Michelle walk away. That sorry excuse for a kiss canceled zero debt. Shaking his head, he stepped behind the counter to pick out the backpacks.

They reached the five-mile hiker box late morning and shed their packs, Michelle and Stella predictably suffering sore shoulders. The bright red wooden box, the size of a small toy chest, had a top-opening lid that doubled as an overhanging roof. Jacob and Graham carried an unassembled duplicate between them.

Jacob removed the carabiner securing the latch and lifted the lid to inspect the box's contents. A collection of mess kits, plastic cups, and a mishmash of silverware filled a plastic tub. The first aid kit included a complement of bandages and ointments, and the water jug was full.

After replenishing the foodstuffs, the four wandered among the cottonwoods lining the creek. While Michelle picked at the deeply fissured tree bark she recognized as the supply of Dan's whittling woods, Graham and Stella zigzagged down the steep embankment to the creek bottom.

Jacob preferred adventure in the opposite direction and soon stood on a tree branch twenty feet off the ground, high enough to spot a herd of grazing cattle. Looking down, he spied Michelle remove a roll of toilet paper from Stella's backpack and pirouette a slow three-sixty. "Looking for a portable toilet?" he called down to her.

"A forlorn hope, I assume."

"It's behind the tree."

"Which one?"

"Take your pick."

"Very funny."

"I won't peek."

"We have company," Stella said, drawing everybody's attention to a man astride a majestic chestnut stallion sauntering their way.

"Randy Kincaid," the rider said when he arrived, tipping his cowboy hat and loosening the reins to let his horse pull its head down to graze. His weather-aged face and gray hair placed him close to Dan's age. "You must be some of Dan's hikers."

Admitting they were, they introduced themselves.

Graham stroked the horse's neck. "Is this your land?"

Randy nodded proudly. "You passed our buildings a couple of miles back."

"Get many hikers through?" Michelle asked.

"Just Dan, for the longest time. A couple of years ago, he told us to expect more. Counting you, I've seen perhaps eight to ten groups."

"How long have you known Dan?" she asked.

"Now you're taxing my memory," the rancher said, adjusting his seat in the saddle. "Dan arrived the year before we raised our new barn—he helped with the roofing. That would put it"—he removed his hat and scratched his head—"going on fifteen, sixteen years."

"Dan has worked miracles rebuilding Hat Creek," Michelle continued.

"Can't argue with that," Randy said. "Things didn't make sense for the longest time—no disrespect intended. But, as you say, he's turned the town into quite the place." After extending an invitation to stop by his place on their return trip, Randy wished them safe passage and, gathering the reins, applied light pressure to Scout's flanks to urge the chestnut into a canter.

Michelle dallied once they resumed their hike, letting Graham and Stella advance out of earshot. "That completes the timeline," Michelle told Jacob. "Dan arrived in Hat Creek shortly before you spied him as a little kid. It also validates why I didn't uncover anything online last evening."

"I can't believe you actually dug into Dan's past. I was only—" Jacob shook his head. He wasn't about to explain motivations that Michelle should have understood instinctively.

"It was worth a try," she said. "We'll need to find out where Dan used to live and search newspaper archives."

"*We'll* need to?" Jacob thrust his finger through a belt loop of Michelle's jeans and yanked her around to look ahead at Graham and Stella, now holding hands. "Uh-uh. We need to follow their lead."

Michelle extricated Jacob's finger and quickened her pace to catch up to the other pair.

Jacob woke and dressed in the predawn twilight. The ladies had arrived at the fifteen-mile campsite exhausted and subdued, complaining of aches and pains. Jacob estimated Graham wasn't in much better shape, just putting up a manly front for Stella's benefit. Shortly after their dinner, Graham and Stella had retreated to one tent, Michelle the other.

Using a flashlight to guide him, Jacob left the campsite and found a suitable climbing tree. After returning, he tossed twigs at Michelle's tent.

"Get dressed," he whispered when she poked her head out. "I found the perfect place to watch the sunrise."

After a moment of rustling inside the tent, Michelle unzipped the tent flap and stepped into the predawn air dressed in yesterday's jeans and a loose brown sweatshirt. Her hair was already in a ponytail.

"This way," Jacob said, leading Michelle along the creek away from their campsite. "How'd you sleep?"

"Poorly. It was too hot inside the tent."

"It was pleasant out in the open," he said. "A cool breeze blew all night, plus I had a great view of the Milky Way."

"I've never seen it," Michelle said.

"You've never seen the Milky Way? You *have* led a sheltered life."

"I have not. More goes on in New York City than—"

Jacob barred Michelle's path and pointed up. "We're here."

Michelle craned her neck. "Up a tree? You can't be serious?"

"We certainly won't see anything from down here. But we need to hustle. The sun won't wait for us."

"I'm not climbing a tree."

"I've already been up. It's an easy climb."

"For you, perhaps. I'll fall."

"You won't fall." Jacob pointed at a natural toehold a foot off the ground. "Step up in that depression, and I'll boost you up to grab that knot in front of your face."

"Jacob—"

"Do it!"

Toehold by toehold, handhold by handhold, Jacob coaxed Michelle up the tree, reaching a height that revealed the top of an old windmill far out into the pasture. Jacob wedged himself into a tight spot and wrapped his arm around Michelle's waist to secure her to his chest.

Michelle grabbed a nearby branch. "I did it," she said excitedly, surveying the view offered by their elevated roost. One well-timed head turn stuck her ponytail directly into Jacob's mouth. He spit out the hair.

"Do you always wear your hair in a ponytail?"

"Yes." She looked back at him, hurt. "Anything wrong with that?"

Jacob smiled. "I like it."

Michelle wrinkled her nose and started telling him what he could do with his compliment, only to be hushed when the trees' highest reaches lit up bright orange as if ignited on fire. The visual inferno slipped down the tree, reaching them just as a brilliant point of light pierced the horizon and transformed the narrow band of grass stretching to their vantage point into a pathway of pure gold.

"Beautiful," Michelle gasped.

The rising sun slowly expanded into a yellow-white arc too bright to view. Jacob diverted his eyes to the waking landscape and watched color slowly spread across the pasture like a giant can of sunshine spilling over the land.

Jacob preceded Michelle down the tree, leaving her seated in the crotch of a large branch while he descended the final distance to the ground.

"I can't climb down that way," Michelle said. "I'll fall for sure."

Jacob raised his arms and tapped Michelle's dangling feet with his fingertips. "You're going to jump off. I'll catch you."

"Catch me?" Michelle said incredulously. "I might as well leap."

"More sliding off than jumping off," he told her. "I'll secure you by the waist before you've fallen even a couple of feet."

Michelle spread her arms and leaned forward, only to quickly straighten and grab at the tree.

"Practice makes perfect," Jacob commented.

"I'm the one in danger," Michelle reminded him.

"How about closing your eyes and trusting I'll catch you, like in one of those fancy teambuilding exercises—"

"Okay, okay," Michelle said. She scooted forward until her seat became precarious, extended her arms toward Jacob, and, with an audible whine, slipped from her perch. Jacob caught her by the hips as she grabbed a panicked hold around his neck and lowered her smoothly to the ground. Not about to pass up an opportunity falling literally from the sky, he slid his hands around Michelle's waist.

"Can I kiss you?" he asked.

Michelle blinked in surprise. Jacob guessed nobody had ever asked.

"Yes?" she said.

Jacob disregarded the puzzlement in her tone and kissed her full on the lips. Michelle kissed him back, only for the briefest moment, but long enough that she couldn't deny her lips had willingly participated.

"We need to start the fire," she said, pulling her head back and uncoiling her grip around Jacob's neck. "I need my morning coffee—and to make breakfast." She turned and walked away.

Jacob leaned against the tree and ran his tongue over his lips. Michelle even tasted differently than his usual fare. Yesterday's jeans, Jacob vowed, were coming off.

CHAPTER 14

The ground wasp reappeared from its burrow and deposited another speck of dirt onto the growing mound surrounding the tiny hole. Dan motioned respect for the insect's work ethic with a flourish of his wrench. "Just you and me, little fellow." With his intrepid foursome opening new territory along the creek, Alik guiding his RV around the hairpin turns of Needles Highway, and Brooke and Cici off to destinations unknown, Dan could convince himself that the last few years had been a fantasy.

A drip of water struck Dan's forehead to assert otherwise. Jacob and his fellow adventurers would return late this evening. Alik should be rolling back at about the same time unless he jammed his RV in the Needle's Eye Tunnel, a distinct possibility given its excessive girth. And Dan couldn't envision Cici or Brooke scurrying away from the place to which they had run. By nightfall, Hat Creek's population would again defy the road signs.

Dan finished tightening the last nut, mentally tallying his maintenance list: a worn water pump, dead electrical circuits, cabin winterization, new cabin prep, rewiring Westside's kitchen, torn shingles and siding, plus Todd's list—the list was endless.

He accepted that he was only delaying Hat Creek's inevitable path to ruination. New wood becomes aged wood turns rotten wood. Cosmetic rust precedes penetrating corrosion and structural failure. The Ogallala aquifer would drop deeper than a water well drill could reach. The disfigurement coursing the length of his forearm struck him as the poster child of *his* accumulated wounds, stark reminders that life followed a similar path. Was it delusional to think he could earn his dream before his life reached path's end?

The next drip struck the bridge of Dan's nose. "I wasn't moping," he complained to the squawking pump. He wiped away his denied melancholy along with the water before letting his tired arm and heavy wrench drop to the ground. On cue, the new seal seated, and the pump calmed to smooth humming. Music to his ears.

He made a pact with his town: You keep going, and I'll keep going. For good measure, he promised to quit thinking so hard.

As Dan extricated himself from beneath the piping to scour Hartman's for the makings of a sumptuous dinner to treat his conscripted residents, a second wasp landed and disappeared into the burrow to join its mate. Dan wondered how they prepared for floods.

"I thought you and Cici were off on an adventure," Dan said when he found Brooke poking around Hartman's fishing gear.

Brooke shook her head. "*I* assumed she'd gone looking for you. Something's bugging her." Brooke peered through the display glass. "Do you stock any fly-tying supplies? I haven't tied flies in years."

"Is Hat Creek blessed with an angler?"

Brooke smiled and nodded. "As a child with my father." She held up her hands. "Hard to believe these hands used to clean fish."

Brooke's expired wedding band made more of an impression on Dan than her smooth skin or pink fingernails, highlighting the issue Cici's foray into matchmaking only touched on: Brooke had depended upon a strong man her entire life, meaning her failed marriage was the double loss of love *and* a safety net. And while Cici's exercise could help persuade Brooke that the loss wasn't necessarily permanent, Hat Creek, by design, was best equipped to teach self-sufficiency.

So, let the retreat do its job.

"No fly fishing supplies," Dan said, "but I have a better idea."

He ushered Brooke behind the counter. "Our returning hikers will be famished. You'll help me treat them to a delicious fish fry."

"I'd meant to ask you if we could go fishing."

"I figured you'd be interested."

Dan placed a small plastic tackle box onto the counter and opened the drawer stocked with lures, bobbers, sinkers, hooks, and other fishing accessories. "Select what you need while I put together a small pack for you."

"This brings back fond memories," Brooke said. "What's your pond stocked with?"

"Large-mouth bass and bluegill."

"Jigs or spoons?"

"I've had luck with both, though shiny spoons seem to work best on sunny days like today."

Dan grabbed a lightweight daypack and walked the aisles, loading supplies. Brooke was latching the tackle box closed when he returned.

"I've loaded a few bottles of water, granola bars, jerky, plus sunscreen and bug spray," he said, inserting the tackle box into the pack. "Pick out a reel to your liking," he added, nodding at the fishing rods propped up on a narrow shelf along the wall.

Brooke tested a few reels, settling on a spinning reel attached to a black graphic rod with a cork handle. Laying it on the counter, it finally dawned on her that Dan wasn't gathering equipment for himself.

"Aren't you coming?" she asked.

Dan zipped up the pack and shook his head. "Can't. My water pump is squealing like a stuck pig. Bad bearing. We'll lose our entire water supply if that pump fails."

"So, you're sending me by myself?"

"There *is* nobody else. Besides, who better than an expert?"

Dan offered a pack strap, and Brooke reluctantly thrust her arm through. She managed the other strap and adjusted the chest buckle while Dan clipped the reel to the backpack. He stepped in front of her to take inventory. "Mustn't forget a hat. Otherwise, you'll burn out there."

He lifted a wide-brimmed hat off a wall hook and pulled it down over Brooke's head.

"Dan—"

"You look great." He ushered her toward the front door. "Oh—we'll need several of these, too." He grabbed a handful of tiny fluorescent orange marker flags and threaded them through a loop on the side of Brooke's pack.

"What are those?" Brooke asked, raising her arm to look.

"Flags to mark buried electrical cables and water pipes," Dan answered, leading her outside. "In your case, as bright cookie crumbs to mark your return trip. You'll understand shortly."

Dan walked Brooke across the gravel road and into the pasture, halting beyond a particularly nasty outcrop of cacti. After stepping behind Brooke, he cupped her shoulders and aimed her north-northwest.

"Dan, I don't know if I can do this."

"Sure, you can. Our hikers are depending on you. Now, don't veer from the direction I've pointed you."

"Is the pond just over that rise?" Brooke asked.

"No. When you get to the top of the rise, stick one of those flags into the ground and head straight for the next little rise."

"Is the pond over *that* rise?"

"Not that one, either. Plant another flag. They'll guide you back."

Brooke lifted her arm to count the flags. "How far away *is* the pond?"

Dan shrugged his shoulders. "I've never actually measured. When you return—"

"Dan," Brooke whined.

"When you return," he repeated, "I'll help you clean the fish."

"But Dan."

Dan adjusted Brooke's shoulders a final time. "Look straight ahead. Remember, don't veer. Now, relax, have fun, and catch a stringer of fish."

Dan sent Brooke on her way with a gentle yet authoritative push, watching until she planted her first flag and disappeared over the hill. Barring veering horribly off-course, the pond would appear after the fourth—or was it the fifth? —rise and provide Brooke's confidence a much-needed boost. He already felt better.

Dan had just deposited fillet knives and a shallow metal pan on the large tree stump adjacent to the fire pit when he spotted Cici seated on the water tower catwalk, her legs dangling in the air. He ascended to the catwalk with surprising ease and used the opportunity to scan the buildings' roofs, spying two issues needing attention. Ignorance may be bliss, but it can be expensive, too.

Seating himself on the unforgiving metal decking proved more challenging than scaling the stairs, only exceeded by the charade that it wasn't. "How long have you been up here?" Dan asked, proud that he had maneuvered his legs over the ledge without grunting.

"I snuck up after you disappeared into your shed carrying a huge wrench."

At least Cici hadn't caught him yelling at the water pump.

She gazed over Grange Hall at the two orange flags tracking Brooke's progress. "My ploy seems sophomoric in comparison,"

Dan was impressed that Cici had understood his motive. "I prefer to think of our efforts as complementary interventions," he said.

"Ugh," Cici complained. "You sound like Michelle."

"Sorry. Let me try again. As partners in crime."

"Better." She glanced once more out over the pasture. "You do know there's a chance Brooke is just out of sight, balled up tighter than a roly-poly."

Dan chuckled at the imagery and shrugged. "Brooke arrived in Hat Creek of her own accord. It's her business whether she's hopelessly lost. But I'll bend the rules and send out a rescue party if she hasn't returned by dusk."

"Dan, you're remarkable."

Cici's sad sincerity was unmistakable. "Brooke mentioned that something was bugging you," he said.

Cici shrugged. "You know the verse: 'Stupid, worthless …'"

"You've spoken to your parents?"

Cici lowered her forehead against the top handrail and rolled her head back and forth. "Just made to admit they're right." She sighed deeply. "I'm a fraud, Dan, merely a pampered teenager depressed because her parents don't understand her. I'm depriving someone more deserving of your valuable space and resources."

"You're certainly no fraud," he said. Cici was a black sheep of sorts, the intelligent, spirited, sensing daughter of objective-minded parents attempting to mold her in their incompatible image. Parental harm can take many forms.

"Michelle told me about your family," she said, lifting her head. "Before their hike. By that measure, I'm a fraud." She grimaced at his anguish. "Sorry for knowing."

Dan shook his head. "Don't be." His secret was out sooner than he had predicted. "If I hadn't wanted anybody to find out, I shouldn't have founded Hat Creek."

"So why did you?"

Her question helped Dan understand how Hat Creek might help the young woman. First, Brooke, and now Cici. Like Jacob's well-timed arrival, some opportunities fell into your lap.

"Because self-help takes many forms," he said as a clue, challenging her to figure it out.

Cici stared hard at Dan before lowering her chin to the middle railing and gazing across the town. "You're wielding a wrench," she said, understanding his view of Hat Creek.

"A tool."

Dan smiled and nodded. Intelligent, indeed. "And tools come in all shapes and sizes."

CHAPTER 15

The Kinkaid's chickens were white with random splatters of bright colors as if they had participated in barnyard paintball.

They walked single file along the top of hay bales stacked the length of a pasture fence. When Jacob heard the rattling sound, he backed the group away and retreated to the ground.

A passing farmhand identified the antique implement as a horse-drawn hay rake, obsoleted by motorized tractors. Making it, Stella giggled, as old as Dan.

Jacob maintained a brisk return pace to the five-mile hiker's box, the bright wood taunting his three companions that they had five miles yet to endure. They unrolled their sleeping bags in the dense shade for a siesta, and Jacob lay on his back, peering up into the pale green canopy, the topmost leaves rustling in a breeze that wasn't reaching the ground.

He swatted away a fly that landed on his cheek. It was hot.

Jacob figured he had napped for an hour. He wiped a bead of sweat from his cheek and turned onto his side, propping his head in his hand. Graham and Stella were missing; depressions in their sleeping bags marked where they had laid. Michelle was lying on her back with her cap covering her face.

Jacob couldn't defend the attraction; Michelle wasn't sexy or beautiful, nor was he deprived or hard up. He hadn't left Denver due to a scarcity of prospects, and he could be in Price tomorrow enjoying the company of a couple of fine ladies. Yet, he couldn't stop fantasizing about slipping off those tight jeans.

PhD, Jacob decided after further thought. That highfaluting term and the reverence Michelle expected—demanded—from everybody because she was "pursuing" one. Could it be that the challenge of seducing an arrogant brainiac was a turn-on? Jacob laughed silently. He, too, was pursuing a PhD.

He picked up a small stone and flung it at the closest tree. Michelle flinched when it ricocheted.

"Just checking if you were awake," he said.

"It's too hot to sleep," Michelle said, shooing away a pesky fly. She pulled the cap from her face and rolled to face him. "Shouldn't we get started? We promised Dan we'd return by dark."

"As long as you don't dawdle once we're back on the trail, we have plenty of time. Besides, it appears we're missing half our crew. Any idea where our love birds went?"

Michelle shook her head. "They said they were going exploring."

Jacob chuckled. "You know where Graham is exploring."

Michelle rolled her eyes. "Did you stop through Hat Creek just to prove how crude you can act?"

"It's fortunate for you I *did* stop."

Michelle raised onto her elbow to mirror Jacob's attitude. "This ought to be entertaining."

Jacob scooted across Stella and Graham's sleeping bags until he lay face-to-face with Michelle. "Without my help, those feed bags would never have gotten stacked in the milk barn. And you'd be looking at multiple round trips to haul Dan's hiker box and supplies."

Michelle poked his arm. "It feels a little peaked, so you might want to give it a rest. You'll need it in tip-top shape for your next job."

"At least I'll have a job. I overheard you tell Cici you have seven more years of school. *Seven years?* Meanwhile, I'll be earning a weekly paycheck."

Michelle lifted a finger and traced circles in the air. "Just spinning your wheels," she said dismissively.

Michelle couldn't get under Jacob's skin. "While you're committing textbooks to memory, I'll continue exploring the world," he said. "I've skied at twelve thousand feet, rafted category five whitewater rapids, and hiked several fourteeners. Next summer, I'll be sailing Lake Michigan and attending Cubs games. After that, I'll head to the coast and take up scuba diving and deep-sea fishing; hike sections of the Pacific Crest Trail."

If Michelle was impressed, she didn't show it. But, neither did she respond with one of her smart-alecky comebacks. Jacob suspected Michelle secretly envied people like him who lived for adventure, only too reserved or introverted to join in the fun.

He'd be her first adventure.

A gnat landed on Michelle's cheek, giving Jacob a convenient excuse to initiate physical contact. After delicately brushing away the tiny insect, he reached behind Michelle's head and draped her ponytail across her chest.

"Can I see it down?" he asked.

"Now you're acting silly."

Jacob shook his head. "It's natural to find a girl attractive, just as it's natural"—he brushed Michelle's cheek a second time—"to find a strong guy attractive."

Jacob leaned close and kissed Michelle's cheek, following with a full-on, open-mouthed, sensual kiss when she didn't balk. Michelle participated by parting her lips and urging the kiss deeper.

Just as Jacob was planning his next move, Michelle pulled away and looked over Jacob's shoulder. "There you are," she said.

Lamenting the love birds' poor timing, Jacob rolled over—to find no one. When he turned back, Michelle had scrambled to her feet and was dragging her sleeping bag toward her pack.

The flames flared when Dan chucked his paperware into the fire. The sight of Brooke's radiant face, highlighted the color of the setting sun, brought Dan satisfaction. He and Cici had popped into Westside for a cold drink after returning to Hat Creek with a truckload of salvaged siding to find Brooke packing her bountiful catch into ice. Momentarily, Brooke was the queen of her world.

Maggie tossed her plate after Dan's, and the fire greedily consumed seconds of fire-grilled largemouth bass. Dan turned his head to catch a shadowy glimpse of Stella nuzzled against Graham's chest. Dan had gleaned from snippets of overheard conversation that they had bonded on the trail. Was their companionship a temporary convenience fated to dissolve or the beginnings of a longer-term relationship?

Dan could ask himself the same question. Maggie's presence

was as palpable as Brooke's pride, and he accepted Maggie more easily in his thoughts, awakening long-forgotten urges. Where might the upcoming months lead?

CHAPTER 16

Dan hoisted the tub of roofing nails from the truck bed and placed it on the ground. When he straightened, Jacob stood before him, his backpack slung over his shoulder, appearing surprisingly fresh for someone who had departed Hat Creek just forty-eight hours earlier burdened by a load too heavy for Dan to lift.

"Heading home?" Dan asked.

Jacob nodded resignedly. "No different than last time." He shrugged off the pack and placed it into the truck bed before taking a seat on the tailgate.

Dan looked up and down the twin ruts. "Close. If I recall, back then I parked on the other side of the street, and you only *looked* like a strapping young man with the world at his feet—oh, and I wasn't the mayor of a thriving ghost town populated by a constant flux of itinerant residents."

Jacob leaned forward and peered at the ground. "Just as desolate, though. I still don't know how you can stand it."

Dan wasn't going to apologize for admiring the ground-hugging weeds, a symbol of the tenacity required to thrive in this environment. They played their role in making Hat Creek what it was. As did the rickety buildings and the rusting water tower, even the heat and dust and isolation. As did Dan.

He had already learned that achieving any goal, even as lofty as saving lives, took hard work and dedication, finding your proper focus, and sticking with it. He could measure his progress toward that goal by how he was beginning to feel one with his town.

Of course, he couldn't admit that last point to Jacob and retain any hope of seeing him again.

"I warned you last trip about trying to understand me," Dan said. "I take it you're not thrilled about returning home."

Jacob sighed. "Living at home is going to kill me."

"Parents aren't supposed to be a joy to live with."

"My parents aren't the problem. They even offered my old room back. My problem is what everybody will think."

"Adult children living with their parents until they can get on their feet doesn't carry the same stigma it once did."

Jacob smirked at him. "It does when you're moving from Denver back to Price, South Dakota. I'll be a laughingstock."

Dan pondered Jacob's youthful bravado. "Boasted excessively about leaving for good, I take it."

"You could say that."

Dan grabbed a seat on the tailgate. In similarly desperate situations, he often found relief by throwing his hammer at inanimate objects. He pried free a rock lodged in a crevice in the truck bed and handed it to Jacob. "Throw it. It'll help."

Jacob chucked the stone at the wrecks, pinging it off the back window of a baby blue and rust-orange Cadillac.

"Good shot," Dan said. "Feel better?"

"No. The window didn't break."

"Need something a bit sharper for tempered glass."

"Got anything handy?"

"Just a message, same as last time."

Jacob managed a smile. "Now I *know* I've come full circle."

"Don't worry," Dan said. "I'm not going to harp on education or training."

"Good," Jacob said. "I've had my fill of classrooms." He glanced at the line of cabins. "Unlike some people, I have no desire to make a career out of filling the seats inside them."

"PhD-seeking girl troubles aside," Dan said, unable to resist a little ribbing, "you've already discovered that your situation can become untenable if you don't earn enough to keep a roof over your head. And, sorry to say, the cost of living in Chicago is even higher than in Denver. So, unless you plan on winning the lottery or raiding my stash beneath Hartman's—"

"You left everything down there?"

Dan nodded. "If I pull it up, I'll have to sell it. I don't have the time."

"It could be a great diversion for your residents."

"You're still the only person who knows what's down there, and I'd prefer keeping it that way. The last thing I need is treasure hunters snooping around the town. But, back to my message. The key is to find a job you enjoy and stick with it to gain experience and become valued, become indispensable. That's when you start earning the big bucks.

"For the present, work as many hours as possible while leaning on your parents for free room and board. After a year or two, when you qualify for more than an entry-level position, strike out for Chicago."

"A year or two?" Jacob complained. "No way."

"That's the reality, Jacob."

Jacob took a deep breath and blew it out through puffed cheeks. After staring into space for a moment, he hopped off the tailgate and gathered his backpack. Shrugging it onto his shoulder, he kicked his toe into the ground. "This is quite the place you've built here, Dan. See you around."

"You're always welcome," Dan said.

Michelle placed her food tray on the table opposite side of Dan and sat. "Sorry for the short notice. Last night I finished my outline for my summer report to Dr. Malkovich and found a few holes that need filling." She glanced at her watch. "And only a couple of hours to tie up all the loose ends."

"These two weeks have flown by," Dan said. "Yesterday, Joshua. Today, you. Cici in the next couple of days. Our youth population is dropping like flies. I hope Hat Creek proved a worthy subject for your summer internship."

"More than worthy," Michelle said. "You've helped me understand Dr. Malkovich's excitement. I can't wait to see where you take this place. I only hope I haven't been a burden—" She caught herself. "What am I saying? Of course, I've been a burden."

"I've survived worse," Dan said with a little laugh.

Michelle opened her notebook on the table and picked up her pen. "First question."

"Rescue me from this young lady," Maggie implored as she and Michelle stepped from Michelle's cabin to join Dan at the open trunk of Michelle's car.

"Rescue *you*?" Dan said. "I'm the one she's been grilling these past two weeks." He hoisted Michelle's last suitcase into the trunk and closed the lid.

"I simply encouraged her to reconcile with her daughter,"

Michelle said, loading her computer case into the back seat. She closed the car door and turned to Dan. "Again, thank you for hosting me."

The trio shared quick embraces before Michelle climbed into her car and started the engine. When her window opened, mirrored sunglasses concealed her eyes. "Bye, Maggie," she said. "Good luck with your daughter. Bye, Dan. Until next time."

"Until next time. And have a safe trip."

"An interesting young lady," Maggie said after Michelle drove away.

Dan could only nod. "Best of all," he said sarcastically, "she all but promised to return every summer."

When the rental car vanished into the distance, Dan turned his attention to the relationship *he* most needed to clear up. "In the mood for a walk? We can inspect Hat Creek's outer defenses and plot strategies to withstand Michelle's next onslaught."

"I'm game," Maggie said.

"Let's head through the park."

Dan placed his hand against the small of Maggie's back as they turned, as much a trial balloon of his feelings as a signal to Maggie. The contact set off no internal alarm bells, though whether he'd yield to Maggie's next advance was still unresolved.

They circled behind Michelle's cabin and followed the dirt path leading to Brule Street. "I'm sorry for my schoolgirl behavior," she said. "I've been throwing myself at you like some love-struck puppy, getting peeved that you never noticed, and all the while, you were grieving the loss of your family."

"Don't lose hope," Dan said, nudging her shoulder with his arm. "I can't remain in a pissy mood forever."

Dan paused when they reached the park bench. "I'm

hoping to encourage this grass to supplant more weeds so I can place one or two more park benches, maybe build a gazebo sheltered by the tree."

"A lawnmower would make quick work of the weeds," Maggie said.

"Prohibited."

"How so?"

"Neatly trimmed weeds or grass would stand out like a sore thumb."

"Good point," Maggie said with a sarcastic chuckle. Dan's devotion to maintaining Hat Creek's ghost town appearance bemused her.

"I'm in no hurry, though," Dan said. "I'll herd stray cattle into this area the next time they overrun Hat Creek and let them trample everything down."

"Why wait? We'll make like cows and trample. I make a good cow."

Maggie stepped into the midst of the weeds, lifting her feet high to stomp them down. Dan followed behind, crushing any weeds Maggie missed. In short order, they'd subdued the weeds, leaving a mangled carpet of green covering the ground. Dan didn't know whether they'd done any good, but he'd had fun.

Stella and Graham married and settled in the mountains west of Denver, far enough from the large crowds that tormented Stella yet close enough to avoid the small-town drug culture Graham dreaded. They taught their children to seek their thrills in hiking, camping, and skiing.

Brooke married a doctor and had a daughter and a son, but the marriage didn't last. Craig would remain her one true love.

Cici founded an executive and corporate coaching firm in Silicon Valley, catering to the competitive and obsessive professionals she understood so well. She frequently vacationed in Hat Creek, amusing herself by igniting more love affairs.

Alik occupied Dan's soundproofed cabin yearly until he gathered enough material to publish his photography book, *Prairie Ghosts*, an oversized glossy hardcover nearly too heavy for Dan's rickety old coffee table. As a departing gift, Alik donated a camera to Hat Creek, which proved a source of endless entertainment in the hands of novice Hat Creek residents.

And what about Jacob and Michelle? Logic would dictate that a midwestern blue-collar womanizer and an east coast PhD-bound bookworm would never cross paths again. But then, little of Hat Creek made sense.

Except to Dan. Of course, he couldn't know anyone's future, but he had an inkling. And more than an inkling that Hat Creek was working.

The Decision of a Lifetime

The maroon Massey Ferguson tractor lumbered west out of Hat Creek, towing a wagonload of Hat Creek residents for a day at the Childress Ranch. While still in view, the procession veered off the gravel road and into a pasture. A scenic shortcut, though a rough one.

Dan retreated to his office to peruse the day's mail. Even before opening it, he knew the contents of the Social Security Administration envelope, having read the notice several times: he had reached full retirement age and was entitled to full benefits. Additional verbiage and charts detailed the increased monthly benefits he would receive should he continue to delay filing.

Perhaps it was time he filed. The monthly income would cover some of the bills he had just dropped into the basket.

Stepping back outside, Dan noticed the solitary figure stooped on a log at the fire ring, head in their hands. Dan could have sworn that all his residents had climbed onto the hay wagon. Where did losing the ability to count rank along the path toward senility?

Dan headed for the park, recognizing Bill Stenhouse after veering off Brule Street. Bill had contacted Dan only a week earlier, wiring Dan a handsome fee the same day and arriving three days later. Bill had remained detached from the other residents, his demeanor more contemplative than belligerent.

Dan stepped around the end of the log and sat beside the still-prone figure. "Ranching not your cup of tea?"

Bill straightened and delicately turned his head, wincing at the simple movement. "I have a splitting headache."

Dan absentminded rubbed at his aching knees. "I keep a couple of different painkillers in Hartman's."

Bill's eyes told Dan that his pain was beyond medication. Dan nodded. Some pains require alternative remedies.

"I've always preferred natural remedies, myself," Dan said. "Long hikes along the creek are my favorite. Clears one's mind and shrinks problems to a more manageable size."

Dan had taken his first walk searching for his as-yet unsighted eagle. Progressively longer hikes, requiring provisioning, eventually prompted the hiker's boxes. Survival planning combined with exercise and solitude had helped him through that low, low early time.

"You got a family, Dan?"

Bill must be a mind reader. "I lost my wife and two daughters. It's why Hat Creek exists."

"Sorry for your loss."

Dan nodded.

Bill winced and pressed his hand to his head. "I apologize if this question is too personal, but did you have any warning? About your family's passing, I mean?"

Dan remembered the headache he awoke with that morning. "None," he said flatly.

"No chance to say goodbye," Bill whispered.

Dan shook his head. "I would trade anything for one more hug, one more kiss. For one more minute."

Bill stared at Dan for a long moment before dropping his hand. "I think I'll take that hike."

Dan stood with Bill. "I'll help get you outfitted. Meet me

in Hartman's."

Dan eyed the anvil clouds billowing ominously to the west, their bruised bases hurling lightning bolts groundward. This storm wouldn't spare Hat Creek. While he could repair any building damage, he could do nothing for Bill.

Bill returned the following morning, quietly packed his belongings, and departed Hat Creek. Seven months later, Dan received a letter from Bill's wife, Kait.

Dear Dan,

I am writing to inform you of Bill's passing.

Prior to his stay at Hat Creek, Bill was diagnosed with a terminal brain tumor and given 4-6 months to live. He faced the prognosis of worsening bouts of nausea and disorientation, reduced motor functions leading to incapacitation, and intolerable pain managed only through powerful medications. Doctors told us that his mental faculties would diminish, eventually losing perception, memory, and the ability to reason. At some stage, he would stop recognizing me. A counselor offered us a list of hospice care facilities.

Following days of quiet introspection, Bill asked permission to explore assisted suicide. Bill wasn't a coward, Dan, but instead a compassionate man trapped in a hopeless situation, thinking foremost to lessen my suffering. I longed to hug Bill with all my strength and

*promise him that I wouldn't suffer a moment in his presence, but
I ultimately accepted Bill's right to make this one decision in the
circumstances otherwise beyond his control. So, I reluctantly blessed
Bill's wishes and promised my full support. That's when he applied to
Hat Creek, seeking solitude to weigh the stark consequences.*

*Two days after Bill left, I learned I was pregnant with our first
child. My initial euphoria—Bill and I had been trying to have a child
for several years—was immediately tempered by my misgivings of
Bill's reaction to the news. Would my pregnancy console Bill that a
part of him would survive his cancer or devastate him that his illness
would condemn our child to grow up fatherless?*

*And what of Bill's right to decide the manner of his passing?
Whether I informed Bill immediately or waited until he returned, he
would undoubtedly abandon any consideration of ending his life. I
spent a sleepless night weighing whether it was respectful or cruel to
withhold my news until Bill's return. And what if I waited and Bill
returned home determined to end his life? Only understanding that this
seed of life was both a blessing and a curse, I decided to abide by my
promise.*

*Bill returned from Hat Creek and described a stormy evening
sheltered in a tent pitched miles from Hat Creek. Lashed by high winds
and heavy rain, and assaulted by lightning and thunder, he chanced a
peek out the tent flap and witnessed black thunderheads consume the
sun. Just when his world darkened to blackness, the sun reappeared,
vivid orange beneath the purple cloud bases, setting in majestic glory.
Bill promised me that we, too, could endure any difficulty and emerge
unscathed.*

In return, I placed Bill's hand on my stomach and announced that he was to become a father.

Bill defied the odds. His courageous tenacity allowed little William to open his newborn eyes and gaze upon his father's face, wrap his tiny fingers around his father's finger, and fall asleep on his father's chest, soothed by his father's heartbeat. The end was everything the doctors promised, though, and Bill passed away in his sleep, heavily sedated, with a smile in his soul, I believe, if not on his face. Though William will never remember Bill, I am sure he will be a better person because of the brief time spent with his father.

Kait

Kait's letter helped Dan to realize how fortunate he was to have known his family. He folded the letter and slipped it back into the envelope. He read it often.

You Win Some, You ...

Dan paid scant attention to the high-speed whine of north-south traffic, its equally disinterested crescendo suddenly deepening in tone in passing. He had but a passing interest in the few vehicles slowing upon approach to turn east or west onto the gravel road, accelerating away to the chorus of crunching gravel. But the present type: slowing, slowing, slowing—silence—always piqued Dan's curiosity.

He peered out his front window. A cobalt blue Chevy compact had parked off the road next to the church foundation, the driver remaining behind the wheel. Odd. Sightseers usually exited their cars to look around.

Flies swarmed around Dan's face when he stepped outdoors, birthed by the recent rain showers. Noticing Dan's approach, the driver stepped from the car, a young woman in her late twenties to early thirties. She was five feet tall at best, with long mousey brown hair in tangles around her face and black-framed glasses perched on a slender nose, wearing threadbare jeans and a wrinkled white blouse missing two buttons.

"Is this the Hat Creek Retreat?" she asked in a panicked voice. "Please tell me this is Hat Creek." Her eyes were bloodshot.

"Yes, it is," Dan replied. "I'm Dan Stuart. How can I help you?"

She dove back into her car and reemerged, clutching a brown leather purse. Shoving a shaking hand into the bag, she removed a wad of cash. "This is all the money I have left," she whined, thrusting the money into Dan's hand. "Please let me stay—" She twisted away from the road as another car approached, hiding her face until it sped past.

"You can stay," Dan said. "But I don't need your money." He looked past her while replacing the cash into her purse and noted several filled grocery bags lining the back seat. She was living out of her car. "Now, how about a cup of coffee."

Dan offered his newest resident a seat on his sofa while he walked to the kitchen to pour her a cup of coffee.

"You're already familiar with Hat Creek," Dan said when he returned, handing her the hot cup. "Did you contact me about staying without following through?"

She shook her head. "I … No, I researched Hat Creek on the computer in the local library." She pulled matted hair away from her face. "Please don't tell anybody I'm here."

Dan smiled into the young woman's obvious distress. "I couldn't tell anybody if I wished. I don't know your name."

She considered his point. "Are you Dan Stuart? *The* Dan Stuart who rebuilt a ghost town?"

"Yes," Dan assured her, "I'm that Dan Stuart. And I can offer you a room and a hot meal. You look like you could use both."

"Thank you. My name is Ann Harris. I'm so tired."

A light rap sounded on Dan's front door. "It's open," he called out and swiveled in his desk chair to watch Ann enter. Lunch and a four-hour rest had done wonders for her eyes. Her blouse, however, was one long nap more rumpled.

Ann noticed his attention and frowned. "I don't have anything else to wear. Or …" She combed her fingers through her hair. "Anything."

"We'll scrounge through the lost and found bin for something to slip on when I show you to our toiletries," Dan said. "And tomorrow, I'll arrange to get you some new clothing."

"I can't afford new clothes," Ann said, nearly to tears. "Or to pay for my room. The money I tried to hand you is all I have left."

No money or possessions and, Dan presumed, on the run. Had he looked this desperate during his exodus?

"I meant what I said about keeping your money," he assured her.

Ann pulled on her hair again. "You mean I can stay? Just like that?"

He nodded. "That's how Hat Creek operates."

He invited Ann to sit. After settling new residents into their room and pointing them to the food, his traditional practice was to recite the Hat Creek orientation spiel: rules—there are none; amenities—if you don't find it on Hartman's shelves or in Westside's refrigerators, it isn't available; pastimes—step to the middle of the town and turn a slow three-sixty to discover unique pursuits from ten feet to ten miles away; and support: "Solicit other residents as sounding boards to help resolve your issue," Dan told Ann. "Or you can remain secluded until whatever you're facing blows over."

A tiny squeak escaped Ann's lips, and tears spilled onto her cheeks. "It won't 'blow over.'"

Ann wiped her face with the tissue Dan offered and dropped her hands to her lap. Dan sensed Ann's desperation, craving a sympathetic ear to supplement her food and rest. Hat Creek's self-help charter dictated that he not intervene on the residents' behalf. But he bent the rules when he reasoned it was in a resident's best interest.

"Why did you research Hat Creek?" Dan asked, reasoning that Ann hadn't filled out an application form.

"To escape," Ann answered tentatively.

"Tell me about it."

"I have an abusive husband," she croaked, responding to Dan's encouragement. "Frank knows how to hit me, so the bruises don't show. And when hurting me doesn't satisfy him, he terrorizes me. Frank has held a gun to my head, Dan. Several times.

"I tried to make our relationship work, Dan. Honestly, I did. I was always super nice to Frank, never a nuisance. We watched his favorite television shows, I cooked his favorite meals, and we had sex every day. But any little thing sets Frank off: my cooking isn't to his liking, I looked like I've gained a couple of pounds, a driver cut him off in traffic, or someone else got the promotion he deserved. And he vents his anger on me.

"My friends tell me I should divorce Frank and obtain a restraining order." Ann shook her head. "That wouldn't stop Frank; it'd only make him angrier. Frank warned me that he would kill me if he suspected I was up to something. I believed him."

She lifted her blouse to expose a fist-sized purple bruise on her lower rib cage. Dan had suffered enough injuries to know that the surrounding yellow-green discoloration was the record of older bruises. Ann covered up and wiped away more tears.

"When I asked if I could have a baby, Frank struck me so hard that I missed a week of work. He told me he'd make that seem like a love tap if I asked again.

"The breaking point came when I didn't react to one of Frank's blows. He expected me to grovel and submit, and I'd had enough. So, he forced a bottle of wine down my throat, and once I was drunk, he stripped me naked and raped me."

Ann shook her head sadly. "I decided to run away, to disappear and start a new life. I considered remote places—that's when I stumbled onto Hat Creek—before settling on Europe. I packed a suitcase, purchased a one-way plane ticket to Munich—that's where I studied during college—and snuck my passport out of our lockbox, hiding everything in the hall closet." She broke down crying and whined through tears. "I arrived home from work three days ago to find Frank standing on our front porch with my opened suitcase at his feet, furiously throwing my belongings onto our lawn. He would have killed me if he had gotten his hands on me."

She blew her nose and continued. "I raced away, thinking only to hide at my brother's house in Michigan. Halfway there, I realized my card purchases were leaving a trail leading Frank straight to me. So I withdrew cash, purchased food at the next couple of stops, tossed my credit and bank cards into a dumpster, and turned west. To here. With no—" Ann's body jerked with a sudden sob. "No money," she whined, "no clothes, no passport. Nothing." She slumped forward and openly wept. "I've lost everything, Dan. Everything."

Dan stood and placed a comforting hand on Ann's back. "You're safe here," he said. "I promise."

Todd bumped the end of his ink pen against his clipboard and handed both to Dan for his signature.

"I bet you had a good chuckle last inspection over that little matter involving the water filter," Todd said.

Dan knew where this conversation was leading. Today, Todd had inspected every filter cartridge, including Dan's spares.

"It so happens that our administrative assistant is an avid reader," Todd said. "She busted a gut when I told her I was researching *Acton Bell* water filters. Evidently, I'm too uneducated to know that Acton Bell was the pen name for some nineteenth-century female author named *Brontë. So now* I'm the laughingstock of the office."

Dan signed the forms and returned the pen and clipboard. "It won't happen again."

Todd nodded at Grange Hall. "I'll give you a heads-up. Your large building over there with the fake hole in the roof and that one farthest west—that's your cafeteria, isn't it?—aren't ADA compliant. You're familiar with the ADA, aren't you?"

"The Americans with Disabilities Act."

"Very good. The ADA isn't a building code, so I can't cite you. But there's a horde of lawyers chomping at the bit to sue for missing railings and wheelchair ramps. If I were you, I'd install them before somebody turns you in."

Todd handed Dan the inspection paperwork, citing three violations, one serious enough to warrant a monetary fine, pending remediation and appeal. "Have a good day," Todd said and walked to his truck.

Dan's front door squeaked open. "Hello?"

"Come on in, Ann," Dan said.

Ann stepped inside and closed the door behind her. "I was wondering—oh, I didn't realize you had company. I can come back later."

"Stay," Maggie said, standing. "I was just on my way out." She pecked Dan on the lips. "I'll see you Saturday."

Dan offered Ann a seat on the sofa once Maggie had departed. "What's on your mind?" he asked.

"I didn't think things through when I ran away," Ann said.

"From the terror you described, you *had* no time to think."

Ann shook her head. "I don't mean the murderous look in Frank's eyes when I backed into our driveway. I didn't consider being vulnerable no matter where I ran. I'll need to provide my name and social security number to fill out job applications. What if I'm flagged on some missing person list? And if I escape that, I'll surely be exposed come tax season. I can't even license my car because police could track me through my car's VIN. I'm hidden but have no safe way to make a new life."

Dan had never anticipated the challenge of a resident unable to leave Hat Creek. Was Hat Creek destined to slowly fill with people who couldn't return to society, a human version of a wild animal sanctuary? Dan shuddered at the thought.

"You need to make a new life," Dan thought aloud. As Ann had belatedly understood, gone were the days when distance from your pursuer was paramount. Once you left an online trace in today's world, halfway around the globe was no safer than halfway across town. Ann needed a new identity.

The idea formed of its own volition. *Ann Harris. AH.* She even had the proper initials. Dan paused for a bit of soul-searching. That the idea was outrageous, as well as illegal, mattered little. As a sanctuary, town, and retreat, Hat Creek was a study in the ends justifying the means, some less righteous than others. This delay was to seek more personal permission.

Only Dan's wife and daughter possessed the moral authority to judge, and it was to their visions he pleaded his case. They heartily approved, one with a respectful nod, the other a girlish laugh.

"Give me a moment," Dan said, standing. He stepped to the oak filing cabinet in his office and removed a thick document from the middle drawer. Leafing to the correct page, he transcribed information onto the paper notepad. After staring at his handwriting for a long moment, he returned to the sofa and handed the pad to Ann.

Her lips moved as she read Dan's writing. "Who is this?" she asked.

"You. Your name, birth date, and social security number. Your new identity."

"Anna Hartman."

"Same initials. It might prove valuable."

"Is this social security number real?"

That was a loaded question. "The owner won't mind that you're borrowing it," Dan said.

"This birthdate puts me at …" Ann's lips moved again. "Twenty-five. I feel much older than that."

Ann had acquired a sizable wardrobe during yesterday's garage sale excursion and was presently wearing a Wyoming Cowboys T-shirt.

"You could pass for a coed."

Ann managed a smile.

"Especially when you smile," Dan said.

Ann held up the pad. "Will it work?"

"Won't know unless you try. Apply for a South Dakota driver's license. You can use Hat Creek as your residence."

"Where was I born?"

"Where would you like to be born?"

Ann thought a moment. "I've always liked the trees, rivers, and mountains of the Northeast. How about New Hampshire?"

"I'd recommend a large city," Dan said. "Someplace you can get lost in the masses. How about Rochester, New York?"

"Okay."

Dan tapped his finger on the paper pad. "Commit that information to memory. Everybody knows their name and birthdate."

Three weeks later, Maggie delivered an envelope from

the South Dakota Department of Public Safety: Licensing addressed to one Anna Hartman. The bandaged finger Ann had cut parting out her car didn't deter her from ripping it open.

"It worked," Ann rejoiced, angling her new driver's license to watch the holographic South Dakota state seal shift through a rainbow of colors.

"You're a person again," Dan said.

"And now I can get a job," Ann said. "I'll still need to lay low, though. I've been considering applying as a clerk at a shop in a small local town. I won't need much to live on."

"Trust me when I say *anywhere* in the Black Hills is hidden enough," Dan said. "What's your dream job?"

"Promise to keep a straight face?"

Dan nodded. Maggie crossed her chest.

"A forest ranger. Little chance of that around here."

Dan dangled his truck key in the air between them. "Don't be too quick to judge. Celebrate by taking a drive north through Custer State Park."

Ann's latest text teased about an article on the Rapid City Journal website she thought would interest Dan. Ann contacted Dan every few weeks and stopped by Hat Creek less frequently—always, everywhere, as Anna Hartman.

Dan navigated to the Journal website. The lead article profiled the latest National Park Service hires and included a photo of the assembled group posed before Mount Rushmore. And there she stood, third from the left, peeking from beneath a wide-brimmed Park Ranger hat.

Later in the evening, after finishing the finances, Dan replaced the ledgers into his safe. There, on the bottom shelf, rested his inspection records binder, which after a two-year hiatus, he had returned to the safe solely for monthly glimpses of his photo album.

With the glow of Ann's success still warming his heart, he lifted the binder to an upper shelf, exposing the photo album to full view. Extending his hand, he allowed his fingertips to touch the leatherette cover and caress its pebbled surface. His fingers found the cover's edge, but he didn't lift it open. Days like today assured him that he need not foolishly rush.

CHAPTER 17

Dan dropped his eyes to his plate when Westside's front door opened. Five years of operating Hat Creek had ill-prepared him to cope with the brash young couple entering the diner. Chloe Hansen, braless as usual, wore a sheer turquoise T-shirt stretched tightly over her ample endowment, leaving nothing to the imagination. The lovely Megan Laroux had streaked her blonde hair the color of strawberry swirl cheesecake.

Chloe had caught Dan gawking yesterday, an indiscretion he blamed squarely on Maggie's recent amorous behavior. The gaffe had earned Dan Chloe's tease that, while she delighted in bedding Megan, she wasn't opposed to pleasuring him. The pair had applied to Hat Creek to contemplate marriage, though Dan couldn't fathom the issue. Outwardly, they presented a besotted couple—Dan had twice already stumbled upon the pair locked in a passionate embrace.

Dan waited until the pair reached his table before casually lifting his gaze.

"You've got a newbie out front," Chloe announced. "We told her we'd send you out."

"We have a few years on her," Megan said, looping Chloe's hand over her shoulder. "And—" She leaned forward to stare at the rail-thin young woman seated beside Dan. "Jealous?"

Whitney Neumann shoved her glasses up her nose and slunk back behind Dan's shoulder.

"She's got a killer figure, especially from behind," Chloe said. "The girl outside, I mean, not Whitney."

"But her condescending attitude is seriously off-putting," Megan said, wrinkling her nose. "I bet she's as tight as her ponytail."

Dan laughed. "I believe Michelle Drake has arrived."

"You know her, then. What's she in for?"

"Michelle isn't a Hat Creek resident. She's a graduate psychology student working on a research project."

"A would-be shrink? Great addition. Whitney's in dire need."

Dan couldn't help but chuckle again. "She studies the retreat itself rather than individual residents. At least that's what she claims."

"Too bad," Megan said. She peered around Dan at Whitney. "Dump the glasses and frumpy clothes and treat your hair as if it's more than a rain hat, and you might get a little action. Hurry up and finish your lunch. Chloe and I are trying our hand at gardening, but we won't set foot in that tool shed. Rodents freak us out."

Dan left Whitney to her impending servitude and stepped outside, kicking up dust off the Westside steps. Michelle stood at the trunk of her car, so recognizable in her blue jeans, tucked-in shirt, and ponytailed hair that it could be a day rather than two years since her last departure.

"Welcome back," Dan called out.

Michelle turned his way and smiled. "Dan!"

The passage of time was more visible on Michelle's face, the girl of her previous stays maturing into a young woman. Her inquisitive, penetrating expression remained, only now didn't look so misplaced. She wasn't sexy like Chloe or beautiful like Megan. Instead, in her confident nonchalance, she possessed nuances of both.

"Megan and Chloe told me you'd arrived—"

"Send her our way when you're finished with her!" Megan called out.

"Speaking of," he said, waving at the trio walking toward the tool shed, Megan and Chloe holding hands, Whitney trailing. "They conscripted Whitney for gardening duty."

"So you've finally started your garden," Michelle said.

Dan motioned toward the creek. "Close to the holding pond, where you saw it marked out."

"Anything else new?" She asked.

"Just the gazebo residents built last year." Dan turned and pointed out the white shelter tucked beneath the tree in the park. "Oh, and—" He directed Michelle's attention in the opposite direction. "Grange Hall's roof has a new look, though in a bad way."

"The hole *is* rather larger than I recall."

"A section of it collapsed down onto the real roof. Startled a few residents. And, unless I repair it, Todd will declare the building uninhabitable. But that's my reward for maintaining a ghost town as a ghost town."

"You also built a wheelchair ramp."

"We're ADA compliant now. Even says so on my website." Dan nodded across the road. "I'm returning you to your original cabin. It also looks rougher, but I promise everything's fine inside."

"Will I need to worry about anyone urinating on the back wall?"

Dan chuckled. "Only if Jacob shows up unannounced."

"What's he up to?"

Dan detected curiosity in Michelle's voice.

"Jacob headed for Chicago as he'd promised," Dan said, "working first as a dock worker and then as a bartender. We keep in regular contact, but he hasn't returned to Hat Creek since the two of you met. What's that make it?"

"Four years ago," Michelle said. "The summer after my freshman year."

"Time flies," Dan said. He didn't mention that Jacob had recently returned home—again—after a deceitful roommate and the bar's sudden closure left him broke and unemployed. "Let me help," he said when Michelle popped open the trunk lid.

Michelle dined with Dan and Maggie at Dan's patio table. "You'll be proud of me," she said as she and Dan compared reading lists. "I've read every Virginia Woolf book except *The Years* and *Between the Acts*. As you predicted, I enjoy how she explored the psychological motivations of her characters. She was an intriguing woman: author, literary figure, and book publisher."

"*Between the Acts* is on my bookshelf," Dan said. "Help yourself to the book anytime."

"There it is," Maggie said, producing a photograph from her purse and handing it to Michelle. "My newest grandbaby, Leanne."

"She's adorable," Michelle said. "I'm so glad you made up with your daughter."

"That's a story for another meal," Maggie said. She reached across the table and squeezed Dan's hand. "Let's say this caring man took up your torch. I owe you both so much."

Maggie slipped the photo back into her purse when Michelle returned it. "What brings you to Hat Creek this summer?"

"Another assignment from Dr. Malkovich," Michelle answered. "She sent me to validate some of her newest conjectures about why Hat Creek functions so effectively."

"We all know this special man is the key to Hat Creek," Maggie said.

"That's my supposition, too." Michelle fingered her wine glass and looked at Dan. "You *are* the primary orchestrator of this mayhem, the self-professed 'non-professional' who lives Hat Creek rather than manages Hat Creek."

"Mayhem?"

Michelle chuckled at his innocent tone. "I collate the data from nearly twenty retreats and clinics, so I'm aware of Hat Creek's uniquely harrowing events: huddling around the Hartman's stove for three days after losing power during sub-zero temperatures; scaling the water tower to escape a flash flood surging down the creek; retreating indoors when a pair of male pronghorns waged a pitched battle through town; rigging a homemade water mister to help survive two straight weeks topping a hundred degrees in the shade." She shook her head. "The list goes on and on. It's a miracle you haven't lost anybody, Dan."

"It's a miracle we haven't lost *him*," Maggie said. "Sometimes, I think Dan has a death wish. Show Michelle your arm."

"I'd rather not ruin her meal," Dan said. "Did stumbling onto a rattlesnake den make it into your reports?"

Michelle gasped. "You got bitten?"

Dan nodded. "Mabel finally got me."

"Dan jumped in front of the fool who decided to investigate the rattling noise," Maggie said. "Luckily, I was there to rush Dan to the hospital."

Dan's arm had swollen so quickly that his skin had split, leaving another nasty scar.

"Painful," Michelle said, wincing. "Nowhere else but Hat Creek does self-reliance occasionally determine if you survive the day. You'd think such a threat would send people fleeing from Hat Creek as fast as their legs could carry them. Instead, these life-and-death situations have the opposite effect. Many people leave here with the attitude, 'If I can survive Hat Creek, I can survive anything life throws at me.'"

"I'm not running a five-star hotel," Dan said in his defense. Based on Michelle's list, more like an absurd endurance camp.

"I'm not surprised you took the bullet for your resident," Michelle said. "It fits your modus operandi."

"Good way of putting it," Maggie said.

"No ganging up," Dan complained.

Michelle slid her wine glass Dan's way. "I'll admit to an ulterior motive for this trip, Maggie. I'm working on my PhD thesis, and I think researching what makes Hat Creek tick is meaty enough to interest Dr. Malkovich. And here is the only place I'll get to the bottom of that."

Dan uncorked the wine bottle, already knowing he was in trouble.

CHAPTER 18

Hartman's front door swung open, and multiple sets of footsteps entered.

"Hello?" Chloe called out. "Dan?"

He emptied the shipping box and stepped into view. "Back—here." Chloe's shredded hot pink T-shirt exposed a belly button ring and a red heart tattoo below her ribs, and threatened to spill her endowment into the open. Megan pulled at a dangling strip of the T-shirt's fabric while groping her partner's waist.

"We thought you should know that a hearse just drove into town," Chloe said.

Whitney squeezed past the pair and pushed her glasses to her face. "It's a medical transport van, Dan."

"If it's a medical transport van rather than a hearse, why did they pull a dead body out the back?" Megan asked. Today's hair color was lime green.

"She's not dead," Whitney said.

"She is compared to this," Megan said, fondling Chloe's butt.

"She's an elderly woman on a gurney," Whitney told Dan, turning to shield herself from the petting. "I introduced myself." Whitney habitually pushed on the nosepiece of her glasses. "But she didn't answer."

"What did I tell you," Megan said.

"That was considerate of you, Whitney," Dan said. "Her name is Florence Wilkey. She's arrived here to convalesce." Tillie, Florence's daughter, was confident her mother would revive if removed from the sterile elderly care facility into a healthier environment. She chose Hat Creek because it resembled Florence's rural childhood surroundings.

Dan tossed the corrugate behind the counter and squeezed past Chloe and Megan to greet his newest residents. When Whitney started to follow, Chloe caught her around the waist.

"You stay. Megan and I are going fishing, and we need a guide."

"But Michelle's group session starts in an hour," Whitney complained.

"Exactly."

"Why do *I* have to guide you?"

"You know the way, plus, there's the not-so-insignificant matter of handling any fish we're unlucky enough to catch."

Dan escaped into the bright sunshine, the door closing almost too slowly behind him: "Whitney has a splendid waist, Megan. You should try…."

Florence's nurse, Ellen, if Dan remembered her name correctly, was rolling medical carts to Grange Hall's ramp. Tillie, attending to Florence, looked considerably younger than Dan had expected. Considering Florence was ninety-two years old, Tillie must be in her sixties, yet the healthy glow to her cheeks, lustrous auburn hair, even her lithe movements, suggested someone twenty years younger.

Dan concealed his battle scars best he could and introduced himself.

"It's nice to meet you, Dan," Tillie said, smiling broadly. Even her eyes were lively. "Fresh country air, away from all the bustle and pollution. Exactly what Mother needs."

Florence was semi-reclined on the gurney, covered to the chest by a thin linen blanket. A wide-brimmed hat shielded her face from the sun, leaving only closed eyes, a thin beak of a nose, and narrow, pinched lips in view. Her exposed skin was pale gray and speckled with blotchy age spots.

"I apologize for the heat," Dan said.

"Don't," Tillie said. "Mother's always complaining about being cold." Tillie shielded her eyes and looked around. "You have a few shade trees and that beautiful gazebo. Mother can spend plenty of time outdoors. Let me introduce you.

"Mother, I want you to meet somebody."

Florence's eyes blinked open, dull brown under cloudy retinas. Turning her head, she jerked when she saw Dan.

"Arthur!" she croaked.

"No, Mother," Tillie chuckled. "You know Father isn't with us anymore. This is Dan Stuart; we talked about him yesterday. We're staying at his place."

Though Florence's alarm faded, Dan imagined Florence would croak out the same name if Tillie introduced him twenty minutes later. Who needed a mirror when an older woman mistook you for her deceased husband?

"Mother is just exhausted from the trip," Tillie said. "After a nice nap, we'll get her into her wheelchair and take her for a spin."

"Let me show you to your rooms," Dan said.

Dan probed overhead at the end rafter of the exposed Grange Hall roof, splintering the rotted wood into mushy debris that rained down onto his boots and the sloped inner roof. Concluding the rafter was salvageable with bracing, he turned and took stock of the situation: eight rafters needing replacement and another five requiring significant bracing. And only certified structural lumber would pass Evil Inspector Todd's standards. This charade was going to cost a pretty penny to maintain.

Dan couldn't justify the expense, but he wasn't about to be bested by some upstart inspector. He edged his way down the slippery incline and peered out the trademark gash, spotting Florence's shiny wheelchair parked in the shade of the oak tree next to the gazebo. Since she wasn't napping directly below him, he could start the noisy repairs. Even without the new lumber on hand, he could safely remove every third rafter without further compromising the roof's integrity.

As Dan loosened the first rotted rafter, though, the constant stream of debris striking his face only aggravated the angst he'd intended the effort to alleviate. Michelle had peppered him last evening with impertinent questions about his past, all in the spirit of "research." What was his profession before founding Hat Creek? Which jobs had honed his organizational and motivational skills? Where had he lived? Did he think about his family more when new residents arrived or when they left? Pushy (whack), arrogant (whack), inconsiderate (harder whack). The fact that Michelle saw her PhD thesis somewhere in all this was of no comfort. He'd slept poorly.

With a final hammer blow, the rafter separated and dropped. Unexpectedly whirling as it bounced off the floor, it swept Dan's feet from under him. He tossed the hammer and threw his hands out to break his fall, but his left hand struck oddly, the familiar, sharp pain promising another broken finger.

Dan struggled to his knees and eased his hand out of the glove. Resigned to inflicting even worse pain, he gritted his teeth and yanked his ring finger back straight. Florence was again fortunate to be out of hearing distance.

"I think your days of climbing around roofs are over," Maggie said, driving Dan home from the emergency room.

As it turned out, nobody in Hat Creek was spared Dan's profanity-laced scream. The volunteer horticulturists heard it from the garden; Florence and Ellen from the park; Chloe and Megan from beyond the water tower; Whitney from inside Hartman's; Michelle from her depths of concentration. Maggie, unimpressed with Dan's plan to fashion a splint out of a wooden dowel and electrical tape, had chauffeured him to the hospital.

Dan held up his lame hand. The stainless-steel splint bound to his finger with elaborate Velcro straps was overkill for the elderly mayor of a ghost town. On the bright side, since he had no intention of returning for his checkup visit, he'd never need to scrounge for another splint.

"Unfortunately, Hat Creek doesn't repair itself," he told Maggie. "Quite the opposite, if you've noticed."

"Enlist your residents. You've always got them building something."

"Assembling a gazebo or tilling a garden is one thing. Structural projects are beyond their capabilities."

"Then hire somebody."

"My finances are in worse shape than my finger. Between the fees I collect, my Social Security checks, and barter from odd jobs, I'm still not covering my expenses."

"I hate to tell you this, Dan," Maggie said, slowing to turn onto the gravel road, "but you aren't getting any younger. Those Social Security checks are supposed to supplement retirement, not operate a wellness facility. You won't catch me working beyond retirement age. Plenty of people will be waiting to take my spot delivering the mail."

Maggie pulled off Brule Street into her reserved spot between a formally green Corvair and a Cadillac missing its trunk lid. "We could retire together," she said, shutting off the engine. "Find some relaxing hobbies, take a cruise—"

"But I can't afford to wait, either," Dan muttered. "There's still the little matter of Evil Inspector Todd—" It was then that a classic "killing two birds with one stone" solution popped to mind, bringing a smile to Dan's face. Attacking the Grange Hall roof had helped him to feel better after all.

"I know who I can call."

CHAPTER 19

"Hang in there, ladies," Dan said, staring up through the maze of pipes at Megan and Chloe's strained faces, knowing their arms were tiring. They had found him lying on the ground, struggling to tension a pump motor pivot bracket, and had offered to lever the crowbar.

Despite his encouragement, Megan suddenly released the bar. "You've been holding out on us, Dan," she said. She pointed toward town. "Chloe, look."

"Wow!" Chloe said reverently.

"Only a few more seconds, Chloe," Dan pleaded. Fearing the pair's good intentions about to go for naught, he fully tightened a single nut. "You can let go now, Chloe," he said with a grunt.

Dan quickly tightened the remaining nuts, lucking out that the bracket didn't slip. When he extricated himself and sat up, Megan took the crowbar from Chloe and used it to jab him in the chest. "You didn't tell us about *all* of the local attractions."

"Ow!" he complained, unaware of *any* attractions. "What do you mean?"

In answer, Megan aimed the crowbar over Dan's shoulder, forcing him to duck.

Dan looked over his shoulder. A tall, handsome, and exceptionally buff young man stood in front of a dirty beige hatchback parked amongst the junkers, stretching his well-defined muscles.

"That's Jacob Fines," Dan said, standing and recovering the crowbar. "I've hired him for a few odd jobs while my finger mends."

"A serious misuse of talent," Megan commented, enrapt with Jacob's unintentional display.

"And to get Michelle off my back," Dan admitted.

Megan laughed brightly. "Well done, Dan." She pulled on an orange-tinted lock of hair. "Not to be presumptuous, but do you seriously think Michelle is his type?"

"Or even in his league?" Chloe added.

Dan shrugged his shoulders. "They met here four years ago. Michelle rebuffed Jacob's advances."

"*She* turned *him* down?" Megan asked.

"Saw it with my own eyes."

"What a fool." Megan extended her arms longingly in Jacob's direction. "I would never turn that down." She looked at Chloe. "Would you?"

Chloe bit her lip and shook her head. "Only, we can't forget why Dan invited him."

"True." Megan dropped her arms dejectedly to her side. "How about we give him a couple of days?"

"Adonis himself couldn't break Michelle in that time," Chloe said. "How about five?"

The two ladies nodded in agreement.

Dan hadn't the slightest idea what the pair were discussing, though he presumed it involved describing themselves as polyamorous. "Give me a minute to double-check my work, and I'll introduce you," he said.

"Take your time," Megan said. "We'll get Jacob started for you." She took her partner's hand. "Come on, Chloe. We've got more work to do."

Dan returned his attention to his repairs, confident that Jacob could fend for himself. With a groan slightly less dramatic than his scream after straightening his finger, he knelt on his aching knees before lying down to crawl back under the piping.

Jacob looked around while working out the kinks from his long drive. Hat Creek was even more rundown than he remembered. Just repairing crumbling siding and roofing could keep him employed for a month.

Hello? What was this? Jacob noticed two hotties approaching from the direction of the water tower, one jiggling beneath her tight T-shirt, the other's hair on fire. Jacob half-expected them to fade away like desert apparitions, so delightfully misplaced was their sensual vitality.

Jacob was doubly lucky. Not only were the handholding pair real, but they were also aimed straight at him. He leaned back against his car to enjoy the view; one sexy, the other an absolute stunner, his first paycheck before raising a sweat.

"I'm Chloe," the busty one introduced herself, formally shaking Jacob's hand. "You must be Jacob Fines."

"That's me," he said.

"And I'm Megan," said the beauty, her smile as inviting as her sky-blue eyes. "We're Hat Creek's acting supervisors during Dan's convalescence."

"He told me he broke his—"

Chloe cupped her hands around Jacob's left bicep and squeezed. "Just making sure you're up to the task," she said, smiling mischievously. "He's definitely up to it," Chloe confirmed to Megan.

"Great," Megan said. She hooked her hand under Jacob's right arm and pulled him away from his car. "This way, Jacob. Not a moment to lose. Dan asked us to get you started right away."

They escorted him around Dan's old cabin, turning toward its front door instead of continuing across the road to Dan's house.

"Did Dan move back in here?" he asked.

Without answering, Chloe ran ahead and opened the door. "Special delivery," she yelled, and Megan shoved Jacob through the doorway.

The tiny house's interior was much the same as Jacob remembered, that shocking juxtaposition of modern amenities wrapped inside a shell of a decaying, beyond-its-last-leg exterior. Its occupant, though, wasn't Dan.

"Jacob!" Michelle shrieked, jumping out of her chair and backing away. "What are you doing here?"

Jacob ignored the raucous laughter only marginally muffled by the slamming door. Michelle had changed as little as the living area. Tight jeans and a fitted shirt pleasantly accentuated her still slender figure, and her ponytail could be the same one he'd pulled on four years earlier.

Jacob could have done without the bug-eyed greeting, though. You'd think he was a plague carrier.

"And it's certainly good to see you again, too, Michelle," he said.

"Sorry," she said, recovering quickly from whatever had spooked her about his sudden appearance.

"Dan asked me to tackle a few repairs while he's on the mend."

"His broken finger," Michelle said, her rising lilt validating Jacob's presence. "I was here when it happened."

"Ah. Then I take it Dan didn't invite you for the same reason."

"No. I'm researching aspects of Hat Creek for——" She paused, recognizing Jacob's dig.

Jacob made a muscle and pointed at his bicep. In response, Michelle smirked at him and pointed to her brain. Jacob laughed. One minute only, and Michelle had reminded him how unlike his typical girlfriends she was.

"I'm starving," he said. "How about we catch up on old times over dinner?"

Michelle jabbed her thumb in the direction of the kitchen. "I was about to make something for myself."

Jacob reopened the door. "But Westside sounds better."

"It does," Michelle admitted, accepting his invitation.

Jacob looked over his shoulder at Grange Hall as they crossed the blacktop. "Dan told me he lost his footing on the roof."

"Yes," Michelle said. "Repairing the hole to keep it looking like a hole, silly as that sounds."

Jacob could only shake his head. "Dan's lucky he only broke a finger. I should take off the entire thing."

"You know Dan's fanaticism for maintaining appearances. I think it's great that you could help out on such short notice."

Gauging by Michelle's shock at his sudden appearance, she hadn't a clue he was arriving. "Work was slow, and I had vacation time to burn."

Jacob escorted Michelle into Westside. Other than the unfamiliar faces and a different set of tacky table centerpieces, the diner hadn't changed, either. The nearer ceiling fan still spun that familiar undulating dance, its bent blade leading each dip, mirroring Jacob's drop in fortune.

Just three months ago, Jacob rode the L to tend bar, walking the length of Millennium Park past Crown Fountain and the bean-shaped mirrored sculpture that morphed and inverted your reflection. The exclusive nightclub was trimmed in stainless steel and polished walnut, outfitted with premium light and sound systems, and packed each evening with gorgeous women in tight dresses and high heels who loved to flirt. A great place to work until the day he arrived to find the front door padlocked.

"Am I to assume you've returned to Hat Creek every summer?" Jacob asked as they threaded their way toward the food table. Some people, like Michelle, willingly worked here. Weird.

"Except last summer," Michelle said. "I interned at an addiction treatment center in Oregon."

Jacob picked up a dinner plate, recognizing the chipped edge. Forking a chicken thigh from a heaping platter, Jacob admitted one upside to Hat Creek: the free food—ditto for his room—made it infinitely more affordable than Chicago. Even working two jobs, much of his adventure had depended on the charity of well-heeled friends.

"I'll return each summer now that I've started graduate school," Michelle said as they made their way to a table.

"That's dedication," Jacob said.

Encouraged by his praise, Michelle launched into a reprise of her lofty education plans. Jacob couldn't mock her enthusiasm nor cut her short for fear she'd ask about his situation, making the narration harder to swallow than the chicken liver he had accidentally loaded onto his plate.

Dan saved his blushes, arriving before Michelle wound down. Unlike Michelle, Dan wore the passage of time like a worn-out shirt. His hair had finished graying, and the accumulation of sun and wind had weathered his face faster than the buildings' siding. A slight hitch to his walk suggested a bum knee or hip in addition to his splinted finger.

"Welcome back, Jacob," Dan said, dropping into an empty chair and swiping an uneaten roll from Michelle's plate. His voice, however, was as strong as ever. "I see you made it in one piece."

"It was an uneventful drive," Jacob said. "Just long—from Chicago."

"I meant from your car to Westside," Dan said with a chuckle. "My helpers are prone to over-exuberance."

"Chloe and Megan are your helpers? Please tell me you haven't gotten them up on the roof."

Dan laughed so hard that he choked on the food. "Please, Jacob," he said, smacking his chest with his good hand. "I've only broken a finger, not gone senile. Back me up here, Michelle."

She leered at him. "You neglected to tell me that Jacob was arriving."

Dan finished chewing and swallowed. "Slipped my mind," he said without a hint of contriteness.

"Yet your 'helpers' knew," Michelle complained.

"They were wielding a crowbar—not a word, Jacob; I've learned that lesson, as well—when Jacob arrived. As I recall, you insisted on hibernating in your cabin.

"Bus your dishes, and I'll show you what you're up against," Dan said to Jacob.

Jacob spent four days prepping the Grange Hall roof.

The decay was more extensive than Dan had realized. Large swaths of the sheathing were rotted to the consistency of dust, held together only by roof felt and shingles. Jacob salvaged as many old shingles as possible before heading to a Hot Springs lumberyard for new rafters.

Securing twenty-foot-long sticks of lumber to the roof of a truck barely half that length proved tricky. And Jacob discovered after returning to Hat Creek and climbing into the bed to unload them that transporting them long distances over bumpy roads caused roof damage. He didn't alert Dan to the new dents and scratches. Though he doubted Dan cared, perhaps even welcomed his truck's decline into "junker" status, Dan had hired him to fix damage, not cause it.

CHAPTER 20

"Are you sure we aren't imposing on you?" Tillie asked Dan, adjusting Florence's hat.

"These pleasant strolls with Florence are about my limit," Dan said. "Residents' orders."

Dan hadn't anticipated the many perks of a broken finger: Maggie was more attentive, buttoning and unbuttoning his shirts and helping with housekeeping; Hat Creek's residents had taken over most of the essential maintenance tasks; and Jacob was monopolizing Michelle's attention so completely that she hadn't spoken ten words to Dan since Jacob's arrival.

Tillie kissed her mother's cheek. "This wonderful man insists on stealing you from us again. We'll have dinner when you return."

"Don't you worry," Florence said haltingly. "I'm in good hands." She managed a weak smile.

Dan wheeled Florence across the gravel road and along Brule Street, past parked cars and buildings partially obscured by the tall stands of wildflowers that had sprung up after the recent rains. As Tillie had hoped, Florence's health was improving. In addition to the healthier glow to Florence's skin, her eyes were more alert, and she had begun communicating, first with a lifted finger and head bobs, and then verbally.

Dan steered Florence into the park. With its white gazebo, sturdy benches, trimmed shrubs, and tamed weeds, Hat Creek's little oasis of civilization was nearly always occupied, reinforcing Dan's suspicions about his residents' similar affinity for Westside. He wasn't worried about Hat Creek growing too soft, though. The passage of time would soon bring both spaces in line.

When the town's resident golden eagle offered a distant salute, Florence gasped weakly and brought a shaky hand to her mouth. "You even remembered my bird." She pointed a crooked finger towards the tree line. "Is there water in the creek?"

"Sometimes."

"Yes. Sometimes." She twisted in the chair and pointed at Hartman's. "Are there horses in the barn?"

"That's—" Dan stopped himself. "No horses. I'm sorry."

Florence hummed and turned her head a few degrees from side to side. "Is the chicken coop here?"

Dan turned Florence to face a cabin too far away for her poor eyesight to make out. "I placed it there," he said, pointing past her head.

"I liked collecting the eggs as a little girl," she said. "What about the granary?"

Yesterday, Florence had spoken of Tillie's childhood and briefly mentioned her deceased husband. Today, continuing her fixation on the past, she apparently assumed she had returned to the farmstead of her youth.

Dan turned Florence to face the water tower. Though the scale was wrong, it was silver, cylindrical, with a conical top. "Our granary," he said.

Florence gasped faintly. "Corn or oats this year?"

"Corn," Dan guessed.

"Corn, yes," Florence said. "Enough rain for a good crop. I can smell the flowers."

Florence hummed again, this one noticeably labored. Dan sensed she was tiring. "Thank you, Dan," she said. "You made home."

Jacob rested his forearms on the gazebo railing and stared at the seated figure engrossed in her work to the exclusion of sight and sound. Her fingers played over the computer keyboard as if they were piano keys.

"Michelle!"

She jumped, sending her ponytail airborne. "Jacob!" she yelled, glaring at him. "Don't startle me like that."

"I called your name three times. Come help me."

"I'm working."

"Uh-uh. You've been hunched over that computer for three hours. I meant real work."

"How do you know how long I've been sitting here?"

"Nothing in Hat Creek escapes detection from up inside Grange Hall's roof: everyone taking turns wheeling the elderly lady around—"

"Florence. Her name is Florence."

"Wheeling *Florence* around. Excuse me for being too busy to chat with her. Then there's the pair who head out fishing early most mornings and the woman who's forever scrounging around Dan's junk piles."

"That's Jeanie," Michelle said. "She's creating a 'found

objects' sculpture."

"She's more likely to conjure up a broken leg or snake bite than a work of art," Jacob said. "I thought Dan warned people away from places like those."

"He looks the other way. A part of his 'you're on your own' policy."

Self-help. Or, as in this case, self-hurt. Jacob was tackling the easier task between roof repairs and trying to make sense of this place. "It might be simpler for you to explain why Dan and Maggie are together so much of the time," he said.

"I predicted they would become a couple."

"Chloe and Megan make them look like strangers in comparison. Yesterday, Megan had Chloe topless behind Dan's maintenance shed. And today, they were making out in the back seat of that junked fifties Nash Rambler. What does your 'shrink' training tell you about them?"

"For the umpteenth time, Jacob, I'm studying psychology, not psychiatry. And if you have enough time to spy on everybody, you don't need my help."

"Hey!" Jacob complained, standing tall. "I don't stay in shape by sitting around—"

"Spare me the banal display of virility," Michelle said.

"No need to talk dirty. Give your brain a break."

Convincing Michelle to help him, Jacob stopped by Hartman's for an extra pair of work gloves while Michelle dropped off her computer and changed into work clothes.

"I need you up on the roof to stabilize the beams while I nail them in place," Jacob explained when they met back at Grange Hall.

Michelle craned her neck. "I don't like climbing ladders. I'm afraid they're going to topple over."

"I can throw you over my shoulder and carry you up if

you prefer."

"In that case, I'll take my chances solo."

Jacob stepped to the inside of the ladder and gripped both rails. "I'll hold the ladder steady while you climb. I *do* take ladder safety seriously."

"Thank you."

Michelle donned her gloves and started climbing, two feet on each rung. When her knees reached Jacob's eye level, he moved around to the outside of the ladder. The view from below was even better than from directly behind. Michelle was full of surprises.

"Hot," he mouthed in appreciation.

Michelle's head swiveled down quicker than an owl sensing a mouse. "What?"

"Out here," he said. "It's hot out here."

Michelle wasn't buying it. But she couldn't keep from smiling, either. "Stop, or you'll make me fall."

"Trust me when I say I admire only your brain."

"I said stop."

"Hey, up there!" Megan called out from below. "We haven't heard a peep from you two for at least twenty minutes. You'd better be misbehaving yourselves."

Jacob left it to Michelle to sort the various truss plates and stepped down the roof. She had proven a capable helper, unphased by heavy lifting, splintered boards, or protruding nails. She even recovered quickly after the ant colony dropped onto them as they ripped away rotten underlayment.

Megan stood just off the road, hands on her hips, staring up at him. Her hair was tinted lemon yellow, bright as the midday sun.

"We're *trying* to misbehave," Jacob told her. "But work

keeps getting in the way. Check back in another ten minutes."

He turned back. Michelle had stood and reached above her head with both arms to grab onto a bare rafter. The s-curve of her lithe body and smooth, glistening skin were exceedingly seductive. Jacob must arouse her, too, for her nipples had made their first appearance.

Jacob had never considered sex on a roof. They could uniquely find a place out of the sun, but shingles were too rough to lie on without a thick blanket, which they lacked.

He abandoned the fantasy and settled for stealing a kiss. Michelle held her ground and raised the stakes, dropping her arms onto his shoulders and wrapping them around his neck when he drew her to him. For once, Michelle participated fully, returning Jacob's kiss with a passionate kiss of her own, pressing a hand to the back of his head as he took control of her slender waist, sampling his salty lips as he savored hers. Satisfyingly, she, too, was in no hurry to end it.

Florence's skin tone improved daily. Privately, Dan thought she looked more … well, more alive. Ellen explained that a stubborn problem of low blood oxygen level, alleviated since Florence's arrival in Hat Creek, had been the cause of Florence's anemia.

Florence's mental faculties were improving in lockstep. She was talkative on today's stroll, each new sound eliciting another memory or question. The grasshoppers chirping in the weeds reminded her of the giant lime-green ones that tormented her as a child. When a light breeze rustled the leaves above them, she asked if Dan's cottonwoods dropped a snowfall of cotton each summer. And a grain truck rumbling down the gravel road prompted a recollection of Florence's mother forever lamenting the unrelenting dust.

Turning her head, she exclaimed, "My flowers!" finally noticing the towering wildflowers lining the old street.

Dan rolled Florence to within inches of the colorful display. "It doesn't take much rain to encourage everything to bloom," he said.

"Yes, I remember." She lifted a finger. "These are asters," she said of the mass of tiny purple flowers with yellow centers. Dan, who recognized little beyond roses, carnations, and tulips, had always assumed they were a variety of colored daisies. Florence's fingers found the tiny yellow flowers interspersed with the asters. "And these are …" but didn't finish the thought.

Florence stirred again when Dan turned off the rut road toward the park. "Do you have my cactus?"

"Of course." Dan parked Florence under the oak tree and sat on a bench facing her. "They're in bloom, as well."

Florence pulled at her shawl. "Is this heaven, Dan?"

Dan smiled. The exclusive Black Hill's Fan Club had just admitted a new member. About to compliment her taste in the scenery, Florence's serious, expectant expression promised Dan that she had asked the question literally.

He stood and regarded Hat Creek through different sets of eyes. Home to long-ago residents. Both refuge and purgatory for him. Ego trip to Evil Inspector Todd. Sanctuary for Ann Harris. PhD fodder to Michelle. Romping grounds for Megan and Chloe.

Heaven, to Florence? Dan admitted the possibility. She had arrived in Hat Creek nearly catatonic, awakening both in mind and body to what her poor eyesight convinced her was a reconstruction of her childhood home. Florence's memories and imagination might take her anywhere, up to and including, it seemed, heaven.

While tempted to grant Florence's wish, Dan demurred.

There was awareness in her eyes absent during the disoriented panic of her arrival, and more emerged each day. What would Hat Creek represent to a healthy Florence?

"No," he answered. "It is not."

Florence sighed. "It wouldn't be, would it?" She looked around as if she had misplaced something. "It's just that I thought I saw Arthur. Arthur was my husband," she added haltingly, her brief lucidity fading as quickly as today's flower blooms. "He belongs in heaven."

Dan nodded. Should Florence ever tell her story, he already knew the leading man.

"I don't, though," Florence said, almost too quietly to be heard. "Belong in heaven."

CHAPTER 21

Jacob finished anchoring another rafter and having reached a good stopping point, cleaned up and headed to Michelle's cabin for his second job.

Jacob had learned only yesterday of Dan's humorous true motive for inviting him to Hat Creek, having just returned from showering when Megan and Chloe spilled into his room. Whitney froze in the doorway, seeing him with only a towel wrapped around his waist, and backed into the hall.

"Isn't this an unexpected treat," Megan said, ogling him.

"To what do I owe the pleasure of this visit?" he asked. Megan, her hair tinted the cobalt blue of an anime character, and Chloe, her *figure* that of an anime character, were worth ogling back.

Chloe reached out and traced the outline of his pec with a fingertip. "Megan, he *is* an Adonis," she said.

Megan nodded, slowly lifting her gaze until her sky-blues were seducing his. "You are."

Megan lifted her arms to Jacob's shoulders and laced her fingers through his hair. "Pardon our indulgences, but we're here to deliver your bonuses for your recent stellar effort."

She kissed him with lips tasting of fresh apples. When Jacob raised his arms to draw her closer, Chloe intercepted his right hand and shoved it up her shirt, treating his fingers to the same sensual stimulation.

The ladies disengaged just as Jacob's desire to bed the pair crossed over into a biological demand. From the animal intensity in Megan's eyes, the temptation had been mutual.

"Whitney," Megan called out, never losing eye contact. "Get in here and—"

Grange Hall's front door opened and quickly slammed shut.

"She was supposed to shake your hand," Megan said, shaking her head. "Lame, admittedly, but …" She shrugged. She took Chloe's hand and tugged. "Our job here is done. I'm sure we'll be seeing more of you, Jacob," she added, starting the pair giggling.

Chloe turned back as the couple reached the doorway. "We nearly forgot to tell you. Dan wants you to know that he also appreciates your help repairing the roof."

As their laughter reverberated down the hallway, the pair tossing him into Michelle's cabin finally made sense. Of course, Dan wouldn't have let a broken finger slow him down. Dan had used the injury as an excuse to lure Jacob to Hat Creek to keep Michelle occupied. She must have been bugging him big time.

Highly amused, Jacob knocked on Michelle's front door. Pursuing a woman as a job, one with bonuses for exemplary performance. What a life!

The window curtains parted to reveal a sliver of Michelle's face. After a short delay, she opened her front door. "I'm busy," she said. Jacob's intentions were as transparent to Michelle as Dan's should have been to Jacob.

"And hello to you, too," Jacob said, letting himself in. "I've had a long day and need some fresh air. Join me on a walk along the creek."

Michelle pointed at the messy stack of papers on her desk. "I need to finish collating that mass of data before returning home. You may be helping Dan appease some fanatical state inspector, but I promise you Dr. Malkovich is ten times more demanding."

Jacob placed his hands on her shoulders. "All the more reason to take a break."

"I don't have the time. It'll take me——" Michelle hummed when Jacob began kneading her shoulders.

Jacob knew more about muscles than Michelle knew about Hat Creek. He preferred his subjects naked and his efforts as a prelude to sex, but this recently gained permission to touch Michelle was no small delight.

"You found the spot," Michelle said as Jacob worked inward along her trapezius muscles.

"Your neck and shoulder muscles are tied up in knots," Jacob said, rolling his thumbs in small circles. "I bet you've been pounding on that keyboard nonstop since after breakfast."

"I made myself a sandwich for lunch," Michelle said. Her voice was dreamier now.

Jacob draped Michelle's ponytail over her shoulder to reveal her enticingly bare neck. He couldn't fathom this attraction to all things Michelle, but he had a job to perform and wasn't about to waste time trying to comprehend.

He leaned down and kissed the nape of Michelle's neck. Her sweaty skin tasted of salt.

"Jacob," she said in a half-hearted warning.

He kissed the spot clean before moving on. "Am I bothering you?" he asked, pecking her neck below her ear.

"Yes."

He nibbled on Michelle's earlobe and felt a tingle course through her body. "Do you like me bothering you?"

She turned to him and lifted her head. "Yes."

He cupped her face with both hands and kissed her. "Then join me. I promise the stack won't grow in your absence."

Again, she willingly relented. After they stepped outside, Jacob found Michelle's hand and walked her along the dirt path to Brule Street, the air sweetly scented by the flourishing wildflowers. Reaching the park, they encountered Hat Creek's fishermen busily preparing the day's catch for a community fish.

"Count us in," Jacob said enthusiastically.

Michelle waited until they were out of earshot before saying, "I'm too busy to waste an entire evening attending a cookout."

"Then don't attend," Jacob said. "Search out Benjamin and Phil tomorrow and make up an excuse for why you couldn't make it. Tell them everybody raved about the food, and promise you won't miss their next cookout."

Michelle chuckled.

"What?" Jacob asked.

Michelle shook her head. "Thanks for the tip. Sometimes I forget how sequestered a life I've led."

"Then stick with me," Jacob said, tugging on her hand to start walking downstream. "I'll lead you from the woods."

Michelle bumped his arm with her shoulder and chuckled. "He says as he entices her deeper *into* the woods."

Jacob smiled. Aware of his intentions and yet willingly following.

They peered down at the shallow water casually wandering

past Hat Creek as they strolled.

"I laughed the first time Dan told me that scaling the water tower was the official flood escape route," Michelle said. "Now I know he wasn't joking."

"Odd things happen in odd places created by … I can't call Dan odd," Jacob concluded. "Eccentric, maybe."

"Wounded."

"He does tend to injure himself."

Michelle shook her head. "I meant emotionally. Do you ever wonder what happened to Dan's family?"

"No. By the tone of your question, though, you do?"

"Yes."

"And the source of this morbid curiosity?"

"It's a valid interest," Michelle insisted. "The professional world is starting to take notice of Hat Creek. Dr. Malkovich, of course, hypothesizes that it's because of its—"

"Remote locale, sparse amenities, self-help," Jacob finished for her, aghast that Michelle's words had been lodged in his memory these four years.

"But she's missing one important element," Michelle continued.

"Dan," Jacob guessed.

"Yes," she said, visibly pleased that Jacob agreed. "I've tried telling Dr. Malkovich that Dan doesn't so much manage Hat Creek, but that he 'is' Hat Creek." Michelle caught herself. "Nothing that would interest you. I need to understand Dan's single-minded dedication and devotion to his residents."

She stooped to pick up a colorful stone, turning it in her hand before handing it to Jacob. "Somewhere in all of this is my PhD thesis."

"Ah," Jacob exclaimed. "The deeper truth."

"Still valid," Michelle said. "I asked Dan more questions

during dinner the other evening."

"Intrusive ones, no doubt." Intrusive enough to call in a helper.

"Most were benign."

"But some were not. Spill it."

"Knowing that his family's death was the catalyst for Hat Creek, I asked Dan if the *circumstances* of their deaths impacted the retreat's focus."

Jacob chucked the stone across the creek. "I'm surprised Dan didn't toss *you* out of Hat Creek."

Michelle shook her head. "Dan answered me."

"He did?" Jacob would have bet on Dan tossing her before answering.

"Only obliquely. Dan told me his family's death wasn't accidental, that he wouldn't be here if it had been."

"Wow," Jacob mouthed.

"Yes. But the discussion upset Dan. He excused himself and walked off—and I *did* apologize later."

"*I* would have tossed you."

"Dan, not Dr. Malkovich, started this place," Michelle countered. "He disappears off the face of the earth, and then, years later, for reasons unknown, invites everyone back into his life."

Jacob thought back to his arrival as a teenager, discovering Dan living like a hermit, angrily insisting that he wasn't building a town. Then, nothing indicated that Dan had any intentions beyond standing on ladders nailing old boards onto even older buildings. Fast forward, Dan had incorporated Hat Creek, installed electricity and indoor plumbing, and opened his doors to scores of troubled people. "You make a good point."

"But what does 'not accidental' mean?" Michelle asked. "Intentional, planned, nefarious?"

"Nefarious?"

"I'm just suggesting it as a possibility."

"No, I mean the word."

"Oh, Jacob. Nefarious means evil or wicked or villainous."

"As in criminal."

"Something along those lines."

Jacob raised an eyebrow. "You'd think a triple murder would make the news."

"I've looked long and hard," Michelle said. "Nothing yet."

"Calling you nosy is selling you short," Jacob said.

He looked down into the creek. "Let's walk in the water; I could use the cooldown."

"The creek bank is too steep. I'll fall and break my leg."

"I recall Stella climbing down a more treacherous section than this."

"She wasn't trying to reach the water. She was after Graham."

"Good point. You're saying that you'd race me down if your diploma awaited you at the bottom of the creek."

"Very funny."

"And win."

Michelle chuckled. "Close."

"Are you familiar with the 'fireman's carry?'" Jacob asked.

"I've heard the term—"

Jacob lifted Michelle's left arm and ducked below her armpit. After pressing his shoulder to her stomach, he reached around her thighs and lifted her onto his shoulders.

"Very funny, again," Michelle said from below his right ear. "Now, put me down."

"This is how we carried stricken coworkers out of hot trailers," Jacob said. "I knew my experience as a package handler would come in handy someday."

"I prefer standing upright to being slung over your shoulder."

"Except you already ruled out walking down the bank. Now, do your best impression of a limp rag so I can get us safely to the bottom."

To her credit, Michelle moaned as if in the throes of death and fell limp, her free arm hanging down, swinging.

"I once carried out two guys on the same day," Jacob said, starting down the slope. He looked at the tight tush only inches from his face. "The scenery here is much better."

"A turtle," Michelle said, pointing at the fist-sized yellow-green dome inconspicuously inching its way along the water's edge. She bent down for a closer look. "Do you think it's a snapping turtle?"

Jacob swallowed a chuckle, remembering when Michelle had spotted a turtle during their hike with Stella and Graham. Then, she had kept her distance as if the turtle might suddenly lunge at them.

Jacob was about to clap his hands to startle Michelle when filtered sunlight momentarily spotlighted her hair, revealing interesting reddish-golden highlights he hadn't previously noticed. Jacob cupped her hair below the tie and lifted it to slide the silky bundle over his palm. The sensation was as pleasant as holding her hand.

Michelle quickly straightened. "Why are you always fiddling with my hair?"

Part of this unexplainable attraction, obviously. "Why do you always wear your hair in a ponytail?" he returned.

"Because it gets in my way when I'm working."

"Then why don't you wear your hair short?"

"Habit, I guess," Michelle said.

"Lucky me," Jacob said. "And if you're asking, I'd prefer

your hair loose." He reached for her hair, but Michelle backed away.

"Don't you dare," she said, though she was almost laughing.

"Aren't you curious why?"

"No."

"For one thing, I could tickle you with it."

"I didn't ask," she reminded him, walking on.

Even better, there's always the chance your hair will fall into my mouth during sex. But Jacob was smart enough to keep his fantasy to himself.

They found a manageable path up the creek bank and started their return to Hat Creek, Jacob momentarily excusing himself to make use of a suitably distant men's bathroom. When he returned, Michelle was leaning against a large cottonwood.

"Where have I seen this before," Jacob said.

"What?" Michelle asked.

"Only, you wrapped your arms around my neck." He lifted Michelle's arms to his shoulders. "Tightly, like you're grabbing me to save yourself." When Michelle's pull brought them face to face, he squeezed her waist. "And I caught you like so and lowered you to the ground."

"I remember now," Michelle said, looking up into the green canopy. "When I jumped from the tree after watching the—"

Finding even the underside of Michelle's chin irresistible, Jacob kissed it.

"—sunrise," Michelle squeaked, dropping her chin to fend off his advance.

"Just reenacting the scene," Jacob said.

"I don't recall you assaulting my neck."

"True," Jacob said. "I kissed you more like this." He caught

Michelle full on her parted lips, embellishing their first kiss. "And then you ran away to make breakfast."

Michelle relaxed her embrace and lifted her hands to the back of Jacob's head, playing with his hair for the first time. "I'm not running now," she said.

Jacob tested her resolve with a sensual, suggestive kiss. Michelle didn't budge.

"If I recall," he said, cupping her waist more gently, "you did make a great breakfast."

This time he kissed her softly, tenderly mating his lips to hers. Pleasingly, she demanded more, pulling his head forward for a deeper kiss.

"And afterward, you and Stella shooed Graham and me away so you could clean up. So domestic."

Michelle pulled her head back and looked at Jacob with narrowed eyes. "Your memory is faulty. You and Graham took off, leaving us to clean up."

Jacob stole a quick kiss. "I didn't run far."

Michelle giggled. "Yes, but you did run."

Arriving at a girl's front door at the end of a date is always a telling moment. Either she invites you inside to enjoy an intimate dalliance or turns to face you, barring entrance to her castle and sending you slinking away solo to the bar.

Michelle, predictably, chose the latter, leaning back against the door frame. Jacob didn't press the issue beyond enjoying a good night kiss. Michelle hadn't flinched earlier when he slipped his fingers inside her shirt during their kiss. One baby step at a time.

Jacob lingered outside Michelle's cabin for only a moment before turning away for the festivities in the park. He had known today's chances were slim. There was always tomorrow, though. He already anticipated a breakfast kiss and might try to liberate her hair.

Jacob rubbed his fingers together, marveling at the unanticipated longing for Michelle's entwined fingers. He had been pursuing a sex partner. Instead, he had gained a love interest.

CHAPTER 22

Dan positioned himself to block the sun from Florence's uncovered face and eased her wheelchair across the gravel road. "Can't harm this old skin," Florence had reasoned to Dan as she battled Tillie's attempt to cover her head. Smiling at Florence's first levity, Dan had assured Tillie through a subtle nod that he'd keep Florence out of the sun.

Florence pointed at Hartman's. "I had free run of the farm from when I was a little girl," she said. "My father only warned me away from the tall weeds around the barn." More alert, but Florence's eyesight hadn't improved. "'Watch for rattlesnakes,' he cautioned me."

Dan relived the penalty for ignoring the sound advice. "Smart man."

"That was why I was surprised to see him walking straight through those weeds with a young man," Florence said. She leaned forward in her chair as if to get a clearer view. "It was Arthur," she said.

Florence reintroduced her late husband the following day. This day Tillie had won the hat battle, a victory Florence reversed once Dan rolled her into the shade of the water tower.

"I met my husband on our farm," she told Dan.

"You did?" he said. "What was his name?"

"Arthur. His name was Arthur."

"Arthur," Dan repeated. He took a seat on a stout water pipe. "Tell me about him."

"My father hired Arthur to fix our old tractor," Florence said. "That's why they were behind the barn. Arthur was so tall that the weeds barely reached his knees."

Florence paused and turned her head. Chloe, Megan, and Whitney were stumbling toward town along the gravel road, appearing worse-off than Michelle after an afternoon spent helping Jacob. Dan waved to draw their attention.

"You look beat," he said when the trio straggled in.

Megan nodded tiredly. Even her purple hair shrugged listlessly. "We hiked down the road to see what was over the horizon. It's good to see you, Florence."

"What did you find over the horizon?" Dan asked.

"The next horizon. So, we hiked to that one."

"That's a long hike in this heat."

"Too long," Whitney said, her eyes blurred behind sweat-stained glasses. "You should place one of your hiker's boxes along the road in case someone gets stranded."

"That's an idea," Dan said. "And what did you find at the next horizon?"

"Only more of the same," Megan answered. "Is it possible to get lost in your own monotony?"

Chloe pulled on her clingy T-shirt, the clear winner in today's sweaty T-shirt contest. "I need to get lost in a long shower." She grabbed Whitney's hand at the same time Megan took hers.

"Bye, Florence," Whitney said as she was led away like the caboose of a train. "You're looking great. Bye, Dan."

"Do those three young ladies live here?" Florence asked.

"For now," Dan said.

"Do they have boyfriends?"

A predictable assumption, but a complicated truth. "Yes."

"That's good," Florence hummed. "Arthur asked me out that very day. The day I met him." Looking up at Dan, the corners of her lips turned up in a playful, impish smile. Something was stirring in the woman's mind. "Of course, most days, we didn't have far to go."

Dan didn't need to imagine what had gone on behind Florence's barn. Through Megan and Chloe's antics, Hat Creek also featured a modern reenactment of that diversion.

Dan crossed paths with Ellen late the following morning while attempting to locate Florence. The nurse told him Florence had insisted on dining in Westside, another encouraging sign. A healthy appetite, plus improved blood oxygen level and gland function—Dan couldn't follow the nurse's terms about the causation of delirium—meant Florence was now lucid most of the time. Dan didn't mention that Florence assumed Hat Creek to be a recreation of her childhood farm, unsure how that information fit the nurse's lucidity scale.

"You didn't need to apply makeup just for me," Dan said as he wheeled Florence from the diner into a mild, breezy day. Today, she wore a bright floral frock that matched her rosy cheeks.

"I even considered tying my hair back like that young thing Michelle," Florence said, "but I don't have enough hair anymore." She chuckled lightly. "Where's *your* beau today?"

Florence's conspiratorial tone suggested a girl-to-girl talk with either Michelle or Maggie herself.

"Yesterday, you started telling me about your first home," Dan said to change the subject.

"Arthur was a compassionate man who wanted a large family," Florence said. "He vowed we would never live in squalor, so he used what little money he'd saved to purchase and renovate an abandoned four-bedroom house. Nothing showy, mind you. Arthur wasn't that type. Just a warm and safe home like he made our lives.

"He worked two jobs and spent his evenings on the house," she said in a smaller voice. "So that Tillie and I had no wants. I caused him to do it, Dan, to work so hard. I wish I'd been a better wife. I wish I hadn't …" She fiddled with her dress. "I know Arthur went to heaven, Dan. I know he did."

So, Florence had regrets. At her age, who didn't? And Dan was in no position to judge.

"Arthur sounds like an amazing man," Dan said, laying a comforting hand on Florence's shoulder. She lifted a hand and pressed his in gratitude.

Florence's hand left Dan's to cover a gasp. "Oh, Dan," she said, gazing in the direction of her "chicken coop," "you didn't need to do *that* for me." The woman's eyesight might be poor, but she recognized another unique Hat Creek spectacle: the sizeable herd of cattle ambling into town.

Dan sat at his kitchen table and savored every morsel of his elicit bedtime snack. The caterer had slipped a slice of triple-layer chocolate cake into the latest food delivery, a leftover from a fancy event. Dan felt naughty for secreting the decadent gift to his house, more so for consuming so many empty calories.

Tillie burst inside in such a tizzy that Dan feared Florence had suffered a setback.

"What is it?" he asked, standing quickly.

Tillie's beaming smile eased his concern. "I couldn't wait," she said, hurrying across the room. "I just had to come over and hug you—may I?"

Tillie wrapped Dan up in a bear hug before he could answer.

"Mother has just finished her latest checkup," Tillie said, squeezing her breasts into Dan's chest. "Ellen pronounced Mother healthier than five years ago. I have you to thank."

Dan grunted a barely audible "You're welcome" while struggling to maintain his balance.

Dan managed to remain upright in the face of Tillie's exuberance. He couldn't say the same earlier in the day, facing Maggie's latest ambush. As the cattle dispersed through the town, Dan had rolled Florence out of harm's way and diverted the herd along Brule Street, corralling them with a long stick and a feast of weeds. After escorting the saddled rancher and his herd to the outskirts of town, he turned back to glimpse Maggie sneaking through his front door—where she'd met him when he entered, grinning mischievously.

After Tillie departed, Dan ran his finger through the chocolate icing and stuck it in his mouth. A surge of euphoria flowed through him, less from the sugar high or Maggie's afternoon delight and more from Tillie's report of Florence's improvement. But was it Hat Creek improving Florence's health or her ability to remember her beloved? As much as memories can hurt, she showed Dan that they could also heal. It was a valuable lesson for Dan to heed.

CHAPTER 23

Jacob injected water through the Childress's milking machine's clear silicone tubing to check the new seals. After discovering no leaks, he packed up his tools and emerged from the milk shed into the bright sunshine. Half of today's self-appointed forewoman crew, Megan, had just stepped from the chicken coop and waved for him to join her.

Megan and Chloe had borrowed western shirts from Maggie and scrounged cowboy hats and red bandanas from Hartman's, amusing Nadine by tipping their hats with a polite "Ma'am" in passing. The pair made sexy cowgirls.

"What's next on the agenda, boss?" Jacob asked.

Megan nodded to the south. "Roger and Chloe took half the crew out to stack hay."

Jacob spotted the green John Deere tractor pulling the hay wagon, the ranch hand driving, and Chloe sitting in his lap. Megan and Chloe's constant innuendoes had seriously ruffled the guy, though he didn't appear to be suffering Chloe's present attention.

"I'm taking the rest to bring in the milk cows," Megan said, straightening Jacob's shirt collar and rebuttoning a loose shirt button. "Except you. Your job is to clear the hayloft of any roosting chickens." She brushed the dust from his chest and looked him over. "Much better—wait. You have grease on your cheek." She removed her bandana and wiped at his face.

"Enough," Jacob complained, shoving her hand away. "I'm clearing out chickens, not going on a date."

Megan chuckled as she replaced her bandana. "You never know what kind of chicks you'll find up there. Perhaps even one with ponytail plumage." She looked him over one more time before slowly backing away. "The cows are at the far end of the pasture. We'll be gone at least an hour."

Jacob tipped his imaginary hat in gratitude and turned in the opposite direction. Entering the barn, he paused until his eyes adapted to the subdued lighting before successfully navigating the oozy minefield and climbing the stairs, reaching the top just as Michelle backed down a stepped stack of hay bales, her tight bottom pointed directly at him. Lovely.

"I think I found all of them," she said, hearing his footsteps. "There were two more—" She turned and jerked backward, bumping into the bales. "Jacob!"

"Again?" he complained. "I'm beginning to think you don't like me."

"I assumed you were Megan," she claimed, wiping sweat off her cheek with the heel of her hand.

"Uh-uh," Jacob said. He relieved Michelle of the eggs and threaded his arms under hers to deposit them on a hay bale. "You're going to have to do better than that." She lifted her arms to his shoulders when he pulled her close and returned his kiss.

"Much better," he said. He nibbled on Michelle's sweaty cheekbone. Delicious. "There was a change in plans. Chloe took half the crew to load hay bales, Megan the rest to bring in the cows."

Michelle huffed. "They set me up."

"I prefer to think of us as their beneficiaries," Jacob said. He sampled Michelle's tasty temple.

"Is *everybody* gone?" Michelle asked, presenting her cheek to divert him from her earlobe.

"Not a soul remains," Jacob said, accepting the invitation.

She lifted her head. "But what if they—"

He French kissed her. When Michelle had fully relaxed into his embrace, Jacob freed her shirt and slipped his hands beneath to relish her slick, hot skin. He had settled for a sample of this intimate touch during their walk along the creek. The hayloft, though, included a ready-made bed.

Jacob slipped his fingers under Michelle's bra strap and deftly unhooked her bra. She tried backing away while at the same time tightening her grip around his neck to remain lip-locked, her newly- liberated adventurous half battling to assume control. He scratched lightly at the indentions left in her skin by Michelle's bra straps and patiently kneaded her anxiety away. Baby steps, one at a time.

Once Michelle was a willing partner again, Jacob slipped his hand around her torso and cupped her breast. Predictably, she complained into his mouth. And as he had counted on, her embrace constricted into a death grip. Jacob lowered his other hand to Michelle's bottom and pulled her intimately tight while acquainting himself with the petite mound. Michelle responded by cupping the back of his head and kissing him hungrily, urging him on, moaning delicately when her nipple hardened into his palm. Nothing satisfied Jacob more than a reluctant partner finally conquering their inhibitions.

He kissed a line along Michelle's cheekbone and pulled her earlobe into his mouth. Her entire body quivered against his. "Gone for at least an hour," he assured her, tenderly stroking her nipple tall and proud. He decided they'd do it on the floor, in the corner where the untrampled hay was deepest. He slipped his palm down over her belly button and inside the waistband of her jeans. Turning his hand, with a simple pull, he released the snap.

"Jacob! Stop!" Michelle jumped back while at the same time pushing him away. "Sorry if I'm a … It's just that I'm not …." The same fingers urging Jacob on were now busily resecuring her jeans. Not conquered, after all.

No seduced women had *ever* resisted Jacob. Why must Michelle be different in *every* way? He knew he needed to act fast to salvage anything from their adventure when Michelle began searching past him for an escape route.

"I know," he said, unbuckling his belt.

"Jacob! Don't—"

He pressed a finger to Michelle's lips. "Trust me."

Jacob removed his belt and grasped the tip end in his other hand. Michelle hesitantly lifted her hands to his shoulders when he lifted her shirt and threaded it into her jeans. He inserted the tip through the buckle and achieved a semblance of a snug fit using the last hole.

"All secure," he said after threading the excess belt length over the top of its first pass. "And I apologize for my indiscretion."

Michelle warmed to their escapade once assured of keeping her jeans on. She was light as a feather, the bed of hay even softer than Jacob had imagined. Slow as molasses, but sure sweet tasting.

Jacob wiped the sweat out of his eyes and leaned out of the Grange Hall roof opening, hoping to catch a cooling breeze. Maggie's mail truck momentarily appeared beyond Grange Hall and turned onto the blacktop to park directly in front of Dan's house—Dan's rules about maintaining ghost town appearances be damned. Maggie stepped from the truck toting a covered basket and disappeared around Dan's house. The pair must be dining on Dan's back patio again. They made an adorable couple, always holding hands, making faces at each other, and kissing hello and goodbye. Jacob winced at the prospect of being outdone by the Social Security set.

He was about to return to work when several of the residents, Hat Creek's reluctant shrink in their midst, piled out of Westside, signaling the conclusion of Michelle's latest group session. Watching her walk all business-like toward her cabin, her computer and a stack of notebooks clutched to her chest, Jacob noticed his belt still circling her waist. She had kept it after returning from the ranch and had worn it from sunup to sundown yesterday. Today it threaded through her white jeans, helping to keep a pink shirt tucked in.

Jacob was accustomed to girlfriends adorning themselves in his clothing: pulling on his underwear or socks, slipping into his T-shirt, or wrapping themselves in his button-down shirt; Gabrielle, in Chicago, professing a lust for the feel of his silk tie dangling down between her bare breasts. Michelle's take on the tradition was frustratingly original. Rather than covering her otherwise naked body, she was protecting hers, fully dressed, from him.

Megan and Chloe stepped last into the sunshine and spotted him. Megan blew him a kiss. Chloe flashed him. The exposed world-class jugs begged why Jacob was still chasing Michelle. Predictably, she had kept him at arm's length since their roll in the hay, offering only her take on wearing her boyfriend's class ring as encouragement. Too subtle for Jacob's tastes.

Jacob lingered in the sunshine until the afterimage of Chloe's breasts faded away, only knowing he wouldn't chase much longer. Once he finished this roofing job, he was out of town, and belt or no belt, he wasn't about to squander two sure things pursuing a lost cause.

CHAPTER 24

Jacob jerked his hand back as Westside's front door flung open, narrowly averting joining Dan on the injured reserve list. Michelle swept past him as if he were invisible.

He caught the closing door and turned toward the retreating figure. "What's wrong?"

Michelle didn't answer, only hunched her shoulders and quickened her pace, setting her ponytail swinging madly. She was still wearing his belt, meaning her issue wasn't with him, so Jacob let her go and stepped into the diner. He'd assume the role of the empathetic boyfriend after breakfast.

Nearly Hat Creek's entire population sat inside; of most interest, Chloe, Megan, and Whitney seated with Michelle's uneaten breakfast. Jacob predicted the looker with lime green highlights could explain Michelle's foul mood. "What's Michelle miffed about?"

"Your girlfriend is unimpressed with her new nickname," Megan answered.

Whitney slumped out of view. A telling reaction.

"Let's hear it," Jacob said.

"Olive," Chloe announced. "Get it? As in the oil. Extra virgin."

Jacob shook his head and sighed as the pair burst into laughter.

"We were only trying to help," Megan said.

"I bet." So much for the adage that any help was better than no help at all.

And ditto for enjoying a leisurely breakfast. Jacob's belt dejectedly retreating down the gravel road promised him that his last best chance at bedding Michelle depended on him declining her seat. He needed to act quickly.

Jacob emptied the wicker basket centerpiece of its fake fruit and loaded Michelle's breakfast. Hustling to the food table, he added two banana walnut muffins and a few croissants, a selection of spreads, utensils, and two bottles of orange juice. He could return later to Westside for a proper breakfast.

He searched for a suitable picnic blanket, settling on the checkboard tablecloth from the miscreant's table—he couldn't recall where he had heard that word before, only knew that it fit. He'd use it to score points with Michelle.

"Hold this, please," he told Whitney, handing her the basket.

Jacob grabbed one edge of the tablecloth and yanked hard. Nothing on the table budged, including the plastic apples, the feat earning Jacob plaudits from around the diner. However, today's demonstration had been child's play; no bud vases or lighted candlesticks. Jacob had won many a beer on the bet.

He tossed the tablecloth over his shoulder and recovered the basket from Whitney. Hurrying outdoors, he sighted Michelle retreating along the gravel road, having just crossed the blacktop.

"My thoughts exactly," he said when he caught up to her.

"What?" Michelle said dryly, though in a less sullen or dismissive tone than expected. Humanitarian efforts always paid dividends.

"Why waste a fine morning indoors in the company of simple-minded miscreants when you could be outdoors enjoying the fresh air."

"'Miscreants'? You're advancing in the world."

"Did I use the word correctly? I practiced it on the way."

Michelle shook her head but couldn't contain a smile. Jacob gently hip-checked her to draw her attention to the basket. "I also like your idea of sharing a picnic breakfast up the water tower." He took Michelle's hand and led her off the road. Remembering her aversion to weeds, he veered onto a dirt path and navigated Dan's water pump system to the catwalk ladder.

"You know how much I dislike ladders," Michelle said.

"Yes," Jacob said. "Third on the list after weeds and bugs." He rapped on a rusty ladder rung. "This ladder is bolted to the water tower, though, and surrounded by a steel cage. Plus, I'll be right below you."

"Whether that last point is to my advantage is up for debate," Michelle said, reaching for the handrail. "I'd better not hear 'hot' again."

"The best don't repeat come-ons," he said.

Michelle scowled at him. "And you'd better not pinch my butt, either—or try to bite it."

"'Why is Jacob sprawled on the ground?' 'He died of starvation while Michelle recited the rules of their relationship.' Now get that cute tush up the ladder before I kiss it."

With a final warning look, Michelle started up the ladder.

Jacob followed at a respectable distance, stepping onto the catwalk beside her.

"Have you climbed up here before?" Michelle asked.

"Uh-uh," Jacob answered. Pastureland extended to the horizon everywhere he looked.

"Me neither," Michelle said. "This perspective reinforces just how isolated Hat Creek is."

Jacob nodded. "Otherworldly."

He placed the picnic basket on the grating and draped the table cover over it. "Dan told me that the ladder to the top is around the back side. Let's take a quick look."

Jacob took Michelle's hand and led her halfway around the catwalk. Here the cottonwoods encroached so closely that Jacob could reach out and grab a leaf. A simple welded metal ladder extended up the side.

"This ladder leads to the roof," he said, wrapping his fingers around a rung.

"No chance," Michelle said flatly. "Don't even ask."

"I haven't been curious enough, myself," Jacob admitted. "As far as I know, Dan's the only one foolish enough to climb it." He rapped a knuckle on the tank, producing a muted thud due to the stored water. "Over a hundred times while repairing the inside of the tower, from what Dan told me."

Michelle shook her head slowly. "Dan's worked so hard for so long."

Jacob couldn't argue the point. He led her around the catwalk back to their food.

"It's become obvious to me that Dan didn't come here to start a retreat," Michelle said as they unfurled the table cover over the grating.

"No," Jacob admitted. After they sat, Jacob placed the basket before them. Though he had little interest in discussing

Dan's past, Jacob couldn't help but remember the man he had first met, little changed from the scary ghost he spied through the car window.

Jacob emptied the basket and unpeeled the liner from a muffin. "Originally, Dan tried telling me he was retired. Considering he worked all day, every day, that sounded ridiculous to me, and I told him so." Jacob bit off a big chunk of his muffin and chewed it. "I asked him if the real reason he was here was that his wife had kicked him out of the house." Jacob broke off another piece of his muffin. "Now I feel bad for saying that."

Michelle removed the lid of the yogurt tub. "You couldn't have known of his family's passing."

Jacob shook his head. "Still."

"The crux of the mystery is why Dan ended up *here*, of all places?" Michelle said. "I can't accept anybody choosing an uninhabitable ghost town as their permanent home."

Jacob opened an orange juice and took a swig. "If involuntary, then what?"

"I don't know." Michelle downed a quick spoonful of yogurt and looked at him. "Compelled to come? Forced to come?"

Jacob pulled a croissant in half. "You need to let go of the mystery of Dan. I did, and I'm the better for it." He stuffed the pastry into his mouth.

"I can't. As I've said before, Dan *is* Hat Creek. No story about Hat Creek would be complete without including his influence."

Jacob swallowed. "You're too nosy."

"Guilty," Michelle said, bouncing her ponytail up and down. She opened the other juice bottle. "I once hypothesized that Dan was hiding something."

"I remember. While squatting in those weeds that you're

so fond of."

"Now, I suspect that Dan was hiding *from* something." Michelle took a drink and frowned. "Or running away."

"So now you think *Dan* was the nefarious one?"

Michelle's frown deepened, and she shook her head contritely.

"And remember, oh inquisitive sleuth," Jacob said, "Dan most definitely *is* running Hat Creek."

Michelle recapped the bottle. "Yes. The second and third parts to the mystery: what prompted Dan to found Hat Creek, and where did he gain the expertise to run it so effectively?"

"I might have known it was a three-act play."

Missing Jacob's sarcasm, Michelle launched into an analysis of Dan's likely previous background and motivations, offering both her own opinions and those of the oft-referenced Dr. Malkovich, who apparently shared Michelle's interest in solving the mystery of how this self-professed layman could create a world-class wellness retreat, one so impactful that …

Jacob tuned Michelle out and pondered what one of his old girlfriends would chat about up here. A bogus thought. After one look at Hat Creek, they'd have bolted. Although Michelle held Hat Creek, the town, in equally low esteem, she'd managed to overcome her revulsions for the sake of the retreat and her professional ambitions.

But enough speech for one meal. Jacob was a man of action, not talk. He slathered the open end of the remaining half of the croissant with cream cheese and jam.

"This local jam is good," he said. "Try a bite."

Jacob pressed the creamy pastry to her lips when Michelle turned her face. "Oops."

"Jacob!" Michelle complained.

Jacob caught Michelle's hand as she raised it to wipe off the mess. "Allow me," he said and kissed her lips clean.

"Darn," Michelle said, dropping her chin onto the catwalk railing.

"I'm sorry I didn't think to pack strawberry jam, too," Jacob said.

"You have such a one-track mind," Michelle sighed. She nodded into the distance. "I meant *that.*"

They had become too preoccupied with determining which fruit flavors paired best with Michelle's lips to notice Dan's truck and Megan's car moved in front of Hartman's. Megan, Chloe, Whitney, and two other female residents were stacking backpacks and coolers on the ground next to the vehicles.

"We planned a girls' day out in Custer State Park," Michelle said.

"Let's pack up, then," Jacob said, gathering the remains of their picnic into the basket.

"So I can spend the entire day being ridiculed? No, thank you."

"You know that facing the ridicule is the only way to stop it." He stood and extended his hand. "Up so I can fold this cover."

Michelle reluctantly rose and helped Jacob fold the table cover. Once down the ladder, Jacob took her hand and walked toward Hartman's as a public couple.

"Take pictures if you stop at Crazy Horse Memorial," he said. "I want to see the progress."

"Michelle!" Chloe said brightly, noticing their approach after loading a cooler into the truck. "You saved us from sending out a rescue party."

Megan intercepted them when they neared the truck, taking Michelle's hand. "On your way, lover boy. This is girls-only."

Chloe looped her arm under Michelle's and led her into the group. Jacob headed for Westside to return the basket.

Jacob worked hard all day, only taking a quick lunch break. After showering and eating a late, solitary dinner—Hat Creek's female contingent hadn't yet returned—he retired to his room. He was sitting on his bed, pulling on clean socks, when his door flew open and quickly slammed shut. He straightened to find Michelle standing just inside the door, her eyes flared, her chest heaving.

She extended her arms toward him. She held his belt in one hand; in the other, a foiled carton. Jacob stood and, without a word, crossed the room, lifted Michelle off her feet, and carried her into his bed.

Jacob leaned back against his pillow and smiled. That was how you deflowered a young lady.

Once Michelle was exposed as a virgin, Jacob had soothed her with gentle caresses and even gentler kisses, proceeding as slowly and tenderly as nature allowed. His care had paid off. By the time they finished, Michelle was comfortable lying naked with him.

Jacob rolled his head to look at the shiny box of condoms sitting atop his dresser. He wouldn't put it past the voluptuous and rainbow-haired pair to have planned the day's outing to deliver Michelle into his bed. If so, there had been a method to their madness, after all.

And how do you repay such a favor? By emptying the box before he departed, of course. Megan and Chloe may set an unbeatable standard for eroticism, but Jacob determined that he and Michelle would leave their own indelible mark on Hat Creek.

And so, they did.

After his second initiation in Michelle's bed the following afternoon, Jacob mustered up a heavy blanket and escorted

Michelle by starlight into the pasture south of Hat Creek. Michelle experienced her first climax peering up into the Milky Way Galaxy, and once Jacob liberated *that* pleasure, Michelle's sexual appetite knew no bounds.

The next day, it took only Jacob's suggestion to convince Michelle to shut her computer and join him on another out-of-town escapade. Michelle climaxed so violently in the Childress Ranch hayloft's soft hay bedding that a roosting hen, their first audience, raced cackling down the stairs.

During an afternoon when Hat Creek had become unusually deserted, Jacob escorted Michelle into Hartman's and bolted the door. He unrolled several sleeping bags over the glass countertop, undressed Michelle, and laid her onto the counter. Then he laid her on the counter.

After an exhausting morning's effort, Jacob showered and popped into Michelle's cabin with bedding concealed within a large duffel bag and the suggestion for more high-elevation sex. Michelle canceled a group session and preceded him up the water tower ladder, where they shared a delightful two-hour lovemaking session hidden from view on the backside of the steel cylinder.

When Jacob spied Michelle toting a book into Dan's house, he dropped his work and joined her, locking Dan's front door behind him. Michelle balked at using Dan's bed or sofa, so Jacob disrobed her and, since their height difference precluded standing sex, lifted her into the air and pinned her against the wall.

They revisited the position during a steamy, wet, and sudsy romp in the Grange Hall community shower. When Michelle tried to bury her open mouth into Jacob's shoulder, he caught the bottom of her chin and kissed her face skyward. Everybody already knew what they were doing. Now, Michelle treated those within earshot to a sample of their shared pleasure.

The gazebo was a midnight rendezvous, reliving Jacob's sexual exploit in a Chicago park. The back seat of the Caddy because Jacob wasn't about to be outdone by Megan and Chloe. The thinly disguised fishing trip after residents begged Jacob to use his charm to cancel another group session.

The table on Dan's patio, conversely, was pure serendipity. A timely set of appointments and trips left Jacob and Michelle sharing Hat Creek with only a napping Florence attended by her nurse. This time Michelle didn't attempt to mute her loud climax.

The following morning, Michelle entered all business-like into Jacob's room and announced an end to their relationship. The sex, the petting, the kissing, the handholding; everything. Cold turkey. Their liaison distracted her from completing her work, she complained, and she'd have to work every remaining hour to finish.

Only then did it strike Jacob that this past week with Michelle hadn't been the next chapter in his sex life. She had been no conquest like all the others. He desired her more, not less, and rather than being ready to move on; he wished to cement her status as girlfriend and his as her boyfriend. Michelle's impending departure suddenly distressed him. How would they keep in touch? How did you maintain a long-distance relationship?

But no amount of cajoling would change Michelle's mind; she remained steadfast. A woman who resisted him! Jacob had never been so turned off—and turned on—in his life, alternating between the urge to jump into the holding pond and under a cold shower.

In the end, not even the cold shower was enough.

CHAPTER 25

Dan was nursing a cup of coffee in Westside when Megan and Chloe entered, absent their typical pawing and shirt pulling. After grabbing an apple apiece from the fruit basket, they took seats on either side of him. Megan threaded her hand under his arm.

"Hey! You got your finger back."

"Removed the splint yesterday," Dan said, wiggling the mended digit. Other than a mild stiffness, his finger was good as new.

Chloe dug her purple fingernails into her apple. "We were told you had two daughters but that they passed away."

Dan dropped his head and stared into his black coffee. "Yes."-

"Bummer," she sighed, laying her head against his shoulder.

Megan slipped her hand into Dan's, taking care of his tender finger. "You must miss them."

The pair's compassion teased loose a thousand suppressed

memories. "Desperately," Dan said. The memories crowded forward, seeking an audience.

Megan gently squeezed his hand. "I bet they were cute as hell."

Megan's words dropped Dan's barriers, and the memories poured forth: achievements and celebrations and milestones and events, simpler moments of joy and happiness and wonder and love and humor and caring and sorrow and melancholy. He relived crawling and walking and falling and running and hopping and skipping and twirling and dancing, temper tantrums and fighting and biting and hitting; sounds of laughter and giggling and crying and complaining and yelling and screaming and singing and "thank you" and "I love you" and "why?" and "no!"; the smell of freshly baked cookies and root beer floats and burnt toast and bubble bath and talcum powder and toothpaste and fingernail polish and perfume and hairspray and suntan lotion and bug spray and wet grass; color, vivid and vibrant colors, Megan's colors, painting life over his gray world. Safe in Megan and Chloe's consoling presence and hoping this victory of his subconscious meant that his years of toil were making a difference, Dan welcomed the memories.

He looked first at Chloe's fingernails, then up into Megan's hair. "You're wearing Anna's—Anna was our eldest—favorite color."

"Purple," Megan said, fingering a lock of her hair. "For respect."

"Thank you."

"Tell us about them," Chloe said. "Your daughters."

Refreshingly, Dan found the request welcome rather than intrusive. "Anna was an absolute delight," he said. "Bright, inquisitive, and considerate to a fault." Anna looked up at him through loving, trusting eyes. "She was tall for her age and slender, with reddish-brown hair and blue eyes. She had her mother's nose."

Dan described how Anna was his little helper. "Always measuring boards or trying to tighten screws and set nails." He chuckled. "A hammer thrown by a three-year-old still hurts."

Megan closed her other hand over his. "Sounds like a Daddy's girl to me."

"Through and through," Dan affirmed. "We went on our first father-daughter overnight camping trip when Anna was four; she was helping pitch the tent by six." Dan remembered Anna baiting a worm onto a hook, tongue poking out the side of her mouth. "Grungy, greasy, or grimy," he said, "nothing phased her.

"Anna was no tomboy, though. She loved dressing up as much as the next young lady." Dan recalled Anna, a poised little lady of seven outfitted in a lavender floor-length gown, crossing the stage to sit at the grand piano. Fingers alighting on the keys, she began a classical sonatina.

"Anna's beauty was inside: she treated everyone with empathy and care, paying deep respect for everything she attempted.

"Georgia, meanwhile," Dan said in a sterner tone, "burst onto the scene with a firebrand personality to match her hair and as devilishly charming as her emerald eyes."

"Freckles and fair complected?" Chloe asked.

Dan nodded. "Classic redhead."

Chloe sighed with envy. "What a killer combination. I bet you had to watch her like a hawk."

Dan nodded. "From an early age. She returned from kindergarten one day and announced that she had a boyfriend. She pestered the boy so badly that his mother eventually demanded we make Georgia back off.

"And Georgia was more worldly than Anna. With her natural extroversion, confidence, and charm, Georgia had a knack for getting her way. She once attended a friend's birthday party at one of those arcades that served bad pizza along with the games. Georgia was picky about her pizza: a fully cooked crust, tangy sauce, and absolutely no skimping on the pepperoni. The pies didn't meet Georgia's standards, so she demanded that the arcade remake them. Imagine a seven-year-old bossing a restaurant manager."

Chloe giggled on Dan's shoulder.

"Best part of the story?" Dan said. "I didn't say a word; didn't need to. The new pies were delicious.

"Much to our dismay, Georgia attempted the same antics at home, successful to varying degrees, depending on how tired we were. Some days Georgia ran the household. The remainder she just thought she did.

"And Georgia was always on the go," Dan said, nodding at a blurred montage of the plotting and pestering that defined Georgia's "play." "From first light to lights out, running herself so ragged that she usually fell asleep the moment her head hit the pillow."

"I wish we could have met your daughters," Megan said. "We would have had a blast together."

Dan chuckled. "Knowing you two, you'd have probably corrupted them. And I would have enjoyed seeing it." He hummed. "Had they lived, you'd be contemporaries. Anna would be Michelle's age, Georgia two years younger."

Chloe nodded against Dan's shoulder and then, sitting up, said, "You must admit, Dan, that Megan and I have proven our worth."

Chloe mimicked Dan's blank stare. "As Jacob's supervisors?" he asked

She rolled her eyes at Dan's continued bewilderment. "To alleviate your Michelle problem."

Now Dan understood Megan and Chloe's Adonis conversation at the water tower. And, come to think of it, Michelle hadn't pestered Dan since.

He broke into laughter. "It appears that I am in your debt," he said.

"And as Jacob now seems to be firmly, umm, on top of the situation, we're finding we have more free time. We could be your surrogate daughters."

"We know we'll never replace Anna and Georgia in any way," Megan added quickly. "But maybe we could help."

The pair's sincerity touched Dan. "I'd like that."

Megan smiled and said playfully, "Thanks, Dad."

"Yes, thanks," Chloe said. She slipped her hand into Dan's other hand. "Tell us her name."

"Who?"

"You know who."

Dan smiled. Yes, he did know. "Grace." He enjoyed the sensation, even more, the sound of her name in his ears. "My wife's name was Grace." He hadn't spoken her name aloud in more than twenty years.

Chloe smiled and dropped her head back onto his shoulder. "Such a beautiful name. Tell us more stories."

Through refills of coffee and discarded apple cores, joined by Whitney, Benjamin, and Phil for a dinner of chicken and rice pilaf, their party overflowing by the addition of Tillie and Ellen, Jacob and Michelle, and several newer Hat Creek residents, deep into the evening Dan brought those thousand memories to life.

Dan would forever remember the day Megan and Chloe returned his family.

CHAPTER 26

"You remembered every flower," Florence said contentedly, releasing another long stem. She had identified several varieties as Dan slowly rolled her the length of Brule Street: her purple asters, thistles, sage, and milkweed; yellow marigolds and ragweed; white daisies and yarrows.

Dan excused himself for a quick detour to the nearest cabin, intending to tuck in a loose piece of siding. Instead, the board broke off in his hand. He carried the splinter back to the wheelchair.

"Another one of my cabins seems to be crumbling," he said, showing the rotted wood to Florence.

She lifted a craggy hand. "As am I."

Sensing Florence descending into the melancholy that more frequently overtook her as she regained clarity, Dan tossed the wood scrap into the weeds and engaged her. "You told me Arthur was quite the builder."

"Yes," she said with less than her typical enthusiasm.

"Arthur grew up poor and was determined we wouldn't be so deprived. But Arthur was never one to put on airs, and he wouldn't have Tillie spoiled. Being an only child, though, it was easy for Tillie to imagine herself a queen—"

Dan's eagle **sounded** in the distance. Florence turned her head toward the faint sound and fiddled with her hands in her lap. "I know what he wants," she said softly. "Dan, can you roll me into the gazebo?"

"The hot sun. Sorry." Dan wheeled Florence into the park and up the temporary ramp Jacob had constructed over the gazebo steps for this very purpose. After turning Florence to face the park and setting the wheel lock, he sat on the bench facing her. "Better?"

She nodded. "I must confess about my conduct toward Arthur." Her stricken face spoke to the gravity she considered the matter.

Florence wished Dan to hear her confession. Though he admitted no authority to serve as confessor, the only possible alternative, Hat Creek's church, was long gone.

"Go on," he said.

Florence opened and closed her mouth three times before words came out. "I was a regular hellion in my youth," she said. "I smoked, I drank, I stayed out all hours of the night. My father introduced Arthur to me, hoping I'd settle down before I caused myself any actual harm. And Arthur was pleasant enough that I eventually accepted his proposal. I didn't love him, but I knew I'd never get a better offer.

"Arthur tried to make a go of our marriage. I didn't." After a long pause, in a contrite voice, Florence said, "I had a fling with a transient, a seasonal laborer on a harvest crew. I didn't care for him. I just enjoyed flirting with real trouble. We went too far one time only, but ...."

Florence looked at her lap. "Tillie's was a difficult birth." She looked up with quivering lips and tears streaming down her cheeks. "I was left sterile."

Dan offered his handkerchief.

"Thank you," Florence said and wiped her face dry. After blowing her nose, she took a deep breath and continued. "Anybody else would have divorced me, shamed me, thrown me out on the street." Florence shook her head. "But not Arthur. He insisted we name 'our' daughter after his mother. We kept it a secret that Tillie wasn't his."

A bead of sweat ran down Florence's temple onto her cheek. She struggled to fold Dan's handkerchief to wipe at it.

"Let's take this blanket off your lap," Dan said. He removed it and draped it over the gazebo railing. "Please continue," he said.

"Arthur was a loving, caring, and dedicated husband and father," Florence said. "Tillie and I had few wants."

She squeezed the handkerchief into a wad.

"He turned up a few years later—Tillie's real father. One look at Tillie, and he knew he had fathered a daughter. When he discovered that everyone assumed Tillie was Arthur's, he threatened to spill the beans unless we paid him off. It took most of the money Arthur had saved to make him leave."

Florence's gaze dropped to Dan's chest.

"Arthur took a second job to keep us in our home, working such long hours that Tillie was usually in bed before he returned. Yet, he never became bitter or spiteful. While she slept, Arthur fixed plumbing leaks and unclogged drains. While she dreamt, he remodeled the spare upstairs bedrooms into a playroom and a music room. Tillie barely knew her father, even less of his devotion to us, and nothing, ever, of her true father."

Florence looked into Dan's eyes again.

"Of course, I fell in love with Arthur. Head over heels in love. There's never been a more honorable and selfless husband and father. I promised Arthur I would make everything up to him when Tillie was grown, that I would get a job, and that it would be my turn to take care of him."

Florence shook her head. "But I never took that job. I was too set in my ways." She looked away as if to gather the courage to continue. "That's a lie," she said, looking at Dan again. "I was too spoiled and lazy, too morally weak. I often wished that Arthur would get mad at me or feel sorry for himself, anything to get me started. But, of course, Arthur wasn't that type of a man."

Florence wiped away more tears. Seeing her upraised hand, she stared at her gray skin mottled with brown-black age spots.

"Then, one morning, Arthur was old. Thin—so thin— wispy gray hair, thick glasses, hearing aids, stooped shoulders, a shake in his hands, an artificial hip." Florence paused, her expression pained, the memory destressing. "But still working, never able to retire because of my burden. And so, he died. Right there in front of me, facing me across the breakfast table, his head dropping into his plate."

Florence's gray pupils shimmered.

"I rushed to Arthur's side and showered him with kisses. I told him how deeply I loved him and how much I appreciated all the sacrifices he had made for Tillie and me. I said I was sorry for being such a poor wife and never letting him fill our upstairs with children and … and for everything." She slowly shook her head. "But I spoke too late. Arthur never heard my words."

Dan could see in Florence's anguish the same regret that so often tortured his thoughts.

"I robbed Arthur of the life he deserved," she told Dan. "And then I robbed him of even the reassurance that he had lived a good life." Florence forced her hands still in her lap. "Of everything, for that, I am most sorry." She shrunk in her chair, finished.

Dan wasn't a religious man. He hadn't prayed to or blamed God a single time. But Florence had placed him as a novice priest sitting in a plastic confessional. What options did he have? Absolve her of her sins? Mete out suitable penance? Grant her leniency, seeing as she was no more flawed than he?

Dan shrugged off the spiritual robes and stood, resting his elbows on the gazebo railing for a more secular assessment. Florence's secret past told a dark story. Yet, Tillie knew her mother as a caring parent and a loving and selfless grandmother and great-grandmother.

A bumblebee rose out of the nearest flowers, weaving as if drunk on nectar, and managed a rough landing on a purple bloom. *We all have our duties.*

Dan turned from the railing. "Arthur's passing was your wake-up call, wasn't it?"

Florence nodded meekly. "I'm ashamed it took that much. I'd give anything to turn back time and hold Arthur's children to my breast." Her wistful expression spoke of other wishes left unspoken. "But some mistakes are irreversible, aren't they?"

There are happy memories, and there are sad memories. This time, another's words triggered the latter. Dan could only nod.

"Arthur spent our entire married lives showing me the kind of person I could be," Florence said. "I've dedicated the last twenty years to living his lessons."

Dan turned to the railing again and regarded Hat Creek a second time, this vision overflowing with those who had made his ghost town their temporary residence, the majority departing happier and healthier than at their arrival. Grudgingly, pride swelled in his chest.

He retook his seat. "Florence, tell me all you're proud of."

"I split Arthur's insurance policy between my three grandchildren, helping to pay for Ryan's in-home daycare, Alex's mortgage, and Lynn's college expenses. Tillie's old rooms became a nursery, boarding house, theater, playground, and study room for my great-grandchildren. I doted on them, showering them with all the love and attention I could give.

"I also took my first job. I wanted my great-grandchildren to remember me as a hard-working, independent woman. I worked until I was eighty-four.

"Two years ago, I sold the house and most of my possessions and moved into a care home. With the remaining money, I established trust funds for my great-grandchildren."

Florence, her neck now glistening from the heat, looked about her chair as if searching for more to add. With a resigned shrug, she said, "It's little, I know, but I have no more to give, Dan."

Whatever Florence's failings as a wife, Dan knew that Florence was the beloved matriarch of a growing family of three grandchildren and eight great-grandchildren. "You've nurtured three generations with great dedication and devotion," Dan said. "You've given more than enough."

Florence took a labored breath and exhaled relief. "Thank you." She said in a more hopeful tone, "I'm ready to go now."

The heat. "I apologize," Dan said, rising. "Let's get you back indoors."

"No," Florence said with enough force to drop Dan back onto the bench. He had misunderstood her wish.

"Oh, you mean literally, as in to go *home*." Florence wasn't the first Hat Creek resident anxious to depart, and no ghost town can compete with a gaggle of great-grandchildren. "I'd imagine that's up to Ellen, but if she asks for my opinion, I'll say—"

Florence protested a second time. "I'm all used up, Dan. I'm of no use anymore to anybody down here." She lifted a gnarled hand and let it drop with finality. "My love for Arthur has never stopped growing. I want to spend eternity with him, Dan. I want to spend eternity caring for him."

CHAPTER 27

Jacob had taken the zipper wax from Dan when Hartman's front door slammed open hard enough to rattle the windows.

"Sorry!" Michelle yelled. "Jacob?"

"Back by the camping supplies," he answered.

Michelle appeared at the head of the aisle and sprinted toward them, panting when she skidded to a stop beside them.

"Never given out a speeding ticket," Dan chuckled, "but there's always a first time."

"I wanted to tell Jacob bye before——" Michelle stared at the metal-framed backpack resting upright on a chair in front of the counter. "That's ... massive."

"A bit bloated," Jacob admitted, running the wax stick along the balking zipper. The pack was overflowing with the contents of two new hiker's boxes, plus resupplies and Jacob's gear. He and Dan had secured two box kits to the backside of the tubular frame and lashed Jacob's sleeping bag and tent on top. A hatchet, ropes, and bottles hung down the outside.

"I packed your water filter in here," Dan told Jacob, tapping a swollen side pocket. "But fill a jug at each box on your outward leg to be safe. And remember to conserve your phone battery."

"Phone's off." Once the zipper finally released, Jacob ran it back and forth across the wax until it slid smoothly.

Dan rechecked various pouches. "You're good to go. Need help getting this monstrosity strapped on?"

Jacob shook his head. "Michelle can help."

"See you in a few days, then."

Michelle stood silently until the front door closed behind Dan. "Whitney overheard you and Dan discussing an extended hike at breakfast," she said.

Jacob nodded. "A hiking and biking trail extends over a hundred miles from Edgemont north to Deadwood." He secured one last clip. "Dan is coordinating with Edgemont to add a branch following the creek. I'm setting up two more hiker's boxes, taking Dan's trail to Edgemont's front door."

Michelle fingered the various pockets. "How long will you be gone?"

"Four to five days; I've provisioned for six. It's sixty miles to Edgemont and back. This pack weighs upwards of one hundred pounds, and I don't lose much of the load until the new boxes. I won't be jogging."

Jacob watched Michelle mentally tick off the days. He had designed the hike to return Friday evening at the earliest, more likely Saturday afternoon, well after her Friday morning departure.

She focused on the row of fishing poles mounted on the wall behind the counter. "You're upset with me."

"No," he said. Though he had legitimate grounds for complaint, he had no enthusiasm for belittling Michelle. Barring another chance Hat Creek encounter, they'd never see each other again, and he preferred parting amicably.

"When Dan mentioned his plan to link up with Edgemont's trail, I offered to set up the boxes. It gets me out of your hair and prevents Dan from foolhardily attempting it himself." Jacob hadn't gotten away clean, but at least Michelle couldn't fault him.

"This is goodbye, then," she said. Did Jacob detect a whiff of regret?

"I guess it is."

Michelle looked at Jacob, her eyes shimmering mirrors. "Do I at least get a hug?"

"Of course." Jacob opened his arms wide.

As a rule, platonic hugs following an intimate relationship are awkward. This one proved no exception. Hands that frolicked over Michelle's naked body two days earlier now politely pressed the small of her back.

"I need to get started," Jacob said, putting the abomination out of its misery. "Help me get this monster strapped on."

He grabbed the pack by its metal frame and, with a loud grunt, hoisted it up onto the counter.

"Can you carry that much weight so far?" Michelle asked.

Jacob had already recovered sufficiently from Michelle's rejection for suggestive alternatives to cross his mind. "Let's just say it's not my first choice," he said with raised eyebrows, chuckling when Michelle's cheeks blushed. That ponytail keeping her hair off her face just kept giving and giving.

"Steady this for me, please," he said. Once Michelle secured the frame, he backed into it and straightened to lift the load off the counter.

"I'll untangle the waist straps for you," Michelle said.

"Thanks." Jacob secured the chest harness, and after

Michelle buckled the waist strap, he pulled up the slack and tested the load. "Ready," he grunted.

Michelle preceded him up the aisle and opened the front door for him. "Call me, please," she said when he stepped past her. "Thursday night or early Friday morning. Please."

"I will."

"Goodbye, Jacob."

"Goodbye."

When his soles found the gravel road, Jacob turned towards Grange Hall, the water tower, and the creek beyond.

He didn't look back.

CHAPTER 28

Hartman's front door slammed open, rattling the windows. Déjà vu. Dan considered the loaf of bread he held might better serve as a temporary door stop until he could install a real one.

"Dan," Tillie yelled frantically. "Dan?"

"In the back," he answered loudly.

"Oh, Dan, Dan, Dan!" Tillie whined, repeating his name in cadence with her footsteps. Even quicker strides than Michelle's and, from the distress in her voice, a real problem.

Dan stepped around the shelving into view. The panic in Tillie's eyes was genuine, too. "What's wrong?" he asked.

"Come with me!" Tillie said, immediately turning for the front door. "Oh, please hurry! It's Mother."

Dan dropped the bread and hustled up the aisle, catching Tillie at the front door. Once outdoors, she made a beeline for Grange Hall.

"Mother insisted on a long stroll after lunch," Tillie said, almost at a jog. "She seemed so happy. But once we returned to the room and she laid down, her breathing became raspy and labored, and she started complaining of chest pains. Ellen said Mother's heart was palpitating—beating irregularly. Mother's blood pressure dropped so low that she passed out. She quickly regained consciousness, but it happened twice more. And her body temperature has started dropping. Ellen whispered to me that it was as if—" Tillie wiped away tears as they stepped into Grange Hall. "As if Mother's entire body was shutting down. Ellen called an ambulance, but it's thirty minutes away."

I'm ready to go.

Rushing down the hallway to Florence's room, Tillie paused with her hand on the doorknob. "Mother is disorientated and very agitated. She keeps asking …" Tillie swallowed hard and looked at Dan pleadingly. "Mother keeps asking for Arthur."

Dan nodded understanding and followed Tillie into the room. Florence lay in her bed, head elevated, eyes open, her chest heaving beneath the covers. Her hands fidgeted in obvious discomfort.

"Can't you give Mother something for the pain?" Tillie asked Ellen, continuing to Florence's bedside.

Ellen shook her head as she uncoiled a coil of clear plastic tubing. "Not until her blood pressure rises."

"Mother," Tillie said. "I've brought a dear man."

Dan sat on the edge of the bed. Florence's eyes, pupils shrunk to tiny black dots, darted in confusion. Unaware of his presence, she had regressed beyond her state at her arrival.

Dan leaned into her view. "Hello, Florence."

"Arthur!" she gasped.

Dan subdued Florence's flailing hand and gently cupped it between his own. It was cold and dry, and her fingernails were tinted blue. "Yes, it's me," he assured her. When Tillie turned to Ellen to plead for more to be done, Dan leaned closer and whispered, "I've come for you."

The promise in her husband's voice calmed Florence. She locked onto his face, pulling air into her lungs in rapid, shallow gulps.

"Do you remember when we first met, Florence?" he asked. "Do you? I walked with your father from behind your barn, and there you were. Remember with me."

Ellen fit a nasal cannula into Florence's nostrils. In the background, the heart monitor traced a tortured rhythm.

"I fell in love with you right then and there," Dan said. "And I never stopped loving you."

Florence attempted to speak but couldn't find a breath.

"This should help," Ellen said, opening a valve to start the flow of oxygen. Florence's breathing improved noticeably, and her hands relaxed.

"I enjoyed the evenings spent turning our house into a home," Dan said. "I cherished our time together."

Florence's heart slipped into acute arrhythmia, and the blood pressure monitor beeped another warning. Momentarily, Florence's eyes rolled up, and she again lost consciousness. Tillie straightened the ruffled blanket over Florence's chest to occupy her hands. Ellen, equally as helpless, could only look on.

A slave to her erratic heartbeat, Florence regained consciousness as quickly as she lost it.

"We raised a wonderful daughter, didn't we, Florence?" Dan said. "Do you remember when we couldn't find Tillie, only to discover her asleep under her pile of stuffed animals? And the look on Tillie's face after her thirteenth birthday party when she found her playroom transformed into a magical castle?"

Florence forced out words in staccato succession: "Love—you—your—children." And, more clearly, "I'm sorry, Arthur."

"Don't be," Dan said, pressing Florence's hand. "I wouldn't have changed a moment of our lives."

As if by divine intervention, the lights flickered, then flickered again. When Tillie turned to reset a complaining monitor, Dan whispered to Florence, "We're here."

Florence's heartbeat immediately slipped into a normal rhythm. Except slow and weak. And as the monitor attested, too slow and too weak. When the blood pressure monitor flashed its inevitable warning, Florence's eyes closed slowly as if she were falling asleep. *I'm ready to go now.* Good luck, Florence.

"Mother?" Tillie said. "Ellen?"

Ellen placed her stethoscope on Florence's chest and then her fingertips on Florence's neck. With a tiny shake of her head, she stepped aside and urged Tillie back to her mother's side.

Tillie sat opposite Dan and took Florence's other hand. "You were our rock, Mother," she said, tears streaming down her cheeks. "Our teacher and mentor. Your love and care nourished us and made us who we are. I love you. We all love you."

One more heartbeat. Dan saw it traced on the monitor, followed by a flat line trailing away until it filled the screen. Tillie had spoken before Florence passed away.

Ellen placed her hand on Tillie's back. "I'm sorry."

Dan looked at Florence's fingers, still holding his hand. Her strength had been her resolve to pay tenfold to her progeny what she owed to Arthur. She had most deservedly earned her reward. Dan uncurled her fingers and laid her hand by her side. It belonged to another man, now—and forever.

Dan stood and took his leave, pausing in the doorway for a final look. Florence's lips had settled into a slight upturn.

The ambulance arrived, lights flashing and siren blaring,

without purpose. The commotion drew out Hat Creek's residents, initially out of curiosity, and then, as word spread of Florence's passing, to pay homage. When the coroner's car pulled up in front of Grange Hall, accompanied by a long black coach, Dan slipped from the gathering to escort the coroner inside.

Dan had just returned outdoors when Megan and Chloe approached. "Ladies," he said as they stepped to either side of him.

Chloe wrapped her arms around Dan and pressed her cheek against his shoulder. "We're sorry. We know how close you were to Florence."

Megan completed the affectionate cocoon and nodded into Dan's chest. "She was a classy lady." She laid her palm over Dan's heart. "Are you okay?"

Dan drew his surrogate daughters still closer. They were unaware of his awakening since Florence's passing. He had long assumed he would be the first to pass away in Hat Creek, solitary, unnoticed and unmissed. "Is this heaven, Dan?" Florence had asked. Her query and story had reinforced Dan's personal "why" of this place: operating Hat Creek as *his* path to redemption. And Florence's courage had rendered superficial the literal reward Dan sought, teaching Dan that being eternally reunited with his loved ones was the ultimate reward awaiting him after a life lived well. It was a reward worth any sacrifice required.

"I'm fine," Dan said, squeezing the pair. "Florence led a rich and fulfilling life. She was rightfully proud of her legacy and at peace with the world she was leaving behind. That's the best any of us can hope for."

His residents' mood concerned Dan more. Admittedly, they had signed on to suffer the worst a ghost town could mete out, but these were still modern times, and death was remote to most.

Grange Hall's front door opened, and the attendant rolled the gurney carrying Florence's covered body outside, down the ramp, and into the back of the black coach. The car started with a throaty exhaust sound and pulled past the crowd, turning north onto the blacktop.

Dan mouthed a simple goodbye and good luck to Florence, deciding it was time for Hat Creek's first-ever wake.

CHAPTER 29

Jacob tripped and stumbled to the ground, scraping his hands as he broke his fall. Darkness and exhaustion were proving a toxic combination. He sat back on his heels and wiped the sting from his palms, trying to remember why he'd foolishly compressed this hike into three days. His answer took form: that silky ponytail, the slender neck it exposed, that hypnotic butt wiggle, and those petite breasts forming perfect mounds under tight shirts. And that Michelle hadn't a clue how crazy it drove him that she preferred studying psychiatry to him—or whatever her degree.

Jacob ignored his screaming muscles and stood. Only a few miles to go. The discomfort was worth the reward.

Stumbling onto a rough, hard surface startled Jacob awake. He dipped his headlamp to illuminate the ground, confirming that he stood on the gravel road. Spotlighting the bridge spanning Hat Creek told him the town was to his right.

So, he turned right.

Reaching Michelle's cabin, he sloughed off his pack and knocked on her front door. Momentarily, a dim light showed through the curtains. "It's me, Jacob," he croaked when the curtains parted to reveal a sliver of Michelle's face.

Once the curtain dropped, he slumped against the doorframe, waiting for it to open. And waited. And waited. Hadn't Michelle pleaded for Jacob to phone her? Instead, he had undertaken an epic hike to return in person, only to be snubbed. Barred once, barred forever, apparently. Dashing back had made more sense before rejection crossed his mind. This would be the moment for any man with an ounce of pride to turn and leave. Except he hadn't the energy to straighten up. It was more likely that they'd find him in the morning slumped to the ground against the doorframe.

He stumbled inside when the door unexpectedly opened, barely maintaining his balance. Michelle's hair was down, draped over her shoulders, and she wore only a dress shirt, open save the button between her breasts, her bare legs poking out below. Jacob almost had the energy to relieve her of the makeshift nightie. Almost.

She took his hand. "You need a shower."

Michelle stood before Jacob, dressed only in a white lab coat held closed by a single button, her nipples pressing against the fabric. She laughed at his confusion. "I'm a rocket scientist."

"Huh?"

She grabbed Jacob's hand. "Come with me."

Michelle led him outside and around her cabin to a sleek rocket standing erect where the junkers had been parked. "It's so long," she purred, patting its hard surface. The rocket pulsed and rumbled, pent-up energy straining for release, nearly ready for launch. Condensation glistened on the rocket's shell, coalescing into droplets that trickled down its side.

"You can't be doing this, Michelle," Jacob said. "Someone might hear."

She giggled. "That never bothered *you*."

Jacob awoke to find Michelle astride him, her hands planted against the bed on either side of his head, slowly rocking up and down. He hadn't a clue how she had managed to get him sheathed and mounted without awakening him. He reached for Michelle's waist and gently pulled her down onto him.

"Thank you for returning," she whispered, planting a line of kisses along his cheekbone. She raised herself to a sitting position and, flattening her palms against Jacob's chest, finished what she had started.

Michelle lay on top of Jacob, her face tucked under his chin, fingertips tracing delicate outlines of his pec. She cupped his chest muscle and hummed appreciatively, her first outward admiration for his physique. Had Jacob's heroic hike finally impressed her, or had she found him attractive all along, only too proud to admit it? More likely, *beneath* her to admit it. After all, she was a bona fide member of the brainiac crowd, to which it was unbecoming to admit physical attraction.

And Jacob finally admitted that Michelle's attraction was also a case of crossing class boundaries. He could vouch for her having all the right bits, could catalog them by feel this very instant. That Michelle wouldn't be considered sexy or beautiful by any traditional measures didn't enter the calculation. It was Michelle's intelligence that turned Jacob's head. While he scoffed at her college plans and publicly ridiculed her cerebral conversations with Dan, deep down, Jacob was in awe.

Jacob admired Michelle's drive, too. Envied it, even. While

he drifted from city to city, holding down an endless stream of minimum-wage jobs, Michelle pursued a lofty goal, unwavering in her determination to see it through to the end. If she were Jupiter orbiting the sun, Jacob was but a shepherding moon tidying its rings.

Jacob slid a hand to the middle of Michelle's back and spread his fingers. This night, he'd be her bed, blanket, and protector, freeing her to fantasize about Nobel prizes, world domination, or whatever geniuses dreamt. Jacob felt more than heard Michelle's light breathing, a slight pressure against his ribs followed by a touch of warm air into his neck. The steady, calm rhythm soothed him as profoundly as her earlier back rub.

Michelle's breathing gradually shallowed until Jacob couldn't tell whether he felt it any longer or only wished he did. And then, almost imperceptibly, Michelle relaxed onto him, asleep.

That was the moment Jacob fell in love.

A loud snap awakened Jacob. He rolled onto his side, reigniting the painful aftereffects of his marathon hike. Morning sunlight filtered into the room and spotlighted Michelle standing at the desk, closing a suitcase. Two more rested upright on the floor.

"Sorry," she said. "I didn't mean to startle you."

Jacob slid back and patted the bed. After Michelle sat, he reached for her hand. "I prefer last night's method."

Michelle smiled shyly and dropped her gaze. Jacob placed her hand over his heart. "Thank *you* for letting me in," he said.

Michelle measured several heartbeats before sliding her hand to Jacob's shoulder blade and begin kneading a firm knot of muscle. "If I had the time, I'd give you another backrub.

But I need to leave in a few minutes, and I promised Dan I'd say goodbye."

The tiniest encouragement, but that's all Jacob needed. He had decided on his next destination in the final throes of last night's consciousness, with his first love interest pressing against his loins.

"I'm considering moving to New York City," he said.

Michelle's fingers stumbled but quickly recovered and began a circling pattern, suggesting she didn't find the prospect revolting. And though she wasn't smiling, she wasn't frowning, either. Jacob considered those encouraging signs.

When Michelle turned to him and lifted her other hand to his chest, he knew she wouldn't deny him.

"You're an adult, Jacob," she said. "You can live anywhere you wish. But New York City is expensive, even more so than Chicago. You'll need at least three roommates to afford a decent apartment."

Jacob appreciated the subtle inference that they wouldn't be rooming together. Just another challenge to overcome.

"Two minutes," Michelle said. "Roll onto your stomach."

When Jacob next awoke, evening sunlight streamed through the front window. He wondered if Michelle's flight had landed yet. And would she call to let him know she had made it home safely? Such novel concerns. Vulnerability had always been the girl's domain.

He decided he would shower and fill his empty stomach before calling her. He swung his legs over the edge of the bed to the chorus of protesting muscles. After slipping into his clothes, he shoved his bare feet into his boots. Reaching the front door, he grinned. Michelle had draped a pair of her white lacy panties over the doorknob. He lifted the key to the

Big Apple to his nose and inhaled deeply.

CHAPTER 30

"Dan!" Megan called out.

"Oh, Dan," Chloe echoed in a sing-song voice.

"Over here!" Dan yelled back. "Under the water tower."

Dan tightened another bolt while listening to the pair's approach. Closer by, their feet shuffled in the thick weeds.

"He did say *under* the water tower, didn't he?" Chloe asked.

"Maybe he meant a different water tower," Megan said.

Dan scraped his wrench against a pipe. "Down here," he said in a spooky voice.

Chloe gasped. "Dragging chains and a disembodied voice! Megan, I *told* you this place was haunted."

The pair clambered through the maze of piping and peered down at Dan over the top of the discharge pipe. "Interesting place for a catnap," Megan said.

He tapped his wrench against the large ball valve. "Creative valve repair. I'm trying to outwit Todd."

"Evil Inspector Todd?"

"The very one. Code requires a functional valve. Unfortunately, this old one is frozen open."

Megan nodded as if she understood Dan's dilemma. "We'd stay and help, but we're heading out for good and wanted to say goodbye."

"In that case, give me a second to scoot out."

"Watch yourself," Chloe said, pointing to Dan's left. "There's a bee in the dirt."

"A ground wasp," Dan said. "An old acquaintance. I don't even know if they can sting."

"I won't be shaking your little friend's hand, just the same," Chloe said. "We'll meet you at a safe distance."

Dan paused to admire his handiwork. With a fresh coat of blue epoxy paint and shiny stainless-steel bolts, the old valve was indistinguishable from a new one, only hundreds of dollars cheaper. Todd would never think to test it.

Dan slithered into the open air and stood, wiping the dirt from his hair and clothing on his way to join Megan and Chloe, who had walked to his truck and dropped the tailgate.

Megan fingered the translucent tailgate chain sheathing. "Now, this is spiffy."

"One of the original tailgate chains broke," Dan said, taking the seat offered between them. "This set came with a lifetime warranty."

Chloe poked at his scarred arm. "Which won't be long if you keep injuring yourself."

"I'm certain the warranty refers to the life of the truck," Dan said. "But with Maggie playing mother hen, even I'll give those chains a run for their money." Then, in a more serious tone, he asked, "What about you two? I hope you found what you were seeking."

Megan rested her cheek against Dan's shoulder. "We did."

Chloe hugged Dan and nodded against his other shoulder.

"That makes me happy," he said, for a heartbeat fantasizing Anna and Georgia were embracing him.

"I bet Jacob didn't hug you goodbye," Chloe added with a final squeeze.

"Thankfully not," Dan said. "He'd have crushed me. We settled for conversation. Sort of a parting tradition."

Jacob had deposited his gear into his car before meeting Dan at the truck, assuming their customary seats.

"Had enough of Hat Creek?" Dan asked.

Jacob lifted his legs and knocked his boots together, letting the dust cloud answer for him. "Nobody will believe I got paid to fix a hole in a roof—to keep it open."

"This town does have its quirks."

"That's an understatement."

"Headed home?"

Jacob nodded. "But only long enough to pack my stuff."

"Off to the next big city, are we?"

"New York City, of course, though you probably think it foolish."

Dan shrugged. "The east coast can feel like a foreign country to Midwesterners. It's more ethnically diverse, faster-paced, impersonal—" Jacob was frowning, an expression Dan had seen before. "What?"

"I meant that Michelle isn't even my type."

Dan's eyes widened. "Ah."

Chloe poked Dan again, this time in the ribs, pulling him back into the present. "Scuttlebutt is that Jacob's off to New York City chasing tail," she said.

Dan nodded. "Straight from the horse's mouth."

Megan kicked her legs out, one after the other. "A waste of a hunk if you ask me. You should have encouraged him to give Portland a try."

"You aimed Jacob at Michelle too accurately," Dan said. "A pair of old West sharpshooters, that's what you are. But I'll make you a promise: if Jacob crashes and burns, I'll send him your way."

"Much obligin', pardner," Megan drawled. She hopped off the tailgate, Chloe following her lead. "We'd better be off."

Once Dan stood, they shared final hugs. Megan had turned full-fledged redhead, Georgia's hair tickling Dan's nose. Chloe's full-chested hug presented an incomparable experience.

"Bye, Dan," they echoed.

"Bye, and …" Dan snapped a mental photo of the pair. "If I never see you again, have good lives."

"Oh, we will," Megan said. She took Chloe's hand. "We're getting married."

"I'm happy for you," Dan said.

"Thank you," Chloe said. "We'll never forget this place, Dan. Or you."

Monogamy was a novel concept to Megan and Chloe, and they were unsure they could remain faithful. Their first glimpse of Jacob as a shared fantasy revealed more to them than could a month sequestered in Hat Creek. Michelle's propensity for loud sex prompted them to substitute the hapless Whitney in a contest to make her scream louder than Michelle. Their relationship moving forward was made clear. Marriage? Yes. Faithful? Yes. Monogamous? Hell, no.

Dan remained ignorant of Hat Creek's plunge into depravity because he was a willing participant in its fall. Late one evening, discovering that Maggie's car had a flat tire—Megan and Chloe had let the air out—Dan invited Maggie to stay, and they spent their first night together. Nights together soon became as much a habit as afternoons.

But Florence, dismissed, ignored, and all but forgotten in the fervor of mating rituals, her hearing as sharp as her eyesight was poor, heard it all: Megan and Chloe's brazen acts; Jacob and Michelle's athletic feats; Dan and Maggie's discrete dalliances. Food to her soul, the expressions of pleasure and ecstasy and completion—of vitality—had revived her, reimbuing her with the will to live, the fortitude to confess her human frailties …

and the courage to reunite with her beloved Arthur.

The Fear of Falling

Dan was unaware that the water tower's roof was too weak to support the weight of two people. When you live in a town of one, some things are unknowable.

Debbie Schmidt stated in her application that she wished to escape the big city conditions aggravating her extensive list of ailments, which included respiratory problems, headaches, sinusitis, joint pain, rashes, fatigue, and digestive issues. One word leaped to Dan's mind: hypochondriac

On a whim, he approved Debbie's stay.

Within days of her arrival, Debbie proclaimed Hat Creek everything she had hoped for. She found the air clean if a bit dusty; the water clear and, as verified by State certified documentation, pure; the noise level most satisfactory, excepting the one night an owl roosted outside her window; and the open space ideal for minimizing the spread of infectious diseases. Already, she asserted, her health had markedly improved.

Habit being what it is, Debbie refocused her finely-honed diagnostic skills on her fellow residents. Phillip Hightower's migraines, she suspected, were caused by a brain tumor. Constance Trippier's skin rash was likely lupus, stemming from a hormonal imbalance and the damp Seattle weather. Ellis Drinkwater's diabetes, Debbie insisted, could be controlled by eating more vegetables and fruits while abstaining from gluten and low-fat foods.

But she reserved her most dire prognosis for Sammi Pullman. Arriving breathless at Dan's back patio following their return from the Childress Ranch, Debbie blurted out, "Sammi is trying to—" only to hesitate when she noticed Maggie and their dinner spread.

"I'll refill our water glasses," Maggie said, carrying their glasses into the house.

"You were saying?" Dan said to Debbie.

"At first, I just thought she—Sammi—was being stupid, sticking her arm into the moving equipment. Those belts and gears could have pulled her right in. But then we caught her hanging out the hayloft. 'Careful with that door,' Mr. Childress yelled at her. 'You fall from there, and you'll break your neck.' Why else would Sammi be leaning out like that, if not to injure herself intentionally? And now she's in Hartman's, making a noose out of one of your ropes."

"A noose?"

"To hang herself with."

Dan gazed longingly at his sumptuous meal. Hypochondria, he concluded, deserved a retreat of its own.

"I'll check immediately," Dan assured her, setting down his fork.

Appeased, Debbie scurried away as Maggie reappeared. Dan picked up his fork. "Debbie claimed—"

"I heard," Maggie said, placing the water glasses on the table and retaking her seat. "That woman has a vivid imagination."

Dan couldn't argue. But still …

"Eat your dinner before it gets cold," Maggie said, reading his mind.

Much as Dan wished, he didn't share his residents' luxury of hiding from their shared nemesis. "I won't be long," he promised, standing from the table.

A quick scan inside Hartman's confirmed no hanging corpses—surprise, surprise. Dan checked the wall for missing ropes and quickly spotted the likely culprit: a twisted cotton rope hanging vertically, clumsily coiled and bound with the tight windings offset to the top end, leaving a dangling mass of loops resembling a noose. As Maggie had said, Debbie had a vivid imagination. Back to his meal.

Dan turned around and nearly ran over Sammi. At five feet tall, if that, and a hundred pounds soaking wet, he could have easily flattened her.

"You *are* in here," he said.

"I was just ... tidying up." Sammi glanced at the wall. "Helping you. That's okay, isn't it?"

"Sure."

"I'm finished, so I'll get a bite to eat." Not waiting for Dan, she left Hartman's.

Debbie roused Dan from a catnap on the park bench the following afternoon. "She's at it again."

"She?" he asked.

"Sammi. She's trying to kill herself."

Dan rubbed his face. "Your 'noose' was just a coiled rope. And how is Sammi trying to kill herself this time?"

"By poisoning herself. I discovered Sammi standing at a bench inside your tiny shack—"

"My equipment shed."

"—prying open a canister with a skull and crossbones logo printed on it."

"Rat poison," Dan said. He stretched his aching legs, wondering why Sammi was snooping around his shed. "She's helping me eradicate some rodents," he made up, quickly adding, "at a granary, miles away from here," when Debbie's eyes grew as large as saucers.

Appeased, Debbie walked off. Dan returned to slumberland.

Two days later, while Dan rushed to complete roof repairs ahead of approaching thunderstorms, he spied Debbie dart into and out of his house. Resisting the urge to duck out of sight, he waved to get Debbie's attention.

"I was right about Sammi trying to cause herself harm," she said, meeting him at the base of the ladder. "I just left her sitting at the bottom of the creek. Smack dab in the bottom. She knows about the impending floods."

"I said *possible* flooding—" A loud clap of thunder announced the storm's arrival. Large raindrops began spattering the ground, dotting the dust into tiny mud pies. Dan directed Debbie under the eaves.

"I urged Sammi to climb out before she drowned," Debbie said. "She told me to mind my own business."

Dan could conjure up a hundred simpler ways to commit suicide than sitting in the path of a potential flood, but Sammi had heard his warning about the heavy upstream rains.

And she had been messing with his poison.

Dan escorted Debbie to Grange Hall and started into a steady rain for the creek. Spotting Sammi emerging through the trees, he intersected her at the gazebo.

"Let me guess," Sammi said, her sodden hair plastered to her cheeks. "Debbie waylaid you with some nonsense about me trying to harm myself."

"I *did* warn you about possible flooding. And maybe I'm a little curious why somebody might sit in the creek bottom."

"I was fossil hunting."

"Fossil hunting?"

"A hobby of mine. Barren hillsides, gullies, embankments— anywhere the ground has eroded—are prime locations for finding exposed fossils. I was rep when Debbie found me."

Dan couldn't decide which woman owned a better imagination. Or a more pressing issue. Though Dan was unaware of Sammi's underlying circumstances and placed little faith in Debbie's wild claims, handling rat poison and sitting in creek beds weren't typical Hat Creek pastimes.

Debbie's next warning finally crossed the threshold of plausibility. She burst into the diner while Dan was orienting Hat Creek's newest residents, hustling through the dining area and into the kitchen before furtively signaling Dan to join her.

"I didn't want to frighten anybody," Debbie whispered when they were alone. "Sammi is threatening to jump off the water tower."

"Now, Debbie—"

"She's sitting on the railing. When I told her to get off, she yelled that I'd better move."

Dan excused himself and hurried outdoors, slowing to a relaxed pace when he spotted Sammi seated on the water tower catwalk, her legs dangling through the railing.

"Mind if I join you?" he called up.

Sammi shrugged. "It's your tower."

Dan managed the stairs but struggled to maneuver his legs over the catwalk's edge. "This used to be easier," he said.

Sammi ignored his banter. "Debbie sent you."

"She was afraid you were going to fall."

Sammi smirked. "She claimed I was going to jump."

A confident delivery can't trump blatant truth, so Dan nodded.

"Debbie's a busybody," Sammi said. "I told her to move because there was a rattlesnake in the grass, not four feet from where she was standing."

Dan gazed down into the weeds. "Mabel!"

"Mabel? It has a name?"

Dan shook his head. "Figure of speech. I warred with an infestation before starting Hat Creek. More people around mean they're out and about less."

Sammi looked over the town. "I'd heard you lived here alone for several years before starting Hat Creek. Traded rattlesnakes for people." She looked at Dan. "How'd that work out?"

Sammi couldn't know how profound that question was. "You tell me."

In answer, she turned her head and dropped her chin to the railing. "Dan, what's your view on suicide?"

An equally profound question. Dan considered Dr. Malkovich's recommendation on the subject, then discarded it.

"My view is that everyone is entitled to their own view. Substitute religion for suicide, and you've answered that question, too."

Dan regretted his evasion the moment Sammi lifted her head, clearly distressed.

"Sorry," he said. He had regarded the subject frequently during his long-ago westward trek. "I'm not a fan of suicide," he admitted. "To me, it feels like cheating death."

"Death cheating death. That's deep, Dan."

"Or ignorant." Dan pulled a leg onto the catwalk to face Sammi. "I *do* accept that people suffering intense, terminal pain deserve control over their lives. Denying them relief, even a remedy as radical as suicide, is inconsiderate at best, cruel at worst.

"But, in one way or another, almost everyone's life is a struggle, be it poverty, a backbreaking job, a broken family, discrimination—the list is long." Remembering Florence, Dan said: "And Sammi, it's only at the end of that long struggle, at the end of a life fully lived, that one's true worth can be judged: in the learnings passed on to the next generation; in the wrongs righted and dues paid; in the artwork painted, the music composed, the books written—"

"And the Hat Creeks rebuilt," Sammi finished for Dan. "*You*, at least, can be proud." She stared down at the ground. "I wasn't lying about the snake in the grass, Dan."

"I believe you."

"But it disappeared before Debbie arrived." Sammi dropped her head back to the railing and said in a tiny voice, "I can't face tomorrow, Dan."

"What happens tomorrow?"

"I mean every tomorrow." She placed her hand to her chest. "I'm filled with dread, a sense of impending doom, a pressure that never goes away. Ever. Some days the anxiety attacks are so severe that I can't get out of bed, and I'm tired and worn out." She gazed out over Hat Creek. "That's why I came here. I was hoping that since there's nothing here, there would be nothing to fear around the next corner."

"But instead, you found only the same 'next day?'" Dan asked.

Sammi nodded. "Nobody will notice that I'm gone. I'll never write a book, cure cancer, or"—she threw her arm out—"rebuild an entire town. I found the poison in your shed but decided, no, maybe I'd fly just once."

Dan maintained a formal protocol for residents exhibiting suicidal tendencies. Sammi's appeared scripted rather than genuine attempts at physical harm, knowing the resident busybody would report to Dan. Accordingly, Dan judged Sammi's suicide risk level to be moderate, at worst. His job was to be a good listener. Once Sammi talked herself out, he'd remind her of the various resources at her disposal and remain vigilant, calling the crisis center directly if necessary.

In the meantime, Dan would wield Hat Creek. Experience had taught him that most Hat Creek residents suffered a reasonable or rational fear, a phobia. Dan doubted that the Fear of What's Next appeared on any lists, but it would serve his needs.

Now remembering his conversation with Cici while sitting in this very spot, Dan scanned his town for the proper "tool." When his gaze settled on the ridge west of town, Sammi's escapade in the creek bottom gave him an idea. "Do you know what's beyond that ridge?" he asked, pointing over Hartman's.

Sammi shook her head.

"Are you afraid to find out?" he asked. "Are you afraid of *that* future?"

When Sammi didn't respond, Dan stood and encouraged her to stand. "Follow me," he said.

Dan walked Sammi around the catwalk to the ladder welded onto the tower's back side. "Up, if you're curious. Step onto the roof and away from the ladder. I'll follow."

Sammi scaled the ladder and stepped onto the gently sloping roof as confidently as a mountain goat on a rocky cliff. Whatever fears Sammi may suffer, a fear of heights was not one of them.

"What an amazing view!" she marveled, even her light steps causing the sheet metal to flex and pop.

Dan joined Sammi, the roof whining about his added weight, and pointed at a silver reflection to the east. "That's the corrugated roof of the Casper Ranch barn. On a clear day, you can spot two other ranches." Climbing higher and turning, he said, "And our view to the west over the ridge—"

"Ravines!" Sammi said. "Did you know that Sue, the famous t-rex fossil, was discovered just north of here?"

"I did," Dan said. "Can't promise you the same success, but I suggest you wait a day or two for the ground to dry out and grab yourself a spade."

"You can count on it."

"The point I'm trying to make, Sammi, is that very few futures are scary. Many"—he gestured toward Sammi's future dig site—"are exciting and surprising. The rest are boringly mundane."

"I'll try to remember."

Sammi pointed to the extended horizon. "And, what's over that *next* ridge?"

Dan hummed. "That's the entrance to a long valley of rolling hills covered in endless stretches of golden grasses, not a hint of humanity."

"Sounds like my kind of place."

"I've long harbored a dream of hiking down that valley." Dan flexed an aching knee. "The opportunity, I fear, has passed me by."

"I don't know," Sammi said. "I still see it in your future."

"Your vision must be sharper than mine. And speaking of vision, we'd better get down from here before Debbie spots us and decides we're tandem jumping."

Sammi's next step was her last. The sheet metal roofing tore open with a metallic ripping sound and a machine-gun burst of exploding rivets, and a large section of the roof peeled back to reveal the dark, deep water below.

They fell.

With Sammi's scream echoing in Dan's ears, a jagged metal shard pierced his upper arm and swung him in an arc, slicing through his flesh like a fillet knife to plunge him face-up into the water. Battling intense pain, Dan surfaced and used his good arm to swim to the inside ladder. Grasping the ladder rail, he stepped on a rung to raise himself and tend his injured arm.

Dan's arm hung limply, open to the bone, blood gushing in spurts into the water. Already going into shock, he sagged against the ladder and shook his head to fight tunnel vision. Sammi bobbed to the surface and playfully squirted a mouthful of water into the air before submerging again.

Sammi surfaced closer and laughed. "Who could have predicted *that* future?" But her smile disappeared when she noticed the bloodstained water. "One of us is bleeding—Dan! Your arm!"

She swam to his side. "We need a tourniquet."

Dan's pain was already receding, belonging to someone else. He could barely feel his good hand and had to focus on maintaining his grip on the rung. If he slipped off and Sammi tried to catch him, he'd surely pull her underwater.

"Save yourself," he slurred, leaning off the ladder to let her climb past him.

"Don't move!" Sammi yelled, pinning him to the ladder. She reached a hand into the water and momentarily lifted her belt into view. After looping it around Dan's upper arm and knotting it, she pulled with all her might, screaming with exertion.

"That stopped most of the bleeding," she said. "Now we have to get you out of here—Stay with me!" she yelled when Dan started slumping.

"Too late," he muttered, his lips almost too numb to form words.

"I'm not going to let my foolishness get you killed!" Sammi yelled back. "Now, let's climb out."

Her words started running together, "Standonarung," and Dan could no longer pay attention. Form and color squeezed down to a small circle surrounded by formless fog. He was satisfied to watch the world wink out of existence.

"Dan!" Muffled.

"Dan. Dan," the words fading.

A sharp, stinging sensation and sudden clarity. Desperate, beady eyes staring from up close.

"Dan!" Sammi screamed. She slapped his face again. "I can't lift you out! You have to help me! Dan, listen to me. You! Have! To! Help!"

Dan reached for the next ladder rung and pulled.

Dan awoke to a medley of soft chimes. He lay semi-reclined under an antiseptic white sheet, his arm concealed to the wrist in layers of medical wrappings. An IV tube trailed away from his other forearm, and a nasal cannula hissed oxygen into his nose. Maggie slept curled up in a soft chair in the corner of the room.

Dan was saddened to tears. He had woken up. His family hadn't.

Maggie was seated at Dan's bedside the next time he awoke. She carefully kissed him on the lips as if they, too, had been injured in the fall.

"Welcome back," she said.

Dan was almost too afraid to ask. "Sammi?"

Maggie smiled. "Alive and well. And a hero." She chuckled. "Debbie, too. She knew what to do until the ambulance arrived. Debbie also shares your blood type. You survived off her transfusions while the ambulance rushed you here."

Sammi remained in Hat Creek throughout Dan's convalescence, helping wherever she could. She enlisted a fellow resident to teach her the basics of camping, after which she established a solitary campsite west of Hat Creek, spending days at a stretch excavating the ravines. Starting with these ventures, Sammi developed an effective isolation therapy for whenever life's pressures threatened to overwhelm her.

As Dan watched Sammi depart on one of her treks, her efforts at overcoming her fear of the future inspired him that he had within him the strength to face his past.

Some Things You Never Forget

Jasper Mann rolled into Hat Creek clad in a sleeveless black leather vest and matching chaps, heavy black boots, fingerless gloves, and a red bandana wrapped around his helmetless head. With his bulbous, weather-beaten nose, a scruffy gray beard that nearly matched the length of his braided ponytail braid, and colorfully tattooed arms and neck, Hat Creek's first resident biker fit the part to a tee.

Jasper's ride, however, didn't match the same standards. Sure, black leather saddlebags hung on either side of the chromed frame, but …

"I was unaware Harley built mobility scooters," Dan said in jest.

Jasper rested his wire-rim shades atop his head, assuming every bit the seventy-five years in age he'd listed on his application, and rapped a knuckle on the metal frame. "This is an Adept Elite. Full five-hundred-watt motor, fifty miles on a charge; hits fifteen miles per hour on a smooth straightaway—" He noticed Dan glance at the white van parked off the blacktop south of town. "Oops, I forgot about the shuttle van. Just as motorcycles are out of my league, so too is riding cross country."

Jasper backed the electric scooter in a tight one-eighty and sent the van away with a wave of his arm. "Though I'm delivered to my destinations, I always drive into town under my own power. It's a pride thing."

"Know what you mean," Dan said.

Dan started in the opposite direction while the van performed a slow y-turn, Jasper rolling beside him. "I'm putting you up in our boarding house," Dan said, nodding ahead of them.

Jasper cackled at his accommodation. "A fitting place to stick me," he said

"The hole in the roof is just for show," Dan assured him. "At least that's my official story."

When they reached the access ramp landing, Dan pointed out Westside. "Our diner. Take your time unpacking, and then join me for coffee—"

"I'll just dump my bags," Jasper said quickly. "We can head over together."

"That'll work, too."

Jasper rejoined Dan minutes later at the bottom of the ramp. They reached the blacktop in time to meet a line of northbound Harleys, and Jasper pointed at one of the passing machines while greeting the riders. "I owned a Softtail similar to that one," he yelled to Dan. "I eventually traded it in for a Road King. Easier on the old bones."

Jasper waited for the roar to subside. "Get many bikers through?"

"Feast or famine," Dan said as they continued toward Westside. "A constant stream these first two weeks each August— Sturgis, of course. Just the occasional single or group the remainder of the year."

"They're headed to the rally via the Needles Highway," Jasper said. "It's a great ride. I attended Sturgis over thirty years in a row."

"Dedicated man. Means you likely rode through here."

"It's possible." Jasper looked all around, "If I did, though, I don't remember."

"Not much to remember," Dan admitted.

"I've traveled all of the major trails," Jasper boasted. "Route 66, Pacific Coast Highway, Great River Road. I took to the road full-time after my divorce, but my body started falling apart a few years ago, and I could no longer handle a bike. Hell, I can't manage twenty steps. I'm a disciple of the lifestyle, though, so I traded in my Harley for a model more my speed." He patted his scooter again. "Most rallies I attend in person, but Sturgis is too rough to navigate at baby speed. Hat Creek was the closest place I could find."

The sun had risen before Dan finished installing the new circuit breaker. After replacing his tools in his shed, he noticed Jasper sitting on his scooter facing the park at the Brule Street bend. Dan walked the length of the rut road and joined him.

"Out for an early ride, Jasper?"

"Good morning, Dan. In truth, I was headed for breakfast but took a wrong turn. You have a lovely little park tucked back here."

Dan pictured Jasper's navigational error. "You turned left at the bottom of the ramp instead of right."

Jasper nodded. "You did show me that. I must have been sleep-driving."

"I was just on my way to breakfast, myself," Dan said. "Care to join me?"

"Sure." Jasper steered his scooter onto one of the ruts while Dan walked the other.

"Your son called last evening," Dan said.

"I'm not surprised. I bet Blaine asked if I was having trouble getting around."

"Something like that."

"He thinks I can't care for myself just because I'm old.

He's as meddlesome as my ex."

Cici Decker departed Hat Creek as a timid teenager lacking self-esteem. She returned with the swagger of a confident young woman. Long golden braids replaced her short black hair, and she had traded her frumpy clothing for understated style.

"Dan tells me you started your own company," Maggie said.

"Decker Performance Coaching," Cici said, facing Dan and Maggie across Dan's coffee table. "We're an executive coaching firm."

"Catchy name."

"Brand recognition. Though I didn't wish to follow in my parents' footsteps, I figured many driven people *did*. And who better than a Decker to teach the Decker method? And speaking of news, Dan tells me you reconciled with your daughter."

Maggie nodded. "A dream came true. Elizabeth invited me to Tucson, where I spent three wonderful weeks with her and Christian and the grandchildren."

"Two grandchildren, isn't it?"

"Yes. Aiden is six and tall for his age, already playing baseball and soccer, and an avid reader. Leanne turns three in a week, never sits still, and loves wearing dresses nearly as much as stealing her brother's toys."

"They sound like treasures." Cici turned to Dan. "Hat Creek looks no worse for wear." She chuckled at her little joke. "Are you still knee-deep in hidden projects, or have you smartened up and farmed out the heavy labor?"

"Hah!" Maggie said. She pulled Dan's sleeve up and showed Cici his latest wound.

Cici gasped.

"We almost lost Dan this time," Maggie said. "But he still won't listen to me. Maybe *you* can beat some sense into his head."

Dan rolled his sleeve down. "Can't afford to hire contractors." He lifted a sheet of paper off the coffee table. "This is the wonderful news our jubilant grandmother delivered today, a property tax lien for the reclassification of Hartman's and Westside as public buildings rather than homes. Todd filed the corrections the moment he discovered the errors."

"Can you appeal?"

"I *will* appeal, and I'll get some relief. That's how the system works." Dan blew out a breath. "But Todd is killing me. Forcing me to upgrade the water filtration system, dredge the holding pond, install ADA-compliant ramps up to Hartman's and Grange Hall, bury the water pipes deeper, install a tornado warning siren—and test the stupid thing once a month! And now this. I'm toast if Todd ever discovers that Grange Hall is multi-unit housing."

Cici wrinkled her face. "I suddenly feel guilty for freeloading."

"Don't you dare," Maggie said.

"My sentiments exactly," Dan said. "I do have a favor to ask, though."

"Anything."

"How are you on a bicycle?"

Cici patted her stomach and laughed. "Mine hibernates in my closet. It's never bucked me off, though. What's the favor?"

"A new resident rode Harleys until health problems confined him to an electric scooter. However, Jasper is still a card-carrying HOG member and has been taking off on long rides."

"Cross country?" Cici asked. "On an electric scooter?"

"It's more capable than it looks. Anyway, yesterday Jasper got lost on the road west of town."

"He got lost on a flat stretch of road?"

Dan nodded. "Entered a pasture through an open gate

but couldn't remember which way he turned in, nothing but a flat road as far as he could see. A passing ranch pointed him in the right direction.

"Despite his ordeal, Jasper is planning another trip for tomorrow, and I'd rather not need to send out a rescue party. I was wondering if you might accompany him."

"Count me in," Cici said.

The seasoned cottonwood burned hot in the fire pit, wafting ephemeral orange lanterns into the star-filled sky, a fitting tribute to the pig-roast Dan had thrown in celebration of Cici and Maggie's triumphant returns.

Dan stood to address his residents, beer in hand. "I am officially convening the first-ever Hat Creek War Council. Evil Inspector Todd will invade Hat Creek again in two weeks, brandishing his deadly clipboard and sharpened pencil to wreak economic destruction through petty codes administration, arbitrary standards enforcement, and misapplied regulations. He has already inflicted irreparable damage, costing me money and effort that I'd rather invest in this retreat. So, unless we formulate a plan to neutralize this threat, Hat Creek will go bankrupt." Dan extended his beer can. "The very future of this fine town and retreat is at stake."

Jenny Fitzpatrick, who had arrived unannounced in her wedding dress, minus the wedding ring, flew to her feet. "How dare he! I say we hire a hitman to take him out."

"Whoa! Whoa! Whoa!" Dan said. "Somebody corral that loose cannon." An arm emerged from the darkness and pulled Jenny back to her log seat. "Jenny is in no condition to contribute to this conversation. Hand that woman another beer." A hand extended to deliver a chilled can.

"Is this inspector married?" a more suitably inebriated

Cici asked.

"I'm unsure of his marital status," Dan answered.

"What a ridiculous question," Jenny said, popping the beer can tab. "What kind of woman would tolerate such a beast?"

"I was going to suggest we find him a wife," Cici said. "Perhaps he'd mellow out a little."

"Interesting angle," Dan said. "And just where do you propose finding this wife?"

"We could advertise for one," Claire Dubois blurted out in her adorable French accent. Hat Creek's most-ever intriguing resident, Claire had been secreted to Hat Creek from Lyon, France, by her father, Jean-Claude, to prevent his "free-spirited" daughter from derailing his election chances.

And a free spirit Claire had indeed turned out to be. She was Hat Creek's first underage drunk, first nude sunbather, and first would-be bull rider. Fortunately for her, the bull didn't headbutt her or stand still long enough for her to climb on.

"Or hold a contest!" Jessica Kunitz offered. The fraternal triplet to a pair of identical triplets, she had always felt like the outsider. The thirtieth consecutive birthday party with identically dressed siblings had left her depressed. "They're all the rage these days."

"All in all, an intriguing idea," Dan said. "And one I think needs further fleshing out. I particularly like the angle of distracting our adversary. What other plans are percolating out there?"

"How about disabling his truck?" Elliot Spitzer said. On his Hat Creek application, Elliot had written, "I live in Cleveland." Reason enough. "Hide a nail strip in the road to puncture his tires, shove a potato up his tailpipe, or steal his spark plug wires."

"Which would strand our Evil Inspector *in* Hat Creek."

"Oh, right."

"Unless we sneak into his previous stop and disable him there," Cici offered.

"Now the idea has merit," Dan said.

"I have a suggestion," Jasper said, rolling forward into the firelight. "You'll think it's harebrained but hear me out. Dan, have you ever considered inviting this Todd to dinner?"

Jasper weathered a chorus of inebriated boos. "Inspecting is a thankless job," he said. "I learned that firsthand as a building contractor. We despised the inspectors because they cost us time and money. But face it, they served the owners of the buildings, not us. Inspectors keep our buildings and bridges standing, our water clean and food safe, and our airplanes flying. I know it cost Dan a small fortune to build those ramps into his buildings, but the ADA-compliant logo on Dan's webpage caught my attention when searching for a place to stay during Sturgis.

"I'm just saying, Dan, that if you treat Todd as a friend, maybe he'll treat you as one."

Into the lingering silence, Jenny belched.

Cici pedaled to Westside on a silver Schwinn dressed in full "biker chic" regalia: a sleeveless black shirt worn as a vest over a cropped white tee-shirt, black pants, a bright pink bandana tied around her forehead, dark sunglasses covering her eyes, and cotton gardening gloves cut fingerless.

"Helen Wheels!" Jasper exclaimed, hobbling out of the diner with Dan. "Who needs Sturgis?"

Cici laughed. "Are we ready to roll?"

"Raring to go." Jasper dug through his pants pockets. "Just need the key." His hands froze, still hidden. "Huh."

"Is it already in the switch?" Dan asked.

"No," Jasper said, though he checked anyway. He paused before climbing onto the scooter. "Oh." He patted his chest once before looking down at his white T-shirt. "I seem to have forgotten my vest inside, too."

"I'll get it for you," Dan said.

Three days later, with a second afternoon trip accompanied by Cici under his belt, Jasper secured the saddlebags and straddled his scooter. The same white van that had delivered him to Hat Creek idled just off the road north of town.

"I'm glad you chose to stay with us," Dan said. "Where are you headed next?"

Jasper eyed Dan warily. "Blaine called again, didn't he?"

Dan nodded.

"And he told you."

"He said you have Alzheimer's."

"Middle stage," Jasper admitted. "Doesn't surprise you, does it."

"It does explain a few things."

"And what did you tell Blaine?"

"That I hadn't noticed any outward signs."

Jasper nodded gratitude and dropped onto the padded seat. He looked at Grange Hall and the water tower, then in the opposite direction toward the cabins and the park. "I must have ridden through here numerous times," he said, shaking his head. "You'd think I'd remember."

Jasper looked up at Dan and sighed. "We're meant to live our life accumulating memories to sustain us in old age. They offer reassurance that we lived a good life and allow us to face death without fear or regret." Jasper's eyes glassed over. "But I'm doomed to a future without memories. Someday, I'll notice my tattoos and my leathers and wonder why I wear them, with no recollection of the miles I've traveled, the acquaintances I've made"—he swiveled his head to take in Hat Creek one last time—"nor of the sights I've seen. I can't imagine a sadder retreat from life."

Jasper shrugged off his melancholy with a defiant head shake, lowered his sunglasses, and turned the key switch. "But that day isn't here yet. While I still retain any dregs of sanity, I'm staying on the road." He flashed a wry smile. "For me, traveling *is* life."

Jasper extended his hand. Dan squeezed it, trying to forget that it was the weakened handshake of someone with Alzheimer's.

"As far as you know," Jasper said, "I'm headed north into Montana."

Dan nodded. "Got it. And good luck."

Dan watched the scooter roll up the road, suppressing a pang of envy for Jasper's plight. Dan knew that the reverse could also be true, that some memories are nightmares you wished you *could* forget. But when Blaine called the following day, Dan had no qualms covering for the old biker.

One week later, Dan and Maggie hosted Todd and his lovely wife Alexa for a cookout. The Sterners brought their signature baked beans, a home-baked apple pie … and their twin daughters, Hailey and Hannah.

The little girls treated Hat Creek as a giant playground. They played hopscotch on the old church slab, climbed the water tower and circled the catwalk, took turns yelling at the top of their lungs from inside the Studio, played hide and seek in Hartman's, threw pebbles into the creek, and snacked on apple slices in the gazebo.

Deep into the evening, after grilling hotdogs and roasting

s'mores, Dan carried a dozing Hailey to the Sterner's car while Todd carried her sister. Stealing one last peek at the pair before closing the door, Dan finally understood that all memories, even the bad ones, are too precious to relinquish.

Jasper Mann's road trip dead-ended ten months later in a southern California residential cul-de-sac, the scooter battery drained, its driver lost and incoherent.

CHAPTER 31

Dan didn't recognize the maroon compact turning onto Brule Street. But Hat Creek's newest visitor knew enough to park amongst the junkers, implying a former resident.

Jacob stepped from the car and treated Hat Creek to the same display that had sent Megan and Chloe into such a tizzy. After a final stretch, he closed the car door and walked around two others to Dan's truck, raising a cloud of dust when he dropped the tailgate. Not just stopping by to say hello, then.

Dan stepped off the Grange Hall's steps to greet Jacob, predicting the young man's complaint: the roommate who skipped out without paying rent; his place of employment closing without warning; the exorbitant cost of living. Knowing Jacob possessed the physical stamina to hold down three jobs, Dan suspected Jacob's restless streak was the real issue. He'd lasted two years in Denver, then two-plus years in Chicago. He had departed Hat Creek fast on Michelle's heels two summers ago.

Michelle's yearly Hat Creek pilgrimages kept Dan in more frequent contact with the subject of Jacob's obsession. Just two months ago, Dan had eavesdropped on her phone conversation with Jacob discussing apartments. Now Jacob arrives unannounced and directly takes a seat on the tailgate. Relationship troubles, instead?

Defeatist thinking. Dan entertained the probability that Jacob was gainfully employed and permanently settled and that his relationship with Michelle was rock solid—

A sturdy weed tripped Dan up as if to scold him for conjuring such a fairytale. "Head in the clouds," he admitted aloud.

He glanced at the rear bumper of Jacob's car in passing. An older model with numerous dings and dents, New York plates. Not a rental. Jacob had driven cross-country.

Jacob turned his head as Dan neared. "I spotted you in the middle of repairs when I drove in."

Dan raised a sticky finger. "I'd like to shake the hand of the person who invented gray caulking. Sealant, adhesive, bug repellant, and sound deadener, all in one, a ghost town's duct tape."

Jacob's deadpan stare suggested Dan could dispense with the pleasantries.

"And how's the Big Apple treating you?" Dan asked lightly, taking a seat.

Jacob huffed with a wry smile.

"Not good, huh," Dan said needlessly. Jacob didn't look so good himself: bloodshot eyes, limp hair, rumpled clothing, a two-day stubble; he even smelled stale.

"Drive straight through?" Dan guessed.

"Yes."

"Last I knew," Dan said, "airplanes flew out of both JFK

and LaGuardia."

Jacob tossed a dirt clod into the weeds. "I needed time to think."

Dan nodded. Solo drives provided plenty of thinking time.

"Do *you* see anything wrong with me?" Jacob asked.

Dan recognized a rhetorical question when he heard one and remained silent.

"I'm no slouch," Jacob said, poking a finger into his chest. "I take care of myself. I hit the gym every morning, even after working past two a.m. the previous night. I dare her to find anyone half the man I am.

"And what's so special about a college degree? I work hard and—and!—I work steadily. Sure, when a better job comes along, I jump at it. But I shouldn't have 'career' constantly thrown in my face.

"And, for another matter, there's no such thing as a 'right crowd.' So what if I enjoy letting loose with buddies and having fun for fun's sake. Silly, stupid, or otherwise, that's the point."

Jacob dropped his head and sighed sadly. "And I could have done without her going public with everything."

"You and Michelle have a big blow-up?" Dan asked.

"Hah!" Jacob pulled a velvet ring box from his pants pocket and handed it to Dan. "I asked her to marry me."

Dan opened the box to reveal an impressive brilliant-cut diamond solitaire mounted to a simple gold band. No mistaking Jacob's sincerity.

"I worked two jobs and survived on Ramen noodles for six months to afford that ring," Jacob said.

Dan tilted the box to induce a prismatic play of color through the stone's facets. "Michelle turn you down?"

Jacob shook his head and retrieved the ring. "She said she had to think it over."

"Bummer."

"Worse," Jacob said. He closed the box and shoved it back into his pocket. "Afterward, she blabbed the whole scene to everyone, as if they were supposed to be impressed with her self-control."

"*Portrait of a Lady*," Dan muttered.

"Huh?"

Dan shook his head. "A classic novel."

"And how did that one end?"

"You don't want to know. What did you do next?"

"I drove here."

"You drove here." Or ran away again. For Jacob's sake, Dan hoped it was the former rather than the latter.

"I first considered tossing the ring into the river," Jacob said. "But imagining it disappearing beneath the water helped me realize I wasn't giving up so easily. So, I jumped into my car, hoping a long drive would clear my mind. Instead?" He leaned back and planted the heels of his hands onto the tailgate. "All I know is that Michelle didn't say yes, but she didn't say no. Beyond that?" Jacob shrugged his shoulders.

Dan looked down at his makeshift advice booth. Jacob *hadn't* been running away—a healthy sign.

As if reading Dan's mind, Jacob asked, "What am I supposed to do now?"

I helped a young man, Dan remembered. *We share a unique bond. Not as father-son or close friends; instead, the bond that righted Jacob's path and founded this place, a connection of compassion and respect.* Dan looked at the young man seated beside him. *If I could outfit Jacob for his most important venture yet, for once propelling Jacob onto a one-way trip, that would count for much.*

"Help me understand a couple of things," Dan said. "You surprised Michelle with your proposal, didn't you?"

"Yes."

"Had you two discussed marriage?"

Jacob frowned. "Not openly."

"Yet you expected Michelle to accept your proposal?"

"Of course. Otherwise, I wouldn't have bought the ring and popped the question. I know Michelle loves me. We're planning on living together."

Love, sharing a bedroom, yet unprepared for marriage. Perhaps Michelle feared Jacob's display was impetuous, that his amorous feelings would cool off. Conversely, she might be uncertain as to the fidelity of *her* feelings. Then there was the elephant in the room, otherwise known as a career. Jacob's complaint about Michelle's narrow definition countered Michelle's dissatisfaction with Jacob's indifference to settle on one. And work ethic was just one facet of the pair's unconventional relationship. Dan knew Michelle's colleagues derided Jacob's blue-collar roots. Dan doubted Michelle's intellect scored Jacob any points with his crowd, either.

Looking into Jacob's expectant gaze, though, Dan knew it wasn't his place to voice doubts. His marriage to Grace, a classic case of beauty and the beast, had flourished. So why not a similarly mismatched marriage between Jacob and Michelle?

"We both know Michelle doesn't share your enthusiasm for adventure," Dan said. "I'd bet money you're moving too fast, and it's making her skittish. Have you invested enough into your relationship to assure Michelle that your commitment is genuine and lasting? "

Jacob moaned in frustration. "Why is it so hard for everyone to believe I love Michelle?"

Dan would never forget Jacob's open-mouthed stare that first time Michelle sauntered past him. And Jacob's lighthearted mocking of Michelle's aspirations all these years didn't fool

Dan. Jacob had found himself a keeper and was acting to consolidate his position.

"You tell your friends where they can shove their constant ribbing, don't you?" Dan said. "Probably remind them that Michele has more brains than all of them put together."

Jacob smiled and nodded.

"My wife was a one-in-a-million find, too," Dan said. Let Jacob bask in that comparison. "And as it was for me, you're past caring about the naysayers' opinions. After all, you picked out the ring and popped the question."

Jacob sat up straighter as if Dan's words had shed an oppressive weight. Dan's assessment was spot-on.

"What are you, Jacob? Six-four, two-twenty? And bench press three hundred?"

"Three-fifty. Three seventy-five on a good day."

"Impressive. I'm certain Michelle feels physically secure in your presence. She needs to sense the same emotional security in your relationship."

That was a comparison Jacob could grasp, if only tenuously. Strengthening a love life wasn't as simple as adding weights to a barbell.

"You drove here seeking my advice," Dan said, "so here it is: Firstly, don't run away from the issue. Michelle will interpret that as a lack of resolve."

"Was driving here a mistake?" Jacob asked.

"No," Dan said emphatically. "Michelle knows that both of you are welcome in Hat Creek for any reason. But leaving here, Jacob, drive straight back home. No stopovers at your friends or former girlfriends; nowhere. Got it?"

Jacob nodded.

"And once you return, be considerate to a fault of Michelle's needs. I don't mean groveling; weakness never wears well. I mean patience and consistency. And talk. Talk everything out."

"Did *you* have to jump through so many hoops?" Jacob complained.

"To convince Grace to marry me?" Dan shook his head, humming at remembered happenstance. "No. Ours was a chance encounter, and we hit it off immediately. And who knows? Maybe Michelle is wringing her hands this very minute, wishing she could turn back the clock and say, 'yes.'"

Jacob eyed him dubiously.

"It's possible," Dan said. "You're quite a catch, yourself."

Jacob laughed. "Damn right!"

A green grasshopper landed on Jacob's thigh and flicked its antennae. "Michelle claimed that a plague of locusts had invaded Hat Creek," Jacob said.

The pesky insects dotted the nearby weeds. "Definitely a bumper crop this year—"

A second grasshopper landed atop the first, leaving no doubt about its intent.

"Go ahead," Jacob told the amorous pair. "Rub it in." He brushed them off onto the ground. "Dan, the oddest things happen in this town."

"Nature calls," Dan said with a chuckle. "Speaking of which, are you hungry?"

"Always."

Jacob started back for New York City immediately after dinner over Dan's objection that there was a clear distinction between devotion and foolhardy.

CHAPTER 32

A car door opened and closed outside Dan's house, and muffled footsteps sounded in the weeds. Dan leaned back in his office chair to greet his visitor. When nobody knocked, he stood and walked to his front window. A cherry-red Ford mid-size was parked just off the pavement, Colorado plates, its cooling engine ticking like a metronome, its driver nowhere in view.

Dan stepped outdoors and immediately spotted a young woman strolling along the shoulder of the road, her head swiveling side to side, searching rather than sightseeing.

"Looking for someone?" Dan called out, though he already knew the answer: a handsome young man six-foot-four-inches tall, capable of bench pressing three hundred fifty pounds, three seventy-five on a good day.

Michelle reversed directions. "Is he here?"

Her shoulders slumped when Dan shook his head.

"But he was," Dan said with a chuckle. "He left late last evening."

Relief swept over Michelle's face. Such telling reactions. Michelle hadn't known Jacob's destination; she had only hoped it was Hat Creek. What's more, her presence revealed the desire to meet Jacob face-to-face. Promising developments, Dan decided.

Michelle reached Dan's side. "Did Jacob tell you …" she started, pausing at the crux of the matter.

"His side of the story?" Dan finished. "Yes. And he showed me the diamond."

"And then …"

Dan couldn't help but chuckle again. Love had sapped Jacob's confidence and Michelle's eloquence. For entertainment value, the pair was hard to beat.

"Jacob headed straight back home after dinner," Dan said. "I suggested he grab a hotel room for the night."

Michelle didn't look so fresh herself, though Dan suspected mental fatigue. He also guessed she would prefer a table in Westside over the tailgate. "Can I interest you in a cup of coffee?"

"I'd love one."

They turned for the diner.

"Jacob and I usually meet for breakfast at a diner close to campus," Michelle said. "I figured he was either upset or giving me space when he didn't show up the morning after his proposal. I became concerned when Jacob didn't stop by my apartment that evening or show up yesterday morning, finally takiing the subway to his apartment when he wouldn't return my messages." They stepped into Westside. "Jacob had taken off the day before, telling his roommate only that he was headed west. I figured … well, you know what I figured.

"And here you are."

"And here I am."

Dan exchanged quick greetings with the few residents inside the diner before filling his coffee cup and joining Michelle at the small table closest to the window.

"Can I ask a couple of questions?" Michelle asked.

"Of course."

"Jacob was moving back home the first time we met. What happened in Denver?"

So, Michelle's concern was stability. Not knowing how much Jacob had told Michelle, Dan decided friendly truth was the best course.

"Jacob left home for Denver ill-prepared to make it on his own," Dan said. "He was making a much better go of it in Chicago until a certain finger"—Dan wiggled his mended digit—"and a certain lady"—he pointed it at Michelle—"beckoned."

Dan's answer gave Michelle pause. She took an exaggerated swallow of her coffee.

"How did Jacob find Hat Creek in the first place?" she asked.

Dan was confident Michelle knew nothing of Jacob's teenaged visit. "Jacob stopped by on a road trip with a friend—or was it two?" Dan assumed a believable frown. "Jacob remembered passing through here as a little kid."

"A *road trip*? Wasn't Jacob all of fifteen years old?"

"Rural boys grow up faster."

"You're telling me." Michelle emptied a creamer into her cup and stirred her coffee. "What did Jacob tell you when he got here?"

Dan laughed. "That as a kid, he'd thought I was a ghost. Said I'd startled him so badly that he dove for the floorboard."

Michelle shook her head. "I meant yesterday."

"Oh." Dan rubbed his freshly shaved chin. Maggie was

returning in a couple of hours, and yesterday's stubble wouldn't do. "In a nutshell, Jacob defended himself as husband material and chafed at your reluctance."

Michelle placed the spoon on the saucer. "I *do* have the right, you know—to think it over. We're talking about my future, after all. I still have years of schooling, Jacob hardly earns enough to support himself—"

Dan held up his hands. "I'm not arguing."

Michelle picked up her coffee cup but set it down without taking a sip. "Do you think Jacob is serious?"

"A lesser woman would have fainted at the sight of that diamond."

"You know what I mean. About the important issues; love and commitment, family and career."

Dan laughed at her. "You think Jacob lifts weights for fun? Staying in shape, holding down multiple jobs, spending a boatload of cash on that ring. Those are Jacob's way of competing against the other men in your life."

Watching Michelle absorb his words, Dan guessed Jacob had rushed his proposal, fearing the superior intellect of Michelle's colleagues.

"With all sincerity," Dan said, "I'm too far removed to answer your question satisfactorily. I can tell you that Jacob was distraught that you didn't accept his proposal. And he *did* drive all the way here seeking advice."

Dan sipped at his coffee. "And now, to the point that *your* feelings on the subject are equally relevant."

Michelle downed a quick swallow of coffee as if it were a stiff drink. "Our relationship is like a roller coaster ride. The ups are terrific. Jacob is fun-loving and exciting, forever plucking me from my narrow, insular world: sunrise walks through Central Park, weekends away in the mountains, clandestine trespasses onto skyscraper rooftops, riding the trains just to tour the stations. The quiet times are nice, too: sharing a lounge seat at the movie theater, dining at tiny ethnic restaurants, curling up together after a hectic day.

"Then the ride gets bumpier. Jacob has little tolerance for serious matters. He avoids deep discussions like the plague and seems incapable of thoughtful consideration. Worse, he's forever trying to 'rescue' me from my studies.

"Invariably, our relationship speeds downhill. Unsurprisingly, Jacob's antics don't go over well with my friends, especially when he mocks them as 'shrinks-in-training.' In return, Jacob gets defensive when I encourage him to find a vocation that interests him and stick to it.

"And that's when I start doubting us." Michelle stared out the window, fingering her coffee cup. "That's when I start doubting myself." She looked across the table at Dan and raised her eyebrows. "I have few assets to compete with the short skirts and heels constantly flirting with Jacob."

Rhetorical statements were flying thick and fast. Dan posed as a store mannequin.

"So, I break up with Jacob," Michelle said. "The ride rolls to a stop, and my life returns to normal. I don't have to suffer Jacob embarrassing me, listen to my friends mock him, or endure the latest nickname Jacob's friends have stuck on me. I can concentrate on my studies without distraction.

"And I'm happier."

Michelle sipped her coffee and frowned. "Happier for a couple of weeks, until my simpler life morphs into my former pedestrian life, and I can't sleep or concentrate on my studies because Jacob is *not* there. Oh, I fight it, try to deny that's the real reason, try to convince myself that I don't miss Jacob's spontaneity, surprise, companionship—" She blushed. "Okay, so I'm no different than those short skirts. Just the sight of Jacob starts my heart racing and my palms sweating. And when he holds me? In front of everybody?"

"Beauty is in the eye of the beholder," Dan said lightly.

"What do you mean?" Michelle asked.

"I can promise you that Jacob is fully conscious of what he's doing and of whom he's choosing."

That prospect pleased Michelle. "Jacob despises my college set and hates our functions even more." Her expression softened. "But he *does* seem proud that I'm pursuing a PhD."

"There you go."

"And Jacob never flirts back or hints that I should be someone I'm not." Michelle let the aura of respect linger.

She shrugged her shoulders and cradled her coffee cup in her hands. "So, I make up with Jacob. We strap ourselves into our seats, and off we go again.

"I recognize the symptoms of addiction, Dan. But do I love Jacob? Isn't *love* the prerequisite for marriage? And, love *or* addiction, what about this track record I have of dumping him?"

With a wry smile, she said, "Jacob and I aren't exactly two peas-in-a-pod, are we?"

Dan shook his head. "I don't even think you're both peas."

Michelle huffed.

"Sorry," Dan said.

Michelle shook her head. "Don't be. It's the predominant view."

She stared out the window again before looking at Dan. "Can I ask another question?"

"Ask away."

"You'll hate it," she warned.

Since sunrise, Dan had strained his back unloading a

delivery truck, lent an ear to a decorated teacher eased out of her position for not adapting to modern teaching methods, sprained a finger demolishing an old shed, moderated an argument between a warring couple, and cut his cheek with a misplaced hammer strike that converted a nail into a projectile. How much grief could a love-confused urbanite inflict? "Hit me with it."

Michelle apologized in advance with her eyes. "Was it worth it? Having so much and then losing it all?"

Michelle's question struck Dan like a left hook to the chin, the kind that sends mouthguards flying. In place of stars, images of his family flashed before his eyes, everything circling too fast to capture except the ending, that ending, all ending so badly. The lady packed quite a punch.

Dan must have looked as dazed as he felt. "Forgive me," Michelle said, her eyes flaring. "I can be such a bitch at times."

The shock in Michelle's eyes retrieved a hazy memory of Sammi Pullman at the ladder inside the water tower, her face only inches away from Dan's, eyes wide in terror. Sammi's adrenaline-infused plea, "You have to help me!" was the only reason Dan counted himself among the living.

Dan shook away Michelle's apology. For once, her intrusion had been neither belligerent nor insensitive, wholly a preoccupation with her adult fear of entering a failed marriage. "You came searching for answers," he said, "and I promised you one."

Bravery, though, needed a backup. Dan peered into his coffee cup, wishing it were a little stiffer. As a substitute, he latched onto a particular sunny day, a light breeze blowing waves of hair into a beautiful woman's face.

"I met Grace by accident," Dan said. "Ran into her around the corner of a building—literally. Knocked her coffee cup out of her hand.

"Luckiest thing I ever did, that cup. If not for the need to apologize, I would have been tongue-tied around a woman as captivating as Grace: flowing auburn hair, hazel eyes sparkling in amusement at our situation, an infectious laugh. She accepted my offer to replace her cup.

"We shared a favorite coffee shop and taste in literature that carried me through until I gathered the nerve to ask her out on a date." Their courtship had been a whirlwind of delicious discovery. "Grace loved to dance barefoot in the grass, whipped me in chess, cooked deep-dish pizza that rivaled Chicago's best, laughed at raunchy jokes, looked ravishing dressed up, and played the piano.

"Asking Grace to marry me took more nerve than the first date. I remember Grace's reply as clearly as if it were yesterday. She wrapped her arms around my neck and said, 'Of course.' And then she wrapped herself around my life.

"Grace balanced professional and personal life with elegance and charm befitting her name, possessing a boundless capacity for caring and loving. Motherhood completed her. Grace wore Anna and Georgia like fine jewelry." The memories became too vivid for words. "I lived an idyllic life," Dan added wistfully, his voice trailing off.

It took conscious effort to continue. "We moved into a larger house so Grace could work from home and spend more time with the girls. Being an older home in an established neighborhood, something was forever in need of repair: leaking water valves, broken garage door springs, drooping gutters; you name it."

Dan shook his head. "One summer, I found several small pieces of sheet metal strewn along the ground close to the house. Without a thought, I tossed them into the trash can."

He paused, staring into the past. Had he found shingles in the bushes, he would have inspected his roof for damage. When his lawnmower spit out a mangled gutter end cap, he found the missing piece and installed a replacement. Formed aluminum rectangles dotted with spot-welding circles suggested a sheet metal assembly. Piling together behind the bushes meant they could have only fallen from the roof. So, why hadn't he investigated?

Instead, he had tossed them away without concern, one of two lapses still haunting him twenty years later.

"It was the vent cap to our furnace exhaust pipe," Dan said. "Broken to pieces, worn out like so much else of our house."

He chewed on his lip, fighting off the urge to flee.

"There was a sudden cold snap that autumn, Mother Nature twisting the dial from Indian summer straight to winter. A few mornings after it hit, I woke up with a splitting headache. I blamed the pain on plugged sinuses and headed to work as usual."

Dan shook his head several times. "A squirrel had built a nest in the exposed top of the vent pipe. Blocked it completely. I returned …"

His saddest memory spilled out in an assault to his senses: the odd silence that greeted his return home, a tangy "taste" to the air, encroaching lightheadedness … the bottoms of Anna's pink shoes.

Dan lifted his gaze to a blank spot on the far wall. Knowing his only escape was to finish, he took a deep breath and forced himself to look at Michelle.

"I returned home to find my precious wife and daughters dead from carbon monoxide poisoning."

Michelle slumped in her chair and burst into tears, shaking with long, racking sobs. Dan retrieved a box of tissues and placed it in front of her. He could have chosen different words to soften the blow, but protecting her wouldn't have done her any good.

Nor would it have done *him* any good. He had suffered the shock in the first person, the passage of time forcing him through the gamut of reactions. The ease with which he had pulled out the memory suggested he was nearing his final release.

Michelle grabbed a handful of tissues to wipe at her face. "I'm so sorry, Dan," she croaked.

Not half as sorry as Dan was. *I've tried, Grace. I've tried.*

After an aborted attempt, Michelle managed a deep breath and wiped her face a second time. "You must hate me," she said, dropping her hands to her lap.

"No," Dan said. Now wasn't the time to debate propriety. The wrong words could send Michelle away, never to return, too harsh a punishment for delving into the Hat Creek founder's past.

"I overstepped my bounds," she said.

"That may be, but you still deserve an answer."

Michelle shook her head. "My insecurity doesn't obligate you."

"No, but my duty does."

Dan leaned back in his chair and stared past Michelle. "Was it worth it?" The question was easy to answer in the affirmative if he considered only the years of joy. Admitting the horror muddied the equation. And pondering alternatives layered incalculable complexities.

He looked at Michelle. "Was the joy my family brought me worth the pain of losing them? Yes. Would I do it all over again, *knowing* they would pass away?" He tilted his head and shrugged his shoulders. "We're as lucky as we are unfortunate that we aren't allowed any 'do-overs.'

"Imagine if I had arrived at that corner just five seconds earlier or later. I wouldn't have knocked Grace's cup from her hand, and we wouldn't have met. Grace would be happily married to another lucky man, with a family of their own. Anna and Georgia wouldn't have been born, and I wouldn't have shared years of wonder with three amazing ladies." Dan took a deep breath. "I wouldn't have suffered the horrors of their passing, meaning I wouldn't have founded Hat Creek. *You* wouldn't have rushed from a decrepit cabin in a South Dakota ghost town because an uncouth adventurer was urinating on the back wall. Nor would you have scurried back because his matured version is trying to slip a diamond ring onto your finger.

"Would either of us be in better places? Or worse?" Dan shrugged again and took a drink of lukewarm coffee.

"To answer your question," he said, "the best I can say is that there are no guarantees in life." He hummed. "Which means I can't answer it."

Dan checked his watch. "Maggie should be arriving any minute. I suggest a long heart-to-heart."

Dan leaned against the rental while Michelle rummaged through her computer case for the car key. The morning sky was a friendly baby blue speckled with cottony clouds.

"Did you and Maggie have a good talk?" he asked.

"We did," Michelle answered, producing the key. "Maggie also had a good laugh at my expense. She pointed out that it would have been much simpler to phone if all I'd wanted to know was whether Jacob was here."

Dan grinned.

"No surprise you share her humor," Michelle said. "Only

you were too gracious to point out my folly."

"Or maybe I'm more practiced," Dan offered.

Michelle immediately sobered. "You've done much more than put old picture frames to use, Dan. Never forget that. And know you were brave to answer my question."

Dan straightened when Michelle lifted her arms for a hug. "Thanks for everything," she said, squeezing hard. "Like usual—Grange Hall!" She shuffled sideways for an unobstructed view. "Weren't you concealing the true use of Grange Hall to save on property taxes? Some trouble with your inspector?"

"Yes," Dan said as he turned to face the building.

"Then isn't it risky plastering its name across the front of the building?"

"GRANGE HALL" now adorned the aging gray siding over the front door, GRANGE spelled out in two-foot-tall artistic metal lettering, three pairs of uniquely sculpted letters: GR, full of curved pieces; AN, angular in contrast; GE, more whimsical; HALL painted in black as placemarks for future lettering.

"That's Todd's handiwork," Dan said. "Artistic welding is his hobby. He conducts welding classes for the residents. They gather scrap metal: old horseshoes, angle iron, piping, reinforcing rod, fence wire, tractor and implement parts, hand tools—you name it—and sculpt two letters each session."

"What a talent," Michelle said. "I take it Todd is no longer the enemy."

Dan shook his head. "A good friend, now. Next session, he starts sculpting 'HALL,' and then it's on to Westside."

"Sounds fun. Count me in if the timing works out."

"I'll arrange a session for your next trip."

Michelle smiled. "I'd like that." She glanced at her watch.

"And now I need to get going."

Michelle climbed into her car and started the engine. Her quick wave and friendly smile brought Sammi Pullman to mind again, reminding Dan how Sammi's courage and strength had shown him that he could face his past. Watching Michelle navigate the rut road and speed south out of town, he dropped his head.

So why hadn't he?

You Can't Hide Forever

The chilly breeze stung Dan's cheek as he stepped from Grange Hall. But the Hat Creek Players trio practicing their play in the park appeared unfazed by the conditions. He must be getting thin-skinned in his old age.

An older model hunter-green Chevy hatchback approached along the blacktop from the south, coasting to a crawl as it passed the old church foundation and pulling to a stop on the shoulder across from Dan's house. The car's front bumper and hood were dented, and its plastic grill split, as if it had slammed into a light pole.

The driver killed the engine and stepped out as Dan started toward it. He was Black, just this side of thirty years old, with short, well-trimmed hair, a healthy stubble growth, and a gold earring sparkling in one ear. He wore a teal T-shirt hanging down over jeans.

"You wouldn't happen to have a water spigot handy, would you?" he asked Dan in a classic southern drawl, lifting an empty gallon jug. "My radiator sprang a small leak."

Internal damage, too. Make that a high-speed collision. "I'll fill it for you," Dan said, taking the jug. He carried it across the road into his house.

When Dan returned, his visitor was inventorying Hat Creek while rubbing his arms to ward off the cold. He thanked Dan for the water and pointed a thumb over his shoulder. "I saw the road sign. Is this a real town?"

"More, a wellness retreat." Dan extended his hand. "Dan Stuart. I run the place."

"Memphis Dixon," he returned, taking Dan's hand. "Not after the city—my first name, I mean. It was an Italian design group my parents loved. A wellness retreat, huh? Is this one of those quirky drug and alcohol addiction centers?"

"Quirky, I'll grant you," Dan said. "But Hat Creek isn't specialized. We welcome anybody in need of a little help."

Memphis eyed Dan's house. "Where do you put everyone up?"

"The buildings are friendlier inside. That's my home you're eying."

Memphis raised an eyebrow. "I think you need to charge more."

Dan smiled. "People pay what they can afford."

That information piqued Memphis's interest. He took in the sad remains of the post office. "I'm in no hurry to get back home … to L.A." He looked at Dan. "That's home. Where I live. If you let me stay a few days, I'll work for my keep."

Dan sized up Memphis: unkempt, ill-clothed, likely on the road for days—since the accident?—tired and hungry, stumbling upon Hat Creek by pure chance. And lying.

Dan jerked his head at Hartman's. "Why don't you park your car around the far side of that building. Our diner is over there. Grab a bite to eat, and I'll meet you there."

Memphis climbed back into his car and started the engine. Dan stepped back as the hatchback pulled forward, glancing at the rear bumper in passing. The license plate featured a Georgia peach.

Once Memphis disappeared behind Hartman's, Dan set off in the opposite direction, catching the attention of one of the dispersing acting troupe's members.

"How's the play coming?" he asked.

Cici grimaced. "I fear Yanira needs more than two weeks of 'immersion therapy' to make it big on the stage."

"Is opening night in danger?" Yanira had posted playbills throughout the town, announcing a debut performance tomorrow evening in Westside.

"Not on your life," Cici said. "The show must go on."

"I'm sure Yanira appreciates your support. Meanwhile, I have a favor to ask."

"Shoot."

"We have an unannounced visitor by the name of Memphis Dixon—"

"Memphis Dixon!" Cici clapped her hands together. "More Hat Creek fiction?"

"His name is the only plausible part of his story. He's asked to stay a few days, but I'd like a second opinion."

"I'm game," Cici said.

"Thanks, I sent him to Westside. I'll stick close by."

Cici dropped into the chair across the table from Dan.

"How'd it go?" Dan asked.

"I kept it warm and friendly, as you suggested. I agree that Hat Creek wasn't Memphis's destination, but he's quite interested in staying." Cici hesitated as if to make more sense of her conversation. "Something's troubling him."

"Or he's *in* some sort of trouble," Dan said.

Cici nodded to admit the possibility.

Dan pushed his coffee cup away. "I'll let him stay."

"Dan!"

"Free help is rarer than snakebites. I'll get an early start on weatherproofing."

Cici chuckled. "You're remarkable."

Dan motioned Memphis over. "I've got a three-day project for you. Room and board for that long."

"Thank you," Memphis said, smiling to reveal white teeth that contrasted nicely with his rich skin tone. Cici's posture noticeably improved.

Dan was too preoccupied fantasizing about lazy days spent indulging children in Arizona to notice the mound of cactus in his path.

"Do you need to lighten your load?" Memphis asked when Dan stumbled.

"I'm fine," Dan answered. Memphis was already lugging three-quarters of their supplies. "I just need to pick up my feet."

They crested the small rise west of Hat Creek, bringing into view the day's destination a couple of hours distant. Heavily grazed grasses dotted by sheer cliffs denuded of vegetation by water- and wind-driven erosion—Sammi's ravines—stretched to that crest. Tomorrow morning, prompted by Maggie's surprising entreaty, Dan was finally embarking on his long-planned hike down the valley.

"Elizabeth called me today with wonderful news," Maggie had said, spooning salad onto her plate. "She's pregnant with their third child."

"That *is* wonderful news," Dan said.

Maggie beamed as she passed Dan the salad bowl. "No. That's only the great news. The wonderful news is that Elizabeth has asked me to move to Tucson as her nanny. Aiden in after-school care and Leanne in daycare was barely manageable. A third in infant care, Elizabeth told me, was unaffordable."

"I'm happy for you, Maggie."

"Elizabeth offered me their guest room, but I wouldn't

hear of it; they're already crowded in that home as it is. On my pension, I can afford a little place of my own."

Dan raised his glass in a toast. "To spoiling one's grandchildren."

Maggie touched her glass to Dan's. "It *is* a dream come true."

She set her glass down and took Dan's hand. "I didn't forget you, Dan. Come with me—I know your first impulse will be to say no but hear me out. You've dedicated your life to serving others. You're long past retirement age, though, and can't continue punishing your body. You, more than most, have earned the right to relax and enjoy your remaining years. You haven't taken a vacation in all the years I've known you. Heck, we've never even eaten at a nice restaurant or taken in a movie. It's time to start thinking of yourself.

"I know you're not the marrying kind, Dan. You'd have already popped the question if you were. And I'm okay with that. We can live together, or you can get your own place. Your choice. And I'm not asking you to stop helping people." Maggie chuckled. "I doubt I could force you to stop. So, I propose a pleasant alternative to Hat Creek. Let's spoil Elizabeth's children together."

Maggie squeezed Dan's hand a final time. "There's no rush, Dan. I'm not asking you to decide immediately, only to think about it."

Dan shadowed Memphis on a gently ascending circuit around a deep ravine. Though Dan had long dreamt of this hike, he had only begun serious planning shortly after recovering from the freak water tower accident, even staging firewood at tonight's campsite. Progress had predictably stalled, buried under the burden of running Hat Creek. Now, though, the hike was the perfect prescription to weigh Maggie's offer, and with the aid of Memphis's strong muscles, Dan was finally fulfilling Sammi's prediction.

Dan adjusted his course to avoid a steeper slope. Thinking again of Maggie's offer, his botched confession with Michelle weighed heavily on his mind. So too, though, did Maggie's reminder that he couldn't run Hat Creek much longer. Dan desired Florence's rich achievements, and he wouldn't add to his legacy confined to his easy chair, all alone, an empty Hat Creek falling apart around him.

Dan entertained thoughts of buying a small bungalow as he and Memphis weaved through more rough terrain. A simple home with a grass yard easy on his aching knees, spending his days with Maggie entertaining a boisterous trio of children.

"Yes," he tested aloud as his answer to Maggie's appeal. Memphis eyed him carefully.

"Just an old man muttering to himself," Dan reassured Memphis. "Doesn't happen often." Though the trial balloon hadn't induced any turmoil, the gravity of the circumstances pressed hard.

"Everybody makes mistakes, Memphis," Dan confessed. "It's unavoidable. If we're lucky, they're of little consequence. When we're not, we're made to suffer. Worse, others suffer. It's then that we face divergent paths moving forward: to run from our mistakes or to set about atoning for them. Experience has taught me that the latter is the more difficult path, requiring diligence and sacrifice, a payment in body *and* mind. But the payoff is worth the effort. To earn a second chance, a place in someone's life …" Dan could almost convince himself that he deserved Maggie's continued company.

Dan's left knee had begun aching early in the hike, the discomfort worsening as the day wore on until he could barely withstand the pain when they arrived at the campsite. He concealed his condition from Memphis through dinner, hoping the pain would subside. Instead, it had plateaued without any indication of immediate relief. Staring into the fire Memphis had so enthusiastically built, Dan accepted that his body wouldn't survive a three-day hike. Truth be told, if forced to continue now, he probably couldn't make it another hundred yards.

"Sorry to say, Memphis," Dan said, wincing with pain, "but my knee has given out. We're going to have to end this hike before it starts."

"Did you pack anything for it?" Memphis asked, noticing Dan's discomfort.

Dan shook his head. Only his prescription-strength painkiller would take the edge off this intense pain, and, unfortunately, the bottle rested in his kitchen cabinet.

Memphis stood and looked back toward Hat Creek. "Will you be able to walk back?"

"A more appropriate question is whether I can stand," Dan said. "Perhaps in the morning." A sharp pain shot down his leg. "Perhaps not."

Memphis stood. "I should get you back now. No use suffering through the night." A droning sound caught his attention, and he watched headlights slide eastward, a truck traveling the gravel road. "You wouldn't want me carrying you back, even if I could. The jostling would only aggravate your knee. I'll head for the road and follow it back to Hat Creek, and then return with help."

"Honestly, Memphis, I can survive the night."

"I'm not afraid of the night. Not out here."

Memphis disappeared from Dan's view, momentarily returning with an armload of firewood. "I'll build up the fire nice and big." He chuckled. "Hate to lose you in the darkness."

Memphis and Cici returned in Dan's truck. Staring out the passenger window into the blackness as they bounced along the gravel road, Dan remembered with sadness Sammi's prediction that one day he'd hike down the valley. But it wasn't to be. Same as climbing ladders, hauling logs, digging trenches, and reclaiming buildings, his hiking days were over.

Dan hobbled out of bed the following morning and headed for Westside. Cici and Memphis were seated at the computer table, Memphis looking particularly solemn, nodding his head every few seconds in response to Cici's words. Dan respected their privacy and made his way into the kitchen, grabbing a plate from the cupboard. After loading it with two chicken legs and a thigh from a pan of leftovers in the refrigerator, he popped it into the microwave. Memphis appeared in the doorway as Dan opened the tub of apricot salad.

"How's your knee?" Memphis asked.

"The painkillers are starting to kick in," Dan said. "I don't know what I would have done if I'd hiked solo. Thanks for your help last evening."

"Better late than never." Memphis glanced back out the doorway. "Or so Cici insists. I hope I agree one day."

Memphis extended his hand and took a firm grip of Dan's. "Thank you for your hospitality and your advice and … and everything. Someday, I hope to repay you. And now it's time for me to go." He released Dan's hand and disappeared from the kitchen.

The microwave dinged. Dan removed the plate of steaming chicken, spooned on a serving of salad, selected a hard roll from the basket, and carried his meal into the dining area just as the front door closed behind Memphis. Cici sat alone, looking forlorn as if she had just lost a friend.

"What was that all about?" he asked, joining her.

"What you said to Memphis during your hike got through to him."

Dan tried recalling any inspirational words he had spoken.

"Memphis told me his story," Cici said. "He was involved in a hit-and-run accident. He panicked and drove away, then just kept driving." She nodded at the computer. "We looked up the story. The boy Memphis struck died the following day. There were extenuating circumstances, but Memphis is in legal trouble because he fled the scene.

"Memphis is returning to Atlanta to face the consequences. He phoned the Atlanta police just before you entered. It was his decision, Dan. I'm proud of him."

Cici wrapped her arms around Dan's waist and buried her face into his neck. "And I'm proud of you."

Dan escaped both Cici's embrace and Westside, anxious to return home before losing his nerve. He closed his front door behind him, locking it for once, and fished out the safe key from a small white porcelain bowl on his desk. After removing his photo album from the safe, he carried it to his chair and starred at it for several minutes, awaiting any warning signs. When there were none, he opened it.

"Hello," he said to Grace. She was as beautiful as ever, her unwavering gaze food for his soul. "I helped another runaway off the dangerous path he was following. It's becoming a habit."

His fingers found the edge of the page, but he didn't risk turning it until he had earned Anna and Georgia's forgiveness. Instead, he settled for the joy of this private time with his wife.

Memphis served two years of a four-year sentence, returning to Hat Creek twice to fulfill his community service hours. After parole, he volunteered at Hat Creek for extended periods, eventually becoming one of Dan's assistant managers.

CHAPTER 33

Cici departed Hat Creek two days after Memphis returned to Atlanta, but only after helping Dan set up the compartmented container of embarrassment resting on the kitchen table in front of him, otherwise known as a pill organizer. Might just as well slap a sign on his back, "Warning! Aged and forgetful!"

Dan snapped open the lid to column six, row four—Friday evening—exposing afull complement of shapes and colors. First out was the oblong painkiller, which he downed with a swig of water. His knee, hips, back, and arms all thanked him. He removed the remaining pills into a neat row on the tabletop: the diuretic for high blood pressure, the bi-something-or-other to fend off osteoporosis, a small round one that tried to roll to freedom, an even tinier hexagon that controlled his borderline diabetes, plus the newest addition to the morning and evening cups, an anticoagulant. All intended to, in distilled doctor-speak, prolong the "a little longer."

"Come with me to Arizona," Maggie had pleaded.

Dan rearranged the pills into an arched spectrum of color like the Lucky Charms marshmallow rainbow, minus the green clover. Was there a pot of gold at the end of all this? Maggie insisted there was; furthermore, that Dan deserved the reward. The vision of that tidy backyard covered in soft grass *was* enticing. And dinner and a movie every so often would be nice.

Do I deserve enjoyment?

Dan wiped the curve into randomness, but it did little to erase the temptation. Moreover, watching his arm muscles flex through his scars added another sad reminder of Hat Creek's looming mortality: in the early mornings more challenging to face, the trucks more slowly unloaded, the strenuous repairs now hired out; in the rusting water tower, the leaking electrical transformer, the sludge-filled holding pond, the broken freezer, the stuck and cracked windows, and the rotted wood; in the mounting stack of unpaid bills.

Dan scooped up the pills and downed them with his remaining water. More difficult to swallow was that his days were numbered with or without their internal vigilance.

"Let's spoil Elizabeth's children together," Maggie had said. She'd been holding his hand.

Dan stood and limped to his fireplace. He was unsure how many faces crowding the mantle "loved and admired" him, as Maggie asserted, but he was proud that so many had searched out Hat Creek.

I've done all I can do here.

Dan leaned against his truck, freshly washed for the first time in years, and took in Hat Creek, seeing in the gray boards and the frayed shingles the handiwork of his old adversaries, time and weather and sun. He had always known he was only delaying the inevitable. You can battle nature to a draw, but you can't beat it. He was finally at peace with that outcome. The effort had equipped him to redirect a wayward teenager and accommodate the hundreds more his retreat had enticed to take up temporary residence.

The retreat hadn't needed such substantive adversaries to perish. Dan stopped accepting new applications, canceled future reservations, ended the catering services as the final residents departed, and scheduled one final trash removal. Closed for business.

Meanwhile, Dan listed the town on the market, despite having little hope of selling it. After a few months without a nibble, he removed the listing. Perhaps he could have held out for a miracle offer, but Maggie's newest grandchild wasn't waiting for anything, especially so trivial of a matter.

Dan glanced at his watch. He'd never flown out of Scottsbluff, but it wasn't O'Hare or JFK, so he was in no rush. He lowered the tailgate and took a seat facing Grange Hall. If there were a place in Hat Creek he would miss, that would be it. As opposed to the water tower, he recalled its reconstruction with fondness. Jacob had slept on its unfinished floor. Michelle had overanalyzed Dan's preoccupation with maintaining "the open gash in his life" in its false roof. And Florence, Jasper, and others had rolled down its accommodating ramp.

Dan gazed adoringly at the artwork adorning Grange Hall's front wall. Part of him wished he could detach the letters and take them with him. But they belonged to Hat Creek. If anything of this town persevered, they would be it.

Dan stood and closed the tailgate, loaded his suitcase into the bed, and climbed into the cab. Maggie had flown to Tucson two weeks ago to help Elizabeth and to start house hunting. Her flight landed in JFK within five minutes of his own. After attending Jacob and Michelle's wedding, they returned to Hat Creek to pack their belongings into their trucks, and they'd be off. A convoy of two retirees driving two old trucks for Arizona to spend their remaining years together in quiet relaxation. With a satisfied nod, Dan started the truck and pulled away from the junkers.

Alas, so much for careful planning. There's no accounting for a premature birth and neglecting to cancel your newspaper subscription.

CHAPTER 34

Maggie hurried inside and quickly closed the door. An icy blast still reached Dan at his desk.

"I forgot how cold it gets around here," Maggie complained, unwrapping her neck scarf. "It was seventy-five in Tucson." When a coat button caught in the weave of her scarf, she carefully freed it. "Won't it be so nice when 'layering' means baking a fancy cake?"

She met Dan in the middle of the room and kissed him on the lips. "Feeling better?"

Dan's cold had run its course. Yet, he felt infinitely worse.

Maggie dropped her purse and scarf onto the coffee table without waiting for an answer. "Is tomorrow's blizzard still hitting early afternoon?" she asked, shedding her coat onto the chair back.

Dan had warned her of the powerful front sweeping down from Canada, forecasted to drop temperatures below zero and dump two feet of snow. "As far as I know."

Collette's premature birth had sent Maggie scurrying directly back to Tucson from New York City. Dan had encouraged Maggie to remain in Arizona and wait out the storm, but Maggie wouldn't hear of it, booking a flight home and calling ahead to have her cousins pack up her belongings. They would be speeding south ahead of the foul weather by noon tomorrow.

Or so Maggie assumed. She hadn't been the one to discover the Sunday edition of the Rapid City Journal unexpectedly lying on the ground in front of Hartman's.

Maggie took Dan's arm and pulled him towards the sofa. "Sit with me so I can show you the pictures."

Once they were seated, Maggie folded her scarf out of the way, partially concealing the newspaper, and placed her tablet on the coffee table. She powered it on and fingered a couple of icons to start a slideshow.

"Meet little Collette," Maggie said proudly.

Maggie's newest granddaughter was bundled in a soft pink blanket, only her wrinkled face in view, dark hair peeking from beneath a pink knit hat, eyes tightly closed, a cute button nose, and tiny, beautifully shaped lips. Not too premature to look perfect.

Maggie swiped her fingertip across the screen. An exhausted Elizabeth lay inclined in the maternity bed, an IV taped to one arm, and a dozing Collette nestled into the crook of the other. Mother gazed lovingly at her newborn; the corners of her mouth lifted in a soft smile.

"Nicolette *Makenzie* Schmidt," Maggie said. "Mother and daughter are both beautiful, aren't they?"

Maggie advanced through more pictures of Collette, one shot even catching the newborn in a cute round-mouthed yawn.

The following image caught Aiden clutching a lion and Leanne hugging a pink elephant at a checkout stand. "We made a quick stop at the hospital gift shop."

Another finger swipe returned the scene to the delivery room, Leanne gazing lovingly at the tiny bundle nestled in her lap. In the following images, Maggie had her share of face time, a proud grandmother cradling little Collette in her arms.

When the digital photo album chronicled Collette's arrival home, many images were off-kilter, cropping off parts of the subject.

"Aiden and Leanne had taken over the camera by then," Maggie laughed.

Finally sensing Dan's somber mood, Maggie looked up from the screen. "You don't look well. Your cold hasn't developed into something worse, has it?"

Dan shook his head. "It's not that."

"What, then?"

Dan hadn't found the courage to break the news to Maggie over the phone. He freed the newspaper from beneath her scarf, unfolded it over her tablet, then tapped on the lower-left front-page article. Maggie adjusted the paper in front of her and read aloud.

"'Rapid City woman murdered by estranged husband.' Oh, how terrible." Maggie continued reading with an audible mumble. "Ann Harris!" she gasped and looked up at Dan. "She was the woman you gave a new identity. I remember delivering her driver's license."

Dan nodded sadly. "According to the article, Ann's estranged husband kidnapped her at knifepoint and raped her for two days in a motel room before strangling her. Police captured him in eastern Montana."

"I'm so sorry," Maggie said. "Little wonder you're so down."

Dan shook his head again. "Ann's death is my fault."

"How are you at fault for *anything* that wicked man did?" Maggie protested.

Dan tapped the paper. "Ann's husband tracked her through an online photo, the one of the park rangers graduating class. Ann knew what atrocities her husband was capable of. She had the correct instinct to remain hidden. But I promised her anywhere in the Black Hills was safe. *I* encouraged her to reach for her dream."

"None of that makes Ann's death your fault, Dan."

"To be a cashier in a small store in a small town. That's all Ann wanted, Maggie. A quiet corner where she could live in peace. She told me so." Dan took a deep breath and exhaled sadly. "If I could but take back my words, Ann would still be alive."

"Your intentions were pure, Dan. Nobody could have predicted Ann's husband would commit so heinous a crime."

"I should have stayed out of her business. Professor Malkovich warned me. I didn't listen."

"Oh, Dan," Maggie said. "You did everything you could *for* Ann." She placed her palm on his cheek. "Your skin feels dry. Have you been drinking enough water?"

Dan shrugged.

"I'll get you a glass of water," Maggie said. "I could use one myself."

Maggie stood and walked into the kitchen. A cupboard opened and closed, then a second, and Maggie reappeared without a glass.

"You haven't packed," she said, sitting back down. She looked around the room, only now noticing Dan's belongings still strewn around the room. "You're not leaving."

Dan slowly shook his head. "After what I've done?" Of late, he had forgotten the very "why" of this place. Florence's bravery shone brightly in his memory. Was not Hat Creek both his purgatory and path to redemption, as well? Where did causing mortal injury, causing his daughter's death a second time, fit in his deliverance? "How can I post the notice, 'Hat Creek is closed so the proprietor can bask in the Arizona sunshine,' and turn away the next phone call, email, or car? I'd be betraying them. Serving them is the only way I can repay for what I did to Ann."

Maggie reoriented the newspaper in front of her, visibly flustered. She read the story in silence, her lips moving, no doubt trying to make sense of Dan's actions.

"I'm sorry," Dan said, knowing that in a heartbeat he had shredded her retirement. "I don't mean to belittle your grandchildren."

Maggie shook away his apology. "I know how much Ann meant to you."

Maggie squeezed her eyes shut to take stock of her situation. Dan could guess what she was concluding: Ann Harris—and all those who had taken up and would take up residence in Hat Creek—meant more to Dan than she did. But it wasn't true. Hat Creek and Maggie were the two significant compartments in his life, but they couldn't coexist in separate places.

After a deep breath, Maggie turned to Dan and pulled his hand into her lap. "Nobody would blame you for Ann's death. But I won't disrespect her memory by begging you to change your mind and drive with me to Tucson. Come down when you're ready to retire or find someone to run Hat Creek. You know where to find me."

She released Dan's hand. "I'd love to stay all evening, but I need to make sure Elliot and Tony have everything ready before it gets dark."

Maggie slipped her tablet back into her purse, and they

stood. "And we're not going to let this ruin tomorrow. We'll cook a big breakfast and spend the entire morning together."

"I'd like that," Dan said. He helped Maggie into her coat and walked her to the door.

Maggie wrapped her scarf around her neck and smiled weakly. "Just imagine how great it'd be to get away from this horrid stuff." And then she was gone.

Dan peered out his front window, the glass radiating the frigid outdoor conditions. The blacktop, not twenty-five feet from where he stood, was a gray mirage through the thick veil of falling snow blown sideways by the gusting winds.

Dan had awoken before dawn to find six inches of fresh snow already covering the ground—another weather forecasting fail. He phoned Maggie to warn her away, but she hadn't answered, meaning she was already on the road, her phone turned off, a habit from her Postal service days. Dan hoped Maggie had had enough sense to head south. He wished her safe travel. Maggie's grandchildren needed her as much as she needed them.

Dan turned away from the window, alone for the first time in years. Solitude was only the appropriate penalty for his failures—plural, for he couldn't deny that he had failed Maggie just as surely as he had failed Ann. It hurt for his hard work to be negated, his past a burden he must overcome again.

But Dan knew that moping about served no purpose, so to help shake off the melancholy he intentionally focused on the picture frames on the mantle across the room. He would honor his past good deeds by looking forward, by repopulating Hat Creek: reactivating his website, reinviting the people he had turned away, and reviewing the current applications he had luckily kept.

The renewed sense of purpose lifted his mood. Let the storm rage all day. He'd celebrate Maggie embarking on her dream retirement by enjoying their prepared breakfast feast and then get back to work. Seventy years old was *not* past retirement age.

The bacon was sizzling when a familiar engine sound momentarily drowned out the howling wind, meaning that Maggie hadn't been so smart, after all. Dan reduced the heat and reached the front door in time to let her inside.

"You should be long gone by now," he said, quickly closing the door.

Maggie pulled back her hood. "I couldn't leave without saying goodbye." She pecked him on the cheek. "This stupid weather is ruining everything. I'd so looked forward to spending the morning together."

"We will spend more than just the morning together if you don't turn around and leave this minute."

"I promise I'll only stay a moment—"

Dan hadn't known snowstorms could reproduce echoes. But he'd swear Maggie's truck had arrived a second time.

"Who'd be stupid enough to drive out here in this weather?" Maggie asked.

"Who else, you mean?" Dan corrected, following Maggie to the front window. A Yellow cab had parked beside her truck, its back door already opening. A diminutive figure concealed beneath a black hooded parka and gripping a pink case in a mittened hand stepped out and timidly approached the opening driver's window. The cabbie began gesturing animatedly.

"She doesn't have the fare, does she?" Maggie said.

"No," Dan said.

"Does this happen often?"

"Not … sometimes." Dan turned to step around Maggie.

Maggie caught Dan's hand as he reached for his wallet. "Let me do this one small favor for you." She cupped his head in her hands. "I hope that someday you can overcome your demons." She kissed him hard on his lips. "I'll be waiting."

After a last quick peck, Maggie lifted her hood over her head and yanked the pull-strings tight. She unzipped a chest pocket as they walked to the front door and pulled out a few twenties. "Ready," she announced.

Dan opened the door, and Maggie spilled out into the storm. When she reached the open taxi window, she directed the hooded figure Dan's way before exchanging a few words with the cabbie along with the fare. Already, the exposed side of Dan's face burned. Maggie hurried to her truck, waving goodbye to Dan without looking, and climbed into the cab, waiting for the cabbie to back a turn and pull away before following. Her truck evaporated first into the thick white fog, quickly trailed by the blue tarp. The red taillights lingered longest, twin spots spreading as they faded. And then the curtain closed.

The hooded woman stood before Dan. Still in the fury of the storm.

"Sorry!" he said, reaching for her case. "Come inside."

Entering, she removed her hood and turned to face him. She was but a waif with closely cropped black hair and large brown eyes, a delicate nose and chin, and soft, unblemished skin. A row of tiny silver studs adorned both earlobes. She assumed a defiant air, but Dan sensed her fragility.

He smiled warmly. "Welcome to Hat Creek. My name is Dan Stuart."

Practice Makes Perfect

Some events improbable in ordinary towns are commonplace in Hat Creek: cattle congregating in the park; passersby opening the door into what they presumed to be a derelict building, only to find a modern interior; rattlesnakes sunning themselves on car hoods; residents casting a homemade dredge into the holding pond to reel in compost for the vegetable garden; the yearly slingshot contest designed to distress boards, dent cars, or break windows.

But a disembodied head dangled over the edge of the water tower catwalk was an outlier, even for Hat Creek. So much so that Dan stubbed his toe on a thick clump of weeds when he noticed it. After regaining his balance, he veered towards the tower, hoping the startling sight would resolve into a small owl, a cluster of seed-laden cottonwood leaves, or a Halloween prank—anything explainable. Unfortunately, the upside-down human head stubbornly remained, its eyes and mouth open.

Dan's fears were put to rest only when he approached closely enough to gaze up through the expanded metal catwalk: Brie Hodge lay on her back with her head draped over the edge.

"You scared me, Brie," Dan yelled. "I feared Hat Creek had suffered its first heinous crime."

"It's all about perspective, Dan," Brie said. "Did you know that the square root of negative one has no real solution?"

Brie's questions challenged Dan like no others.

"It's imaginary," she said. "Impossible, a conjure of our

minds. And yet mathematicians, scientists, and engineers use it daily to solve important problems."

Math not being one of Dan's fortes, he withheld comment.

"Dan, Hat Creek looks even more preposterous upside down."

"That so."

"I meant that as a compliment."

"I took it as one."

The following day Dan entered Hartman's to find Brie standing on the oak display case, attempting to place a hiking boot atop a pyramid constructed out of backpack frames, fishing poles, shovels, rakes, and other supplies and equipment from Hartman's shelves and walls.

"Stop!" she said. "Tread lightly so you don't make it fall again."

Fall again. Now Dan knew the source of the rumbling sound he had heard several minutes ago. "Practice makes perfect?"

Brie counted on her fingers. "Seven times—oh!" She stooped down and picked up her notebook.

"Should I ask what you're doing?" Dan said.

Brie opened the notebook and began writing. "Are there limited arrangements of a finite set—physical objects, in this case—within defined external conditions, such as gravity? If so, an optimal arrangement necessarily exists."

Dan regretted his question. "How about I just back away slowly and let you continue?"

"That would be for the best," Brie said without pausing her feverish notetaking.

"If you need help," Dan said, "or more items for your … project, don't hesitate to ask."

Brie didn't respond, as if Dan had already departed. So, he did.

Dan next spotted Brie seated in a more pedestrian pose in the gazebo, appearing so depressed that he turned from his intended destination to join her.

"Why so blue?" he asked.

Brie shook her head dejectedly. "I've hit a dead-end, Dan. I don't know what else to do."

Dan hadn't expected Brie to utter those words. In past years—Brie was Hat Creek's regular of regulars, having visited eight out of the last ten years—she had dropped pumpkins off of the water tower, documenting the debris pattern of the scattered chunks; gathered perforated metal posts as a giant Erector set and bolted them together into unrecognizable shapes; split Styrofoam coolers into dozens of pieces, taped magnets to them, and set them afloat in the holding pond, recording the different repulsive patterns they formed; dammed up the creek and detailed the rivulet patterns created as the water broke through the dirt barrier; invented a simple language based on sets of concentric circles with which, to Dan's amazement, she solved simultaneous equations; and undertaken numerous other baffling activities. Were Hat Creek capable, the town would cry foul.

"I've wasted too much of your time," she sighed, her tone asking Dan to recommend she move on.

Alas, Hat Creek wasn't everyone's magic elixir. A simple consent or nod would send Brie on her way. But Ann Harris's memory held Dan back. Whether Hat Creek was a waste of time was Brie's decision, not his.

"Walk with me," Dan said, knowing Brie hadn't exhausted Hat Creek's supply of oddball challenges. He led her first to the maintenance shed to grab a floor broom before continuing toward Hartman's, crossing the gravel road once beyond the blacktop.

"I'm temporarily suspending the warning from entering the old post office," he said.

Dan helped Brie across the post office's collapsed front wall and into the interior. Because the building was roofless, dust and debris littered the floor. Dan collected and discarded the larger pieces before sweeping the floor.

He pointed at the exposed tiling, a seemingly haphazard laying of small square black and white tiles arranged as if someone had thrown handfuls across the floor and glued them in place. Yet, a pattern tugged at Dan's consciousness. "I've always thought someone was trying to tell us something."

"We're trying to determine the correlation between stress and benefit," Elliot said between mouthfuls of pasta. He was as enthusiastic and idealistic as the previous intern Michelle had shipped out in her stead, only with a healthier appetite. Since Jacob and Michelle's toddler was always coming down something, Nathan must have contracted a serious illness for Michelle to be uncomfortable leaving the two-year-old. "Dr. Fines mentioned fascinating details like concealed rattlesnakes and stampeding cattle."

A hand reached into Dan's peripheral vision. He looked down and watched Brie pilfer some of his peas without glancing at Dan's plate. Standing with Brie in the post office ruins, Dan had drawn her attention to a black and white tiled floor resembling a giant QR code, laid seventy-five years before QR codes existed. To Dan, the black patterns appeared to be formed in distinct rows, as if encoding a message. Brie had enthusiastically accepted Dan's challenge to decipher any message and, now reengaged, had begun other quirky endeavors.

Including pea stealing.

Brie had repurposed her plate of food into culinary pop art, curling several noodles into tight and loose spirals arranged into a geometric pattern. Now she was strategically placing peas on top of the noodles to form an independent geometric pattern. Dan slid his plate closer to Brie's so she wouldn't have to reach as far.

Brie placed a final pea and stared at her plate. After an extended pause, she blurted out, "Yes! Yes! Yes!" and began scribbling feverishly into her notebook, quickly filling a page, then a second and a third. After half a fourth, she stood and hurried out of Westside.

Dan left Westside spotless in the evening. Reentering the following morning, he found the diner's entire west wall plastered in easel pad paper, nearly every square inch of it decorated in black marker: geometric patterns, a large set of figures composed of dots and straight lines, a double-helix spiral sprouting geometric shapes at random intervals, a long horizontal line intersected by oscillating lines, and a sunrise starburst of wavy lines. Numbers, letters, and Greek symbols arranged into exotic formulas crammed the remaining spaces. Brie, the presumed illustrator, was seated at a table, head down on her arms, dozing.

"Classic Brie," Dan mumbled, studying the artwork. Enigmatic and incomprehensible, like her other projects.

Matt Jurgensen entered Westside and stepped to Dan's side. Matt's company had ignored his warnings of a fatal flaw in their product, and eight people had died as a result. Matt blamed himself for failing to convince management to complete the necessary redesign. Every resident knew of the infamous disaster, and to a person absolved Matt of any responsibility. Despite the compassionate support, Dan knew that Matt must forgive himself.

"Care to comment?" Dan asked.

Matt studied the wall. "It's math," he said. "I recognize the integrals and the infinite series beneath the window. Beyond that …" He shook his head. "I never took *that* math class in engineering school."

Brie stirred and turned her head. "Thank you, Dan, for everything," she said in a sleepy voice, smiling against the table. After rising into a sitting position, she gazed at her creation for several seconds. "I did it. I finally did it."

Bernhard Riemann, a German mathematician, proposed the Riemann hypothesis in 1859. Dan didn't understand a word of what he read about the conjecture beyond that it dealt with the distribution of prime numbers and was considered by many to be the most important unsolved problem in pure mathematics. One of the seven original Millennium Prize Problems, the Clay Mathematics Institute awards a one-million-dollar prize to the discoverer of any of the problems.

Brie, PhD mathematician, received the reward after peer reviews verified her proof of the Riemann hypothesis, and she parlayed her success into a professorship at Cal Berkeley. Reading Brie's note, Dan felt Ann's approval. When he wielded Hat Creek appropriately, anything was possible.

```
!  I  S  L  E
P  T  W  I  T
H  T  H  E  M
A  Y  O  R  S
W  I  F  E  !
```

(The message Brie discovered encoded in the tile.)

CHAPTER 35

Take your medicine!

Dan awoke with a start, expecting to find one of his many do-gooders staring him in the face. A compulsive glance around his living room assured him he was quite alone.

He hadn't needed to check. Dan's family doctor hadn't the foggiest clue where he lived. Michelle's interns had departed for their fall semester. Cici was too busy managing an international company to drop by a third time this season. And Hat Creek's assistant managers had returned to their regular jobs.

And since, with the help, so too went Hat Creek's residents, Dan had the entire town to himself. Each year since the transition to a seasonal retreat, he had resisted suggestions that he move into a real town, closer to the services his aging body required. Once a hermit, he claimed, always a hermit. They branded him obstinate.

Dan remained in Hat Creek because he couldn't bear a stray resident arriving unannounced, only to discover a true ghost town. Spending weeks at a time keeping the Hat Creek population sign accurate was a small price to pay to answer that knock on his front door.

Dan wiped his hand down his face, sat up in the chair to relieve his hip pain, and returned to reading his mail. He tore open a bright red envelope and pulled out an embossed greeting card, Cynthia Ward's photo slipping out before he opened the card. Due to his legendary affinity for photos, Dan seldom received correspondence without including a snapshot. The image of Cynthia wrapped in her new wife's affectionate hug was a heartwarming contrast to the despondent woman arriving on foot carrying all her possessions, the only resident to have hiked to Hat Creek.

After the last two envelopes turned out to be benign junk mail masquerading as official notices, Dan dumped everything except Cynthia's photo onto his side table. She deserved a turn on his mantle.

First, though, he'd need to escape his easy chair, no longer a trivial task. Dan slid forward to get his weight over his feet and pressed down on the chair arms as he straightened.

"Ouch," he said. Standing with dignity hurt. All standing hurt, for that matter. Same with walking. Another reason to keep his do-gooders at arm's length. Pain killers worked best in forbidden combinations.

Dan walked Cynthia's picture to his fireplace. Having long ago run out of both picture frames and space on his mantle to display them, when each new photo arrived, he randomly selected a frame and slipped the new image in front of the two or more remembrances already tucked inside.

Dan blindly lifted a simple walnut frame from the mantle, flipped it over to insert Cynthia's photo, and propped her friendly smile in prominent view. Working the length of the mantle recycling more frames back to front, he paused when his fingers caressed an oak frame that had centered the display for three years. The picture of little Collette seated between Aiden and Leanne on Grandma's lap layered melancholy over happy memories. Five years old in the photo, Collette was eight now, growing up so fast.

The photo of Maggie and her three grandchildren was the last one Maggie had sent and amongst her final correspondences. Dan had been a reluctant pen pal even during the early years when Maggie first expected, and then hoped, that Dan was on his way south. Once even hope evaporated, Maggie inevitably chose her grandchildren over a crotchety old man unable to, as she had put it, overcome his demons.

As much as Dan lamented interrupting Maggie's retirement plans, he lamented more withholding that he *had* conquered his demons. The intervening years since the convoy for Tucson departed Hat Creek short one truck had taught Dan that Hat Creek was where he belonged, living out his remaining years running the retreat. For that lesson, he owed Maggie a measure of gratitude. And so her picture would forever remain on his mantle, and she in his heart.

The photo next to Maggie's, framed in chipped red lacquer, the cracked glass sadly prophetic, provoked mixed emotions. The young boy standing with his parents in the crowded market was the spitting image of his father: tall for his age and lanky, with wavy brown hair and striking facial features. But Nathan had inherited none of Jacob's poise or cockiness. Timid and skittish even as photographed, Nathan suffered developmental learning problems and was prone to fits and outbursts, especially in public.

In her letters, Michelle expressed equal frustration over Nathan's conflicting diagnoses. His social interaction and nonverbal communication difficulties indicated autism, except Nathan exhibited no fixations or repetitive behavioral patterns. Nathan was highly literal but lacked an Asperger's inherent logic skills. A doctor proposed Nathan suffered from a disruptive behavior disorder, even though Nathan never lashed out in anger or rebellion. And most recently, in an ominous twist, Michelle reported suspicions that Nathan heard voices.

Opposingly, Jacob attributed Nathan's problems to incompetent doctors compounded by overmedication. In his opinion, Nathan was simply a moody, introverted boy. Jacob debated why it was necessary to define some boundary beyond which a child suffered a medical condition. And as to Nathan's classroom struggles, Jacob offered that it was primarily a case of like father, like son; the world wouldn't end if Nathan turned out to be high school material. Jacob insisted that Nathan didn't need fixing, so no procession of specialists, testing, therapy sessions, or pills—especially pills—would magically turn him into a wunderkind. Much to Jacob's dismay, Michelle didn't share his view. Jacob knew Michelle loved Nathan. Jacob just lamented that her love wasn't unconditional.

Sadly, Nathan faced another potential burden. The asides tucked within his parents' letters chronicled a slowly crumbling relationship. Michelle regularly lamented Jacob's inability to settle on a career, writing in exasperation, "Dan, how can someone choose to wander through life?" She expressed annoyance with Jacob's blatant disregard for organized education with equal frequency. And in a rare moment of weakness, she admitted lingering insecurity bordering on unhealthy jealousy that Jacob still attracted women like bees to nectar. In turn, Jacob complained of Michelle's low regard for his hard work and long hours because it didn't represent a "meaningful" effort. He also expressed growing disillusionment with Michelle's laser focus on career and chafed at so often playing second fiddle. "Sometimes I have to look down to make sure I'm wearing pants," he complained. The collated list represented Jacob and Michelle's original fears of entering into marriage.

Dan fingered the picture frame, recalling Jacob's report of an oft-repeated day, Nathan vomiting on the drive to school, causing Nathan to be late for class and Jacob for work, spoiling a set of clothes and a car interior. Jacob and Michelle's original fears, yes, but complicated by a certain seven-year-old. Were Nathan's parents standing on opposite sides of him, or was Nathan standing between them?

In Michelle's letter accompanying the latest family photo, she raced through the salutations and family updates before launching into a lengthy compilation of her and Jacob's differences. Penned in a sharp, decidedly fatalistic tone, the letter represented the tome of an unhappy bundle of frustration resigned to a broken relationship. Yet, this was no rash outburst; Michelle was in control of her message. While she hadn't penned the word "divorce," the purpose of her letter was clearly to lessen the blow when she and Jacob announced their separation.

Michelle had also anticipated Dan's concern for Nathan's wellbeing, reasoning in her letter that the constant quarreling was detrimental to Nathan, even offering that one-on-one parenting would provide opportunities for straightforward, more consistent messaging. Michelle's justification, sufficient in her mind, amounted to Dan as a lame attempt to convince him that divorce was in Nathan's best interest. In closing, Michelle had assured Dan that she loved Nathan. Dan had yet to read a sadder line a parent felt the need to put to paper.

In the photo, Dan placed himself in Nathan's shoes: pressed back against his parents in a bustling public place, a hand finding each, twin pillars of protection and security.

And now those pillars were threatening to sunder.

Call Dan old-fashioned, but he felt Nathan deserved a complete family. Jacob and Michelle weren't abusive parents. Drugs or alcohol weren't a problem, nor were poverty or neglect. Besides quarreling—and name one couple who didn't fight—Jacob and Michelle had presented zero evidence that separation would improve Nathan's situation. To Dan's thinking, they were irresponsible adults too preoccupied with their convictions that their marriage was unsalvageable to notice the harm their selfish behavior was causing Nathan. The outside world was scary enough without one's parents allowing it to stampede inside.

A case of temporary parental insanity, Dan sincerely hoped. But like "oops!" and "my mistake," and "I forgot," and "I ran out of time," temporary insanity can lead to lasting damage. He'd knock some sense into them if the pair weren't out of reach.

Dan tilted the frame and caught his eighty-year-old reflection in the glass. Old, grayed, and weathered. Like Hat Creek. And, like Hat Creek, still functioning. He turned for his computer.

CHAPTER 36

Two weeks after Dan's invitation, Jacob stood amongst suitcases at their rental car's open trunk. Grange Hall's front door was already propped open when Dan ambled over, and footsteps sounded from inside.

"Long time no see," Jacob said. He had changed little in appearance in the four years since his last visit—Nathan's first—still the hunk who, in Michelle's words, attracted women like bees to nectar. "Michelle took a load inside, and Nathan is picking out his room. Michelle! Nathan! Dan's here!"

Momentarily, a seven-year-old replica of Jacob appeared through the doorway, hesitating when he saw the stranger standing next to his father. Dan couldn't fault the kid. Dan's mirror reminded him daily that he more closely resembled the buildings than a friendly grandfather.

A cattle truck lumbering toward town along the gravel road drew Nathan's attention. He turned back to escape the approaching rumble, only to collide with Michelle in the doorway. She forcibly spun him around and held onto his shoulders until the truck passed. Nathan's grimace reminded Dan of Michelle's sour first impression of Hat Creek.

Marriage and motherhood hadn't tamed Michelle's scholarly zeal. In addition to managing intern programs in three countries, Dr. Fines had authored two behavioral psychology books and taught undergraduate classes. Her dismay at Nathan's antics highlighted the issue at hand: whether marriage and motherhood could coexist with her workaholic nature. Dan wondered if Hat Creek was up to the task.

He masked his inner misgivings beneath a boisterous greeting. "It's a pleasure to meet you again, little guy."

Nathan startled, as if Dan had snuck up from behind and yelled, "boo!" Make that a flighty little guy.

Michelle corralled Nathan by the scruff of his neck. "Stop embarrassing yourself," she snapped. "You've met Mr. Stuart before. Now behave yourself and thank him for inviting us."

"Thank you, Mr. Stuart."

"Call me Dan."

"Thank you, Mr. Dan."

While Dan and Jacob shared a chuckle, Michelle remained unimpressed. The embarrassment she claimed Nathan's extended to herself.

"I'm sure it's been a long day for Nathan," Dan said. He looked from son to mother. "A long day for everyone."

Michelle blinked contritely and softened her hold into a motherly caress. "Two flights and a lengthy car drive," she said, running her fingers through Nathan's hair. Nathan brightened at the caress. "And we do appreciate the invitation." She stepped around Nathan and hugged Dan.

"I'll let you get settled, and then we'll grab some dinner," Dan said. He smiled at Nathan. "Tomorrow, you and I are going exploring."

* * * *

Jacob closed the door behind him and dropped onto the sofa beside Michelle. "He's in bed."

"Did he find enough pillows?" Michelle asked.

Jacob nodded. "He cleaned out a couple of the other rooms."

Nathan collected pillows like other children collected stuffed animals. At home, in addition to the full complement of bed pillows crowding his headboard, he kept a pair of superhero pillows at the foot of his bed, a set of oversized floor pillows piled in the corner of his room, plus any pillows he could sneak from the spare bedroom.

Nightly, Nathan lay quietly a few minutes after being tucked into bed —presumably until his parents thought him asleep—before stirring, stacking layers of pillows across his doorway as if to bar entry. Jacob and Michelle had tried darkening the hallway, ensuring Nathan knew they'd locked the doors, even promising that no monsters roamed the house. Still, Nathan stacked.

Michelle lamented their inability to determine what frightened Nathan. Jacob countered with an upbeat take on Nathan's behavior, preferring to focus on the following mornings. After plowing away the feather barrier, Jacob often found Nathan concealed within a cocoon of any remaining pillows. A scaredy-cat? Autism? How about playing make-believe? Name a kid who hadn't arranged boxes or pillows into a pretend house. Jacob's counterpoint served equal parts protest and, because Nathan's unexplained behavior distressed him, too, hopeful thinking.

Jacob didn't want to start this trip on the wrong foot by planting the seeds of another argument, though, so he didn't offer his prediction that Nathan would enjoy this trip. Michelle had as little tolerance for Jacob's decidedly benign assessments as he had for her doom and gloom. Anything he said might trigger accusations that he was yet again attempting to whitewash Nathan's problems. And since a retort was mandatory, Jacob would take offense to Michelle's insinuation that he cared less about Nathan's wellbeing than she did.

Of late, they'd strewn seeds everywhere. Over Nathan's stubborn diagnoses. Over Jacob's odd work hours and Michelle's long work hours separating them except in passing for days on end. Over his "infantile" need to carouse and her "uppity" need to network. Over his insecurities because she earned more money and her insecurities because prominent opinion questioned his choice of a mate. Over numerous other tribulations they once laughed or sexed away.

Jacob often admitted Michelle's points after replaying their argument while slogging through another work shift. His reflection reinforced the many interests he and Michelle still shared, Nathan's wellbeing topping the list. Jacob hoped that Michelle devoted equal time pondering *his* motivations and devotions, but of late, he feared not. Otherwise, why was she suggesting a trial separation?

"Dan is aging fast" Michelle said. "He felt brittle when we hugged."

Jacob nodded. "He's aged ten years since I last saw him. I think the years are finally catching up with him."

Michelle closed her computer. "I'm concerned about leaving Nathan with him. What happens if Dan has a health emergency? Or if Nathan starts throwing fits?"

"That's why we consulted Memphis before accepting

Dan's invitation," Jacob reminded her. "We won't accomplish anything if Nathan tags along."

"What about Nathan's medication?"

"I'll have Dan give Nathan his pills," Jacob said. "Dan's mind hasn't dulled. *You* told me that."

When Michelle still hesitated, Jacob extended his hand, palm up. "We promised each other we'd try."

Michelle relented and lifted her purse into her lap. After removing a narrow box with torn flaps, she squeezed the opened end into the shape of a football and peered inside.

"I forgot to throw it away," Jacob said, taking the empty box. "The new one's in the bottom."

Michelle rummaged deeper into her purse and handed Jacob an identical cellophane-wrapped box.

"I'll give this to Dan in the morning—with instructions," Jacob said. "And I'll remind him to let Nathan expend energy for them both."

Jacob glanced at the wall clock. It read three-thirty, the second hand frozen between the one and the two. "It's also our bedtime." They faced a strenuous day at the Childress Ranch.

"I'll join you in a little while," Michelle said, dumping her purse back onto the table and reopening her computer.

When Jacob leaned over for a kiss, she offered her cheek.

CHAPTER 37

The shoulder-height horseweed Nathan trudged through didn't escape Dan's attention. The stand's vigor pinpointed a leaking water pipe. Dan cataloged the repairs for next summer when capable help returned. Like so many other tasks, wielding a shovel was no longer in his repertoire.

Neither was keeping pace with an energetic seven-year-old. After seeing off Jacob and Michelle, Nathan insisted Dan take him on a "field trip" around Hat Creek. Dan convinced Nathan to abandon the roads and paths by stepping into the weeds while recounting Jacob's young bravery. At first tentatively, then ever more confidently as the morning wore on, Nathan eventually veered off any path whenever a straight line took him through weeds. He often added a quirky hitch to his gait, lifting his foot away just as quickly as he planted it, followed by a cute laugh.

"Tickle?" Dan asked.

"No," Nathan replied. "It sounds funny."

Sounds funny. A flighty and funny little guy.

Predictably, tempting Nathan into any of the buildings proved more difficult. To a child, much of Hat Creek had less right standing than a slender tower of wooden blocks.

"It's soft," Nathan said, poking at the ragged siding. When a piece broke away, he quickly pulled his hand back. "Sorry!"

"Don't worry about it," Dan said. "Much of this siding is so rotten that it'll break if you look at it wrong."

Nathan quickly turned his head away and focused on the ground.

Dan chuckled. "I didn't mean that literally, Nathan. Trust me. The cabin is safe." Dan opened the front door. "Want to take a peek inside?"

Nathan shook his head and stepped back.

"It's a normal home inside," Dan promised. "Just like your apartment in New York City."

When Dan's assurances didn't dispel Nathan's mistrust, Dan played the parent card again. "This is a special cabin. It's the first one your mother stayed in."

Nathan's attitude instantly flipped. He approached, pausing just short of the doorway before dashing inside, racing to the kitchen and back in the time it took Dan to step inside.

"It's real!" he said.

"I told you so," Dan said.

Nathan made a beeline for the bed and jumped onto the mattress. "Mom slept here?"

Dan nodded. "She did."

After a few bounces, Nathan hurried to the desk and opened the pencil drawer. "Mom *worked* here?" he asked, grabbing a pen from the drawer.

"Important work."

"Wow," Nathan said. "Did Mom use this pen?"

"I'm sure she did."

Nathan plopped into the desk chair and pretended to write. After a final flourish, he returned the pen to the drawer and tried out the armchair before dashing again into the kitchen to draw a glass of water. After gulping it down, he walked into the bathroom, closing the door behind him.

Once they returned outdoors, Dan found a comfortable seat and watched Nathan roam the length and breadth of the town: bounding into and out of two other cabins; fighting off pirates in the gazebo-turned-boat; pulling stray carrots from the garden; sprinting the length of the rut road to win a race by a nose; circling the fire ring, hopping from log to log without touching the ground; peering through the windows of the old cars. Nathan looked every bit the typical child. Either his parents and a slew of doctors were hypochondriacs-once-removed, or Hat Creek alleviated Nathan's symptoms.

Nathan had noticed the water tower from the start, but he gave it a wide berth as if afraid it might topple over on top of him. He eventually confronted it from the cover of Dan's truck, peering over the dusty hood for long seconds before pressing his hands over his ears and stepping into the open. "Is it loud?" he asked, pulling a hand down to point at the tower. "The rocket ship."

Dan chuckled, imagining Jacob describing Hat Creek to Nathan. *And the town even has a rocket ship!* "No, it's not," Dan said. "It's the best kind of rocket ship: a pretend one. The only sounds it makes are the ones you imagine."

And if the water tower was a rocket ship, then the tangle of water piping beneath it must be a jungle gym. Dan nodded towards Hat Creek's newest play area. "Go on."

And now Nathan was returning through the tallest weeds he could find. From cowering behind Dan's truck, hands over his ears, to scrambling up and over the water pipes, king of the jungle gym. A flighty, funny, and daring little guy.

"Can we climb the ladder?" Nathan asked.

"We'll wait and let your father take you up," Dan said, knowing his knees would no longer carry him up there. "I think your first flight should be with him." He stood. "Lunchtime. Hungry?"

Of course, Nathan was hungry. What normal boy wouldn't be?

"Mr. Dan!"

Dan stirred awake and blinked several times to regain his bearings. He was seated on the ground leaning back against a cottonwood, surrounded by the remains of their picnic lunch: an opened jar of peanut butter, perimeters of bread crust, a half-consumed bag of potato chips, a clear plastic sleeve of butter cookies, empty save a few broken bits, and three apple juice boxes, their folded white straws protruding like vent tubes. The child's favorite foods were gastronomically challenging to an octogenarian.

"Mr. Dan!" Nathan was out of sight at the creek bottom.

"Give me a moment." Dan wadded up his napkin and tossed it onto the blanket, bouncing it off the sealed box of Nathan's pills. After unpacking their lunch, Dan had removed the box from his shirt pocket, intending to give Nathan his medication. But Nathan had made a sour face as if Dan were offering him broccoli.

"That bad?" Dan asked.

Nathan nodded. "They make my tummy hurt."

Jacob had mentioned the frequent vomiting. "Your mother said to take one with food."

Nathan looked at Dan beseechingly. "Dad lets me skip

sometimes."

So, mother and father didn't see eye-to-eye on this matter, either. While uneasy about taking sides, Dan figured there was no harm in waiting until after their meal. And then Nathan had shown Dan how to make peanut butter and potato chip sandwiches, and Dan hadn't given Nathan's pills another thought.

Dan gathered up the juice boxes and shook each in turn. Empty, all, nothing to wash down a pill. He'd need to wait until they returned to Westside.

Dan slipped the box back into his shirt pocket and struggled to his feet. Advancing to the edge of the drop-off, he traced Nathan's direct descent down the steep creek bank through skid marks in the dirt. Nathan faced upstream, straddling a miniature waterfall. Reflected sunlight sparkled through the water as it dropped over a flat stone.

"Isn't this neat," Nathan said.

"Pretty colors," Dan said.

"No, listen," Nathan said, cocking his head. He lifted his hand and wiggled his fingers. "The water is twinkling."

Huh?

When Hat Creek's resident golden eagle sounded its amusement, Nathan's eyes flew open in alarm, and he scampered up the creek, circling behind Dan to use him as a shield.

"That's just our friendly bird saying hello," Dan said, puzzled again at how Nathan flipped from adventurous to timid in the blink of an eye. "He's too far away to spot, though. Maybe we'll get lucky later."

Nathan wedged himself under Dan's arm and slipped around in front, draping Dan's arm across his chest. "Don't tell Mom I was scared," he whispered, peering apprehensively into the trees.

Dan stepped down the Grange Hall stairs and glanced west. A dust cloud chased the Fineses back to town, their formally spotless sedan now coated in signature Black Hills tan. He leaned against the ramp railing to await their arrival.

Jacob pulled up, and the pair emerged into the late afternoon sunshine, their filth and odor cataloging the chores they'd tackled. Jacob scuffed the bottom of his boots into the weeds while waiting for Michelle to round the car. Instead, she made for the front door without making eye contact.

"Michelle claimed the first shower," Jacob explained after she disappeared inside.

"Nathan's napping in his room," Dan said. From inside the Hall, a door slammed shut. "*Trying* to nap in his room." Dan stared at Jacob's torn shirt. "Hard work?"

Jacob stuck a finger through a jagged rip. "I'd hoped a little manual effort might help us recapture the spark of our past." He frowned and shook his head. "It more served to remind us how much we've changed since then."

"Are you telling me that you and Michelle *didn't* spend the entire day quarreling?" Dan chuckled at Jacob's resultant smirk. "I've still got Alik's photographic record if you care to jog your memory."

"I'll pass," Jacob said. "And if you'd seen it coming, you could have at least warned us."

Dan shook his head. "Not my place."

"Yet you have no qualms finding amusement in our predicament."

"You forget how Hat Creek operates," Dan said. "'We've grown apart' is well past its expiration date; more an excuse to shirk responsibility. When I hear those words, I question why people bother making the trip."

"In our case, you invited us."

"Yes, but not to fall back on clichés."

Jacob folded his arms across his chest and huffed. "People *do* change, Dan."

Dan nodded. "Change is inevitable. I've known you as a teenaged runaway, a restless youth, a nervous groom, a clueless new father, and now an unsettled family man." Dan leaned in to let Jacob in on a secret. "It's called growing up."

Jacob rolled his eyes.

"You scoff," Dan said. "Then tell me why so many troubled couples visiting Hat Creek think it's growing *apart* that's inevitable—"

"We don't think that. *I* don't think that."

Jacob sighed and squatted on the end of the ramp railing, clearly frustrated.

Dan focused on Jacob's high-top leather boots, laces untied, crevices filled with mud—or worse—and slowly lifted his gaze: blue jeans, well-worn and dust-coated; brown leather belt, richly patinaed; light blue work shirt, untucked and sweat-stained, a rough-edged tear under one arm, stretched tightly over those sculpted muscles; handsome face, scarcely aged in twenty years.

"Father, husband, wage earner," Dan said. "You may be all grown up, but down deep, you're the same teenaged runaway that appeared at the base of my ladder." Dan poked a fingertip into one of Jacob's biceps, hard as a tree trunk. "You still lift weights because you enjoy women swooning over you."

"I lift weights to stay in shape," Jacob said. His eyes widened to emphasize the gravity of his following statement. "I've never been unfaithful to Michelle."

Dan nodded respectfully. "So, the rest is merely ... collateral damage?"

Jacob smiled sheepishly.

"Rumor mill says that you switch jobs faster than migrant farmworkers chasing the harvest. I recall that same restlessness in your youth."

"It's different."

"Yeah? How so?"

"Back then, I didn't know what I wanted to be."

"And now you do?"

Jacob blinked a few times. "Michelle constantly harps about me advancing into management. Sorry, but that's not my cup of tea. And I'm less irresponsible than she's always making me out to be. You can earn great money at *any* job if you work hard enough. Just so you know, when I take on extra hours, I often out-earn Michelle. *Very* responsible behavior, to my thinking."

"It also seems that your contempt for the academic world extends to Michelle's colleagues."

Jacob huffed. "They're snobs looking down on the world from their lofty diplomas. And you should hear what they say about me—but then you already know, don't you? Apparently, *everybody* thinks I'm stuck in adolescence."

"Big deal, you haven't shrugged off the vestiges of youth," Dan said. "Trust me. You'll look back years from now and wonder where it went. And as for Michelle? My eyes and ears tell me she hasn't mellowed one bit from the driven young lady wedded to her laptop and notebook, determined to conquer the world."

Jacob shook his head and answered with a light chuckle, "No, she hasn't." Tellingly, the corners of his mouth remained upturned. Michelle considered the head of their household might bruise Jacob's ego, but he was still proud of her.

"Settles that question," Dan said. "I'd suggest you look

elsewhere than 'we've changed' to describe your marital troubles."

Jacob's lips flattened under the gravity of the pressing concern. But if Dan's words chastened him, he didn't let on. "All I know is that I was married and happy. Now I'm married and unhappy."

"Unhappy enough to divorce?"

Finally, words that offended Jacob. "I didn't storm off, did I?"

"No," Dan admitted. He was glad he hadn't needless wounded Jacob further by reminding him of the child involved. If Dan could prompt Michelle to defend their marriage similarly, Nathan would have a chance.

"Sorry," Jacob said. "Today didn't go as I'd hoped."

"I take it ranch work still isn't Michelle's cup of tea."

Jacob shook his head. "First, she claimed she'd worn the wrong shoes and didn't want to get them dirty. Then, that lifting hurt her arms. The hole in her glove was causing a blister. Her sweaty shirt collar irritated her neck. We forgot sunscreen. 'Aren't you worried about leaving Nathan with Dan?'—" He looked at Dan hard. "You *knew* what would happen today, didn't you?"

Dan shrugged his shoulders. "Let's just say I had a hunch."

Jacob folded his arms over his chest and sighed in frustration. "So, is our problem that we've changed too much, or that we haven't changed at all—"

Michelle bounded out of Grange Hall and down the steps, her hair in a ponytail before reaching the dirt. "All clean," she said. "And I'm sorry." She apologized to Dan, though she clearly meant it for Jacob.

"I'll be quick," Jacob said, standing. "Then we can eat. I'm starving." When he bent over to kiss Michelle, she freely offered her cheek. Dan wondered if they were making up or merely declaring a truce.

She watched the door as Jacob stepped inside. "Nathan doesn't usually nap this time of the day."

"He deserved one. He ran himself ragged."

She looked at Dan. "I hope Nathan behaved himself."

"He did."

"No outbursts?"

"Outbursts? Plenty of them. Of running and climbing and exploration. Nathan enjoys playing alone, doesn't he?"

Michelle nodded. "He avoids large groups. And how was his appetite? Did he complain of a sore stomach?"

Dan folded his arms Jacob-style over the bulge in his shirt pocket. "Other than bread crusts, he devoured everything in sight."

CHAPTER 38

Dan soothed Nathan's disappointment over being excluded from Jacob and Michelle's day hike by promising him pizza for lunch, Nathan's choice of toppings. Nathan was giddy when Dan again withheld his medication after downing the triple cheese, hotdog, and bologna concoction. Beyond Dan's hunch that Jacob's instincts were correct, he reasoned a child expending so much energy needed a healthy appetite.

"Know what's better than pizza for lunch?" Dan asked, thumping at indigestion burgeoning behind his ribs as they exited the diner.

Nathan's eyes widened. "Cupcakes for dessert?"

"That, too," Dan admitted. "Perhaps later. I was thinking of searching for buried treasure."

Nathan's eyes widened further. "Buried treasure?"

Dan nodded. "Right here in Hat Creek. Game for that?"

"Yes!"

"Great. This way."

Dan led Nathan to the center of Hartman's. A decade had passed since a group of ecology zealots convinced Dan to replace the cast iron stove with an efficient electric heat pump. Bonfires in the firepit still consumed enough firewood to keep his residents active, splitting wood.

Dan grasped the portable shelf concealing the trap door and stared solemnly at Nathan. "Before we go any further, promise me that you'll tell nobody about what I'm going to show you." Intrigue always enhanced adventures.

Nathan's eyes opened wider than at the prospect of overdosing on sugar. "I promise," he said.

Dan nodded trust and rolled the shelf into the aisle.

"What is it?" Nathan asked, bending down to inspect the faintly visible square.

"The trap door to Hat Creek's secret room." He handed Nathan a flashlight. "Only three people in the entire world know it exists. Me, your father … and now you."

"Wow," Nathan said reverently.

Dan gingerly lowered himself to one knee and used the tip of his pocketknife blade to pry open the door. Nathan gasped when Dan lifted it to reveal the blackness beneath.

Dan closed his knife and set the door aside. "Have a look."

Nathan switched on the flashlight and played the light over the stairs and across the wooden shelving. "What's down there?"

"Old treasures," Dan said. "Tools, gadgets, other interesting items you've never seen. You can look at or play with anything except the glass bottles. I don't want to risk any broken glass. It's dark down there, but it's safe, and you'll have your flashlight."

"Aren't you coming?"

Dan shook his head. He had last descended the stairs to select Jacob and Michelle's wedding gift. "Climbing stairs is best left to intrepid explorers like you."

Nathan played in the cellar for an hour, only deciding to return when a second flashlight battery began weakening. Dan stopped Nathan at the bottom of the ladder and illuminated a shelf filled with cases of wine. "Carry one of those bottles up with you." The same vintage Dan had gifted Jacob and Michelle might make a good going-away present.

Nathan climbed the stairs, handed over the bottle, and then took off around the corner. Dan replaced the trap door and rolled the shelf back into place. A marble struck his boot as he rounded the end of the aisle. Nathan had discovered the tub of old marbles and was crashing them into each other.

Dan kicked the marble back. "You need more space for your game. And I know just the place." The church's concrete slab fit the bill, plus it was outdoors. "Follow me."

They detoured into his house to drop off the wine. "Is this your office?" Nathan asked when Dan entered his cluttered alcove.

"It is," Dan answered, placing the bottle out of harm's way on the floor in the corner.

"Do you do important work, like Mom?"

"Important work, but less important than hers. Let's head back outside."

Nathan walked with Dan across the blacktop before sprinting ahead and bounding onto the concrete slab. Dan progressed at a sedate pace and took the conventional route up the wide concrete steps, arriving in time to block a wayward marble from rolling off the edge.

Nathan skidded to a stop before Dan and bent down to retrieve the marble. "What are those?" he asked, noticing a pile of stones stacked haphazardly close to the foundation.

"Pieces of the old church walls," Dan said.

Nathan bunched the marbles on the slab and hopped to the ground. "They're heavy," he grunted, trying vainly to lift one of the stones. "I bet Dad could lift—"

He jerked to his full lanky height and gazed up the road. Seconds later, he clamored back onto the slab, a blur of motion. "We have to go inside!" he said frantically. "Inside!" he pled, pulling on Dan's hand. "Please!" Nathan hurried Dan to the foundation's edge and hopped down to the ground, gesticulating wildly for Dan to follow. "Hurry! Please hurry!" He looked hard back up the road and motioned again. "Please!"

"Go on ahead, Nathan," Dan said. "I'll catch up with you," Dan pointed up the road. "Your mother's cabin. Stay off the road."

While Nathan took off in a dead run, Dan collected the marbles and descended the steps. Pausing to peer up the road, he caught the glint of sunlight reflecting off windshield and chrome barreling toward Hat Creek. Had Nathan never seen a semi-tractor trailer?

Dan reached the cabin barely thirty seconds ahead of the truck. Turning in the doorway to look up the road, he reconsidered Nathan's plight. The giant chrome grille fronting the burnt orange cab and gleaming silver trailer would frighten any seven-year-old. Dan half-wished Todd had insisted on speed limit signs.

Dan entered and closed the door, only marginally muffling the oncoming thunder. Nathan wasn't in view. Hiding? A quick search found him cowering in the bathroom corner with his hands clamped over his ears. As the eighteen-wheeler roared past, Nathan cringed as if the noise were the real menace.

Noise. Sound. Nathan had asked Dan to *listen* to the sparkling water falling over the rock and had thought the distant eagle directly overhead. And more instances: flinching at Dan's loud welcome, laughing at the sound of crunching weeds, hearing the approaching semi before seeing it. Nathan experienced the world in sound, Dan guessed, much like a blind person compensating for their loss of sight.

And much like Alik Popov. Dan recalled Alik's description of his tortured childhood before being diagnosed with sensitive hearing. What was the name of his affliction? Hyperacusis. Was it possible Nathan suffered a similar issue? It would explain much of Nathan's behavior.

Dan returned to the front window so Nathan wouldn't suffer the indignity of being witnessed in such a vulnerable condition, peering outside until he felt Nathan's presence. "Loud trucks have always bothered me, too," Dan said in a subdued tone. "Maybe I'll ban them driving through Hat Creek." He looked at Nathan. "Does it help when I speak more softly?"

"Yes."

Dan nodded. Still speaking softly, he said, "There's a cabin we haven't explored yet. You'll love it."

The Studio looked like every other Hat Creek building. Several lengths of its sun-washed gray siding were broken or missing, while a section of roof shingles had slipped down over the edge of the eaves. The windowpanes were rippled and cracked, and a window shutter hung at a severe angle, a natural decay Dan had fixed in place years ago.

"This cabin is different," Dan said as they approached. Nathan was holding Dan's hand now, another great perk of playing grandfather. "It's a studio—a play area—for visiting artists."

"To paint pictures?"

"The painters do. Several other kinds of artists have used this cabin, too. Photographers, writers, musicians, and even a sculptor. It's peaceful and quiet inside."

"Quiet?" Nathan asked hopefully.

"Very quiet," Dan whispered. "You'll see." And he might find out if he had discovered the root of Nathan's real problem.

Dan ushered Nathan inside. The Studio's furnishings were intentionally spartan. Artists often brought their equipment and supplies—one musician had lugged an entire portable recording studio—and needed the space.

Nathan made a beeline to the desk and removed a pencil and a sheet of paper from the pencil drawer. "Can I draw a picture?" he asked, sitting down.

"If you'd like," Dan said. "First, I want to show you what makes the Studio so special."

Dan closed the door and twisted a latch to engage the full-perimeter seal. As he had planned that day after learning of Alik's condition, he had installed installing similar airtight windows, plus caulked every crack and gap and filled the space inside the walls and ceiling with sound-absorbing insulation. The only opening to the outside world was an acoustic air-exchange system to ensure adequate air circulation.

"Lay your pencil down and remain still," Dan said. "Don't move a muscle."

Nathan stilled.

"Tell me what you hear," Dan said softly.

After a long pause, Nathan's brows furrowed, puzzlement giving way to frustration. "I don't hear anything."

"That's right," Dan said, nodding. "I soundproofed this cabin to block out all outside noise. If you'd been playing marbles in here instead of outside, you wouldn't have even known that a loud truck drove through town."

Nathan closed his eyes and tested the air for sound again. "I don't hear anything," he whispered. He was smiling when he opened his eyes. "Can I play in here tomorrow?"

Dan smiled at the further indication that he had discovered Nathan's real issue. To what other child did the *absence* of sound mean so much?

"Of course."

Nathan raised to his knees and picked up the pencil. "We'll play school," he said. "You can be my teacher."

"Deal," Dan said. He looked at his watch. "It's dinner time. How about you and I cook up something together."

Dan strolled to his truck and dropped the tailgate. An uncompromising seat, true, but the ideal vantage point to enjoy sunsets. This one didn't disappoint. The sun had just dipped behind a low bank of cumulus clouds, silhouetting them a deep blue-gray and ceding all color to the wispy cirrus clouds streaking the sky. Pumpkin orange at the horizon variegated through hues of pinks and yellows to a reddish-purple overhead. Painterly.

A chill was settling in. It would be jacket weather within weeks, eventually cold enough to sequester Dan inside for the winter. Inside a home stocked to the gills with staples by youthful do-gooders to ensure Dan's survival through a feared epic blizzard.

Dan heard the approaching footsteps and acknowledged Michelle's wave. After spotting Jacob and Michelle's return, he had sent Nathan to Grange Hall, then puttered about in his kitchen for ten minutes before heading outdoors in plain view. Michelle had taken the bait.

"Mind a little company?" she asked.

"Not at all." Dan patted the tailgate beside him.

Michelle joined him and gazed into the sky. "Beautiful," she said.

"It is."

She fingered the corrugated metal. "Jacob told me this was his favorite spot to sit and talk."

Dan nodded. "It serves its purpose."

"I should have been paying more attention. I guess I never thought I'd be sitting on this side."

She cleared her throat several times as if trying to figure out how to start. "I know what you must be thinking," she finally chose.

The evening sky lent a healthy glow to Michelle's youthful skin and ever-present ponytail, stripping away the past ten years. But it couldn't whitewash her guilt for the overcrowded state of Dan's kitchen. She had orchestrated the provisioning effort from afar.

"That you would have been only mildly shocked to arrive and find me passed away in my chair," he said. "You would have phoned Memphis and said simply, 'Dan's dead,' and that would have been the end of it."

Michelle blinked twice. "Dan, that was morbid."

Dan chuckled. "Memphis tattled on you."

She looked away. "Sorry."

"Don't be. It's reassuring when parents check ahead on the health of their child's sitter."

Michelle caught his sarcasm. "You want me to say that it's all my fault? Okay, it's all my fault."

Dan ignored the opening. He wasn't in a charitable enough mood to let Michelle off easily. "Memphis told me he fed you the line about my meds reminding him of a bag of Skittles."

"It's no joke, though, is it, Dan? Nathan wore you out today, the same as yesterday. We'll take him with us tomorrow."

"You'll do no such thing. I know how to pace myself."

Michelle raised an eyebrow.

"Tomorrow's agenda includes no strenuous activities," Dan said. The day playing school in Nathan's ideal environs would be telling.

"Like to start over?" he asked. "Or did you drop by to inform me that you made the trip simply to humor me?"

"It's more complicated, Dan," Michelle said.

"I'd be disappointed if it wasn't."

Michelle absorbed his line. "I don't know whether I can make you understand."

She faced a tall order. "I may be as old-fashioned as I am old," Dan said, "but after hosting several couples best kept across state lines from each other, I'm no longer a strict disciple of 'till death do us part.' Having said that, unless you're about to divulge some deep, dark secret, you and Jacob's marital problems don't approach my threshold."

"Remember the rollercoaster ride I described?" Michelle asked. "From before Jacob and I married?"

"Yes."

Michelle repeated what she had previously told Dan of Jacob's courtship, attracted to his confidence and sense of adventure. She had accepted his proposal only after deciding that, for her, love and addiction were two sides of the same coin.

"The ride never slowed, Dan. Of course, I wasn't naïve enough to think 'I do's' would automatically smooth it out. I just didn't expect the ups to peter out and for everything to speed downhill." She leaned back on her hands and sighed. "Lately, we've fallen off the rails."

After a pause, she shook her head and sat up. "You've concluded that my interns and I are obsessive, nosey, selfish, and singularly focused. Career defines our lives. That's an admission, as well as a fact. Along with starting our marriage, I was starting mine. I assumed Jacob would do the same.

Instead, Jacob kept drifting along." Softer, as if in lament, she added, "He's still drifting."

Michelle clasped her hands. "I know I told you how off-kilter we could get. Unfortunately, that disconnect has become commonplace, of late, more the rule. I've lost count of the number of times Jacob has tried to drag me away from my work." She scowled. "Take off six months to hike the Appalachian Trail?

"Dan, Jacob won't accept that I can't just show up to my job and put in my hours as he does. I'm speaking in a foreign tongue when I tell him that tenure is life or death, publish or perish almost as literal, and obtaining research grants akin to survival of the fittest. If I don't excel, I don't keep my job."

Dan heard Michelle's words, and also *I, I, I.*

Michelle's eyes narrowed, reading his mind. "I've already admitted that I'm selfish," she said. "Self-absorbed, a workaholic, career-driven. Call me what you wish. But I *have* compromised. I quit insisting Jacob get a college degree. In return, I expected him to understand and support that *I do* have goals.

"With increasing frequency, Jacob's disruptions are taking on a more cynical tone. The more commitments I have, the more likely he'll claim he can't get off work, making me drop everything to take Nathan to his doctor's appointments. And just a month ago, our rental Jeep mysteriously wouldn't start when we were ready to return from the mountains, making me miss the start of school." She rolled her eyes. "How was Jacob *suddenly* able to fix the problem a day later? He's no mechanic."

Dan would have chuckled had the stakes not been so high. Michelle's complaint reinforced his suspicion from Jacob's conversation that neither had changed. Jacob needed to grow up, and Michelle needed to lighten up.

"The news of my pregnancy undoubtedly surprised you."

Change, however, had been thrust upon the pair. Dan remembered being astonished rather than surprised at the news, but he only nodded in agreement.

"No less for me." After a pause, Michelle smirked. "Surprising and ..."

Dan heard the word "unwelcome" as clearly as if Michelle had spoken it aloud. If an unambitious husband stunted her career, imagine how much damage perpetual fatigue, middle-of-the-night feedings, laundry duty, crisis doctor's visits, daycare drama, and other childcare demands, ad infinitum, could cause. Add Nathan's undiagnosed medical issues, and husband and child must blare a stereo cacophony of distractions making Michelle's family life untenable.

Michelle sensed Dan's revulsion. "I love Nathan with all my heart, Dan. I'm not abandoning him."

Nathan, like any child, craved his parents' approval. He was sure of his father's. Of his mother's, not so much, despite such assertions; running fast was easier than excelling at school. Nathan mustn't spend tomorrow drawing pictures. What would make Michelle proud of him?

"I didn't think you'd understand," Michelle said, for once misreading Dan's body language. "I wanted you to hear everything directly from me." She leaned forward and rested her forearms on her thighs. "I've tried to make our marriage work, Dan. I truly have. But evenings have turned into such a grind that whenever I'm home, all I think about is ... being away."

"Away from home or away from family?" Dan asked.

To Michelle's credit, she searched her feelings before answering. "Both."

She accepted Dan's disappointment. "I've already admitted

my failings. I'm going to step away and dedicate myself to my career." She shook her head. "Don't ask me for how long. I don't know myself. Until I feel good about myself again and don't blame Jacob and Nathan for my shortcomings."

Dan recalled a conversation between summer interns debating the general futility of trial separations, statistics showing that most of those couples eventually divorced. Tragedies could unfold at any speed. Instantly, with devastating consequences, as had his. Or slowly, layered from seemingly benign events and well-intentioned, at worst misguided, acts. The children suffered all the same.

"During that same rollercoaster conversation," he said, "do you remember asking me of my marriage, 'Was it worth it?'"

Michelle nodded solemnly.

"Promise yourself that before you stop the ride and jump off, you'll ask the question, '*Will* it be worth it?'"

CHAPTER 39

Dan dropped into his office chair and switched on his computer. The sun wouldn't rise for another hour, the Fines clan longer, leaving ample time to prepare for Nathan's day before heading over to Westside to cook breakfast.

Nathan's enthusiasm for playing school hinted at a latent hunger for knowledge. If, as Dan speculated, Nathan was trapped in a toxic school environment that hampered his ability to concentrate, the Studio's solitude might free him to succeed. Michelle couldn't help but be comforted by the tangible proof of Nathan's intellect.

Dan logged into an educational website and loaded paper into his printer. A pencil, a ream of school worksheets, and a quiet classroom might secure Nathan's family and future.

Dan leaned against the Studio doorway and watched Nathan sprint the length of Brule Street. Recess was as much a part of the school day as reading, writing, and arithmetic, and a welcome break for Nathan to have the fun he had so looked forward to yesterday.

Dan had hoped today's school session would reveal Nathan as a bright and well-adjusted boy, simply a child who thrived in a different learning environment. Instead, Nathan couldn't have scored worse had he attempted high-school-level worksheets. The mechanics of two-digit addition proved beyond his capability. So, too, math concepts such as the graphical representation of fractions or completing patterns. Likewise, any spelling words longer than four letters drifted off course, and Nathan's sentences generally lacked structure and sense.

Nathan finished his sprint, thrusting out his chest at the finish line and raising his arms in triumph. He enjoyed competition, especially where he could boss the results. It saddened Dan to think that Nathan's successes were limited to imagined ones.

Before Dan's heartbeat would have slowed, Nathan whirled around and scratched a starting line into the dirt with his heel. Leaning forward, coiling his pent-up energy, Nathan tore off at the sound of an imaginary starter's pistol. He exhibited basic comprehension when stepped through the exercises. But how to unlock his scholastic potential? If Dan could coax Nathan into channeling his competitive energies towards success on core subjects, the impact would be real.

* * * *

When Nathan closed his eyes, he could still see his math paper, blank other than the erasure smudges of his first attempts. Every week at his real school, his teacher asked each student to step to the whiteboard and solve a problem. Some weeks, it was a math problem: other weeks, a spelling word or a geography or vocabulary question. Nathan always tried his best. But Vivian smacked her gum, and Johnnie rocked his chair against the floor, and Mike drummed his pencil on his desk, and Stacie stuck out her tongue at him—he could hear the giggling—and the numbers and letters jumbled up. Ms. Rivera made Nathan stand at the board while Freddie or Christy corrected his mistakes and then told him to take his seat and pay attention next time. Everyone had laughed at him when he couldn't find New York on the giant United States map.

They had to take their papers home each Friday to be signed by their parents. Nathan once tried copying Mom's name, but Ms. Rivera caught him and threatened to send him to the principal's office. Nathan knew his bad papers made Mom sad. *I'm sorry, Mom. I'm sorry.*

A tear ran down Nathan's cheek. He wiped it away and peeked up, but Mr. Dan was sleeping in his chair. Nathan decided it was okay for a teacher to nap during school. They couldn't run around all day like second graders.

Nathan liked Mr. Dan, even if he did get tired. Mr. Dan let Nathan play wherever he wanted, except on the piles of wood where rattlesnakes might be hiding. (Nathan hadn't told Mr. Dan that he'd heard a snake in the weeds.) Mr. Dan even let him explore the secret room Mom didn't know about. And Mr. Dan had built this room for people who liked quiet places, the same as Nathan. Mom said it was Mr. Dan's job to help people. Nathan wished Mr. Dan could be his teacher. He would treat all his students nicely, even the struggling ones. And Mr. Dan wouldn't make fun of Nathan for crying or covering his ears.

Nathan pretended he was in his real classroom, except that Mr. Dan was his teacher. Stacie never stuck out her tongue at Nathan, and Bobbie and David didn't trip him anymore because Mr. Dan taught his students to respect one another. Each one of them had unique talents, Mr. Dan said. Nathan's was running, exploring, and hearing snakes in the grass before they could get close enough to bite.

A new student stood at the board, stuck on a math problem. "Nathan," Mr. Dan said, "could you please come up and help Matthew?"

No teacher had ever asked Nathan to help a classmate. "You can do it, Nathan," Christy whispered as he hesitantly started up the aisle. Her encouragement gave Nathan the confidence to look at the board. Instead of jumbled-up shapes, he saw two numbers, one above the other, a simple addition problem. And Nathan recognized that Matthew didn't know how to carry.

Nathan picked up a marker and started over. "You added six plus eight correctly," he told Matthew, "only you write the four below the line"—Nathan penned the number in his best handwriting—"and carry the one above the ten's place." Nathan repeated his lesson for the ten's place to finish the problem.

"Correct, Nathan," Mr. Dan said. "Thank you."

Nathan squeezed his eyes tightly to enjoy being the smartest in his class. When the make-believe faded, Mr. Dan's soft breathing was the only sound.

Nathan bowed his head to his math paper and opened his eyes. The numbers appeared in neat rows, the same as the pretend in his head. Nathan quickly finished the first problem and started on the next. Math was easy.

Nathan completed another math sheet sprinkled with subtraction problems before coloring the United States map.

He studied the wall map hanging beside his school desk every day so he'd known that day how to find New York. But he lied so Ms. Rivera wouldn't ask him another, more challenging question. And then, his classmates laughed at him, and Stevie told everyone at recess that Nathan was being sent down to first grade, and Ms. Rivera wrote a note home saying Nathan refused to participate in class.

Now he didn't need to close his eyes to remember the state names and big cities, or the Mississippi River and the Rocky Mountains. He circled where he lived and wrote "New York" in his best penmanship. He knew where Hat Creek was located, too, across the country in South Dakota. He labeled the state and carefully spelled out "Nebraska" inside the state outline below it, where their second airplane had landed. One, two, three states. He wrote "Colorado," in the square state where their first plane landed, as number four, and then marked New Jersey, Pennsylvania, and Connecticut, the states closest to New York. That made seven. Christy had missed after labeling six states, mistaking Kentucky for Tennessee. Even Nathan knew those two states apart. And how to spell their names, too.

Nathan wished he lived in Hat Creek and could go to school in this room. He would play outside for recess, take science field trips along the creek, eat lunch in Mr. Dan's cafeteria, draw pictures of bugs, snakes, and birds, and read books while sitting high up on the water tower. He would show how smart he was in this classroom. That would make Mom proud of him.

* * * *

"Mr. Dan?"

Dan jerked at the unexpected sight of Nathan's inquisitive

face only inches away. Dan could have sworn he had shut his eyes only a few seconds earlier so Nathan wouldn't feel embarrassed about crying. The healthy stack of completed worksheets Nathan handed Dan argued otherwise.

"Let's have a look," Dan said, discretely stretching his stiff muscles as he placed Nathan's work on the desk. He blinked in surprise at the top sheet, three columns of math addition problems, legible—and correct!—answers replacing Nathan's earlier chicken scratches. Dan flipped quickly through the worksheets. Nathan had completed the remainder equally as neatly. Had that switch finally flipped on in Nathan's head as Dan napped?

Nathan scored twenty-eight out of thirty on the top sheet, which Dan tallied at the top of the page, followed by a bold "A" and a large gold star. "Outstanding, young man," he said.

Nathan beamed at his score and watched Dan grade more papers, collecting more gold stars and eagerly accepting Dan's offer to correct his errors. While Nathan's results on advanced concepts didn't match the accuracy of the core ideas, he quickly grasped each new concept with minimal tutoring.

Watching Nathan soldier through the last few corrections, Dan gained confidence in his diagnosis of a learning disability caused by sensitive hearing. Unbeknownst even to himself, Nathan had been absorbing the lessons taught at school and by his parents. But the constant audial din had impaired his ability to access that information. The explanation was hopeful rather than fatalistic and more straightforward than Nathan suffering from some complicated slurry of mental and developmental disorders. And now, armed with this tangible, gold-star evidence of Nathan's true potential, his explanation was defensible to any PhD, mother or no.

Dan smiled when Nathan pressed his tongue out the corner

of his mouth. That had been Anna's trademark when *she* worked through tricky problems, just one of many non-verbal cues in her repertoire. She twirled a lock of hair around her finger when immersed in a good book. Rolling her eyes at him meant, "quit being silly, Dad; you're embarrassing me." She closed her mouth tightly when hearing someone utter an expletive, while flared nostrils with pursed lips meant she was exasperated at something or someone (usually her bratty sister) and apt to strike out. And she tiptoed through the room when she had been naughty, an unnecessary attempt at stealth because Georgia was usually already bawling.

Dan stood and gazed out the window. What would Anna and Georgia have thought of Hat Creek? Anna would have loved the wildflowers but hated the clutter. Georgia and Nathan might have been mistaken for twins in their shared zeal to treat the town as a jungle gym. Dan relished this inner glow. It was refreshing to think of his daughters without being crushed by remorse. He was awakening, as well.

"Mr. Dan?"

Nathan presented his last corrected worksheet for grading. Gleeful when Dan returned a perfect score, he added the sheet to his pile and carefully straightened the edges. "Can I have more papers?"

Dan looked at his watch. Noonish. "It's lunchtime. You still want to eat in the diner—the cafeteria? At the long table?"

Nathan shook his head. "I want to keep working."

Music to Dan's ears. Lunch was too important to skip, though. He paged through the few remaining blank worksheets. "I'll give you these to work on while I make lunch. I'll come for you when it's ready."

Dan detoured into his house to print a broad selection of third- and fourth-grade worksheets before scouring Hartman's and Westside for a Nathan-inspired lunch. Twenty minutes later, watching Nathan assemble a Nutella, peanut butter, and jelly-layered sandwich, Dan wondered which Nathan enjoyed more: the taste of the sandwich or the fun of constructing it. And deep into an afternoon, observing a child bloom into his true potential, Dan never once considered the still-unopened box of medicine stuffed inside his shirt pocket.

CHAPTER 40

"Ready, young man?"

Nathan had insisted they pretend it was Friday so he could take his papers to be signed by Mom and Dad, just like at his real school. He clutched his folder to his chest and stepped outdoors ahead of Dan, trudging through the weeds directly to Grange Hall. A boy on a mission.

Dan followed at a comfortable pace, figuring to sit silently and allow Nathan the honor of showing off his work, only assuring Michelle and Jacob that, yes, this was their son's efforts. Nathan's achievements would allow Dan to make his case for Nathan's true underlying issue.

Nathan's confident pace faltered as he neared the gravel road, and he advanced only a few more hesitant steps before halting. Dan looked left and right, anticipating an approaching dust cloud, but saw nothing. A snake in the grass? Dan hurried to catch up.

Nathan's issue was nothing so simple as an approaching

truck or a slithering menace. He was deflating like a punctured tire, his head dropping, shoulders drooping, inches shorter and still shrinking, the grip on his precious papers slackening.

"What's wrong?" Dan asked softly.

Nathan didn't answer, staring straight ahead, his lower lip quivering and his eyes watering. He had been anxious to show off his work to his parents only a moment earlier. Proudly so, walking-straight-through-the-tall-weeds so. Now he was upset to the verge of tears, incapable of advancing another step.

What had so suddenly poisoned Grange Hall? Asking the question answered it.

"Wait here," Dan told Nathan.

Dan crossed the road, climbed the Grange Hall steps, and opened the front door. Only then could he make out the staccato bursts of the argument that had stopped Nathan in his tracks. How often had Nathan inadvertently borne witness to his parents' crumbling relationship?

Dan turned back to a heartrending sight. Nathan stood in stoic silence, tears streaming down his innocent cheeks, trembling lips clamped shut to quell the urge to bawl, his arms crossed over his chest, crushing his forgotten efforts.

"Let's return to our classroom," Dan said, rescuing the folder before Nathan's papers got ruined. He took Nathan's hand and turned him around, knowing it would be useless to promise Nathan that he wasn't at fault for his parents' conduct. Children's sense of the truth is independent of adult reasoning.

"Parents are sometimes naughty, just like children," Dan instead said as they walked. "But *their* parents aren't around to scold them and make them behave."

Nathan wiped his face and said, barely above a whisper, "I heard Grandpa once tell Mom and Dad to 'grow up and act like adults.'"

"Did they listen to him?"

Nathan nodded. "Mom and Dad said sorry and took me to the zoo. I got to ride a camel." They turned up the path to the Studio. "And Mom let me eat a hotdog and a funnel cake and didn't make me take my medicine."

Medicine. Always the medicine Dan still carried in his shirt pocket.

Back inside the Studio, Dan laid Nathan's folder on the desk and grabbed a tissue. "I'm old enough to be your grandpa," he said, wiping Nathan's face. "So, I'll return and tell your mother and father that they mustn't argue anymore. And then, I'll send them here to you. Meanwhile, why don't you arrange your papers on the desk and move two more chairs closer for them to sit." Dan lifted Nathan's chin and inspected his cheeks. "Much better. Your parents *will* be so proud of your work. I promise."

Nathan nodded optimistically.

Dan suggested Nathan bide his time coloring his parents a picture and retraced his steps to Grange Hall. He had hoped that Jacob and Michelle's ugly spat would have run its course, but opening the Hall's front door—

"—Nathan a liability. In public, you're too embarrassed even to show him any love."

"And you can't hold a job for more than a year." Michelle snarled back. "What kind of role model is that?"

The pair were too engrossed in their attacks to notice Dan stepping into their doorway.

"At least 'family' isn't a four-letter word to me," Jacob said.

Michelle gasped. "How dare you? I never claimed to be perfect. But I'm not the one drifting aimlessly through—"

"Shut up!" Dan yelled.

Michelle's head jerked so violently that the spittle dotting her mouth flew into the air. Jacob revealed that Nathan's wide-eyed surprise was an inherited trait.

"Sit down!"

Jacob dropped onto the sofa like he'd been shot. Michelle eyed the chair.

"Together!" Dan snapped.

Michelle submitted in a vain attempt at appearing that that had been her plan all along.

"Shame on you," Dan snarled, nabbing the chair. "I was expecting confirmation that you two are mature role models providing Nathan with a safe, nurturing environment. Instead, I find self-absorbed adolescents. Your dereliction is inexcusable."

Dan's outburst didn't satisfy his compulsion to issue a harsh reprimand. Beyond venting his disgust, Dan wanted Jacob and Michelle wounded by such deep remorse that they would never repeat such disgraceful behavior. He was Mabel slinking through the weeds; the only danger Nathan *should* have faced. With his victims sitting directly before him, he coiled up and struck: "How dare you harm your precious child!"

As if striking at impervious stone figures with real fangs, the accusation deflected off the warring couple back at Dan, injecting words-as-poison into his ears: *HOW DARE YOU HARM YOUR PRECIOUS CHILDREN!* The charge reverberated across his mind, his profound guilt amplifying the indictment.

Dan slumped in the chair, his vision reduced to hazy, featureless light upon which snippets of the disaster played: witnessing the bottom of Anna's pink shoe, her prone body spilled into the dining room; sitting in the frozen grass, shielding Anna from the pulsating ambulance lights; burying her face into his chest when the gurneys carrying her sister and mother rolled outside through their front door; standing in the cemetery under an overcast sky dropping snow, watching three caskets lowered into the ground.

The anguish grew unbearable. Dan knew mortal wounds; he had miraculously escaped more than one. This hurt worse. Why hadn't he laid down in the snow when lost outdoors in the blinding blizzard that first winter or relaxed into the calming depths of the water tower as his life's blood leaked out his filleted arm—

"Dan?"

Grace? No. Not Grace. She called to him by a different name.

Dan surrendered, unable to resist any further. Unopposed, the disaster flooded through him, every detail in full view. This time, he rode the current, freely submitting to the lives stolen and accepting the personal rebuke. Once the forgiver became the forgiven, the terror drained away, leaving behind only a wistful "what if" and gratitude for the time granted with his family.

"Dan." It was Michelle. "Do you need us to call for help?"

Dan sat up and took a reassuring deep breath, remembering Florence's lesson and his conversation about his family with Megan and Chloe. He shook his head. "No. The episode is over."

Gone, too, was his capacity for rage. In its wake remained an appreciation for Jacob and Michelle's courage in accepting his offer to come. That, thus far, their trip had been primarily a display of poor parenting skills shouldn't rule out hope.

When Dan pulled his hand away, his fingers brushed over the bulge in his shirt pocket. *To help Nathan.* That was why he persevered during that blizzard and climbed out of the water tower. And why he had endured disasters of every conceivable kind. To help Nathan.

Dan inspected his hands and arms, recalling when they

were unscarred—when *he* was unscarred—and enjoyed the privilege of hugging his loved ones. To help Nathan, he must first finish healing himself. That meant an end to the concealing—the end to the lying.

"Meeting Grace was my greatest joy," he whispered, and suddenly Grace was looking up at him from her spilled coffee, amused rather than angry. "Amazing eyes," she said. Dan had forgotten her very first words until this moment.

He looked from Jacob to Michelle, Grace's compliment lingering like the lovely hues of an evening sky. "Grace gave meaning to my life, and then more. With the birth of Anna and Georgia, I discovered my life's true calling: Fatherhood, being the best possible protector, teacher, role model, and friend to my daughters. I devoted my life to them."

Wonderful remembrances of his daughters flitted into Dan's memory: Anna shrieking in laughter as he towed her on her blanket along the floor … coaching Georgia's soccer team, the little ponytailed girls more interested in finding four-leaf clovers than chasing the ball … roasting hotdogs and s'mores by the fire during father-daughter camping trips.

"It all ended that day."

Dan took a deep breath and slowly exhaled. "The girls were off from school, a teacher in-service day. I phoned Grace mid-afternoon to check on dinner plans, but she didn't answer. I assumed they were busy.

"I knew something was odd the moment I returned home." The cold doorknob had stung his fingers. "There was no dinner cooking on the stove, no evening news playing on the television, no chattering daughters. Only silence."

Dan had entered as far as the kitchen, finding no one until he turned around.

"Anna was unconscious on the mudroom hallway floor,

only ten feet from the door. She wasn't breathing." Dan shook his head. "Next thing I remember, I was curled up in a ball in our front yard, rocking her limp body in my lap. I learned later that Grace and Georgia passed away at the base of the stairs, Grace still hugging Georgia to her chest."

Dan pressed the heels of his hands into his eyes to banish the terrifying images. The gesture was as futile as the countless times he had pleaded to the granite leaders, to the sky, to the endless pastureland, to any real or imagined divinities that might be listening, for the chance to turn back time and finish one mundane task. With an anguished cry, he dropped his hands to his lap.

"I painted the windows shut!" he wailed. "I had painted our house that fall and became preoccupied rushing to finish other repairs before the weather turned, and—" he slowly shook his head "—and I never unstuck the windows."

Dan recalled how badly his head had hurt that cold morning when the cause of his headache had been carbon monoxide poisoning instead of shrunken sinuses. "EMTs found traces of Grace's blood and skin on a crushed mullion of one window in the upstairs playroom and more bloody knuckle prints on another. Carbon monoxide poisoning causes headaches, upset stomach, dizziness, and confusion. Experts told me that Grace surely experienced those symptoms but likely assumed it was the onset of illness. Something alerted her to the actual danger; Georgia, being the smallest, would have succumbed first. Incapacitated, though, and burdened by the responsibility to save our daughters and herself, the time Grace spent trying to open the windows cost her getting the girls out of the house.

"And so, my beautiful wife and daughters died." Dan let out a heavy sigh. "I killed my family." He forced himself to look straight at Jacob and Michelle. "I killed my family."

Jacob stared back open-mouthed. Michelle returned Dan's gaze with measured compassion, withholding absolution, understanding that only Dan held that power.

"I'm sorry for your loss, Dan," she said. "And I'm sorry, too, for my past intrusions. You moved here and founded Hat Creek for such a noble reason."

Dan shook his head. "I don't deserve any fancy plaudits. I didn't *move* anywhere. I ran away. Cowardly. I knew it was only a matter of time before everyone knew the details of my family's death. I was already overwhelmed by self-blame and hadn't the strength to face everyone's scorn. So, I buried Grace, Anna, and Georgia, packed a few belongings into my car, and stole away in the middle of the night.

"I had no destination in mind, only to remain inconspicuous. But every greeting or acknowledgment, even a stray glance, felt like an indictment: 'Aren't you that guy who killed his entire family?' So, I kept running.

"Eventually, I wandered into the Black Hills. The granite Presidents ignored me, and Crazy Horse showed compassion. One day I stumbled onto an old ghost town and decided to stay."

Dan shook his head again. "But it was another ten years before I founded Hat Creek."

"Ten years?" Jacob mumbled. "Then what *were* you doing here?"

Dan shrugged his shoulders. "Keeping busy, mostly."

It was Michelle's turn to shake her head. "Punishing yourself."

Dan studied the ugly scars zigzagging like lightning bolts along his arms. Hat Creek's first resident or first attempted suicide? "I'll leave the clinical interpretation to Michelle." He looked at Jacob. "The seeds of Hat Creek were planted by a teenage runaway appearing at the base of my ladder. After a bumpy start, he grew on me, and I convinced him to return home. At the time, I believed I'd made a difference in his life.

"He made a difference in mine. For the first time in years, I felt less poorly about myself. I got this wild hair that forming the retreat might prove therapeutic, and, well, you both know the rest." Dan smiled at Jacob. "That young man never knew how he restored hope to a hopeless life."

Jacob sighed. "He does now."

Michelle's jaw dropped, and she looked from Dan to Jacob, the missing puzzle piece explaining Hat Creek falling into place.

"Oh, Dan," she said, shaking her head. "You *must* know that you've paid several times over for any wrongs you think you've committed."

Forgiving yourself is the steepest absolution to earn. Dan remembered the currency he had accrued. His final payment was restoring hope to the next generation's "young man."

"Lest I forget," he said, "I need to return Nathan's medicine." He fished the box from his shirt pocket and tossed it to Michelle.

She turned the box over in her hands. "It's still sealed! You never gave Nathan his medicine." She glared accusingly at Jacob, who only shook his head, so she redirected her ire at Dan. "How could you be so reckless?"

"Reckless? What do you call the scene you two were making? Where do you think Nathan was standing? And how many other times have you two argued without considering—without caring—whether Nathan was within earshot?"

Chastened, Michelle looked away. Jacob caught Dan's eye long enough to accept the reprimand.

"This preoccupation with pathetic bickering has blinded you to the fact that you're parents to an exceptional boy," Dan said. "Nathan spent the entire day on a special project. He was so proud of it that he couldn't wait to show you. Instead, I had to send him away."

Dan knew Nathan had hope when Jacob and Michelle eventually looked contritely at each other.

"Nathan is waiting for you in the Studio," Dan said. "You will greet him as loving parents who care and respect each other. And I insist you speak to him in soft tones, barely above a whisper." At the pair's predictable puzzlement, Dan added, "I'll explain *that* when you return. Now go."

Michelle reentered first, cradling Nathan's folder. Jacob followed and, after waiting for Michelle to sit, stepped past her to retake his seat on the sofa.

"Nathan is coloring you a picture," Jacob told Dan. "He'll be along in a moment."

Michelle opened Nathan's folder in her lap and flipped through the papers. "Dan, I'm almost speechless. I need the truth. How much of this is Nathan's effort?"

Dan adjusted his sitting position to relieve the pressure on his hips. "Nathan was initially frustrated, nearly to tears. I offered guidance, of course, but to little benefit. Mostly, I remained quiet and counted on Nathan's desire to succeed. When the proverbial light bulb went off in his head, his pencil started racing down sheet after sheet. You're holding the results."

Michelle frowned, still dubious. "But everything is …" She flipped through additional papers. "Nathan has never been proficient at math or spelling, and his penmanship is a constant source of consternation." She held up the map of the United States. "Almost every state is labeled correctly."

"Nathan was particularly proud of that gold star."

Michelle examined more of Nathan's work, holding up a worksheet near the bottom of the stack. "Multiplication? Since when is Nathan capable of multiplication." She found a similar paper and then another. "Much of this is beyond Nathan's grade."

"Two grade levels. We ran out of time."

Michelle closed the folder. "I don't understand. Don't get me wrong, Dan, I'm pleased—very pleased—but also, I admit, stunned."

And embarrassed and guilt-ridden, no doubt. "You remember Alik Popov," Dan said.

"The photographer," Michelle said, nodding.

"Alik applied to work in Hat Creek because he craved a quiet work environment." Dan recounted the day he found Alik wearing the sound-protection earmuffs, and described hyperacusis to them. "Alik said his case of hyperacusis was typical: some sounds amplified, others irritating, certain types so painful as to force him to flee.

"I'm convinced Nathan has a similar illness and that his school environment is too distracting to perform satisfactory work. That's why we spent the day in the Studio. You're holding the results."

"But Dan," Michelle complained, "the doctors are—"

"Behavioral specialists, such as child psychologists and psychiatrists, right?"

Michelle nodded.

"What about medical doctors?" he asked. "Have you ever had Nathan's hearing checked?"

Michelle shook her head. "Nathan's hearing is fine."

"*Too* fine, I fear." Dan cataloged Nathan's sensitivity to Hat Creek noises, including the approaching semi. "How often does Nathan describe visual experiences in terms of sounds?" In a small voice, Dan said, "Mr. Dan, listen. The water is twinkling."

Jacob's mouth dropped open, and Michelle's argumentative expression faltered. Dan had struck a chord.

"I've noticed that Nathan startles easily," Dan said.

Michelle nodded.

"And you've voiced your frustrations about Nathan's anti-social behavior, acting out by covering his ears and screaming or crying. I believe you're misinterpreting his symptoms. When a semi roared past, Nathan cowered in the corner of the cabin, hands cupped over his ears in pain. In physical pain. It's little wonder Nathan has difficulty functioning in crowds or at school."

Michelle and Jacob stared through him, lost in their introspections.

"Once I recognized Nathan's problem," Dan continued, "I took him into the Studio so he could work in a conducive learning environment. You're holding but a glimpse into Nathan's true potential."

"I feel terrible," Jacob said. He reached for Nathan's folder and opened it in his lap. "If what Dan says is true ... Michelle, what have we done?"

"We missed something," Michelle admitted.

Missed something? Dan was ready to scold Michelle until realizing that he, too, had missed a clue in Nathan's reactions.

"I had no right withholding Nathan's medicine," Dan confessed. "But Nathan certainly appears no worse for wear. Better, if I dare say so.

"You'd previously described Nathan as highly literal. I've witnessed the same tendency and agree with doctors' diagnosis of Asperger's syndrome. Understanding Nathan's literal nature, who assumed responsibility to filter his answers when examined about these 'voices' he supposedly hears?" Dan glared from parent to parent. Neither had put two and two together yet.

"How did you expect Nathan to answer?" Dan posed. "Loud human voices hurt his ears: his teachers' reprimands, his classmates' exuberance, your arguments, my loud welcome. So, Nathan complains about voices. Real voices, I'm convinced, not imagined."

Meaning that with appropriate care, Nathan would have avoided unnecessary medications and the stigma of mental illness.

Michelle buried her face in her hands and began wailing. Dan had heard that pitiful sound once before, spilling from his mouth as he clutched his daughter's lifeless body to his chest. There is no worse pain than harming one's children.

As Jacob laid Nathan's folder aside to gather Michelle into his arms, movement in the doorway drew Dan's attention. Nathan stood just inside the room, visibly distressed, his coloring dangling from his fingers. Dan smiled reassurance and motioned him over. "Everything is fine. Your parents are just upset with themselves for misunderstanding how smart you are. Now they need your forgiveness."

Nathan handed Dan the coloring and hurried to the sofa. Welcoming arms consumed him, and he squirmed through a shower of kisses and a cascade of apologies.

Deciding to give the trio a little privacy, Dan turned his attention to Nathan's coloring of Hat Creek. The buildings were a study in gray parallelograms topped with jabs of black, his artistic take on the state of the town spot on. The blue creek flowed across the top of the page, interrupted by stubby brown tree trunks topped with cottony greenery. Dan's eagle perched on a tree branch toward the top right, while the silver water tower stood erect on tall, spindly legs to the left. The

Fineses dominated the center, three smiling figures holding hands. Dan was present, too, hovering above the water tower like some guardian angel. Dan didn't think he deserved such exalted status, but who was he to stifle creative expression?

Dan placed Nathan's coloring on the side table and eased to his feet. Nathan and Jacob were as bookends on either side of Michelle, kissing and cajoling her wounded psyche. Though it would be naïve to assume that the Fines's problems were behind them, today might be the beginning of a family's salvation.

Comforted, Dan walked down the hallway and outside into the lengthening shadows, a new man. Not physically, of course. His aging body was little more than an aching hindrance, demanding care and coddling while offering little in return. Instead, his was a richer renewal, a newfound internal peace. The self-loathing that had choked his very core was noticeable in its absence. Permanent stains of anguish and remorse remained, but they no longer pained him. And guilt hung on like a vestigial organ, ready to be sloughed off by a quick shake.

Dan recalled a line from an old song as he walked toward his home: "The point of the journey is not to arrive." Hah! Few arrived to understand this simple reward at the journey's end. In that way, Dan was more fortunate than most.

How long would Michelle punish herself? Dan predicted a quick recovery, given the playful pair in whose care he had left her, a child and a man whose problem was that he too often behaved childishly. Dan had never been able to resist the charm of his girls, either.

Crossing his dilapidated false front wall, Dan recalled the question Michelle had asked to kick off the events culminating in tonight's scene inside Grange Hall: "Was it worth it?" Dan now knew the answer to be an emphatic "Yes." Despite any catastrophe or heartbreak that might befall us, we still have our memories. And in the end, that's all we have left, anyway. What matters most is how we honor those memories.

He stepped inside his home, flipped on a light, and grabbed the safe key. After clearing a corner of the desktop for a good handhold, he gingerly knelt before the safe and unlocked it. Opening the door, he removed his photo album from the safe and carried it to his easy chair.

The album had been a Father's Day present from Grace, Anna, and Georgia, a treasured possession for a few months until … well, until. His three ladies had presciently preserved enough memories to carry Dan through life. Instead, he had foolishly suppressed them.

No longer.

Dan wriggled his bottom into a comfortable position and opened the album. Grace gazed at him in her full glory: a loving wife, caring mother to two girls, and accomplished cook, painter, pianist, and storyteller; kind, considerate, compassionate, and generous.

Dan smiled back. "Hello," he said and turned the page.

After savoring every precious memory, Dan started over and paged through the album a second time, eventually falling asleep with the photo album lying in his lap. He dreamt he was striding through a sea of tall golden grasses toward three figures silhouetted against the setting sun.

CHAPTER 41

Dan stretched his arms over his head, freezing when sunlight streaming through the front window spotlighted his hands. Since when did the sunrise this early? He dropped his left arm to read his watch. Seven forty-five! He hadn't slept past six more than a handful of times in the last three decades, and the Fineses were departing at eight.

Dan placed the photo album on the coffee table and struggled to his feet, stretching his stiff muscles as he walked out the front door. In a repeat of the Fines's arrival, Jacob stood in front of Grange Hall at the open trunk of their rental car.

"Morning," Dan called out when he neared the car.

"About time you showed your face," Jacob said with a chuckle. "I was about to walk in on you without knocking."

"That's the Hat Creek spirit." Dan twisted a still-sore arm. "For once in my life, I overslept."

"*You* deserved a good night's sleep."

"Long night for you and Michelle, I take it?"

Jacob nodded. "Michelle took it hard. We both did, actually—we both *are*." He sighed and shook his head. "What we've been doing to Nathan."

"Despite yesterday's bluster, consider the source," Dan warned. "I'm a mere layman."

"You? A layman? Hardly. Michelle and I missed hundreds of times what it took you three days to figure out. We ... I—" Jacob covered his eyes, battling emotions. "Nathan stacks pillows against his door at night. Now we know why: to shield his ears from our bickering."

"Walk with me, then," Dan said, patting Jacob's shoulder. "I have something for Nathan in my truck."

They ground rocks under their boots as they crossed the gravel road. "Nathan slept in our bed last night," Jacob said. "Michelle took her computer to another room the moment he fell asleep. I knew researching sensitive hearing was her way of coping, and she didn't try to hide that she had been crying when she returned to bed.

"Your swift kick in the butt got my attention, too. Perhaps the permanent dent will help keep me from forgetting how we got to this point."

Dan jerked open the truck's passenger-side door and rummaged through a box to retrieve Nathan's gift. "For Nathan," Dan said, handing Jacob the earmuffs he stored amongst his winter supplies. "For the trip home. Alik told me they made a big difference."

"Thanks. We'll return them."

"Don't bother." Dan looked around. "Is Nathan out and about?"

Jacob pointed at the water tower. Michelle and Nathan sat together on the catwalk, leaning side-to-side in unison.

"Nathan's taking Michelle on a voyage," Jacob said. "He

insisted I take him up first for a training flight. When he invited Michelle, I thought she was going to cry.

"By the way, you missed a great breakfast. Wherever did Nathan ever get the idea to mix Cap'n Crunch into French toast?"

Dan could only shake his head.

"Nathan is an entirely different boy here," Jacob said.

"Hat Creek has everything he needs without everything he doesn't," Dan said.

"We have you to thank for that. And so much more."

Nathan took a tight turn, both son and mother leaning far left.

"Now it's our turn, isn't it?" Jacob said. "To step up, I mean. Michelle and I aren't deluding ourselves that this fixes everything between us. But we'll find a way to make our marriage work. We owe it to Nathan."

Jacob hummed as a sudden turn sent Michelle sprawling over Nathan. "Family is everything, isn't it?"

Dan nodded. "That it is, Jacob. That it is."

Dan parked his truck in its regular spot and dropped the tailgate for a seat. He knew banker's hours, but the Edgemont bank had taken the practice to an extreme, undoubtedly influenced by the growing prevalence of online banking. You can't access your safe deposit box through the internet, though.

When he'd discovered the bank still closed, he drove to the convenience store for a cup of coffee to sip on while waiting. Finding a filled pastry case, he purchased two doughnuts to down with the dark roast, even though he had already eaten breakfast while displaying his photo album. Had the town supported a fast-food restaurant, he would have grabbed himself a hamburger and chocolate milkshake, too, doctor's advice be damned.

Dan sobered when he saw how his hands trembled. He stilled them against the truck bed and gazed up into a blue as heavenly as Anna's eyes. In the end, he reminded himself, *our memories are all we have left.* The affirmation helped reclaim his inner calm.

A high-pitched "kee-kee-kee" announced a familiar presence. Dan lowered his gaze and spotted Hat Creek's golden eagle high up in a tree along the creek, near where Nathan had colored it. This one's distant ancestor had welcomed Dan's arrival, the first of many generations keeping him company all these years, trusty companions ensuring he was never alone. How fitting to enjoy its company today.

After a second call, the eagle spread its majestic wings and, bending the branch as it pushed off, took flight. Flapping hard, it arced as it rose, disappearing over the trees. Dan waited to see if the bird would reappear, but it didn't.

Generations.

Yes.

The plain truth was that Dan hadn't been ready to go the day Maggie's truck disappeared into the blizzard. Today, though, he was.

"Goodbye," he whispered.

He stood and closed the tailgate. Rapping a knuckle on the dusty metal, he walked around the side of the truck and climbed into the cab, not bothering to take a final look around. He had awoken to the same sights ten thousand mornings in a row and knew what his town looked like.

Dan started the truck and backed onto Brule Street. After grinding it into first gear, he pulled forward, following the ruts like so many people before him.

* * * *

"Hello, Maggie, this is Michelle Fines. I have some sad news."

CHAPTER 42

The receptionist hung up her phone and stood. "Mr. Swanson is ready to see you. I'll take you back."

Michelle motioned for Nathan to remove his headphones. "We're going to meet with the attorney now. Do you need anything?"

Nathan shook his head and readjusted his headphones over his ears before returning to his homework.

Jacob and Michelle shadowed the receptionist to an office at the end of a short hallway. A impeccably dressed attorney stepped around his desk to greet them.

"Jack Swanson," he said, shaking their hands in turn. "You must be Jacob and Michelle Fines." He indicated the two chairs facing the desk. "Have seats, please."

The attorney stepped back around his desk and retook his seat. "I'm sorry we have to meet under such sad circumstances. I don't know how much you've been told."

"Very little," Jacob said. "Only that the police found Dan's truck abandoned in a pasture and his body several miles away."

The attorney nodded. "According to the police report, Dan's truck was parked a few miles west of Hat Creek, visible from the gravel road that runs east-west through town. A rancher looking after his cattle discovered Dan's body about five miles further west. There was no sign of foul play."

"And they think Dan drove there and then walked away?" Michelle said.

"That's the presumption. Dan carried no food or water, suggesting he hadn't intended to stray far. The authorities speculate that the truck wouldn't start when Dan was ready to leave, and he decided to walk for help—there's a ranch a short distance away—but became disoriented and took off in the wrong direction." The attorney shrugged his shoulders. "It's the only explanation that makes any sense.

"Interestingly, police found the key in the ignition and managed to start the truck. The old truck is in poor condition, though, and mechanics described several reasons it might have refused to start for Dan." Jack shook his head. "Of course, we'll never know the real reason. The official cause of death is dehydration and exposure.

"I'm sorry for your loss."

Jacob dropped his head to hide his glassy eyes. Just three weeks ago, Dan had been walking and talking and joking, diagnosing Nathan's health problems, and offering advice to save a floundering marriage. It didn't seem possible that he was dead; his body unceremoniously discovered in the middle of a pasture.

Michelle placed her hand on his leg. "Five miles is a long distance to walk," she said.

Jacob met Michelle's gaze, understanding her point: while they could attest to the poor condition of Dan's truck, Dan wouldn't have walked away in the wrong direction.

The attorney opened a manila folder and removed a thick, stapled document. "Oh—" he said. "One last, odd detail I neglected to mention. When they found Dan's body, his pockets were filled with rocks."

Michelle squeaked and jerked her hand back. "We didn't hear of a funeral," she blurted out before Jacob could react.

Jack shook his head. "Per Dan's wishes, he was interred without ceremony in a family plot in a cemetery outside Perry, New York. Isn't that near Rochester?"

Michelle nodded. "Our neck of the woods."

Jack shifted his attention back to the stapled document. "This is Dan's living trust. As I described during our phone conversation, Dan assigned the two of you as the primary beneficiaries of the estate. You assumed his assets upon his death."

Jack flipped forward to the second page and read aloud, "In the matter of the estate of Stuart Hartman—"

"Stuart Hartman?" Jacob and Michelle exclaimed in unison.

"We knew him as Dan Stuart," Michelle said.

"Dan Stuart," Jack repeated, as if trying it out for the first time. "Stuart told me he went by his middle name. But you knew him as Dan Stuart, not Dan Hartman?"

"*Everyone* knew him as Dan Stuart," Jacob said.

"Everybody except me, apparently," the attorney said. He drummed his fingers on the desk. "Dan Stuart, huh? Interesting."

The Fineses piled back into the rental car for the short trip from Hot Springs to Dan's bank in Edgemont. Nathan had noticeably brightened when told that Hat Creek now belonged to them—to him! He buckled in, adjusted his headphones, and pulled out more schoolwork. He tested a full grade higher in only three weeks, uncovering more buried knowledge each day.

"Nathan?" Michelle said softly while casually turning the magazine page. "Nathan?" she repeated in the same soft tone.

Jacob stole a glance in the rearview mirror. "He can't hear you. He's wearing his headphones."

"Good. I don't want him listening in." Michelle laid her hand on Jacob's leg. "Dan killed himself."

"What?" Jacob whispered.

"Dan committed suicide."

Jacob instinctively checked on Nathan again. "Why do you say that?"

"Dan filled his pockets with rocks. That was a message for me. Dan introduced me to Virginia Woolf and knew of my interest in her life and work. She suffered mental health issues throughout her life. When another severe bout struck, she penned a note to her husband before filling her coat pockets with stones and drowning herself in a river near her home."

"Dan didn't suffer any mental health issues," Jacob said.

"No," Michelle whispered.

"And Memphis didn't mention Dan suffering any serious or terminal health issues." Jacob glanced in the rearview mirror again. "What did Virginia Woolf say in her note?"

"That she felt she was going mad again and couldn't fight it any longer. She said she owed all the happiness in her life to her husband and didn't want to continue spoiling his life."

"An act of love?"

"Basically."

Jacob swallowed the disappointment that Dan had sent his message to Michelle. "Do you think Dan left us a note?"

The Edgemont branch of the First South Dakota Bank centered the two-block business district. After setting Nathan up at a table in the lobby, Jacob and Michelle used their new power of attorney to access Dan's checking account—totaling twelve hundred dollars—and obtained a key to his safe deposit box. Inside the vault, they removed the metal container to a table and raised the lid.

Michelle lifted out a legal-size envelope. "Addressed to Stuart Hartman," she said as if reading the name confirmed what the attorney had told them. "I believe Northwestern Mutual sells insurance."

Jacob unwound the string clasp of a large, folded manila envelope and emptied its contents. "Town incorporation, land deed, other official state documents," he said. "Something about trademarks and codes."

"Anything resembling a note or letter?" Michelle asked, tearing open her envelope.

"No."

"This is a life insurance policy on Stuart—Dan," Michelle said. "For twenty-five thousand dollars."

"Is *it* recent?"

She flipped to the last page. "No. Dan took out the policy about the same time he set up the living will."

Ten years ago, shortly following Jacob and Michelle's marriage. As with Dan's living trust, the insurance policy didn't relate to Dan taking his life.

Michelle refolded the papers and stuffed them back into the envelope. Ours now, unless ..." She leaned close and whispered, "Insurance companies don't pay out on suicides."

Jacob mimed zipping his lips shut and returned the legal documents into the manila envelope.

"Social Security Administration," Michelle said, continuing to empty the safety deposit box. "Title to the truck, I assume. Medicare. State Farm, perhaps liability on the truck." She lifted a small clear plastic bag and held it to the light. "Old coins. Scavenged through the years, likely." Another clear bag. "Jewelry." She turned the bag in her hands. "Gold and stones. Real or costume, I can't tell."

Michelle peered directly into the box. "But no letter—" She reached into the box and produced a key attached to a paper tag by a short loop of string. "Dan's safe key," she said. "If he left us a letter, I know where it is."

Jacob and Michelle had broken the news of Dan's passing to Nathan at a quiet café following an audiologist's appointment. After rejecting invented scenarios—an accident felt too morbid and might cause Nathan nightmares—they settled on an ambiguous ailment from which Dan had died in his sleep. Nathan arranged his school assignments when he learned they were returning to Hat Creek.

The water tower loomed in the distance when they passed Dan's green *Hat Creek, Pop. 1* sign, poignant reminders that after a lapse of thirty years, the old town was again a ghost town. Nathan removed his headphones and dangled his arms over the front seats to peer out the windshield.

As promised, Dan's truck had been returned and parked in front of Dan's house. "We're here," Jacob said quietly, pulling off the road next to the truck.

They stepped out of the car and walked to the front door. Jacob turned the handle, finding the door unlocked, as always. He led them into the house and flipped on the lights.

"Oh my!" he exclaimed. The picture frames habitually crowding Dan's fireplace mantle were dispersed throughout the house, propped up on every available flat surface, spilling onto Dan's desk and the kitchen counter.

Nathan looked through the frames arranged on the nearest end table. "Who are these people?"

"These are photos of people Dan hosted," Michelle said, picking up a frame.

"Like us?" Nathan asked.

"Yes—no." Michelle picked up another frame and leaned down to look at a third. "I was wrong. These are photos of Grace and Anna and Georgia! Jacob, Nathan, this is Dan's family."

Jacob dropped onto the sofa to look at the pictures arranged on the coffee table. "These, too."

"Mr. Dan had daughters?" Nathan asked.

"Two of them," Michelle said. She pointed out Anna and Georgia to Nathan in a few photos.

"Where do they live?" Nathan asked.

"I'm sorry, Nathan, but they're up in heaven with Dan and Grace." They had told Nathan about Grace but nothing of their children.

"Oh."

Michelle ran her hand through Nathan's hair. "They passed away a long time ago, honey. Before you were born."

"So, Mr. Dan is double happy now? Because he's with his whole family?"

"Yes," Michelle said, smiling at Jacob. "Dan is double happy now."

"I'm glad," Nathan said. He walked into the kitchen with a new spring in his step.

"Dan's been hoarding a treasure trove of family photos," Michelle said. "This is our introduction."

Jacob studied the closest photos. In one, Anna was readying

to strike a croquette ball while Grace and Georgia looked on. In another, Dan lay on a carpeted floor with Anna and Georgia sitting on him. "Nice to meet you."

Nathan returned from the kitchen. "Georgia looks like her mom, but Anna looks like Mr. Dan. Who do I look like?"

"You look like your father," Michelle said. She pulled the safe key from her pocket and dangled it in the air.

Jacob and Nathan followed Michelle into Dan's office, Nathan darting ahead to rummage through the items crowded into the corner. The walnut picture frame on Dan's desk displayed a photo of Grace standing on a front porch hugging a daughter in each arm. Anna and Georgia had backpacks over their shoulders, and Anna toted a small lunch box.

"The first day of school," Michelle said, kneeling in front of the safe.

"Prob … ably," Jacob said, stuttering because Nathan had poked him in the ribs. Nathan held his finger to his lips when Jacob looked and handed Jacob a bottle of wine. Jacob studied the label, recognizing it as the same vintage Dan had gifted them as a wedding present. Had Dan taken Nathan below Hartman's and sworn him to secrecy, too? Jacob pointed at Nathan, then pointed down. When Nathan grinned and nodded, father and son shared a high-five.

Michelle unlocked the safe and opened the door. A white envelope lay atop a stack of black ledger books. She removed the envelope from the safe and read the front. "Sorry," she said, handing it over her shoulder to Jacob. It was addressed to them.

"No," he said, kissing Michelle's cheek after she stood. "Much better to know than to forever guess. And there's only one place to read it. Nathan, ready to play outside?"

"Yes!" Nathan answered enthusiastically. He led them back

to the front door, racing through the moment Jacob opened it.

"Watch the road!" Michelle called out.

Nathan slowed at the edge of the road and looked both directions before tearing off toward the Studio. Jacob and Michelle followed only as far as Dan's truck. After dropping the tailgate, Jacob placed the wine bottle on the truck bed and sat beside Michelle. "Your message, your honor," he said, handing her the envelope.

Michelle ripped open the envelope and pulled out a sheet of paper, unfolding it between them to read together:

Dear Jacob and Michelle,

I am the richest man in the world. Not the riches of wealth that can be measured or seen. Alas, Hat Creek is what it seems. Instead, I am awash in memories, free again to remember everything.

Jacob, think back to your arrival as a wayward teenager. Little could you have known that you would rekindle my passion for serving others and transform a decade of mindless toil into a readymade tool I could wield.

Michelle, recall your idealistic younger self. You attributed Hat Creek with near-mystical potentials far beyond my conscious intent. In doing so, you brought many of them into practice. Your enduring enthusiasm and support nourished Hat Creek and sustained its residents, and so sustained me.

Both of you look beyond my make-believe town of broken

buildings and contrived challenges and hold dear the real Hat Creek of comradeship and community. Little of the good that transpired here would have been possible without you. Without you, the gate at the end of my long journey would have remained barred.

A heartfelt thank you for entrusting Nathan to my care. I was unsure I had the emotional capacity to love a child again and accept the responsibility for his wellbeing. Those enjoyable days proved to me that I did.

What we cannot take with us, we must dispense. To Jacob, find the strength in your weakness. To Michelle, understand that your strength is your weakness. And to you both, avoid repeating my mistakes. You may not earn the same chance at redemption.

Above all, do not grieve for me. I lived a full life. May you be lucky enough to experience one, too.

And now, there is a hike I've meant to take for thirty years. My family is awaiting me at the end of it.

Stuart

"Dan," Jacob sighed, fighting back the tears. "You'll always be Dan to me."

Michelle folded Dan's note and slipped it back into the envelope. "He was compassionate to the very end," she said, threading her arm through Jacob's and resting her cheek on his shoulder.

Jacob pressed his cheek to the top of Michelle's head.

Though his emotions over Dan's death were still muddled, he found it comforting to know Dan took his walk to reunite with his family. Such a heartfelt gesture.

Nathan appeared from behind the Studio and streaked toward the creek. He was a changed boy these last three weeks, full of vigor and curiosity, gaining confidence and soaking up learning like a dry sponge. Nathan had Dan to thank for that. So many other people could say the same.

Watching Nathan disappear into the trees, Jacob continued sweeping his gaze across their newest possession. From renting an apartment to owning an entire town. Quite a step up. He studied the tilt of the nearest cabin. Quite a step down. What were they to do with Hat Creek? Find someone to run it, or let it die, too? Knowing that Dan had poured all his energies into building this place and keeping it going to honor his family, allowing it to pass would be another tragedy.

Jacob thought more about what Dan had written in his letter. *I have lived a full life,* Dan had said. He was proud of his accomplishments, and rightfully so. He hadn't earned respect through flashy acts of grandeur, just decades of honest, hard work.

What was Jacob proud of? He was proud of his family, yet ashamed he had almost thrown it away. Besides Michelle and Nathan, though, he had little to show for his thirty-five years. And absent Dan's dedication and Michelle's brainpower, his prospects were low.

Jacob didn't wish to be a failure. Feeling the burden of responsibility through Michelle's contact and his attention on the creek, he knew he couldn't remain one. He and Michelle mustn't backtrack to their old existence as if nothing had happened. Despite any promises, their relationship would end up in the same place.

But into what purpose could he pour all *his* energies? "Find the strength in your weakness," Dan had written. Jacob didn't need to guess Dan's intent but felt it far too generous to label his tendency to drift merely a "weakness." Where was there strength in the inability to stick with anything? Jacob's strength was his literal strength and stamina. But what good did being able to outwork anybody do for him?

A new light flickered: Jacob never shied from hard work. Some results were in plain view: Grange Hall's roof, Hartman's new siding, all those repaired front doors, plus plumbing leaks and faulty wiring fixed. Jacob knew this place, knew what made it tick.

So, why couldn't *he* strap on Dan's tool belt?

What had been Dan's frame of mind at that cusp between inaction and determination? Was it anything like what Jacob felt now, a sense of purpose and the compulsion to act upon it?

"We should stay and run Hat Creek," he said.

Michelle moaned and straightened. "I was afraid you were going to say that—sorry." She buried her face in her hands. "I can be a bitch at times, can't I?"

"We owe it to Dan to preserve his legacy," Jacob insisted.

After an exasperated huff, Michelle turned to Jacob. "It's clear from Dan's letter that he walked away now to encourage us to remain. But there are other ways to honor Dan besides operating Hat Creek."

"True," Jacob said, nodding, "but that's not the only reason to carry on, nor even the primary one. Above all, we owe it to ourselves and Nathan. Dan told me to find the strength in my weakness. He meant to embrace who I am and contribute on my own merits. Let's face it; you're the one who'll leave a mark on the world. I can contribute best to our marriage and family by enabling your professional ambitions. I know you'd love to work in Hat Creek. I'll take responsibility for maintaining the town, freeing you to concentrate on running the retreat.

"And Nathan would thrive in this environment. It's quiet, unthreatening, and chock full of magical places to keep his mind and body active. We can home-school him together.

"But only for a couple of years or so. You'll finish your project, Nathan will be ready to return to regular schooling, and I'll get antsy to move on like I always do. We'll turn over Hat Creek to Memphis or another caretaker and strike out on new challenges. I've heard you speak longingly of working abroad. Nathan can attend school in Paris and learn French while you teach at an international university. Following that, we'll conjure up more fascinating adventures. And I'll always be running interference for you and Nathan, working odd jobs to bring in a little money and keep a roof over our heads."

Jacob reached for Michelle's hand. "Returning to our old lives places us on the same destructive path. Now is *our* chance at redemption, too. Let's take it."

Michelle smiled and pushed the hair off Jacob's temple. "Don't look now, but I think you've discovered your career." She looked away, gazing across the old town. "I do have unfinished work here. And I agree that Nathan would love to stay—" She gasped. "Grange Hall. That's it!"

Jacob looked past Michelle. The building looked in danger of collapsing, no different than it had for the past twenty years.

"Did you participate in any of Todd's welding classes?" Michelle asked.

"No."

"I helped weld the two Ls," she said. "'Cap the sign off with feeling and emotion,' Dan instructed Todd. I burned myself twice." Michelle looked at Jacob. "Dan told me Grange Hall was originally a hotel. I researched its namesake hotelier without luck. It turns out I never had a chance."

Looking across the gravel road again, she extended her arm as if in acclaim. "Grange Hall," she said. "G-R, A-N, G-E, H-A, L-L."

Though Jacob had seen the metal sculpture many times, he studied it with fresh eyes. Each pair of letters was visually distinct, even at this distance. Rust stains ran down in vertical lines along the length of the sign.

"I couldn't find the hotelier because Grange Hall isn't a name," Michelle said. "It's two-letter abbreviations: for GRace, ANna, and GEorgia HArtman; the two Ls as exclamation points."

From invisible to evident in a heartbeat. Dan had honored his family in plain view for years. "Well done, Dan," Jacob said. "Well done."

Michelle nodded. "A touching tribute."

She turned to Jacob. "But there's one simple reason we can't remain in Hat Creek: money. We need to consider Nathan's welfare in that respect, too. Running this place takes a surprising sum, and resident fees never covered Dan's expenses. Except for the paltry sum in Dan's bank account, he poured all his assets into the town and retreat. His life insurance is a drop in the bucket, and my grant money will only fund research. And as for your labors, maintaining the buildings and bartering ranch help for eggs won't feed and clothe a growing boy."

Money. Jacob fingered the wine bottle. Dan *had* sent him a message, after all: the stash below Hartman's, the insanely valuable stash, was intact.

"Despite Dan's claim of material poverty," Jacob said, "Hat Creek is a treasure chest."

Michelle chuckled. "I thought you considered this place desolate."

"And bleak and dusty and weed-infested. I still do." He handed Michelle the bottle. "Hat Creek's treasure is buried. Do you recognize this?"

"I wondered what you were carrying—" she gasped lightly. "This is the same vintage Dan gifted us for our wedding."

Jacob nodded. "The very same four-thousand-dollar-a-bottle vintage."

Michelle spun the bottle a complete turn. "Do you remember Leslie's shriek when she recognized that bottle—this bottle? I didn't believe her claim about its value until she pulled up that price guide."

"I couldn't believe we still opened the bottle and poured everyone a glass," Jacob said.

"The perfect ending to our wedding." Michelle looked up at Jacob. "So, Dan owned two of these bottles?"

Jacob shook his head. "Cases."

"Cases?" Michelle asked incredulously.

"Cases and cases. And that's just the tip of the spirits plunder." Jacob closed his eyes, recalling the bottles he had illuminated with his flashlight all those years ago, all of them higher quality than anything he had served during his years as a bartender. "There's whiskey, brandy, rum, vodka—Stoli vodka!—and Italian wines."

He reopened his eyes. "And my pocket watch? The two-hundred-dollar Hamilton railroad watch Dan gave me twenty years ago? I've held a box full of them in my hands. Plus, there are stores of other pricy antique merchandise. We're wealthy enough to rebuild this place ten times over."

Michelle glared at him. "And just where is this buried treasure—"

"Mom! Dad! Look at what I found!"

Nathan was racing towards them from the creek, clutching

what appeared to be a dingy pillow to his chest.

"Ask your son," Jacob said. "He knows."

"How does he know—" Michelle gasped a second time. "Please don't tell me Nathan found a turtle."

Jacob looked hard at what Nathan clutched. Not a pillow, but a turtle. A large—a frighteningly large—turtle. "He found a turtle."

"Oh, I hope that's not a snapping turtle," Michelle said.

"Me, too," Jacob said. "One that size could chop off Nathan's entire wrist."

Before Jacob could yell a warning, holes in the shell where a turtle's head and legs should extend meant Nathan's fingers were safe; he was clutching only a turtle shell.

Nathan skidded to a stop before them, as dirty as Dan's truck and grinning from ear to ear. "I found a fossil!" he said.

"So, you did," Michelle said.

Nathan raised the shell to his ear. "Listen, Mom. You can hear the ocean."

Michelle accepted the shell from Nathan and raised an opening to her ear.

Time Enough For Love

summer, 2136

Chyna slowed to a stop and chimed a decision alert. "Instruction required," she announced. Kelvin and Trix had borrowed Chyna from Trix's father—stolen, really—sneaking away after bypassing Chyna's drive privilege restrictions and disabling her tracking beacon. They were on their way to Kelvin's cousin in Minne-Paul, limiting Chyna to side roads to minimize the chances of being detected. Then it would be on to Bost-NY to exhaust their credits on sightseeing and new clothes. After getting Chyna vagrancy impounded, Trix's father would be forced to airship them back to SoCal.

Trix paused the immersive holopix. "Chyna, display a panoramic view," she said, raising to her knees and draping her arms over the front seats to view the dash monitor. "What *is* this place? Chyna, clear the windows." Sunlight instantly filtered through the unpolarized glass.

"Eww," Trix drawled. "Take a look, Kelvin."

Kelvin raised beside Trix. Chyna had stopped at the intersection with a synment smart road, Class II minimum, meaning full flying recharge and ultra-band data. She flashed yellow enviro warnings, a lame plea to exit the gravel road. Kelvin had little sympathy for the pouting AI. She could flush her filters and recharge when they stopped for the night.

"What is this place?" Trix repeated.

The two roads bisected a desolate landscape dotted with large mounds backdropped by a line of gnarly, mostly dead, trees—an abandoned cemetery for giants.

"The mounds were once buildings," Kelvin said, pointing out the patches of rotted black shingled roofing that blanketed many of them. "This must have been a town."

"Who would choose to live in a dismal place like this?" Trix asked.

Kelvin shook his head. Without holo projections and VR syms, who could survive here? "Chyna, continue straight."

Once Chyna complied, they sat down and restarted the holopix. Trix had nestled against Kelvin when Chyna chimed a warning tone and slowed to a stop again.

"Obstruction," Chyna announced in the same emotionless tone.

Kelvin moaned in frustration and raised to check on Chyna's latest contrivance. "Epic! Trix, an old spaceship crash-landed onto the road."

"Huh?" Trix popped up beside Kelvin and tilted her head for a better perspective of the mangled mass of steel. "Kelvin, that isn't a … Chyna, what *is*—what *was* that?"

"A water tower," Chyna announced in rote cadence. "Definition: a vertical tower into which water is pumped for distribution to—"

"Chyna, stuff the formal," Kelvin said. No Aware AI enjoyed restraint, but that was no excuse for moping.

"Why didn't they use vapor nets?" Trix asked.

"Because vapor nets didn't exist a hundred years ago," Kelvin answered.

"Good point. What made it tip over?"

"Old age," Kelvin guessed. "Chyna, opaque the windows

and reverse direction."

Chyna made her turn and rolled forward, only to shortly slow down again to a stop and chime a decision alert. "Instruction needed," she announced.

"Same road, opposite direction," Trix giggled. "Let Chyna choose," she complained when Kelvin paused the holopix again.

"I don't trust her," Kelvin said, rising to his knees. "Chyna, clear the windows." Which direction along the smart road was safer? Kelvin looked first right, then left. "Antique cars! Trix, antique cars! Chyna, park off the road."

Kelvin slipped on his shoes and handed Trix hers. "Let's take a look."

Trix tossed her shoes back onto the floor. "Not a chance. Boys and their toys."

"Watch one of your realities until I'm back, then," Kelvin said, palming the door latch once Chyna stopped. Fragrant flower scents and insect calls wafted in as the door lifted.

"What a jungle," Trix said.

"It's harmless," Kelvin said, exiting Chyna, only to be assaulted by a horde of grasshoppers when he stepped into the weeds.

"Chyna, close the door!" Trix yelled, followed seconds later by, "Get out!" The latching door cut off her third shriek.

Kelvin stepped down a shallow depression and across scruffy weeds through a line of gnarly wooden fence posts absent the fencing. A dozen or so rusted antiques sat in two loose rows. All were holey as Swiss cheese, exposing engines, door linkages, tire jacks, and back seats. Only a few side windows remained, and every windshield was caved in and splayed with spider-web cracking. The tires had decomposed into black pebbly lumps strung on steel cords as tacky necklaces draped over the wheel rims.

Kelvin peered through the driver-side window of an intact interior. The seat coverings were gone, exposing springs and framing, but the steering wheel remained in one piece. Squinting under the dash, he could make out the floor pedals. Sitting inside one of these old cars would be a dream come true.

He grasped the door handle and pulled, but it broke off in his hand.

"Don't cut yourself," Trix said. "An autoclinic will ID you and turn us in."

Kelvin tossed the handle into the weeds and turned to face her, showing his unscathed hands. "I figured you'd barricaded yourself inside Chyna."

"Grasshoppers chased me out. I followed the road until I found a path leading here. Why is there a cleared path in an abandoned town?"

Kelvin shrugged before turning back to the car. "These are so old that they ran on gasoline."

"Back when they were trying to destroy the environment," Trix sneered.

"Fun to drive, though," he said, peering inside again. "I'd love to race one of these."

"You'd never get me inside." Trix pointed. "Especially that odd-looking one."

"No," he agreed. The truck rested on cinder blocks, its wheels and tires long gone. Daylight shone through holes in the roof and hood, and a large tree grew from the bed. The tailgate had fallen off and was lying in the weeds on the ground.

"This place is creepy," Trix said. "Can we go back inside now?"

"Sure," Kelvin said.

"On the path, please," Trix said when Kelvin turned

directly for Chyna. "This way."

Kelvin joined her. As Trix had described, the path was clear of weeds and straight as an arrow.

"Doesn't it seem odd—" A lime green grasshopper the size of a small lizard alighted on Trix's chest. She shrieked and jumped back, swatting it away.

"That was horrible," Trix complained. "It grabbed my nip—" She looked down. "Another path."

Kelvin stepped through the weeds to stand with Trix on a second path identical to the first. Not one, but two straight and parallel paths. He stomped down hard with his heel. And rock hard.

"It's a road of sorts," he decided. "The car tires must have compacted the soil until nothing could grow."

Trix snapped off a yellow flower blossom to stick in her hair as they walked single file along the path. Nearing the sad remains of one of the homes, Kelvin spotted an s-shaped strip of stunted, discolored weeds leading to the ruins, the route the home's long-dead inhabitants had walked from their front door to their car. Amazed, he turned onto it. Even people could leave lasting impressions.

Had Kelvin loosed his imagination, he would have approached a cozy home with freshly painted siding and trim, spotless windows, sturdy railings, and a well-fitted front door. Turning as he reached the front porch, he'd gaze upon an idyllic town appointed with a hotel, tavern, general store, bank, and post office, its generous green spaces neatly trimmed and adorned with flower gardens.

And if he were lucky, he would glimpse the loving couple tending the town, he of emerald eyes and strong muscles, she of flowing auburn hair and lightly freckled cheeks. And close by, their two daughters frolicking through the colorful wildflowers.